Brend⋯⋯⋯⋯⋯⋯⋯⋯est-
selling author of ⋯⋯ than one hundred romance ⋯les,
⋯ retiree from a major insurance company and now
⋯ time between family, writing and travel. You may
⋯da at PO Box 28267, Jacksonville, Florida 32226,
⋯ail at authorbrendajackson@gmail. com or visit
⋯ at www.brendajackson.net.

⋯ lives in Texas with her husband of many years and is
⋯ of three grown children. She has a master's degree
⋯ A&M at Kingsville, Texas, and is a former English
⋯ is a founding board member of the Romance Writers
⋯ and a frequent speaker at writers' groups.

⋯ ebsite at www.annmajor.com.

⋯**tes** has always pursued creative passions such as
⋯d handicrafts. She still does, but only one of her pas-
⋯ gratifying enough, consuming enough, to become
⋯g career—writing.

⋯e's not writing, she is a doctor, a wife to her own alpha
⋯d a mother to one brilliant girl and one demanding
⋯cat. Visit Olivia at www.oliviagates.com.

The Best Kept Secrets...

BRENDA JACKSON
ANN MAJOR
OLIVIA GATES

MILLS & BOON

First Published in Great Britain 2018
by Mills & Boon, an imprint of HarperCollins*Publishers*
1 London Bridge Street, London, SE1 9GF

THE BEST KEPT SECRETS... © 2018 Harlequin Books S. A.

The Secret Affair © 2014 Brenda Streater Jackson
Her Pregnancy Secret © 2014 Ann Major
Claiming His Secret Son © 2015 Olivia Gates

ISBN: 978-0-263-26715-0

05-0518

MIX
Paper from
responsible sources
FSC® C007454

This book is produced from independently certified FSC™ paper to ensure responsible forest management.

For more information visit: www.harpercollins.co.uk/green

Printed and bound in Spain
by CPI, Barcelona

THE SECRET AFFAIR

BRENDA JACKSON

To the man who will always and forever be the love of my life, Gerald Jackson, Sr.

Special thanks to Dr Dorothy M. Russ of Meharry Medical College for your assistance in providing information on medical schools and residency programs.

In whom are hid all the treasures of wisdom and knowledge.
—*Colossians* 2:3

Prologue

Jillian Novak stared across the table at her sister, not believing what she'd just heard.

Jillian placed the glass of wine she'd been holding on the table, barely keeping the drink from spilling. "What do you mean you aren't going with me? That's crazy, Paige. Need I remind you that you're the one who planned the trip?"

"A reminder isn't needed, Jill, but please understand my dilemma," Paige said in a rueful tone, her dark brown eyes shaded with regret. "Getting a part in a Steven Spielberg movie is a dream come true. You can't imagine what I was feeling—happiness at being chosen one minute, and then disappointment the next, when I found out that shooting starts the same week I was supposed to be on the cruise with you."

"Let me guess, your happiness overpowered your disappointment, right?" Jillian felt a pounding pressure in her head and knew why. She had been looking forward to the Mediterranean cruise—for many reasons—and now it appeared she wouldn't be going.

"I'm sorry, Jill. You've never gone on a cruise and I know it's one of the things on your bucket list."

Paige's apology only made Jillian feel worse. She'd

made her sister feel awful for making a choice Jillian would have made herself if given the chance. Reaching across the table, she grabbed Paige's hand.

"I'm the one who should be apologizing, Paige. I was only thinking of myself. You're right. Getting that part in the movie is a dream come true and you'd be crazy not to take it. I'm truly happy for you. Congratulations."

A bright smile spread across Paige's lips. "Thanks. I wanted so much for us to spend time together on the cruise. It's been ages since me, you, Pam and Nadia have had sister time."

Nadia, a senior in college, was their youngest sister. At twenty-one she was two years younger than Paige and four years younger than Jillian. Pamela, their oldest sister—who Jillian, Nadia and Paige were convinced was the best older sister anyone could ever have—was ten years older than Jillian. A former actress, Pam had given up the glitter of Hollywood to return home to Gamble, Wyoming, and raise them when their father died. Now Pam lived in Denver. She was married, the mother of two and the CEO of two acting schools, one in Denver and the other in Gamble. Paige had followed in Pam's footsteps and pursued an acting career. She lived in Los Angeles.

With Pam's busy schedule, she'd said accompanying them on the cruise would have been close to impossible. Nadia had wanted to go but finals kept her from doing so. Jillian had wanted sister time with at least one of her siblings. And now that she had completed medical school, she needed those two weeks on the cruise as a getaway before starting her residency. But there was another reason she wanted to take that two-week cruise.

Aidan Westmoreland.

It was hard to believe it had been a little over a year since she'd broken things off with him. And every time she remembered the reason she'd done so her heart ached. She needed a distraction from her memories.

"You okay, Jill?"

Jillian glanced up at Paige and forced a smile. "Yes, why do you ask?"

"You zoned out on me just now. I was talking and you appeared to be a million miles away. I noticed you haven't been yourself since I arrived in New Orleans. More than once you've seemed preoccupied about something. Is everything okay?"

Jillian waved off Paige's words. The last thing she wanted was for her sister to start worrying and begin digging. "Yes, everything is okay, Paige."

Paige didn't look convinced. "Um, I don't know. Maybe I should forget about being in that movie and go on that cruise with you after all."

Jillian picked up her wineglass to take a sip. "Don't be silly. You're doing the right thing. Besides, I'm not going on the cruise."

"Why not?"

Jillian was surprised at her sister's question. "Surely you don't expect me to go without you."

"You need a break before starting your residency."

Jillian rolled her eyes. "Get real, Paige. What would I do on a two-week cruise by myself?"

"Rest, relax, enjoy the sights, the ocean, the peace and quiet. And you might luck up and meet some nice single guy."

Jillian shook her head. "Nice single guys don't go on cruises alone. Besides, the last thing I need right now is a man in my life."

Paige laughed. "Jill, you haven't had a guy in your life since you dated Cobb Grindstone in your senior year at Gamble High. I think what's missing in your life is a man."

Jillian bristled at her sister's words. "Not hardly, especially with my busy schedule. And I don't see you with anyone special."

"At least I've been dating over the years. You haven't. Or, if you have, you haven't told me about it."

Jillian schooled her expression into an impassive facade. She'd never told Paige about her affair with Aidan, and considering how it had ended she was glad she hadn't.

"Jill?"

She glanced up at her sister. "Yes?"

A teasing smile spread across Paige's lips. "You aren't keeping secrets, are you?"

Jill knew Paige had given her the perfect opportunity to come clean about her affair with Aidan, but she wasn't ready. Even after a year, the pain was still raw. And the last thing Jillian needed was for Paige to start probing for more information.

"You know the reason I don't have a man in my life is because of time. My focus has been on becoming a doctor and nothing else." Paige didn't have to know that a few years ago Aidan had wiggled his way past that focus without much effort. That had been a mistake that cost her.

"That's why I think you should go on that cruise without me," Paige said. "You've worked hard and need to rest and enjoy yourself for a change. Once you begin your residency you'll have even less time for yourself—or anything else."

"That's true," Jillian said. "But—"

"No buts, Jillian."

Jillian knew that tone. She also knew that whenever Paige called her by her full name she meant business. "If I were to go on that cruise alone I'd be bored stiff. You're talking about two weeks."

Paige gave her a pointed look. "I'm talking about two weeks that I believe you need. And just think of all the fabulous places you'll get to see—Barcelona, France, Rome, Greece and Turkey." Now it was Paige who reached out to take hold of Jillian's hand. "Look, Jill, there *is* something going on with you, I can feel it. Whatever it is, it's tearing you apart. I picked up on it months ago, the last time I came to visit you."

A wry smile touched Paige's lips when she added, "Perhaps you *are* keeping secrets. Maybe there's some doctor in medical school that caught your eye and you're not ready to tell me about him. One who has blown your mind and you don't know how to handle the intensity of such a relationship. If that's the case, I understand. All of us at some time or another have issues we prefer to deal with alone. That's why I believe two weeks on the open seas will be good for you."

Jillian drew in a deep breath. Paige didn't know how close she was to the truth. Her problem *did* center on some doctor, but not one attending medical school with her.

At that moment the waitress returned with their meal, and Jillian appreciated the interruption. She knew Paige would not be happy until Jillian agreed to go on the cruise. She'd heard what Paige had said—Paige knew something was bothering Jillian. It would only be a matter of time before Pam and Nadia knew as well, if they didn't already. Besides, Jillian had already taken those two weeks off. If she didn't go on the cruise, the family would expect her to come home and spend that time with them. She couldn't do that. What if Aidan came home unexpectedly while she was there? He was the last person she wanted to see.

"Jill?"

Jillian drew in another deep breath and met Paige's gaze. "Okay, I'll do it. I'll go cruising alone. Hopefully, I'll enjoy myself."

Paige smiled. "You will. There will be plenty for you to do and on those days when you feel like doing nothing, you can do that, too. Everybody needs to give their mind a rest once in a while."

Jillian nodded. Her mind definitely needed a rest. She would be the first to admit that she had missed Aidan—the steamy hot text messages, the emails that made her adrenaline surge and the late-night phone calls that sent heat sizzling through her entire body.

But that had been before she'd learned the truth. Now all she wanted to do was get over him.

She sighed deeply while thinking that Paige was right. Jillian needed that cruise and the time away it would give her. She would go on the cruise alone.

Dr. Aidan Westmoreland entered his apartment and removed his lab coat. After running a frustrated hand down his face, he glanced at his watch. He'd hoped he would have heard something by now. What if...

The ringing of his cell phone made him pause on his way to the kitchen. It was the call he'd been waiting for. "Paige?"

"Yes, it's me."

"Is she still going?" he asked, not wasting time with chitchat.

There was a slight pause on the other end and in that short space of time knots formed in his stomach. "Yes, she's still going on the cruise, Aidan."

He released the breath he'd been holding as Paige continued, "Jill still has no idea I'm aware that the two of you had an affair."

Aidan hadn't known Paige knew the truth, either, until she'd paid him a surprise visit last month. According to her, she'd figured things out the year Jillian had entered medical school. She'd become suspicious when he'd come home for his cousin Riley's wedding and she'd overheard him call Jillian *Jilly* in an intimate tone. Paige had been concerned this past year when she'd noticed Jillian seemed troubled by something that she wouldn't share with Paige.

Paige had talked to Ivy, Jillian's best friend, who'd also been concerned about Jillian. Ivy had shared everything about the situation with Paige. That prompted Paige to fly to Charlotte and confront him. Until then, he'd been clueless as to the real reason behind his and Jillian's breakup.

When Paige had told him of the cruise she and Jillian had planned and had suggested an idea for getting Jillian on the cruise alone, he'd readily embraced the plan.

I've done my part and the rest is up to you, Aidan. I hope you can convince Jill of the truth.

Moments later he ended the call and continued to the kitchen where he grabbed a beer. Popping the top, he leaned against the counter and took a huge gulp. Two weeks on the open seas with Jillian would be interesting. But he intended to make it more than just interesting. He aimed to make it productive.

A determined smile spread across his lips. By the time the cruise ended there would be no doubt in Jillian's mind that he was the only man for her.

Moments later, he tossed the empty can in the recycle bin before heading for the shower. As he undressed, he couldn't help but recall how his secret affair with Jillian had begun nearly four years ago....

One

Four years earlier

"So, how does it feel to be twenty-one?"

Jillian's breath caught in her throat when Aidan Westmoreland's tall frame slid into the seat across from her. It was only then that she noticed everyone had gone inside. She and Aidan were the only ones on the patio that overlooked a beautiful lake.

This birthday party had been a huge surprise and Aidan's attendance even more so since he rarely came home from medical school. She couldn't imagine he'd come home just for her birthday. With her away at college most of the time as well, their paths rarely crossed. She couldn't recall them ever holding what she considered a real conversation during the four years she'd known him.

"It feels the same as yesterday," she said. "Age is just a number. No big deal."

A smile touched the corners of his lips and her stomach clenched. He had a gorgeous smile, one that complemented the rest of him. If there was such a thing as eye candy he was certainly it. She had the hots for him big-time.

Who wouldn't have the hots while sitting across from

this hunk of sexiness? If his lips didn't grab you then his eyes certainly would. They were deep, dark and penetrating. Jillian's heart missed beats just looking into them.

"Just a number?" He chuckled, leaning back in his chair, stretching long legs in front of him. "Women might think that way but men think differently."

He smelled good. When did she start noticing the scent of a man?

"And why is that, Aidan?" she asked, picking up her glass of lemonade to take a sip. It suddenly felt hotter than usual. It had nothing to do with the temperature and everything to do with her body's heated reaction to him.

She watched him lift a brow over those striking dark eyes. A feral smile edged his lips as he leaned forward. "Are you sure I'm Aidan and not Adrian?"

Oh, yes she was sure he was Aidan. She'd heard about the games he and his identical twin would play on unsuspecting souls, those who couldn't tell them apart. "I'm sure."

It was Aidan and not Adrian who stirred her in places she'd rather not think about at the moment.

He leaned in even closer. So close she could see the pupils in his dark eyes. "And how are you so certain?" he asked.

Was she imagining things or had the tone of his voice dropped to a husky murmur? It was rumored that he was a big flirt. She had seen him in action at several Westmoreland weddings. It was also a fact that he and his twin were womanizers and had developed quite a reputation at Harvard. She could certainly see why women were at their beck and call.

"Because I am," she replied. And that's all she intended to say on the matter.

There was no way she would tell him the real reason, that from the moment her brother-in-law Dillon had introduced her to Aidan, before he'd married Pam, she had developed a full-blown crush. She'd been seventeen at the time, a senior in high school. The only problem was the crush hadn't lessened much since.

"Why?"

She glanced back up at Aidan. "Why what?"

"Why are you so certain? You still haven't said."

She inwardly sighed. Why couldn't he leave it alone? She had no intention of telling him. But since she had a feeling he wouldn't let up, she added, "The two of you sound different."

He flashed another sexy smile, showing the dimples in his cheeks. Her hormones, which always acted out of control around him, were erratic now. "Funny you say that. Most people think we sound a lot alike."

"Well, I don't think that."

There was no way she could think that when it was Aidan's voice, and not Adrian's, that stroked her senses. Deciding it was time to take charge of the conversation to keep his questions at bay, she inquired, "So how is medical school going?"

He didn't let on that he suspected her ploy, and as she took another sip of her lemonade, he began telling her what she had to look forward to in another year or so. Becoming a neurosurgeon had been a lifelong dream of hers ever since her mother died of a brain infection when Jillian was seven.

Aidan told her about the dual residency program at hospitals in Portland, Maine, and Charlotte, North Carolina, that he planned to pursue after completing medical school. His dream was to become a cardiologist. He was excited about becoming a doctor and she could hear it in his voice. She was thrilled about becoming a doctor one day as well, but she had another year left before she finished her studies at the University of Wyoming.

While he talked, she nodded as she discreetly gave him a slow, appreciative appraisal. The man was too handsome for words. His voice was smooth as silk, with just enough huskiness to keep her pulse rate on edge. Creamy caramel skin spread across the bridge of a hawkish nose, sharp cheekbones, a perfect sculptured jaw and a mouth so sensual she enjoyed watching it in motion. She could imagine all the things he did with that mouth.

"Have you decided where you're going for medical school, Jillian?"

She blinked. He had asked her a question and was waiting on an answer. And while he waited she saw that sexy mouth ease into another smile. She wondered if he'd known she was checking him out.

"I've always wanted to live in New Orleans so working at a hospital there will be at the top of my list," she said, trying to ignore the eyes staring at her.

"And your second choice?"

She shrugged. "Not sure. I guess one in Florida."

"Why?"

She frowned. Why was he quizzing her? "I've never been to Florida."

He chuckled. "I hope that's not the only reason."

Her frown deepened. "Of course that's not the only reason," she said defensively. "There are good medical schools in Louisiana and Florida."

He nodded. "Yes, there are. How's your grade point average?"

"Good. In fact my GPA is better than good. I'm at the top of my class. In the top ten at least."

Getting there hadn't been easy. She'd made a lot of sacrifices, especially in her social life. She couldn't recall the last time she'd gone out on a date or participated in any school activities. But she was okay with that. Pam was paying a lot of the cost for her education and Jillian wanted to make her sister proud.

"What about the entrance exam—the MCAT—and admission essays? Started on them yet?"

"Too early."

"It's never too early. I suggest you prepare for them during your free time."

Now it was her turn to smile. "Free time? What's that?"

The chuckle that erupted from his throat was smooth and sexy and made her pulse thump. "It's time you should squeeze in regardless of whether you think you can or not. It's essential to know how to manage your time wisely, otherwise you'll get burned-out before you even get started."

She grudgingly wondered what made him an expert. Then she pushed her resentment aside. He *was* giving her sound advice and he had gone where she had yet to go. And from what she'd heard, he was doing pretty well at it. He would graduate from Harvard Medical School at the top of his class and then enter a dual residency program that any medical student would die for. He would get the chance to work with the best cardiologists in the United States.

"Thanks for the advice, Aidan."

"You're welcome. When you get ready to knock them out of the way, let me know. I'll help you."

"You will?"

"Sure. Even if I have to come to you to do it."

She lifted a brow. *He would come to her?* She couldn't imagine him doing such a thing. Harvard was in Boston and that was a long way from her university in Laramie, Wyoming.

"Hand me your phone for a second."

His request jarred her thoughts back into focus. "Why?"

"So I can put my numbers into it."

Jillian drew in a deep breath before standing to pull her cell phone from the back pocket of her jeans. She handed it to him and tried to ignore the tingling sensation that flowed through her when their hands touched. She watched him use deft fingers to key in the numbers. Surgeon's fingers. Long, strong, with precise and swift movements. She wondered how those same fingers would feel stroking her skin. She heated just thinking about it.

Moments later his phone rang, interrupting her thoughts. It was then that she realized he'd called himself to have her number, as well. "There," he said, handing her phone back to her. "You now have my number and I have yours."

Was she jumping to conclusions or did his words hold some significance? "Yes, we have each other's numbers," she agreed softly, shoving the assumption out of her mind.

He stood, glancing at his watch. "Adrian and I are meeting up with Canyon and Stern in town for drinks and to shoot pool, so I best get going. Happy birthday again."

"Thanks, Aidan."

"You're welcome."

He walked away but when he got to the French doors he turned and looked back at her, regarding her through his gorgeous dark eyes. The intensity of his gaze made her stomach quiver and another burst of heat swept through her. She felt something…passion? Sexual chemistry? Lust? All three and more, she decided. She'd thought all the Westmoreland males she'd met since Pam married Dillon were eye candy, but there was something about Aidan that pulled at everything female inside of her.

She cleared her throat. "Is anything wrong?" she asked when the silence began to stretch.

Her question seemed to jar him. He frowned slightly before quickly forcing a smile. "Not sure."

As he opened the French door to go inside, she wondered what he meant by that.

Why, of all the women in the world, have I developed this deep attraction for Jillian Novak?

The first time he'd noticed it was when they'd been introduced four years ago. He'd been twenty-two, and she only seventeen, but still a looker. He'd known then that he would have to keep his distance. Now she was twenty-one and still had the word innocent written all over her. From what he'd heard, she didn't even have a boyfriend, preferring to concentrate on her studies and forgo a love life.

And speaking of life, Aidan was fairly certain he loved every part of his, especially his family. So why was he allowing himself to be attracted to Pam's sister? He didn't want to cause any trouble for Dillon.

Pam Novak was a jewel and just what Dillon needed. Everyone had been shocked when Dillon announced he had met a woman who he intended to marry. That had been the craziest thing Aidan had ever heard.

Dillon, of all people, should have known better. Hadn't his first wife left him when he'd refused to send the youngest four members of the Westmoreland family— namely him, Adrian, Bane and Bailey—to foster care? What had made Dillon think Pam would be different? But it didn't take Aidan, his siblings and cousins long to discover that she *was* different.

As far as Aidan was concerned, she was everything they'd *all* needed; she knew the value of family. And she had proven it when she'd turned her back on a promising acting career to care for her three teenaged sisters when her father passed away.

To say the Westmorelands had undergone a lot of family turmoil of their own was an understatement. It all started when Aidan's parents and uncle and aunt died in a plane crash, leaving his cousin Dillon in charge of the family, along with Aidan's oldest brother, Ramsey, as backup. Dillon and Ramsey had worked hard and made sacrifices to keep the family together—all fifteen of them.

Aidan's parents had had eight children: five boys— Ramsey, Zane, Derringer and the twins, Aidan and Adrian—and three girls—Megan, Gemma and Bailey. Uncle Adam and Aunt Clarisse had had seven sons: Dillon, Micah, Jason, Riley, Canyon, Stern and Brisbane.

It hadn't been easy, especially since he, Adrian, Brisbane and Bailey had been under the age of sixteen. And Aidan would admit the four of them had been the most challenging of the bunch, getting into all sorts of mischief, even to the point that the State of Colorado ordered they be put in foster homes. Dillon had appealed that decision and won. Lucky for the four youngest Westmorelands, Dillon had known their acts of rebellion were their way of handling the grief of losing their parents. Now Aidan was in medical school; Adrian was working on his PhD in engineering; Bane had joined the navy and Bailey was taking classes at a local university while working part-time.

Aidan's thoughts shifted back to Jillian, although he didn't want them to. The birthday party yesterday had been a surprise, and the shocked look on her face had been priceless—adorable and a total turn-on. If he'd had any doubt about just how much he was attracted to her, that doubt had been dispelled when he saw her.

She had walked out onto the patio expecting a going-away party for his sister Gemma, who had married Callum and was moving to Australia. Instead it had been a surprise birthday party for her. After shedding a few happy tears, which he would have loved to lick away, she had hugged Pam and Dillon for thinking of her on her twenty-first birthday. From what he'd heard, it was the first time Jillian had had a party since she was a little kid.

While everyone had rushed over to congratulate her, he had hung back, checking her out. The sundress looked cute on her and it was obvious she wasn't the seventeen-year-old he'd met four years ago. Her face was fuller, her features stunning and her body...

Where had those curves come from? There's no way he would have missed them before. She was short compared with his six-foot-two-inch height. He figured she stood no taller than five feet three inches in bare feet. And speaking of her feet, her polished toes, a flaming red, had been another turn on. Pam might not want to hear it, but her sister was Hot with a capital *H*.

When he realized he had been the only one who hadn't wished her a happy birthday, he was about to do so when his phone rang. He had slipped off the patio to take the call from a friend from college who was trying to fix him up on a blind date for next weekend.

When he returned to the patio after finishing his call, everyone else had gone inside to watch a movie or play cards, and she'd been alone. She would never know how hard it had been for him to sit across from her without touching her. She looked good and smelled good, as well.

Jillian Novak had definitely caught his eye.

But Dillon and Pam would pluck out that same eye if he didn't squash what he was feeling.

Everybody knew how protective Pam was when it came to her sisters. Just like everyone knew Aidan wasn't one to take women seriously. And he didn't plan to change his behavior now. So the best thing for him to do while he was home for the next three days was to keep his distance from Jillian as he'd always done.

So why did I get her phone number and give her mine, for crying out loud?

Okay, he reasoned quickly, it had been a crazy moment, one he now regretted. The good thing was he doubted she would ever call him for help and he would make it a point never to call her.

That was a good plan, one he intended to stick to. Now, if he could only stop thinking about her that would be great. Glancing down at the medical journal he was supposed to be reading, he tried to focus on the words. Within a few minutes he'd read one interesting article and was about to start on another.

"Will you do me a *big* favor?"

Aidan glanced up to stare into the face of his sister Bailey. She used to be the baby in the Denver Westmoreland family but that had changed now that Dillon and Pam had a son, and Aidan's brother Ramsey and his wife, Chloe, had a daughter.

"Depends on what the favor is?"

"I promised Jill that I would go riding with her and show her the section of Westmoreland Country that she hasn't seen yet. Now they've called me to come in to work. I need you to go with Jillian instead."

"Just show her another day," he said, quickly deciding that going horseback riding with Jillian wasn't a smart idea.

"That was my original plan but I can't reach her on her cell phone. We were to meet at Gemma Lake, and you know how bad phone reception is out there. She's already there waiting for me."

He frowned. "Can't you ask someone else?"

"I did but everyone is busy."

His frown deepened. "And I'm not?"

Bailey rolled her eyes. "Not like everyone else. You're just reading a magazine."

He figured there was no use explaining to Bailey that his reading was important. He just so happened to be reading about a medical breakthrough where the use of bionic eyes had been tested as a way to restore sight with good results.

"Well, will you do it?"

He closed the medical journal and placed it aside. "You're positive there's no one else who can do it?"

"Yes, and she really wants to see it. This is her home now and—"

"Her home? She's away at school most of the time," he said.

"And so are you, Adrian, Stern and Canyon, and this is still your home. So what's your point?"

He decided not to argue with her. There were times when his baby sister could read him like an open book and he didn't want her to do that in this instance. It wouldn't take her long to figure out the story written on his pages was all about Jillian.

"Fine. I'll go."

"Act a little enthused, will you? You've been kind of standoffish with Jillian and her sisters since Dillon married Pam."

"I have not."

"You have, too. You should take time to get to know them. They're part of the family now. Besides, you and Jill will both become doctors one day so already you have a common interest."

He hoped like hell that would remain their only common interest. It was up to him to make sure it did. "Whatever," he said, standing and walking toward the door, pausing to grab his Stetson off the hat rack.

"And Aidan?"

He stopped before opening the door and turned around, somewhat annoyed. "What now?"

"Try to be nice. You can act like a grizzly bear at times."

That was her opinion. Deciding not to disagree with her, because you could never win with Bailey, he walked out of the house.

Two

Jillian heard the sound of a rider approaching and turned around, using her hand to shield her eyes from the glare of the sun. Although she couldn't make out the identity of the rider, she knew it wasn't Bailey.

The rider came closer and when her heart began pounding hard in her chest, she knew it was Aidan. What was he doing here? And where was Bailey?

Over breakfast she and Bailey had agreed to go riding after lunch. Because the property was located so far from Denver's city limits and encompassed so much land, the locals referred to it as Westmoreland Country. Although Jillian had seen parts of it, she had yet to see all of it and Bailey had volunteered to show it to her.

Dropping her hand to her side, Jillian drew in a deep breath as Aidan and his horse came closer. She tried not to notice how straight he sat in the saddle or how good he looked sitting astride the horse. And she tried not to gawk at how his Stetson, along with his western shirt, vest, jeans and boots, made him look like a cowboy in the flesh.

When he brought the horse to a stop a few feet from where she stood, she had to tilt her head all the way back to look up at him. "Aidan."

He nodded. "Jillian."

His irritated expression and the cutting sound of his voice made her think he was upset about something. Was she trespassing on a particular part of Westmoreland land where she had no business being?

Thinking she needed to give him an explanation, she said, "I'm waiting for Bailey. We're going riding."

"Yes, those *were* your plans."

She lifted a brow. "Were?"

He nodded. "Bailey tried reaching you but your phone is out of range. She was called in to work and asked that I take her place."

"Take her place?"

"Yes, take her place. She indicated you wanted to tour Westmoreland Country."

"I did, but…"

Penetrating dark eyes held hers. "But what?"

She shoved both hands into the pockets of her jeans. There was no way she could tell him that under no circumstances would she go riding anywhere with him. She could barely be around him for a few minutes without becoming unglued…like she was becoming now.

The reason she had placed her hands in her pockets was because they were already sweaty. And then there was that little ball of fire in her stomach that always seemed to burst into flames whenever he was around. Aidan Westmoreland oozed so much sexiness it was driving her to the edge of madness.

"Jillian?"

She blinked when he said her name. The sound of his voice was like a caress across her skin. "Yes?"

"But what? Do you have a problem with me being Bailey's replacement?"

She drew in a deep breath. She couldn't see him being anyone's replacement. It was easy to see he was his own man, and what a man he was. Even now, the weight of his penetrating gaze caused a heated rush to cross her flesh. So, yes, she had a problem with him being Bailey's replacement, but that was something she definitely wouldn't tell him.

"No, I don't have a problem with it," she lied without even blinking. "However, I would think that you do. I'm sure you have more to do with your time than spend it with me."

He shrugged massive shoulders. "No, in fact I don't, so it's not a problem. Besides, it's time for us to get to know each other better."

Why was her body tingling with awareness at his words? She was sure he didn't mean them the way they sounded, but she thought it best to seek clarification. "Why should we get to know each other better?"

He leaned back in the saddle and she couldn't help noticing the long fingers that held the reins. Why was she imagining those same fingers doing things to her, like stroking her hair, splaying up and down her arms, working their way across her naked body? She tried to downplay the shiver that passed through her.

"Dillon married Pam four years ago, and there's still a lot I don't know about you and your sisters," he said, bringing an end to her fantasizing. "We're all family and the Westmorelands are big on family. I haven't been home to get to know you, Paige and Nadia."

With him naming her sisters his earlier statement felt less personal. It wasn't just about her. She should be grateful for that but for some reason she wasn't. "Because of school I haven't been home much, either, but

we can get to know each other another time. It doesn't
have to be today," she said.

She doubted she could handle his closeness. Even the
masculine scent of him was overpowering.

"Today is just as good a day as any. I'm leaving to
go back to Boston tomorrow. There's no telling when
our paths will cross again. Probably not until we come
home for Christmas or something. We might as well do
it now and get it over with."

Why did she get the feeling that getting to know her
was something he felt forced to do? She took offense at
that. "Don't do me any favors," she all but snapped at
him while feeling her pulse pound.

"Excuse me?" He seemed surprised by her remark.

"There's no need to get *anything* over with. It's obvious Bailey roped you into doing something you really
don't want to do. I can see the rest of Westmoreland
Country on my own," she said, untying her horse and
then mounting it.

When she sat astride the mare she glanced back over
at him. "I don't need your company, Aidan."

He crossed his arms over his chest and she could tell
by the sudden tensing of his jaw that he hadn't liked her
comment. She was proven right when he said, with a
degree of smoldering intensity that she felt through her
clothes, "I hate to tell you this, Jillian Novak, but you
have my company whether you want it or not."

Aidan stared hard into Jillian's eyes and couldn't help
but feel they were waging a battle. Of what he wasn't
sure. Of wills? Of desire? Passion? Lust? He rubbed his
hand down his face. He preferred none of those things

but he had a feeling all of them were fighting for the number one spot right now.

He all but saw steam coming from her ears and figured Jillian didn't like being ordered around.

"Look," he said. "We're wasting time. You want to see the land and I have nothing better to do. I apologize if I came across a little gruff earlier, but by no means did I want to insinuate that I am being forced into showing you around or getting to know you."

There was no need to tell her that Bailey had asked him to be nice to Jillian and her sisters. He'd always been cordial and as far as he was concerned that was good enough. Getting too close to Jillian wasn't a good idea. But then, he was the one who had suggested she call him if she needed help preparing for medical school. He now saw that offer had been a mistake. A big one.

She studied him for a moment and he felt something deep in his gut. It was a lot stronger than the kick in his groin he'd experienced when he'd watched her swing her leg over the back of the horse to mount it. He'd taken a long, explosive breath while fighting the sexual hunger that had roared to life inside of him. Even now, with those beautiful full lips of hers frowning at him, a smoldering spike of heat consumed him. One way he knew he could put a stop to this madness was to get her out of his system, since she seemed to have gotten under his skin.

But the way he would do that wasn't an option…not if he loved his life.

"You're sure about this?"

Hell no, he wasn't sure about anything concerning her. Maybe the main reason behind his attraction to her, in addition to her striking beauty, was that he truly didn't know her that well. Maybe once he got to know her he'd discover that he didn't like her after all.

"Yes, I'm sure about this, so come on," he said, nudging his horse forward to stand beside hers. "There's a lot to see so I hope you're a fairly good rider."

She gave him a smile that made him appreciate the fullness of her mouth even more. "Yes, I'm a fairly good rider."

And then she took off, easing her horse into a canter. He watched in admiration as she flawlessly jumped the horse over a flowing creek.

He chuckled to himself. She wasn't a fairly good rider; she was an excellent one.

Jillian slowed her pace and glanced over her shoulder to see Aidan make the same jump she had. She couldn't help but be impressed at his skill, but she shouldn't be surprised. She'd heard from Dillon that all his brothers and cousins were excellent horsemen.

In no time, he'd caught up with her. "You're good," he said, bringing his horse alongside hers. The two animals eased into a communal trot.

"Thanks," she said, smiling over at him. "You're not bad yourself."

He threw his head back and laughed. The robust sound not only floated across the countryside, but it floated across her, as well. Although she'd seen him smile before, she'd never seen him amused about anything.

"No, I'm not bad myself. In fact there was a time I wanted to be a bronco rider in the rodeo."

For some reason she wasn't surprised. "Dillon talked you out of it?"

He shook his head, grinning. "No, he wouldn't have

done such a thing. One of Dillon's major rules has been for us to choose our own life goals. At least that was his rule for everyone but Bane."

She'd heard all about Aidan's cousin Brisbane Westmoreland, whom everyone called Bane. She'd also heard Dillon had encouraged his baby brother to join the military. He'd said Bane could do that or possibly go to prison for the trouble he'd caused. Bane had chosen the navy. In the four years that Pam had been married to Dillon, Jillian had only seen Bane twice.

"So what changed your mind about the rodeo?" she asked when they slowed the horses to a walk.

"My brother Derringer. He did the rodeo circuit for a couple of summers after high school. Then he got busted up pretty bad. Scared all of us to death and I freaked out. We all did. The thought of losing another family member brought me to my senses and I knew I couldn't put my family through that."

She nodded. She knew about him losing his parents and his aunt and uncle in a plane crash, leaving Dillon— the oldest at the time—to care for all of them. "Derringer and a few of your cousins and brothers own a horse-training business right?"

"Yes and it's doing well. They weren't cut out to work in the family business so after a few years they left to pursue their dreams of working with horses. I try to help them out whenever I come home but they're doing a great job without me. Several of their horses have won important derbies."

"Ramsey resigned as one of the CEOs as well, right?" she asked of his oldest brother.

He glanced over at her. "Yes. Ramsey has a degree in agriculture and economics. He'd always wanted to be a sheep farmer, but when my parents, aunt and uncle died in that plane crash he knew Dillon would need help at Blue Ridge."

Jillian knew that Blue Ridge Land Management was a Fortune 500 company Aidan's father and uncle had started years ago. "But eventually he was able to pursue his dream, right?"

Aidan nodded. "Yes. Once Dillon convinced Ramsey he could handle things at the corporation without him. Ramsey's sheep ranch is doing great."

She nodded. She liked Ramsey. In fact, she liked all the Westmorelands she had gotten to know. When Pam married Dillon, the family had welcomed her and her sisters with open arms. She'd discovered some of them were more outgoing than the others. But the one thing she couldn't help but notice was that they stuck together like glue.

"So how did you learn to ride so well?" he asked.

"My dad. He was the greatest and although I'm sure he wanted at least one son, he ended up with four girls. He felt we should know how to do certain things and handling a horse was one of them," she said, remembering the time she'd spent with her father and how wonderful it had been for her.

"He evidently saw potential in me because he made sacrifices and sent me to riding school. I competed nationally until he got sick. We needed the money to pay for his medicine and doctor bills."

"Do you regret giving it up?" he asked.

She shook her head. "No. I enjoyed it but making sure Dad got the best care meant more to me…more to all of us…than anything." And she meant it. There had been no regrets for any of them about giving up what they'd loved to help their father.

"Here we are."

She looked around at the beauty of the land surrounding her, as far as her eyes could see and beyond. Since Dillon was the oldest, he had inherited the main house along with the three hundred acres it sat on. Everyone else, upon reaching the age of twenty-five, received one hundred acres to call their own. Some parts of this area were cleared and other parts were dense with thick foliage. But what took her breath away was the beautiful waterway that branched off into a huge lake. Gemma Lake. She'd heard it had been named after Aidan's great-grandmother.

"This place is beautiful. Where are we exactly?"

He glanced over at her and smiled. "My land. Aidan's Haven.

Aidan's Haven, she immediately decided, suited him. She could see him building his home on this piece of land one day near this huge waterway. Today he looked like a cowboy, but she could see him transforming into a boat captain.

"Aidan's Haven. That's a nice name. How did you come up with it?"

"I didn't. Bailey did. She came up with all the names for our one-hundred-acre plots. She chose names like Stern's Stronghold, Zane's Hideout, Derringer's Dungeon, Ramsey's Web and Megan's Meadows, just to name a few."

Jillian had visited each of those areas and all the homes that had been built on the land were gorgeous. Some were single-story ranch-style designs, while others were like mansions with several floors. "When do you plan to build?"

"Not for a while yet. After medical school I'll probably work and live somewhere else for a while since I have six years of residency to complete for the cardiology program."

"But this will eventually be your home."

A pensive look appeared on his face. "Yes, Westmoreland Country will always be my home."

She'd always thought she would live in Gamble, Wyoming. Although she knew she would leave for college, she figured she would return one day and work in the hospital there before setting up a practice of her own. After all, she had lived there her entire life; all her friends were there. But after Pam married Dillon things changed for her, Paige and Nadia. They were close to their oldest sister and decided to leave Wyoming and make their homes close to Pam's. It had worked out well for everyone. Nadia was in her last year of high school here in Colorado and Paige was in California attending UCLA.

"What about you? Do you ever plan to return to Gamble, Wyoming, to live, Jillian?"

Again, she wondered why her stomach tightened whenever he said her name. Probably had something to do with that deep, husky voice of his.

"No, I don't plan to return to Gamble. In fact, Nadia and Paige and I talked a few weeks ago and we plan to approach Pam about selling the place. She would have done so already, but she thinks we want to keep it as part of our legacy."

"You don't?"

"Only because we've moved on and think of Denver

as home now. At least Nadia and I do. Paige has made a life for herself in Los Angeles. She's hoping her acting career takes off. We're hoping the same thing for her. Pam has done so much for us already and we don't want her to feel obligated to pay more of our college tuition and expenses, especially when we can use the money from the sale of the house to do so."

He nodded. "Let's take a walk. I want to show you around before we move on to Adrian's Cove."

He dismounted and tied his horse to a nearby tree. Then he turned to help her down. The moment he touched her, awareness of him filled her every pore. From the look in his eyes it was obvious that something similar was happening to him.

This was all new to her. She'd never felt anything like this before. And although her little lovemaking session with Cobb Grindstone on prom night had appeased her curiosity, it had left a lot to be desired.

As soon as her feet touched the ground, she heard a deep moan come from Aidan's throat. Only then did it become obvious that they'd gotten caught up in a carnal attraction that was so sharp it took her breath away.

"Jillian…"

He said her name again and, like all the other times, the deep, husky sound accentuated his sexiness. But before she could respond, the masculine hand planted around her waist nudged her closer and then his mouth lowered to hers.

Three

All sorts of feelings ripped through Aidan, making him totally conscious of the woman whose lips were locked to his. Deep in the center of his being he felt a throb unlike any he'd ever felt before—an intense flare of heat shooting straight to his loins.

He knew he had to stop. This wasn't any woman. This was Jillian Novak, Pam's sister. Dillon's sister-in-law. A woman who was now a part of the Westmoreland family. All that was well and good, but at the moment the only thing his mind could comprehend was that she had desire clawing at his insides and filling his every cell with awareness.

Instead of yielding to common sense, he was captivated by her sweet scent and her incredible taste, and the way her tongue stroked his showed both boldness and innocence. She felt exquisite in his arms, as if she belonged there. He wanted more. He wanted to feel her all over, kiss her all over. Taste her. Tempt her with sinful enticements.

The need for air was the only reason he released her lips, but her flavor made him want to return his mouth to hers and continue what they'd started.

The shocked look in her eyes told him she needed time to comprehend what had just happened between them. She took a step back and he watched as she took a deep breath.

"We should not have done that."

Aidan couldn't believe she had the nerve to say that while sultry heat still radiated off her. He might have thought the same thing seconds ago, but he couldn't agree with her now. Not when his fingers itched to reach out and pull her back into his arms so he could plow her mouth with another kiss. Dammit, why did her pouty lips look so inviting?

"Then why did we do it?" he countered. He might have made the first move but she had definitely been a willing participant. Her response couldn't lie. She had enjoyed the kiss as much as he had.

"I don't know why we did it, but we can't do it again."

That was easy for her to say. "Why not?"

She frowned at him. "You know why not. Your cousin is married to my sister."

"And?"

She placed her hands on her hips giving him a mind-boggling view of her slim waist line. "And we can't do it again. I know all about your womanizing reputation, Aidan."

Her words struck a nerve. "Do you?"

"Yes. And I'm not interested. The only thing I'm interested in is getting into medical school. That's the only thing on my mind."

"And the only thing on mine is getting out of medical school," he countered in a curt tone. "As far as Dillon being married to Pam, it changes nothing. You're still a beautiful woman and I'm a man who happens to notice such things. But since I know how the situation stands between us, I'll make sure it doesn't happen again."

"Thank you."

"You're welcome. Glad we got that cleared up. Now I can continue showing you around."

"I'm not sure that's a good idea."

He watched her and when she pushed a lock of hair away from her face, he again thought how strikingly beautiful she was. "Why not? You don't think you can control yourself around me?" he asked, actually smiling at the possibility of that being true.

Her look of anger should have warned him, but he'd never been one to heed signs. "Trust me, that's definitely not it."

"Then there's no reason for me not to finish showing you around, is there, Jillian? Besides, Bailey will give me hell about it if I don't. There's a lot of land we still have to cover so let's get started."

He began walking along the bank of the river and figured that after cooling off Jillian would eventually catch up.

Jillian watched Aidan walk ahead and decided to hang back a moment to reclaim her common sense. Why had she allowed him to kiss her? And why had she enjoyed it so much?

The man gave French kissing a whole new definition, and she wasn't sure her mouth would ever be the same.

No one had ever kissed her like that before. No one would have dared. To be honest, she doubted anyone she'd ever kissed would know how. Definitely not Cobb. Or that guy in her freshman year at Wyoming University, Les, that she'd dropped really quickly when he wanted to take her to a hotel and spend the night on their first date. He might have been a star on the school's football team, but from the couple of times they had kissed, compared to what she'd just experienced with Aidan, Les had definitely dropped the ball.

But then, regardless of how enjoyable Aidan's kiss had been, she was right in what she'd told him about not repeating it. She had no business getting involved with a guy whose favorite sport was messing around. She knew better. Honestly, she didn't know what had come over her.

However, she knew full well what had come over him. More than once she'd overheard Dillon express his concern to Pam that although the twins were doing well at Harvard, he doubted they would ever settle down into serious relationships since they seemed to enjoy being womanizers. That meant Aidan's interest in her was only because of overactive testosterone. Pam had warned Jillian numerous times about men who would mean her no good, and her oldest sister would be highly disappointed if Jillian fell for the ploy of a man like Aidan. A man who could take away her focus on becoming a doctor just to make her his plaything.

Feeling confident she had her common sense back on track, she began walking. Aidan wasn't too far ahead and it wouldn't take long for her to catch up with him. In the meantime she couldn't help but appreciate his manly physique. His faded jeans emphasized masculine thighs, a rock-solid behind, tight waist and wide shoulders. He didn't just walk, he swaggered, and he did it so blatantly sexily, it increased her heart rate with every step he took.

Moments later he slowed and turned around to stare at her, pinning her with his dark gaze. Had he felt her ogling him? Did he know she had been checking out his rear big-time? She hoped not because his front was just as impressive. She could see why he was in such high demand when it came to women.

"You coming?"

I will be if you don't stop looking at me like that, Jillian thought, getting closer to where he stood. She felt the heat of his gaze on every inch of her. She came to a stop in front of him. She couldn't take looking into his eyes any longer so she glanced around. In addition to the huge lake there were also mountains surrounding the property. "You have a nice mountain view in this spot and can see the lake from here," she said.

"I know. That's why I plan to build my house right here."

She nodded. "Have you designed it yet?"

"No. I don't plan on building for several more years, but I often come here and think about the time when I will. The house will be large enough for me and my family."

She snapped her head around. "You plan on getting married?"

His chuckle was soft but potent. "Yes, one day. That surprises you?"

She decided to be honest. "Yes. You do have a reputation."

He leaned one broad shoulder against a Siberian elm tree. "This is the second time today that you've mentioned something about my reputation. Just what have you heard about me?"

She took a seat across from him on a huge tree stump. "I heard what hellions you, Adrian, Bailey and Bane used to be."

He nodded solemnly. "Yes, we were that. But that was a long time ago, and I can honestly say we regretted our actions. When we grew older and realized the impact we'd had on the family, we apologized to each one of them."

"I'm sure they understood. You were just children and there was a reason you did what you did," she said. She'd heard the full story from Pam. The deaths of their parents, and aunt and uncle, had been the hardest on those youngest four. Everyone had known that their acts of rebellion were their way of handling their grief.

"Sorry I mentioned it," she said, feeling bad that she'd even brought it up.

He shrugged. "No harm done. It is what it is. It seems the four of us got a reputation we've been trying to live down for years. But I'm sure that's not the reputation of mine that you were really referring to."

No, it wasn't. "I understand you like women."

He chuckled. "Most men do."

She raised a brow, not in the least amused. "I mean you really like them, but you don't care about their feelings. You break their hearts without any concern for the pain it might cause."

He studied her for a long moment. "That's what you heard?"

"Yes. And now you want me to believe that you're seriously considering settling down one day, marrying and having a family?"

"Yes. One doesn't have anything to do with the other. What I do now in no way affects any future plans. I need to clarify something. I don't deliberately set out to break any woman's heart. I tell any woman I date the truth up front—my career as a doctor is foremost. However, if she refuses to take me at my word and assumes that she can change my mind, then it's not my fault when she finds out otherwise."

"So in other words…"

"In other words, Jillian, I don't intentionally set up any woman for heartbreak or lead her on," he answered curtly.

She knew she should probably leave well enough alone and stop digging, but for some reason she couldn't help herself. "However, you do admit to dating a *lot* of women."

"Yes, I admit it. And why not? I'm single and don't plan to get into a committed relationship anytime soon. And contrary to what you believe, I don't date as many women as you might think. My time is pretty limited these days because of medical school."

She could imagine. How he managed to date at all while in medical school was beyond her. He was definitely into multitasking. She'd discovered most relationships demanded a lot of work and it was work she didn't have time for. Evidently he made things easy by not getting serious with any woman. At least he'd been honest about it. He dated women for the fun of it and didn't love any of them.

"I have one other question for you, Aidan," she said, after drawing in a deep breath.

"What's your question?"

"If all of what you said is true, about not getting serious with any woman, then why did you kiss me?"

Now that was a good question, one he could answer but really didn't want to. She did deserve an answer, though, especially after the way he had plowed her mouth earlier. She was twenty-one, five years younger

than him. And although she'd held her own during their
kiss, he knew they were worlds apart when it came to
sexual experience. Therefore, before he answered her,
he needed to ask a few questions of his own.

"Why did you kiss me back?"

He could tell by her expression that she was surprised
by his counterquestion. And, as he'd expected, she tried
to avoid giving him an answer. "That's not the issue
here."

He couldn't help but smile. Little did she know it *was*
the issue, but he would touch on that later. "The reason
I kissed you, Jillian, is because I was curious. I think
you have a beautiful pair of lips and I wanted to taste
them. I wanted to taste you. It's something I've wanted
to do for a while."

He saw her jaw drop and had to hold his mouth closed
for a second to keep from grinning. She hadn't expected
him to answer her question so bluntly or to be so direct. That's something she needed to know about him.
He didn't sugarcoat anything. *Straightforward* could be
his middle name.

"So now that you know my reason for kissing you,
what was your reason for kissing me back?"

She began nibbling on her bottom lip. Watching her
made him ache, made him want to take hold of those
lips and have his way with them again.

"I—I was…"

When she didn't say anything else, he lifted a brow.
"You were what?"

Then she had the nerve to take her tongue and lick
those same lips she'd been nibbling on moments ago. "I
was curious about you, too."

He smiled. Now they were getting somewhere. "I can

understand that. I guess the reason you asked about the kiss is because I told you I'm not into serious relationships when it comes to women. I hope you don't think a deep kiss constitutes a serious relationship."

From the look on her face, which she quickly wiped off, that's exactly what she'd thought. She was more inexperienced than he'd assumed. He wondered just how inexperienced she was. Most twenty-one-year-old women he knew wore desire, instead of their hearts, on their sleeves.

"Of course I knew that."

If she knew that then why were they having this conversation? If she thought he was looking for something serious just because he'd kissed her then she was so far off the mark it wasn't funny.

"How many boyfriends have you had?"

"Excuse me?"

No, he wouldn't excuse her. There were certain things she needed to know. Things experience had nothing to do with. "I asked how many boyfriends you've had. And before you tell me it's none of my business, I'm asking for a reason."

She lifted her chin in a defiant pose. "I can't imagine what reason you would have for needing to know that."

"So you can protect yourself." He thought she looked both adorable and sexy. From the way her curly hair tumbled down her shoulders to the way the smoothness of her skin shone in the sunlight.

She lifted a brow. "Against men like you?"

"No. Men like me would never mislead you into thinking there was anything serious about a kiss. But there are men who would lead you to think otherwise."

She frowned. "And you don't think I can handle myself?"

He smiled. "Not the way I think you should. For some reason you believe you can avoid kisses until you're in a serious relationship and there are certain kisses that can't be avoided."

He could tell by her expression that she didn't believe him. "Take the kiss we shared earlier. Do you honestly think you could have avoided it once I got started?" he asked her.

Her frown deepened. "Yes, of course I could have."

"Then why didn't you?"

She rolled her eyes. "I told you. The only reason I allowed you to kiss me, and the only reason I participated, is because I was curious."

"Really?"

She rolled her eyes again. "Really. Truly."

"So, you're not curious anymore?"

She shook her head. "Nope, not at all. I wondered what kissing you was like and now I know."

Deciding to prove her wrong and settle the matter once and for all, he moved away from the tree and walked toward her.

Figuring out his intent, she stood with a scowl on her face. "Hold it right there, Aidan Westmoreland. Don't you dare think you're going to kiss me again."

When he reached her, he came to a stop directly in front of her and she refused to back up. Instead she stood her ground. He couldn't help but admire her spunk, although in this case it would be wasted.

"I do dare because I don't just think it, Jillian, I know it. And I also know that you're going to kiss me back. *Again*."

Four

Jillian doubted she'd ever met a more arrogant man. And what was even worse, he had the nerve to stand in front of her with his Stetson tipped back and his legs braced apart in an overconfident stance. How dare he tell her what she would do? Kiss him back? Did he really believe that? Honestly?

She tilted her head back to glare up at him. He didn't glare back, but he held her gaze in a way that was unnerving. And then his eyes moved, slowly raking over her from head to toe. Was that desire she felt rushing through her body? Where had these emotions inside of her come from? Was she getting turned on from the way he was looking at her? She tried to stiffen at the thought but instead she was drawn even more into the heat of his gaze.

"Stop that!"

He lifted a brow. "Stop what?"

"Whatever you're doing."

He crossed his arms over his chest. "So, you think I'm responsible for the sound of your breathing? For the way your nipples have hardened and are pressing against your shirt? And for the way the tip of your tongue is tingling, eager to connect with mine?"

Every single thing he'd pointed out was actually happening to her, but she refused to admit any of them. She crossed her arms over her own chest. "I have no idea what you're talking about."

"Then I guess we're at a standoff."

"No, we're not," she said, dropping her hands to her sides. "I'm leaving. You can play this silly game with someone else."

She turned to go and when his hand reached out and touched her arm, sharp spikes of blood rushed through her veins, filling her pores, drenching the air she was breathing with heated desire. And what on earth was that hunger throbbing inside of her at the juncture of her thighs? And what were those slow circles he was making on her arm with his index finger? She expelled a long deep breath and fought hard to retain control of her senses.

Jillian wanted to snatch her arm away but found she couldn't. What kind of spell had he cast on her? Every hormone in her body sizzled, hissed and surged with a need she'd never felt before. She couldn't deny the yearning pulsing through her even if she wanted to.

"You feel it, don't you, Jillian? It's crazy, I know, and it's something I can't explain, but I feel it each and every time I'm within a few feet of you. As far as I'm concerned, Pam and Dillon are the least of our worries. Figuring out just what the hell is going on between us should be at the top of the agenda. You can deny it as long as you want, but that won't help. You need to admit it like I have."

She did feel it and a part of her knew there was real danger in admitting such a thing. But another part knew he was right. With some things it was best to admit there was a problem and deal with it. Otherwise, she would lay awake tonight and regret not doing so.

His hand slowly traveled up her arm toward her lips. There he cradled her mouth in the palm of his hands. "And whatever it is has me wanting to taste you and has you wanting to taste me. It has me wanting to lick your mouth dry and you wanting to lick mine in the same way."

He paused a moment and when he released a frustrated breath she knew that whatever this "thing" was between them, he had tried fighting it, as well. But he had given up the fight and was now ready to move to the next level, whatever that was.

"I need to taste you, Jillian," he said.

As much as she wished otherwise, there was a deep craving inside of her to taste him, too. Just one more time. Then she would walk away, mount her horse and ride off like the devil himself was after her. But for now she needed this kiss as much as she needed to breathe.

She saw him lowering his head and she was poised for the exact moment when their mouths would connect. She even parted her lips in anticipation. His mouth was moving. He was whispering something but instead of focusing on what he was saying, her gaze was glued to the erotic movement of his lips. And the moment his mouth touched hers she knew she had no intention of turning back.

Nothing could have prepared Aidan for the pleasure that radiated through his body. How could she arouse him like no other woman could? Instead of getting bogged down in the mystery of it all, he buried his fingers in her hair, holding her in place while his mouth mated hungrily with hers.

And she was following his lead, using her tongue with the same intensity and hunger as he was using his. It was all about tasting, and they were tasting each other with a greed that had every part of his body on fire.

He felt it, was in awe of it. In every pore, in every nerve ending and deep in his pulse, he felt it. Lowering his hand from her hair he gently gripped her around the waist and, with their mouths still locked, he slowly maneuvered her backward toward the tree he'd leaned against earlier. When her back rested against the trunk, her thighs parted and he eased between them, loving the feel of his denim rubbing against hers.

Frissons of fire, hotter than he'd ever encountered, burned a path up his spine and he deepened the kiss as if his life depended on him doing so. Too soon, in his estimation, they had to come up for air and he released her mouth just as quickly as he'd taken it.

He tried not to notice the thoroughly kissed look on her face when she drew in a deep breath. He took a step back so he wouldn't be tempted to kiss her again. The next time he knew he wouldn't stop with a kiss. He wouldn't be satisfied until he had tasted her in other places, as well. And then he would want to make love to her, right here on his land. On the very spot he planned to build his house. Crap! Why was he thinking such a thing? In frustration, he rubbed a hand down his face.

"I think we need to move on."

Her words made him look back at her and an ache settled deep in his stomach. She was beautiful and desire escalated through him all over again. Giving in to what he wanted, he took a step forward and lowered his mouth to hers, taking a sweep of her mouth with his tongue. His groin swelled when she caught his tongue and began sucking on it.

He broke off the kiss and drew in a ragged breath. "Jillian! You're asking for trouble. I'm within two seconds of spreading you on the ground and getting inside of you." The vision of such a thing nearly overpowered his senses.

"I told you we should go. You're the one who kissed me again."

He smiled. "And you kissed me back. Now you understand what I meant when I said there are some kisses that can't be avoided. You didn't want me to kiss you initially, but then you did."

She frowned slightly. "You seduced me. You made me want to kiss you."

His smile widened. "Yes, to both."

"So this was some sort of lesson?"

He shook his head. "Not hardly. I told you I wanted to taste you. I enjoyed doing so."

"This can't become a habit, Aidan."

"And I don't intend to make it one, trust me. My curiosity has more than been satisfied."

She nodded. "So has mine. Are you ready to show me the other parts of Westmoreland Country?"

"Yes. We're headed for Adrian's Cove next and then Bailey's Bay and Bane's Ponderosa."

He backed up to give her space and when she moved around him, he was tempted to reach out and pull her back into his arms, kiss her some more, until he got his fill. But he had a feeling that getting his fill would not be possible and that was something he didn't want to acknowledge.

* * *

"So, how did the tour go with Aidan yesterday?"

Jillian glanced up from her breakfast when Bailey slid into the chair next to her. Pam had shared breakfast with Jillian earlier before leaving for the grocery store, and had asked her the same thing. It had been hard to keep a straight face then and it was harder to do so now.

"It went well. There's a lot of land in Westmoreland Country. I even saw the property you own, Bailey's Bay."

Bailey smiled. "I can't claim ownership until I'm twenty-five so I have a couple years left. But when I do, I plan to build the largest house of them all. It will even be bigger than this one."

Jillian thought that would be an accomplishment because Dillon and Pam's house was huge. Their house was three stories and had eight bedrooms, six bathrooms, a spacious eat-in kitchen, a gigantic living room, a large dining room with a table that could seat over forty people easily, and a seven-car-garage.

"I can't wait to see it when you do." Jillian liked Bailey and had from the first time she'd set foot in Westmoreland Country to attend Pam's engagement party. And since there was only a couple years' difference in their ages, with Bailey being older, they had hit it off immediately. "What happens if you meet and marry a guy who wants to take you away from here?"

"That won't happen because there's not a man alive who can do that. This is where I was born and this is where I'll die."

Jillian thought Bailey sounded sure of that. Hadn't Jillian felt the same way about her home in Wyoming at one time? Although it hadn't been a man that had changed her mind, it had been the thought of how much money Pam would be paying for three sisters in college. Although her older sister had married a very wealthy man, it still would not have been right.

"Besides," Bailey said, cutting into her thoughts. "I plan to stay single forever. Having five bossy brothers and seven even bossier male cousins is enough. I don't need another man in my life trying to tell me what to do."

Jillian smiled. When she'd heard the stories about all the trouble Bailey used to get into when she was younger, Jillian had found it hard to believe. Sitting across from her was a beautiful, self-confident woman who seemed to have it going on. A woman who definitely knew what she wanted.

"I hope Aidan was nice and didn't give you any trouble."

Jillian lifted a brow. "Why would you say that?"

Bailey shrugged. "Aidan has his moods sometimes."

"Does he?"

"Yes, but if you didn't pick up on them then I guess he did okay."

No, she hadn't picked up on any mood, but she had picked up on his sensual side. And he had definitely picked up on hers. She was still in a quandary as to exactly what had happened yesterday. It was as if she'd become another person with him. She'd discovered that being kissed senseless wasn't just a cliché but was something that could really happen. Aidan had proven it. Even after brushing her teeth twice, rinsing out her mouth and eating a great breakfast Pam had prepared, the taste of him was still deeply embedded on her tongue. And what was even crazier was that she liked it.

Knowing Bailey was probably expecting a response,

she said. "Yes, he was okay. I thought he was rather nice."

Bailey nodded. "I'm glad. I told him he needed to get to know you and your sisters better since he's rarely home. And we're all family now."

All family now. Bailey's words were a stark reminder of why what happened yesterday could never be repeated. They weren't just a guy and a girl who'd met with no connections. They had deep connections. Family connections. And family members didn't go around kissing each other. Why of all the guys out there did she have to be attracted to one with the last name Westmoreland?

"So, besides Bailey's Bay where else did he take you?"

To heaven and back. The words nearly slid from Jillian's lips because that's where she felt she'd actually been. Transported there and back by a kiss. Amazing. Pulling her thoughts together, she said, "First, we toured Aidan's Haven."

"Isn't it beautiful? That's the property I originally wanted because of the way it's surrounded by Gemma Lake. But then I realized it would have been too much water to deal with. I think the spot where Aidan plans to build his house is perfect, though, and will provide an excellent view of the lake and mountains, no matter what room of the house you're in."

Jillian agreed and eradicated the thought from her mind that Aidan's wife and kids would one day live there. "I also saw Adrian's Cove. That piece of property is beautiful, as well. I love the way it's surrounded by mountains."

"Me, too."

"And from there we visited Bailey's Bay, Canyon's Bluff and Stern's Stronghold."

"Like the names?"

Jillian smiled. "Yes, and I heard they were all your idea."

"Yes," Bailey said, grinning. "Being the baby in the family has its benefits. Including the opportunity to play musical beds and sleep at whatever place I want. I was living with Dillon full-time, but after he married I decided to spread myself around and check out my brothers', sisters' and cousins' abodes. I like driving them crazy, especially when one of my brothers or cousins brings his girlfriend home."

Jillian couldn't help but laugh. Although she wouldn't trade her sisters for the world, it had to be fun having older brothers and male cousins to annoy.

"What's so funny?"

Jillian's heart skipped a beat upon hearing that voice and knowing who it belonged to. Aidan leaned in the kitchen doorway. Wearing a pair of jeans that rode low on his hips and a muscle shirt, he looked too sexy for her peace of mind. She couldn't help studying his features. It was obvious he'd just gotten out of bed. Those dark eyes that were alert and penetrating yesterday had a drowsy look. And she couldn't miss the dark shadow on his chin indicating he hadn't shaved yet. If he looked like that every morning, she would just love to see it.

"I thought you'd already left to return to Boston," Bailey said, getting up and crossing the room to give him a hug. Jillian watched the interaction and a part of her wished she could do the same.

"I won't be leaving until tomorrow."

"Why did you change your plans?" Bailey asked, surprised. "Normally, you're in a rush to get back."

Yes, why? Jillian wondered as well and couldn't wait for his answer.

"Because I wasn't ready to go back just yet. No big deal."

"Um," Bailey said, eyeing her brother suspiciously, "I get the feeling it is a big deal and probably has to do with some woman. I heard you, Adrian and Stern didn't get in until late last night."

Jillian turned her gaze away from Bailey and Aidan and took a sip of her orange juice. The spark of anger she suddenly felt couldn't be jealousy over what Bailey had just said. Had Aidan kissed Jillian senseless, then gone somewhere last night and kissed someone else the same way? Why did the thought of him doing that bother her?

"You ask too many questions, Bay, and stay out my business," Aidan said. "So, what's so funny, Jillian?"

Jillian drew in a deep breath before turning back to Aidan. "Nothing."

Bailey chuckled. "In other words, Aidan, stay out of *her* business."

Jillian heard his masculine grunt before he crossed the room to the coffeepot. The kitchen was huge, so why did it suddenly feel so small now that he'd walked in? And why did he have to walk around with such a sexy saunter?

"Well, I hate to run but I promised Megan that I would house-sit for a few hours so I'm headed for Megan's Meadows. Gemma is decorating the place before leaving for Australia and is sending her crew over to hang new curtains."

Megan and Gemma were Bailey and Aidan's sisters,

whom Jillian liked tremendously. Megan was a doctor of anesthesiology at one of the local hospitals and Gemma was an interior designer who owned Designs by Gem.

Bailey turned to Jillian. "You're here until tomorrow, right?"

"Yes."

"Then maybe Aidan can show you the parts of Westmoreland Country that you missed yesterday."

Jillian could feel Aidan's gaze on her. "I wouldn't want to put him to any trouble."

"No trouble," Aidan said, "I don't have anything else to do today."

Bailey laughed. "Until it's time for you to go and hook up with the woman who's the reason you're staying around an extra day."

"Goodbye, Bay," Aidan said in what Jillian perceived as an annoyed tone.

Bailey glanced over her shoulder at him while departing. "See you later, Aidan. And you better not leave tomorrow before telling me goodbye." She swept out of the kitchen and Jillian found herself alone with Aidan.

She glanced over at him and saw him leaning back against the counter with a cup of coffee in his hand, staring at her.

She drew in a deep breath when Aidan asked, "How soon can we go riding?"

Five

Aidan couldn't help staring into Jillian's eyes. He thought she had the most beautiful eyes of any woman he'd ever seen. And that included all those women who'd thrown themselves at him last night.

"I'm not going anywhere with you, Aidan. Besides, I'm sure the reason you changed your plans to remain in Denver another day has nothing to do with me."

Boy was she wrong. It had everything to do with her. He had spent three hours in a nightclub last night surrounded by beautiful women and all he could think about was the one he considered the most beautiful of all. Her.

A possibility suddenly hit him. Was she jealous? Did she actually believe that crap Bailey had just spouted about him changing his schedule because of some woman? He didn't know whether to be flattered or annoyed that she, or any woman, thought they mattered enough that they should care about his comings and goings. But in all honesty, what really annoyed him was that she *was* beginning to matter. And the reason he had decided to hang in Denver another day was because of her.

Instead of saying anything right away, for fear he might say the wrong thing, he turned and refilled his coffee cup. Then he crossed the room and slid into the chair across from her. Immediately, he sensed her nervousness.

"I don't bite, Jillian," he said, before taking a sip of coffee.

"I hope not."

He couldn't help but smile as he placed his cup down. He reached out and closed his fingers around her wrist. "Trust me. I prefer kissing you to biting you."

She pulled her hand back and nervously glanced over her shoulder before glaring at him. "Are you crazy? Anyone could walk in here!"

"And?"

"And had they heard what you just said they would have gotten the wrong impression."

He leaned back in his chair. "What do you think is the *right* impression?"

Her hair was pulled back in a ponytail and he was tempted to reach out, release the clasp and watch the waves fall to her shoulders. Then he would run his fingers through the thick, black tresses. He could just imagine the light, gentle strokes on her scalp and the thought sent a sudden jolt of sexual need through him.

"I don't want to make any impression, Aidan. Right or wrong."

Neither did he. At least he didn't think he did. Damn, the woman had him thinking crazy. He rubbed a frustrated hand down his face.

"It was just a kiss, nothing more."

He looked over at her. Why was he getting upset that she thought that way when he should be thinking the same thing. Hadn't he told her as much yesterday?

"Glad you think that way," he said, standing. "So let's go riding."

"Didn't you hear what I said?"

He smiled down at her. "You've said a lot. What part in particular are you asking about?"

She rolled her eyes. "I said I'm not going anywhere with you."

His smile widened. "Sure you are. We're going riding because if we don't, Bailey will think it's because I did something awful and got you mad with me. And if she confronts me about it, I will have to confess and tell her the truth—that the reason you wouldn't go riding with me is because you were afraid I might try to kiss you again. A kiss you can't avoid enjoying."

She narrowed her gaze at him. "You wouldn't."

"Trust me, I would. Confessing my sins will clear my conscience but will they clear yours? I'm not sure they would since you seem so wrapped up in not making any right or wrong impressions."

She just sat there and said nothing. He figured she was at a loss for words and this would be the best time for him to leave her to her thoughts. "Let's meet at the same place where we met yesterday in about an hour," he said, walking off to place his cup in the dishwasher.

Before exiting the kitchen he turned back to her and said, "And just so you know, Jillian, the reason I'm not leaving today to return to Boston has nothing to do with some woman I met at the club last night, but it has everything to do with you."

It has everything to do with you.

Not in her wildest dreams had Jillian thought seven little words could have such a huge impact on her. But they did. So much so that an hour later, she was back in the same place she'd been yesterday, waiting on Aidan.

She began pacing. Had she lost her mind? She wasn't sure what kind of game he was playing but instead of putting her foot down and letting him know she wanted no part of his foolishness, somehow she got caught, hook, line and sinker.

And all because of a kiss.

She would have to admit, it had been more than just a kiss. The fact that he was a gorgeous man, a man she'd had a secret crush on for four years, probably had a lot to do with it. But she'd always been able to separate fact from fiction, reality from fantasy, good from bad. So what was wrong with her now? An association with Aidan would only bring on heartache because not only was she deceiving her sister and brother-in-law, and no doubt the entire Westmoreland family, but she was deceiving herself, as well. Why would she want to become involved with a man known as a womanizer?

But then, she really wasn't involved with him. He was taking her riding, probably he would try to steal a few kisses and then nothing. Tomorrow he would return to Boston and she would return to Wyoming and it would be business as usual. But she knew for her it wouldn't be that simple.

She turned when she heard his approach. Their gazes connected and a luscious shiver ran through her body. He rode just like he had yesterday and looked basically the same. But today something was different. Now she knew he had the mouth of a very sensual man. A mouth he definitely knew how to use.

"I was hoping you would be here," he said, bringing his horse to a stop a few feet from her.

"Did you think I wouldn't after what you threatened to do?"

"I guess not," he said, dismounting.

"And you have no remorse?"

He tipped his Stetson back to gaze at her. "I've heard confession is good for the soul."

"And just what would it have accomplished, Aidan?"

"Putting it out there would have cleared your conscience, since it obviously bothers you that someone might discover I'm attracted to you and that you're attracted to me."

She started to deny what he'd said about her being attracted to him, but decided not to waste her time. It was true and they both knew it. "A true gentleman never kisses and tells."

"You're right. A true gentleman doesn't kiss and tell. But I don't like the thought of you cheapening what happened yesterday, either."

She placed her hands on her hips and leaned in, glaring at him. "How is it cheapening it when the whole thing meant nothing to you anyway?"

Jillian's question stunned Aidan. For a moment he couldn't say anything. She had definitely asked a good question, and it was one he wasn't sure he could answer. The only response he could come up with was that the kisses should not have meant anything to him, but they had. Hell, he had spent the past twenty-four hours thinking about nothing else. And hadn't he changed his plans so that he could stay another day just to spend more time with her?

She was standing there, glaring at him, with her arms crossed over her chest in a way that placed emphasis on a nice pair of breasts. Full and perfectly shaped. He could just imagine running his hands over them, teasing the nipples before drawing them in his mouth to...

"Well?"

She wanted an explanation and all he wanted to do was erase the distance separating them, take her into his arms and kiss that glare right off her face. Unfortunately, he knew he wouldn't stop there. Whether she knew it or not, Jillian Novak's taste only made him want more.

"Let's ride," he said, moving toward his horse. Otherwise, he would be tempted to do something he might later regret.

"Ride?" she hissed. "Is that all you've got to say?"

He glanced back over at her as he mounted his horse. "For now."

"None of this makes any sense, Aidan," she said, mounting her own horse.

She was right about that, he thought. None of it made any sense. Why was she like a magnet pulling him in? And why was he letting her?

They had ridden a few moments side by side in total silence when she finally broke it by asking, "Where are we going?"

"Bane's Ponderosa."

She nodded. "Has he built anything on it?"

"No, because legally it's not his yet. He can't claim it until he's twenty-five."

"Like Bailey. She told me about the age requirement."

"Yes, like Bailey."

He wished they could go back to not talking. He needed the silence to figure out what in the hell was happening to him. She must have deciphered that he was not in a talkative mood because she went silent again.

Aidan glanced over at her, admiring how well she handled a horse. He couldn't help admiring other things, as well. Such as how she looked today in her jeans and western shirt, and how the breasts he had fantasized about earlier moved erotically in rhythm with the horse's prance.

"There is a building here," Jillian said, bringing her horse to a stop.

He forced his eyes off her breasts to follow her gaze to the wooden cabin. He brought his horse to a stop, as well. "If you want to call it that, then yes. Bane built it a while back. It became his and Crystal's secret lovers' hideaway."

"Crystal?"

"Yes. Crystal Newsome. Bane's one and only."

Jillian nodded. "She's the reason he had to leave and join the navy, right?"

Aidan shrugged. "I guess you could say that, although I wouldn't place the blame squarely on Crystal's shoulders. Bane was as much into Crystal as Crystal was into Bane. They were both sticks of dynamite waiting to explode."

"Where is she now?"

"Don't know. I'm not sure if Bane even knows. He never says and I prefer not to ask," Aidan said, getting off his horse and tying it to the rail in front of the cabin.

He moved to assist her from her horse and braced himself for the onslaught of emotions he knew he would feel when he did so.

"You don't have to help me down, Aidan. I can manage."

"I'm sure you can but I'm offering my assistance anyway," he said, reaching his arms up to her.

For a minute he thought she would refuse his offer, but then she slid into his embrace. And as expected the moment they touched, fire shot through him. He actually felt his erection throb. He didn't say anything as he stared into her face. How could she arouse him to this degree?

"You can let go of me now, Aidan."

He blinked, realizing her feet were on the ground yet his arms were still around her waist. He tried to drop his arms but couldn't. It was as if they had a mind of their own.

Then, in a surprise move, she reached up and placed her arms around his neck. "This is crazy," she whispered in a quiet tone. "I shouldn't want this but I'm not thinking straight."

He shouldn't want it, either, but at that moment nothing could stop him. "We're leaving tomorrow. When we get back to our respective territories we can think straight then."

"What about right now?" she asked, staring deep into his gaze.

"Right now all I want to do is taste you again, Jillian. So damn bad."

She lifted her chin. "Then do it."

He doubted she knew what she was saying because her lips weren't the only thing he wanted to taste. He lowered his mouth to hers, thinking that she would find that out soon enough.

At that particular moment, Jillian couldn't deny herself the enjoyment of this kiss even if her life had depended on it.

She was getting what she wanted in full force—Aidan Westmoreland–style.

She stood with her arms wrapped around his neck and their lips locked, mesmerized, totally captivated, completely enthralled. How his tongue worked around in her mouth was truly remarkable. Every bone, every pore and every nerve ending responded to the way she was being thoroughly kissed. When had she become capable of such an intense yearning like this, where every lick and suck of Aidan's tongue could send electrical waves through her?

"Let's go inside," he whispered, pulling back from the kiss while tonguing her lips.

"Inside?" She could barely get the question past the feeling of burning from the inside out.

"Yes. We don't need to be out here in the open."

No they didn't. She had gotten so caught up in his kiss that she'd forgotten where they were. But instead of saying they shouldn't even be kissing, in the open or behind closed doors, she didn't resist him when he took her hand and tugged her toward the cabin.

Once the door closed behind them she looked around and was surprised at how tidy the place was. Definitely not what she'd expected. It was a one-room cabin with an iron bed. The colorful bedspread matched the curtains and coordinated with the huge area rug.

She turned to Aidan. "This is nice. Who keeps this place up?"

"Gemma promised Bane that she would and of course she had to put her signature on it. Now that she's getting married and moving to Australia, Bailey will take over. This place is important to Bane. He spends time here whenever he comes home."

Jillian nodded. "How's he doing?"

Aidan shrugged. "Okay now. It was hard for him to buckle down and follow authority, but he has no other choice if he wants to be a SEAL."

She'd heard that was Bane Westmoreland's goal. "So no one usually comes out this way?" She needed to know. There would be no turning back after today and she needed to make sure they didn't get caught.

"Rarely, although Ramsey uses this land on occasion for his sheep. But you don't have to worry about anyone showing up if that's what you're worried about."

She turned to face him. "I don't know why I'm doing this."

He touched her chin and tilted her head back to meet his gaze. "Do you want me to tell you?"

"Think you got it all figured out?"

He nodded. "Yes, I think I do."

"Okay then, let's hear it," she said, backing up to sit on the edge of the bed.

He moved to sit down on a nearby stool. "We're attracted to each other."

She chuckled slightly. "Tell me something I don't know, Aidan."

"What if I say that we've sort of gotten obsessed with each other?"

She frowned. "*Obsessed* is too strong a word, I think. We've only kissed twice."

"Actually three times. And I'm dying for the fourth. Aren't you?"

She knew she had to be honest with him and stop denying the obvious. "Yes, but I don't understand why."

He got up from the stool and stood. "Maybe it's not for us to understand, Jillian."

"How can you say that? How do you think our family would react if they knew we were carrying on like this behind their backs?"

He slowly crossed the room to stand in front of where she sat. "We won't know how they'd react because you're determined to keep this a secret, aren't you?"

She tilted her head to look up at him. "Yes. I couldn't hurt Pam that way. She expects me to stay focused on school. And if I did get involved with a guy, I'm sure she wouldn't want that guy to be you."

He frowned. "And what is so bad about getting involved with me?"

"I think you know the answer to that. She thinks of us as one big family. And there's your reputation. But, like you said, we'll be leaving tomorrow and going our separate ways. What's happening between us is curiosity taking its toll on our common sense."

"That's what you think?" he asked, reaching out and taking a lock of her hair between his fingers.

"Yes, that's what I think." She noticed something in the depths of his eyes that gave her pause—but only for a second. That's all the time it took for her gaze to lower from his eyes to his mouth.

She watched as he swept the tip of his tongue across his lips. "I can still taste you, you know," he said in a low, husky tone.

She nodded slowly. "Yes, I know." Deciding to be honest, she said, "And the reason I know is because I can still taste you, as well."

Six

Aidan wished Jillian hadn't said that. After their first kiss, he'd concluded she had enjoyed it as much as he had. When they'd gone another round he'd been sure of it. Just like he was sure that, although her experience with kissing had been at a minimum, she was a fast learner. She had kept up with him, stroke for stroke. And now, for her to confess that she could still taste him, the same way he could still taste her, sent his testosterone level soaring.

He took a step closer, gently pulled her to her feet and wrapped his arms around her waist. He truly didn't understand why the desire between them was so intense but he accepted that it was. The thought of Dillon and Pam's ire didn't appeal to him any more than it did to her, but unlike her, he refused to believe his cousin and cousin-in-law would be dead set against something developing between him and Jillian.

But he didn't have to worry because *nothing* was developing between them. They were attracted to each other; there was nothing serious about that. He'd been attracted to women before, although never to this degree, he would admit. But after today it would be a while before they saw each other again since he rarely came home. This would be a one-and-done fling. He knew for certain that Pam and Dillon would definitely *not* like the thought of that. They would think he'd taken advantage of her. So he agreed they did not need to know.

"I won't sleep with you, Aidan."

Her words interrupted his thoughts. He met her gaze. "You won't?"

"No. I think we should get that straight right now."

He nodded slowly. "All right. So what did you have in mind for us to do in here?" To say he was anxious to hear her answer was an understatement.

"Kiss some more. A lot more."

Evidently she didn't think an intense kissing match could lead to other things, with a loss of control topping the list. "You think it will be that simple?"

She shrugged. "No. But I figure if we both use a reasonable degree of self-control we'll manage."

A reasonable degree of self control? Jillian had more confidence in their abilities than he did. Just being here with her was causing a hard pounding in his crotch. If only she knew just how enticing she looked standing in front of him in a pair of jeans and a white button-up blouse that he would love to peel off her. Her hair was pinned up on her head, but a few locks…like the one he'd played with earlier…had escaped confinement.

"Is there a problem, Aidan?"

He lifted a brow. "Problem?"

"Yes. You're stalling and I'm ready now."

He fought to hide his grin. Was this the same woman who only yesterday swore they would never kiss again? The same woman who just that morning had refused to go riding with him? Her enthusiasm caused something within him to stir, making it hard to keep his control in check. His body wouldn't cooperate mainly because her scent alone was increasing his desire for her.

And she thought all they would do was some heavy-duty kissing?

Deciding not to keep her waiting any longer, he slanted his mouth over hers.

When had she needed a man's kiss this much? No, *this* much, she thought, leaning up on her toes to become enmeshed in Aidan's kiss even more. Jillian felt his arms move from around her waist to her backside, urging her closer to the fit of him, making her feel his hard erection pressing against her middle. She shouldn't like how it felt but she did.

The tips of her nipples seemed sensitized against his solid chest. When had she become this hot mass of sexual desire?

When he intensified the kiss even more, she actually heard herself moan. Really moan. He was actually tasting her. Using his mouth to absorb hers as if she was a delectable treat he had to consume. She was losing all that control she'd told him they had to keep and she was losing it in a way she couldn't define.

When he groaned deep in his throat and deepened the kiss even more, it took all she had to remain standing and not melt in a puddle on the floor. Why at twenty-one was she just experiencing kisses like these? And why was she allowing her mind to be sacked with emotions and sensations that made it almost impossible to breathe, to think, to do anything but reciprocate? Their tongues tangled greedily, dueling and plowing each other's mouths with a yearning that was unrelenting.

When she noticed his hands were no longer on her

backside but had worked their way to the zipper of her jeans, she gasped and broke off the kiss, only to be swept off her feet into Aidan's strong arms.

Before she could ask what he was doing, he tumbled them both onto the huge bed. She looked up into his dark eyes as he moved his body over hers. Any words she'd wanted to say died in her throat. All she could do was stare at him as intense heat simmered through her veins. He leaned back on his haunches and then in one quick movement, grasped her hips and peeled the jeans down to her knees.

"What—what are you doing?" she managed to ask, while liquid fire sizzled down her spine. She was lying there with only bikini panties covering her.

He met her gaze. "I'm filling my entire mouth with the taste of you." And then he eased her panties down her legs before lifting her hips and lowering his head between her thighs.

The touch of his tongue had her moaning and lifting her hips off the bed. He was relentless, and he used his mouth in a way that should be outlawed. She wanted to push his head away, but instead she used her arms to hold him in place.

And then she felt a series of intense spasms spread through her entire body. Suddenly, he did something wicked with his tongue, driving her wild. She screamed as a flood of sensations claimed her, tossing her into an earth-shaking orgasm. Her very first. It was more powerful than anything she could have imagined.

And he continued to lap her up, not letting go. His actions filled her with more emotions, more wanting, more longing. Her senses were tossed to smithereens. It took a while before she had enough energy to breathe through her lungs to release a slow, steady breath. She wondered if she had enough energy to even mount her horse, much less ride away from here.

Aidan lifted his head and slowly licked his lips, as if savoring her taste, while meeting her eyes. "Mmm, delicious."

His words were as erotic as she felt. "Why? Why did you do that?" she asked, barely able to get the words out. She felt exhausted, totally drained. Yet completely and utterly satisfied.

Instead of giving her an answer, he touched her chin with the tip of his thumb before lowering his lips to hers in an open-mouth kiss that had fire stirring deep in her stomach. Tasting herself on his lips made her quiver.

When he finally released her lips, he eased back on his haunches and gazed down at her. "I did it because you have a flavor that's uniquely you and I wanted to sample it."

She lifted her hips off the bed when he pulled her jeans back up. Then he shifted his body to pull her into his lap. She tilted her head back to look at him. "What about when we leave here tomorrow?"

"When we leave tomorrow we will remember this time with fondness and enjoyment. I'm sure when you wake up in your bed in Wyoming and I wake up in mine in Boston, we will be out of each other's systems."

She nodded. "You think so?"

"Yes, I'm pretty sure of it. And don't feel guilty about anything because we haven't hurt anyone. All we did was appease our curiosity in a very delectable way."

Yes, it had been most delectable. And technically, they hadn't slept together so they hadn't crossed any lines. She pulled away from him to finish fixing her clothing, tucking her shirt back into her jeans.

"Um, a missed opportunity."

She glanced over at him. "What?"

"Your breasts. I had planned to devour them."

At that moment, as if on cue, her breasts began to ache. Her nipples felt tight, sensitive, pulsing. And it didn't help matters when an image of him doing that very thing trickled through her mind.

"We need to go," she said quickly, knowing if they remained any longer it would only lead to trouble.

"Do we?"

He wasn't helping matters by asking her that. "Yes. It's getting late and we might be missed." When he made no attempt to move, she headed for the door. "I can find my way back."

"Wait up, Jillian."

She stopped and turned back to him. "We don't have to go back together, Aidan."

"Yes, we do. Pam knows of our plans to go riding together."

Color drained from Jillian's face. "Who told her?"

"I ran into her when I was headed to the barn and she asked where I was headed. I told her the truth."

At the accusation in her expression, he placed his hands in the back pockets of his jeans. "Had I told her I was going someplace else and she discovered differently, Jillian, she would have wondered why I had lied."

Jillian nodded slowly upon realizing what he said made sense. "What did she say about it?"

"Nothing. In fact I don't think she thought much about it at all. However, she did say she was glad you were about to start medical school and she would appreciate any advice I could give you."

Jillian swallowed tightly. He'd given her more than advice. Thanks to him, she had experienced her first orgasm today. "Okay, we'll ride back together. I'll just wait outside."

She quickly walked out the door. He'd claimed what they'd done today would get them out of each other's systems. She definitely hoped so.

When the door closed behind Jillian, Aidan rubbed a hand down his face in frustration. He couldn't leave Denver soon enough. The best thing to do was put as much distance between him and Jillian as possible. She felt uncomfortable with the situation and now he was beginning to feel the same. However, his uneasiness had nothing to do with Dillon and Pam finding out what they'd been up to, and everything to do with his intense attraction to Jillian.

Even now he wanted to go outside, throw her over his shoulders and bring her back inside. He wanted to kiss her into submission and taste her some more before making nonstop love to her. How crazy was that?

He'd never felt this much desire for any woman, and knowing she was off-limits only seemed to heighten his desire for her. And now that he'd gotten an intimate taste of her, getting her out of his system might not be as easy as he'd claimed earlier. Her taste hadn't just electrified his taste buds, it had done something to him that was unheard of—he was no longer lingering on the edge of wanting to make love to her but had fallen off big-time.

Every time his tongue explored her mouth, his emotions heated up and began smoldering. And when he lapped her up, he was tempted to do other things to her, as well. Things he doubted she was ready for.

Drawing in a deep breath, he straightened up the bed-covers before heading for the door. Upon stepping outside, he breathed in deeply to calm his racing heart. She stood there stroking his horse and a part of him wished she would stroke him the same way. He got hard just imagining such a thing.

He didn't say anything for a long moment. He just stood there watching her. When his erection pressed uncomfortably against his zipper, he finally spoke up. "I'm ready to ride."

She glanced over at him and actually smiled when she said, "You have a beautiful horse, Aidan."

"Thanks," he said, walking down the steps. "Charger is a fourth-generation Westmoreland stallion."

She turned to stroke the horse again and didn't look up when he came to stand next to her. "I've heard all about Charger. I was warned by Dillon to never try to ride him because only a few people could. It's obvious you're one of those people."

Aidan nodded. "Yes, Charger and I have an understanding."

She stopped stroking Charger to look at him. "What about you and me, Aidan? Do we have an understanding?"

He met her gaze, nor sure how he should answer that. Just when he thought he had everything figured out about them, something would happen to make his brains turn to mush. "I assume you're referring to the incidents that have taken place between us over the past two days."

"I am."

"Then, yes, we have an understanding. After today, no more kissing, no more touching—"

"Or tasting," she interjected.

Saying he would never again taste her was a hard one, but for her peace of mind and for his own, he would say it. "Yes, tasting."

"Good. We're in agreement."

He wouldn't exactly say that, but for now he would hold his tongue—that same tongue that enjoyed dueling with hers. "I guess we need to head back."

"Okay, and I don't need your help mounting my horse."

In other words, she didn't want him to touch her. "You sure?"

"Positive."

He nodded and then watched her move away from his horse to get on hers. As usual, it was a total turn-on watching her. "I want to thank you, Aidan."

He took his gaze away from the sight of her legs straddling the horse to look into her face. "Thank me for what?"

"For introducing me to a few things during this visit home."

For some reason that made him smile. "It was my pleasure." And he meant every word.

Seven

"You're still not going home, Jillian?"

Jillian looked up from eating her breakfast to see her roommate, Ivy Rollins. They had met in her sophomore year when Jillian knew she didn't want to live in the dorm any longer. She had wanted an apartment off campus and someone to share the cost with her. Ivy, who had plans to attend law school, had answered the ad Jillian placed in the campus newspaper. They'd hit it off the first time they'd met and had been the best of friends since. Jillian couldn't ask for a better roommate.

"I was home last month," she reminded Ivy.

"Yes, but that was a couple of days for your birthday. Next week is spring break."

Jillian didn't want to be reminded. Pam had called yesterday to see if Jillian would be coming home since Nadia had made plans to do so. Paige, who was attending UCLA, had gotten a small part in a play on campus and needed to remain in Los Angeles. Guilt was still riding Jillian over what she and Aidan had done. She hated deceiving her sister about anything. "I explained to Pam that I need to start studying for the MCAT. She understood."

"I hate leaving you, but—"

"But you will," Jillian said, smiling. "And that's fine. I know how homesick you get." That was an under-statement. Ivy's family lived in Oregon. Her parents, both chefs, owned a huge restaurant there. Her two older brothers were chefs as well and assisted her parents. Ivy had decided on a different profession than her parents and siblings, but she loved going home every chance she got to help out.

"Yes, I will," Ivy said, returning her smile. "In fact I leave in two days. Sure you'll be okay?"

"Yes, I'll be fine. I've got enough to keep me busy since I'm sitting for the MCAT in two months. And I need to start working on my essays."

"It's a bummer you'll be doing something other than enjoying yourself next week," Ivy said.

"It's okay. Getting into medical school is the most important thing to me right now."

A few hours later Jillian sat at the computer desk in her bedroom searching the internet. She had tossed around the idea of joining a study group for the MCAT and there appeared to be several. Normally, she preferred studying solo but for some reason she couldn't concen-trate. She pushed away from the computer and leaned back in her chair knowing the reason.

Aidan.

It had been a little over a month since she'd gone home for her birthday, and Aidan had been wrong. She hadn't woken up in her bed in Wyoming not thinking of him. In fact she thought of him even more. All the time. Thoughts of him had begun interfering with her studies.

She got up and moved to the kitchen to grab a soda from the refrigerator. He should have been out of her system by now, but he wasn't. Memories of him put her to sleep at night and woke her up in the morning. And then in the wee hours of the night, she recalled in vivid detail his kisses, especially the ones between her legs.

Remembering that particular kiss sent a tingling sensation through her womanly core, which wasn't good. In fact, nothing about what she was going through was good. Sexual withdrawal. And she hadn't even had sex with Aidan, but she hadn't needed sex to get an orgasm. That in itself showed the magnitude of his abilities.

Returning to her bedroom she pushed thoughts of him from her mind. Sitting back down at her desk, she resumed surfing the net. She bet he hadn't even given her a thought. He probably wasn't missing any sleep thinking of her, and he had probably woken up his first day back in Boston with some woman in his bed. Why did that thought bother her?

She had been tempted to ask Pam if she'd heard from Aidan, but hadn't for fear her sister would wonder why Jillian was inquiring about Aidan when she hadn't before.

Jillian turned around when she heard a knock on her bedroom door. "Come in."

Ivy walked into the room, smiling. "I know you have a lot to do but you've been in here long enough. Come grab a bite to eat at the Wild Duck. My treat."

Ivy wasn't playing fair. She knew the Wild Duck was one of Jillian's favorite eating places. They had the best hamburgers and fries. "You've twisted my arm," she said, pushing away from the desk.

Ivy chuckled. "Yeah. Right."

Jillian stood, thinking she did need a break. And maybe she could get Aidan off her mind.

* * *

"How are you doing, Dr. Westmoreland?"

Aidan smiled over at the doctor who'd transferred in to the medical school during the weekend that he'd gone home. He really should ask her out. Lynette Bowes was attractive, she had a nice figure, and she seemed friendly enough. At times almost too friendly. She enjoyed flirting with him and she'd gone so far as to make a few bold innuendos, which meant getting her into his bed probably would be easy. So what was he waiting on?

"I'm fine, Dr. Bowes, and how are you?"

She leaned over to hand him a patient's chart, intentionally brushing her breasts against his arm. "I would be a lot a better if you dropped by my apartment tonight," she whispered.

Another invite. Why was he stalling? Why wasn't he on top of his game as usual? And why was he thinking that the intimate caress she'd purposely initiated just now had nothing on the caresses he'd experienced with Jillian?

"Thanks, but I have plans for tonight," he lied.

"Then maybe another night?"

"I'll let you know." He appreciated his cell phone going off at that moment. "I'll see you later." He made a quick escape.

Later that night while at home doing nothing but flipping TV channels, he couldn't help wondering what the hell was wrong with him. Although he'd asked himself that question, he knew the answer without thinking.

Jillian.

He'd assumed once he was back in Boston and waking up in his own bed that he would eradicate her from his mind. Unfortunately, he'd found out that wasn't the case. He thought about her every free moment, and he even went to bed thinking about her. And the dreams he had of her were double X-rated. His desire for her was so bad that he hadn't thought twice about wanting anyone else.

And it hadn't helped matters when he'd called home earlier in the week and Dillon mentioned that Jillian wasn't coming home for spring break. She told Pam she had registered to take the MCAT and needed the time to study and work on her admissions essays. He applauded her decision to make sacrifices to reach her goal, but he was disappointed she hadn't reached out to him liked he'd suggested. He'd made a pretty high score on the MCAT and could give her some study pointers. He'd even keyed his contact information into her phone.

Yet she hadn't called to ask him a single question about anything. That could only mean she didn't want his help and had probably pushed what happened between them to the back of her mind. Good for her, but he didn't like the fact that she remained in the center of his.

Tossing the remote aside he reached for his cell phone to pull up her number. When her name appeared he put the phone down. They'd had an agreement, so to speak. An understanding. They would put that time in Denver behind them. It had been enjoyable but was something that could not and would not be repeated. No more kissing, touching…or tasting.

Hell, evidently that was easy for her to do, but it was proving to be downright difficult for him. There were nights he woke up wanting her with a passion, hungering to kiss her, touch her and taste her.

The memories of them going riding together, especially that day spent in Bane's cabin…every moment of that time was etched in Aidan's mind, making his brain cells overload.

Like now.

When he'd pulled down her jeans, followed by her panties, and had buried his head between her legs and tasted her…the memory made his groin tighten. Need for Jillian clawed at him in a way that made it difficult to breathe.

Aidan stood and began pacing the floor in his apartment, trying to wear down his erection. He paused when an idea entered his mind. He had time he could take off and he might as well do it now. He'd only been to Laramie, Wyoming, a couple of times, and maybe he should visit there again. He would take in the sights and check out a few good restaurants. And there was no reason for him not to drop in on Jillian to see how she was doing while he was there.

No reason at all.

Three days later, Jillian sat at the kitchen table staring at the huge study guide in front of her. It had to be at least five hundred pages thick and filled with information to prepare her for the MCAT. The recommendation was that students take three months to study, but since she was enrolled in only one class this semester she figured she would have more time to cram and could get it done in two months. That meant she needed to stay focused. No exceptions. And she meant none.

But her mind was not in agreement, especially when she could lick her lips and imagine Aidan doing that very same thing. And why—after one month, nine days and twenty minutes—could she still do that? Why hadn't she been able to forget about his kisses and move on? Especially now when she needed to focus.

The apartment was empty and felt lonely without Ivy. It was quiet and just what she needed to get some serious studying done. She had eaten a nice breakfast and had taken a walk outside to get her brain and body stimulated. But now her mind wanted to remember another type of stimulation. One that even now sent tingles through her lower stomach.

She was about to take a sip of her coffee when the doorbell sounded. She frowned. Most of her neighbors were college students like her, and the majority of them had gone home for spring break. She'd noticed how vacant the parking lot had looked while out walking earlier.

Getting up from the kitchen table she moved toward the front door. She glanced through her peephole and her breath caught. Standing on the other side of her door was the one man she'd been trying not to think about.

Shocked to the core, she quickly removed the security chain and unlocked the door. Opening it, she tried to ignore the way her heart pounded and how her stomach muscles trembled. "Aidan? What are you doing here?"

Instead of answering, he leaned down and kissed her. Another shock rammed right into the first. She should have pushed him away the moment their mouths connected. But instead she melded her body right to his and his arms reached out to hold her around the waist. As soon as she was reacquainted with his taste, her tongue latched onto his and began a sensuous duel that had her moaning.

In all her attempts at logical thinking over the past month, not until now could she admit how much she'd missed him. How much she'd missed this. How could a man engrain himself inside a woman's senses so deeply and thoroughly, and so quickly? And how could any woman resist this particular man doing so?

She heard the door click and knew he'd maneuvered her into her apartment and closed the door behind him. Noticing that, she almost pulled back, and she would have had he not at that moment deepened the kiss.

This had to be a dream. Is that why the room felt as if it was spinning? There was no way Aidan was in Laramie, at her apartment and kissing her. But if this was a dream she wasn't ready to wake up. She needed to get her fill of his taste before her fantasy faded. Before she realized in horror that she was actually kissing the short and bald mailman instead of Aidan. Had her fascination with him finally gotten the best of her?

The thought had her breaking off the kiss and opening her eyes. The man standing across from her with lips damp from their kiss was definitely Aidan.

She drew in a deep breath, trying to slow the beat of her heart and regain control of her senses.

As if he'd known just what she was thinking, he said, "It's really me, Jillian. And I'm here to help you study for your MCAT this week."

She blinked. *Help her study?* He had to be kidding.

Aidan wanted nothing more than to kiss the shocked look off Jillian's face. But he knew that before he could even think about kissing her again he had a lot of explaining to do since he'd gone back on their agreement.

"I talked to Dillon a few days ago and he mentioned you wouldn't be coming home for spring break and the reason why. So I figured I could help by giving you a good study boost."

She shook her head as if doing so would clear her mind. Looking back at him, she said, "There's no way you could have thought that. And what was that kiss about? I thought we had an understanding."

"We did. We still do. However, based on the way you responded to my kiss just now, I think we might need to modify a few things."

She lifted her chin. "There's nothing for us to modify."

That response irritated him to the core. "Do you think I want to be here, Jillian? I have a life in Boston, a life I was enjoying until recently. Ever since the kisses we shared on your birthday, I've done nothing but think about you, want you, miss you."

"That's not my fault," she snapped.

"It is when you're not being honest with yourself. Can you look me in the eyes and tell me that you haven't thought of me? That you haven't been wanting me? And be honest for once because if you deny it then you need to tell me why your kiss just now said otherwise."

He watched as she nervously licked her tongue across her lips and his gut clenched. "Tell me, Jillian," he said in a softer tone. "For once be honest with me and with yourself."

She drew in a long breath as they stared at each other. After several tense moments passed between them, she said, "Okay, I have been thinking of you, missing you, wanting you. And I hated myself for doing so. You're a weakness I can't afford to have right now. It's crazy. I know a lot of guys around campus. But why you? Why do I want the one guy I can't have?"

Her words softened his ire. She was just as confused

and frustrated as he was. "And why do you think you can't have me?"

She frowned. "You know why, Aidan. Pam and Dillon would be against it. In their eyes, we're family. And even if you were a guy she would approve of, she would try to convince me not to get involved with you and to stay focused on becoming a doctor."

"You don't know for certain that's how she would feel, Jillian."

"I do know. When Pam was in college pursuing her dream of becoming an actress, I asked her why she didn't date. She told me that a woman should never sacrifice her dream for any man."

"I'm not asking you to sacrifice your dream."

"No, but you want an involvement during a time when I should be more focused than ever on becoming a doctor."

"I want to help you, not hinder you," he stressed again.

"How do you think you can do that?"

At least she was willing to listen. "By using this week to introduce you to study techniques that will help you remember those things you need to remember."

She nervously licked her tongue across her lips again. "It won't work. I won't be able to think straight with you around."

"I'll make sure you do. I'm not asking to stay here, Jillian. I've already checked into a hotel a mile or so from here. I'll arrive every morning and we'll study until evening, taking short breaks in between. Then we'll grab something to eat and enjoy the evening. Afterward, I'll bring you back here and then leave. Before going to bed you should review what was covered that day, making sure you get eight hours of sleep."

She looked at him as if he was crazy. "I can't take time from studying to enjoy the evening. I'll need to study morning, noon and night."

"Not with me helping you. Besides, too much studying will make you burned out, and you don't want to do that. What good is studying if that happens?"

When she didn't say anything, he pushed harder. "Try my way for a couple of days and if it doesn't work, if you feel I'm more of a hindrance than a help, I'll leave Laramie and let you do things your way."

As she stared at him, not saying anything, he could feel blood throb through his veins. As usual she looked serious. Beautiful. Tempting. He wanted her. Being around her would be hard and leaving her every night after dinner would be harder. He would want to stay and make love to her all through the night. But that wasn't possible. No matter how hard it would be, he needed to keep his self-control.

"Okay," she finally said. "We'll try it for a couple of days. And if it doesn't work I intend for you to keep your word about leaving."

"I will." He had no intention of leaving because he intended for his plan to work. He had aced the MCAT the first time around, with flying colors. Once he'd gotten his act together as a teenager, he'd discovered he was an excellent test taker, something Adrian was not. Determined not to leave his twin behind, he'd often tutored Adrian, sharing his study tips and techniques with his brother. Aidan had also done the same with Bailey once she was in college. Unfortunately, he'd never gotten the chance to share his techniques with Bane since his cousin hadn't been interested in anything or anyone but Crystal.

"Now let's seal our agreement," he said.

When she extended her hand, he glanced at it before pulling her into his arms again.

He was taking advantage again, Jillian thought. But she only thought that for a second. That was all the time it took for her to begin returning his kiss with the same hunger he seemed to feel. This was crazy. It was insane. It was also what she needed. What she'd been wanting since leaving Denver and returning to Laramie.

Kissing was something they enjoyed doing with each other and the unhurried mating of their mouths definitely should be ruled illegal. But for now she could handle this—in the safety of her living room, in the arms of a man she thoroughly enjoyed kissing—as long as it went no further.

But what if it did? He'd already shown her that his definition of kissing included any part of her body. What if he decided he wanted more than her mouth this time? Her hormones were going haywire just thinking of the possibility.

He suddenly broke off the kiss and she fought back a groan of disappointment. She stared up at him. "Okay, where's the study guide?" he asked her.

She blinked. Her mind was slow in functioning after such a blazing kiss. It had jarred her senses. "Study guide?"

He smiled and caressed her cheek. "Yes, the MCAT study guide."

"On my kitchen table. I was studying when you showed up."

"Good. And you'll study some more. Lead the way."

* * *

Aidan leaned back in his chair and glanced over at Jillian. "Any questions?"

She shook her head. "No, but you make it seem simple."

He smiled. "Trust me, it's not. The key is to remember that you're the one in control of your brain and the knowledge that's stored inside of it. Don't let retrieving that information during test time psych you out."

She chuckled. "That's easy for you to say."

"And it will be easy for you, as well. I've been there, and when time allows I tutor premed students like yourself. You did well on the practice exam, which covers basically everything you need to know. Now you need to concentrate on those areas you're not so sure about."

"Which is a lot."

"All of them are things you know," he countered. He believed the only reason she lacked confidence in her abilities was because the idea of failing was freaking her out. "You don't have to pass on the first go-round. A lot of people don't. That's why it's suggested you plan to take it at least twice."

She lifted her chin. "I want to ace it on the first try."

"Then do it."

Aidan got up from his chair and went over to the coffeepot sitting on her kitchen counter. He needed something stronger than caffeine, but coffee would have to do. He'd been here for five hours already and they hadn't stopped for lunch. The key was to take frequent short breaks instead of one or two long ones.

She had taken the online practice exam on verbal reasoning and he thought she'd done well for her first time. He'd given her study tips for multiple-choice exams and gone over the questions she had missed. Personally, he thought she would do fine, although he thought taking the test in two months was pushing it. He would have suggested three months instead of two.

"Want some coffee?" he asked, pouring himself a cup.

"No, I'm okay."

Yes, she definitely was. He couldn't attest to her mental state with all that she'd crammed into that brain of hers today, but he could definitely attest to her physical one. She looked amazing, even with her hair tied back in a ponytail and a cute pair of reading glasses perched on her nose. He was used to seeing her without makeup and preferred her that way. She had natural beauty with her flawless creamy brown skin. And she looked cute in her jeans and top.

He glanced at his watch. "Jillian?"

She glanced up from the computer and looked over at him. "Yes?"

"It's time to call it a day."

She seemed baffled by his statement. "Call it a day? I haven't covered everything I wanted to do today."

"You covered a lot and you don't want to overload your brain."

She stared at him for a moment and then nodded and began shutting down her computer. "Maybe you're right. Thanks to you, I did cover a lot. Definitely a lot more than I would have if you hadn't been here. You're a great tutor."

"And you're a good student." He glanced at his watch again. "What eating places do you have around here?"

"Depends on what you have a taste for."

He had a taste for her, but knew he had to keep his promise and not push her into anything. "A juicy steak."

"Then you're in luck," she said, standing. "There's a great steak place a few blocks from here. Give me a few minutes to change."

"Okay." He watched her hurry off toward her bedroom.

When she closed the door behind her, he rubbed a hand down his face. Jillian was temptation even when she wasn't trying to be. When he'd asked about her roommate she'd told him that Ivy had gone home for spring break. That meant…

Nothing. Unless she made the first move or issued an invitation. Until then, he would spend his nights alone at the hotel.

Eight

Jillian glanced across the table at Aidan. It was day three and still hard to believe that he was in Laramie, that he had come to give her a kick-start in her studying. Day one had been frustrating. He'd pushed her beyond what she thought she was ready for. But going to dinner with him that night had smoothed her ruffled feathers.

Dinner had been fun. She'd discovered he enjoyed eating his steaks medium rare and he loved baked potatoes loaded with sour cream, bacon bits and cheddar cheese. He also loved unsweetened tea and when it came to anything with chocolate, he could overdose if he wasn't careful.

He was also a great conversationalist. He engaged her in discussions about everything—but he deemed the topic of medical school to be off-limits. They talked about the economy, recent elections, movies they had enjoyed, and about Adrian's plans to travel the world a few years after getting his PhD in engineering.

And Aidan got her talking. She told him about Ivy, who she thought was the roommate from heaven; about Jillian's decision two years ago to move out of the dorm; and about her first experience with a pushy car salesman. She told him about all the places she wanted to visit one day and that the one thing she wanted to do and hadn't done yet was go on a cruise.

It occurred to her later that it had been the first time she and Aidan had shared a meal together alone, and she had enjoyed it. It had made her even more aware of him as a man. She'd had the time to look beyond his handsome features and she'd discovered he was a thoughtful and kind person. He had been pleasant, treating everyone with respect, including the waitress and servers. And each time he smiled at her, her stomach clenched. Then he would take a sip of his drink, and she would actually envy his straw.

After dinner they returned to her apartment. He made her promise that she would only review what they'd covered that day and not stay up past nine, then he left. But not before taking her into his arms and giving her a kiss that rendered her weak and senseless—to the point where she was tempted to ask him to stay longer. But she fought back the temptation. Knowing she would see him again the next day had made falling asleep quick and easy. For the first time in a long time, she had slept through the night, though he'd dominated her dreams.

He arrived early the next morning with breakfast, which she appreciated. Then it was back to studying again. The second day had been more intense than the first. Knowing they couldn't cover every aspect of the study guide in one week, he had encouraged her to hit the areas she felt were her weakest. He gave her hints on how to handle multiple-choice questions and introduced her to key words to use when completing her essays.

For dinner they had gone to the Wild Duck. She had been eager to introduce him to her favorite place. A dinner of hamburgers, French fries and milk shakes had been wonderful. Afterward they went to Harold's Game Hall to shoot pool, something she had learned to do in high school.

When he'd brought her home, like the night before, he took her in his arms and kissed her before he left, giving her the same instructions about reviewing what they'd covered that morning and getting eight hours of sleep. Again, she'd slept like a baby with him dominating her dreams.

She enjoyed having him as a study coach. Most of the time she stayed focused. But there were a few times when she felt heat simmering between them, something both of them tried to ignore. They managed it most of the time but today was harder than the two days before.

Aidan was tense. She could tell. He had arrived that morning, like yesterday, with breakfast in hand. Since he believed she should study on a full stomach and not try eating while studying, they had taken their meal outside to her patio. It had been pleasant, but more than once she'd caught him staring at her with a look in his eyes that she felt in the pit of her stomach.

He wasn't as talkative today as he'd been the past two days, and, taking a cue from his mood, she hadn't said much, either. On those occasions when their hands had accidentally touched while he'd been handing her papers or turning a page, she wasn't sure who sizzled more, her or him.

That's why she'd made up her mind about how today would end. She wanted him and he wanted her and there was no reason for them to suffer with their desires any longer. She'd fallen in love with him. After this time together, she could admit that now. That little crush she'd had on him for years had become something more. Something deeper and more profound.

The thought of Pam and Dillon finding out was still an issue that plagued her. However, since Aidan didn't feel the same way about her that she felt about him, she was certain she would be able to convince him to keep whatever they did a secret. He was doing that now anyway. He'd told her that neither Pam nor Dillon knew where he was spending this week. That meant Jillian and Aidan were already keeping secrets from their family, and she would continue to do so if it meant spending more time with him.

That night they went to a restaurant she had never visited because of its pricey menu. The signature dishes had been delicious and the service excellent. But the restaurant's setting spoke of not only elegance but also romance. Rustic wood ceilings with high beams, a huge brick fireplace and a natural stone floor. Beautiful candles adorned the tables and even in the dim light, each time she glanced over at Aidan he was looking back at her.

Getting through dinner hadn't been easy. They conversed but not as much as they had the previous two nights. Was she imagining things or did his voice sound deeper, huskier than usual? His smiles weren't full ones but half smiles, and just as sexy.

Like he'd done the previous two nights, he walked through her apartment, checking to make sure everything was okay. Then he gave her orders to only review what she'd studied that morning and get into bed before nine because at least eight hours of sleep were essential.

And then, as had become his habit, he pulled her into his arms to kiss her goodbye. This is what she had anticipated all day. She was ready for Aidan's kiss. Standing on tiptoe she tilted her open mouth toward him, her tongue ready. He closed his full mouth over hers and their tongues tangled, almost bringing her to her knees.

The kiss lasted for a long, delectable moment. It was different than any they'd shared before and she'd known it the moment their mouths fused. It was hot, heavy and hungry. He wasn't letting up or backing down—and neither was she.

Jillian felt herself being lifted off her feet and she immediately wrapped her legs around his waist while he continued to ravish her mouth in a way that overwhelmed her and overloaded her senses. His hunger was sexual and greedy. She could tell he was fighting hard to hold it together, to stay in control, to keep his sanity in check. But she wasn't. In fact, she was deliberately trying to tempt him every way that she could.

She felt the wall at her back and knew he'd maneuvered them over to it. He broke off the kiss and stared at her, impaling her with the flaming fire in his eyes. "Tell me to stop, Jillian," he said. "Because if you don't do it now, I won't be able to stop later. I want to tongue you all over. Lick every inch of your body. Taste you. Make love to you. Hard. Long. Deep. So tell me to stop now."

Her pulse jumped. Every single cell in her body sizzled with his words. Hot, sparks of passion glowed in his gaze and when a powerful burst of primal need slammed through her she didn't want to escape.

"Tell me to stop."

His plea made the already hot sexual tension between them blaze, and she knew of only one way to put out the fire.

"Stop, Aidan!"

His body went still. The only thing that moved was the pulse throbbing in his throat. He held her gaze and she was convinced she could hear blood rushing through both of their veins.

When she felt him about to untangle her legs from around his waist and lower her feet to the floor, she said, "Stop talking and do all those things you claim you're going to do."

She saw the impact of her words reflected in his eyes. While he seemed incapable of speaking, she released her arms from around his neck and tugged at his shirt, working her hands beneath to touch his bare chest. She heard the groan from deep in his throat.

"If you don't take me, Aidan Westmoreland, then I'll be forced to take you."

That was the last thing Aidan had expected her to say. But hearing her say it intensified the throbbing need within him. His crotch pounded fiercely and he knew of only one way to remedy that. But first…

He lowered her to her feet as a smile tugged at his lips. Only for a moment, he gazed down at her shirt, noticing the curve of her breasts beneath the cotton. In an instant, he tugged the shirt over her head and tossed it aside.

He drew in a deep breath when his eyes settled on her chest, specifically her skin-tone colored bra. Eager beyond belief, he touched her breasts through the lace material. When his fingers released the front clasp, causing the twin globes to spring free, the breath was snatched from his lungs.

Mercy. He eased the bra straps from her shoulders to remove it completely from her body and his mouth watered. Her breasts were one area that he hadn't tasted yet, and he planned on remedying that soon.

Deciding he wanted to see more naked flesh, he lowered to his knees and slid his fingers beneath the elastic waistband of her skirt to ease it down her legs. She stepped out of it and he tossed it aside to join her shirt and bra. His gaze raked the full length of her body, now only covered by a pair of light blue bikini panties. His hands actually trembled when he ran them down her legs. He felt as if he were unveiling a precious treasure.

She stepped out of them as she'd done her skirt and she stood in front of him totally naked. He leaned back on his haunches while his gaze raked her up and down, coming back to her center. He was tempted to start right there, but he knew if he did that, he wouldn't get to taste her breasts this time, either, and he refused to miss the chance again.

Standing back on his feet, Aidan leaned and lowered his head. He captured a nipple between his lips, loving how the tip hardened in his mouth as his tongue traced circles around the rigid bud. She purred his name as she cradled the back of his head to hold his mouth right there.

He continued to taste her breasts, leaving one and moving to the other, enjoying every single lick and suck. Her moans fueled his desire to possess her. To make love to her. And what he loved more than anything else was the sound of her moaning his name.

Aidan eased his lips from her breasts and moved his mouth slowly downward, tasting her skin. As he crouched, his mouth traced a greedy path over her stomach, loving the way her muscles tightened beneath his lips.

A slow throbbing ache took hold of his erection as he eased down to his knees. This was what he'd gone to bed craving ever since he'd first tasted her between her thighs. He'd fallen asleep several nights licking his lips at the memory. Her feminine scent was unique, so irresistibly Jillian, that his tongue thickened in anticipation.

Knowing she watched him, he ran his hands up and down the insides of her legs, massaged her thighs and caressed the area between them. His name was a whisper on her lips when he slid a finger inside of her. He loved the feel of her juices wetting him. He stroked her.

Hungry for her taste, he withdrew his finger and licked it. He smiled before using his hands to spread her feminine core to ready her for an open-mouth kiss.

Jillian released a deep, toe-curling moan the moment Aidan latched his hot tongue onto her. She grabbed his head to push him away, but he held tight to her legs while his tongue went deep, thrusting hard. Then she pressed herself toward his mouth.

She closed her eyes and chanted his name as spasms ripped through her, making her thighs tremble. He refused to let go, refused to lift his mouth, as sensations overtook her. Her body throbbed in unexpected places as an orgasm shook her.

When the last spasm speared through her, she felt herself being lifted into strong arms. When she opened her eyes, Aidan was entering her bedroom. He placed her on the bed, leaned down and kissed her, sending rekindled desire spiking through her.

When he ended the kiss and eased off the bed, she watched as he quickly removed his clothes. She could only lie there and admire his nakedness. He was a fine specimen of a man, both in and out of clothes. Just as he'd appeared in her dreams. Thick thighs, muscular legs and a huge erection nested in a patch of thick, curly black hair.

How will I handle that? she asked herself when he pulled a condom packet from his wallet and quickly sheathed himself. He took his time and she figured it was because he knew she was watching his every move with keen interest.

"You have done this before right?" he asked her.

"What? Put on a condom? No. One wouldn't fit me."

He grinned over at her. "Funny. You know what I'm asking."

Yes, she knew what he was asking. "Um, sort of."

He lifted a brow. "Sort of?"

She shrugged slightly. "I'm not a virgin, if that's what you're asking," she said softly. "Technically not. But…"

"But what?"

"I was in high school and neither of us knew what we were doing. That was my one and only time."

He just stood there totally naked staring at her. She wondered why he wasn't saying anything. What was he thinking? As if he'd read her mind, he slowly moved toward her, placed his knee on the bed and leaned toward her. "What you missed out on before, you will definitely get tonight. And Jillian?"

She swallowed. He'd spoken with absolute certainty and all she could do was stare back at him. "Yes?"

"This will not be your only time with me."

Her body reacted to his words and liquid heat traveled through her body. He hadn't spoken any words of love but he'd let her know this wasn't a one-time deal with them.

She didn't have time to dwell on what he'd said. He pulled her into his arms and kissed her. She closed her eyes and let herself be liquefied by the kiss. Like all the other times he'd used his expertise to make everything around her fade into oblivion, the kiss was the only thing her mind and body could comprehend. His hands were all over her, touching her everywhere. She released a deep moan when she felt his knees spreading her legs.

"Open your eyes and look at me Jillian."

She slowly opened her eyes to look up at the man whose body was poised above hers. He lifted her hips and his enlarged sex slid between her wet feminine folds. He thrust forward and her body stretched to accommodate his size. Instinctively, she wrapped her legs around him and when he began to move, she did so, as well.

She continued to hold his gaze while he thrust in and out of her. Over and over he would take her to the edge just to snatch her back. Her inner muscles clamped down on him, squeezing and tightening around him.

As she felt new spasms rip through her, he threw his head back and let out a roar that shook the room. She was glad most of her neighbors had gone away for spring break; otherwise they would know what she was doing tonight.

But right now, all she cared about was the man she loved, and how he was making her feel things she'd never felt before.

He kissed her again. Their tongues dueled in another erotic kiss and she couldn't help but remember the words he'd spoken earlier.

This will not be your only time with me.

She knew men said words they didn't mean to women

they were about to sleep with, and she had no reason to believe it was any different with Aidan.

Besides, considering that she needed to stay focused on her studies, it was a good thing he wasn't serious.

Aidan watched the naked woman sleeping in his arms and let out a frustrated sigh. This was not supposed to happen.

He wasn't talking about making love because there was no way such a thing could have been avoided. The sexual tension between them had been on overload since the day he'd arrived at her apartment and neither of them could have lasted another day.

What was *not* supposed to happen was feeling all these unexpected emotions. They had wrapped around his mind and wouldn't let go. And what bothered him more than anything else was that he knew he was not confusing his emotions with what had definitely been off-the-charts sex. If he hadn't known before that there was a difference in what he felt for Jillian, he definitely knew it now.

He had fallen in love with her.

When? How? Why? He wasn't sure. All he knew, without a doubt, was that it had happened. The promise of great sex hadn't made him take a week's vacation and travel more than fifteen hundred miles across five states to spend time with her. Sex hadn't made him become her personal test coach, suffering the pains of being close to her while maintaining boundaries and limits. And sex definitely had nothing to do with the way he felt right now and how it was nearly impossible for him to think straight.

When she purred softly in her sleep and then wiggled

her backside snugly against his groin he closed his eyes
and groaned. It had been great sex but it had been more
than that. She had reached a part of him no woman had
reached before.

He'd realized it before they'd made love. He'd known
it the minute she told him she'd only made love once
before. As far as he was concerned that one time didn't
count because the guy had definitely done a piss-poor
job. The only orgasm she'd ever experienced had been
with Aidan.

But in the days he'd spent studying with her he'd
gotten to know a lot about her. She was a fighter, determined to reach whatever goals she established for herself. And she was thoughtful enough to care that Pam not
bear the burden of the cost of sending Jillian to medical
school. She was even willing to sell her family home.

And he liked being with her, which posed a problem
since they lived more than a thousand miles apart. He'd
heard long-distance affairs could sometimes be brutal.
But he and Jillian could make it work if they wanted to
do so. He knew how he felt about her but he had no idea
how she felt about him. As far as he knew, she wasn't
operating on emotion but out of a sense of curiosity.
She'd said as much.

However, the biggest problem of all, one he knew
would pose the most challenge to the possibility of anything ever developing between them was her insistence
on Pam and Dillon not knowing about them.

Aidan didn't feel the same way and now that he loved
her, he really didn't want to keep it a secret. He knew
Dillon well enough to know that if Aidan were to go to
his cousin and come clean, tell Dillon Aidan had fallen in
love with Jillian, Dillon would be okay with it. Although

Aidan couldn't say with certainty how Pam would feel, he'd always considered her a fair person. He believed she would eventually give her blessing…but only if she thought Jillian was truly in love with him and that he would make Jillian happy.

There were so many unknowns. The one thing he did know was that he and Jillian had to talk. He'd given her fair warning that what they'd shared would not be one and done. There was no way he would allow her to believe that her involvement with him meant nothing, that she was just another woman to him. She was more than that and he wanted her to know it.

She stirred, shifted in bed and then slowly opened her eyes to stare at him. She blinked a few times as if bringing him into focus—or as if she was trying to figure out if he was really here in her bed.

Aidan let her know she wasn't seeing things. "Good morning." He gently caressed her cheek before glancing over at the digital clock on her nightstand. "You woke up early. It's barely six o'clock."

"A habit I can't break," she said, still staring at him. "You didn't leave."

"Was I supposed to?"

She shrugged bare shoulders. "I thought that's the way it worked."

She had a lot to learn about him. He wouldn't claim he'd never left a woman's bed in the middle of the night, but Jillian was different.

"Not for us, Jillian." He paused. "We need to talk."

She broke eye contact as she pulled up in bed, holding the covers in place to shield her nakedness. Aidan thought the gesture amusing considering all they'd done last night. "I know what you're going to say, Aidan. Although I've never heard it before, Ivy has and she told me how this plays out."

She'd made him curious. "And how does it play out?"

"The guy lets the woman know it was just a one-night stand. Nothing personal and definitely nothing serious."

He hadn't used that particular line before, but he'd used similar ones. He decided not to tell her that. "You weren't a one-night stand, Jillian."

She nodded. "I do recall you mentioning that last night wouldn't be your only time with me."

He tightened his arms around her. "And why do you think I said that?"

"Because you're a man and most men enjoy sex."

He smiled. "A lot of women enjoy it, as well. Didn't you?"

"Yes. There's no need to lie about it. I definitely enjoyed it."

A grin tugged at Aidan's lips. His ego appreciated her honesty. "I enjoyed it, as well." He kissed her, needing the taste of her.

It was a brief kiss and when he lifted his lips from hers, she seemed stunned by what he'd done. He found that strange considering the number of times they had kissed before.

"So, if you don't want to say last night was a one-night stand, what is it you want to talk about?" she asked.

He decided to be just as honest as she had been, and got straight to the point. "I want to talk about me. And you. Together."

She raised a brow. "Together?"

"Yes. I've fallen in love with you."

Nine

Jillian was out of the bed in a flash, taking half the blankets with her. She speared Aidan with an angry look. "Are you crazy? You can't be in love with me. It won't work, especially when I'm in love with you, too."

Too late she'd realized what she'd said. From the look on Aidan's face, he had heard her admission. "If I love you and you love me, Jillian, then what's the problem?"

She lifted her chin. "The problem is that we can't be together the way you would want us to be. I was okay with it when it was one-sided and I just loved you and didn't think you could possibly return the feelings, but now—"

"Hold up," Aidan said, and her eyes widened when he got off the bed to stand in front of her without a stitch of clothes on. "Let me get this straight. You think it's okay for me to sleep with you and not be in love with you?"

She tossed her hair back from her face. "Why not? I'm sure it's done all the time. Men sleep with women they don't love and vice versa. Are you saying you love every woman you sleep with?"

"No."

"Okay then."

"It's not okay because you're not any woman. You're the one that I *have* fallen in love with."

Why was he making things difficult? Downright complicated? She had to make him understand. "I could deal with this a lot better if you didn't love me, mainly because I would have known it wasn't serious on your end."

"And that would not have bothered you?"

"Not in the least. I need to stay focused on my studies and I can't stay focused if I know you feel the same way about me that I feel about you. That only complicates things."

He stared at her as if he thought she was crazy. In a way she couldn't very much blame him. Most women would prefer falling in love with a man who loved them, and if things were different she would want that, too. But the time wasn't right. Men in love made demands. They expected a woman's time. Her attention. All her energy. And being in love required that a woman give her man what he wanted. Well, she didn't have the time to do that. She was in medical school. She wanted to be a doctor.

And worse than anything, an Aidan who thought he loved her would cause problems. He wouldn't want to keep their relationship a secret. He was not a man to be kept in the closet or denied his right to be seen with her. He would want everyone to know they were together and that was something she couldn't accept.

"I still can't understand why you think me loving you complicates things," Aidan said, interrupting her thoughts.

"Because you wouldn't want to keep our affair a secret. You'll want to tell everyone. Take me out anyplace you want. You wouldn't like the thought of us sneaking around."

"No, I wouldn't." He gently pulled her into his arms. She would have pushed him away if he hadn't at that moment tugged the bedcovers from her hands leaving her as naked as he was. The moment their bodies touched, arousal hit her in the core. She was suddenly reminded of what they'd done last night and how they'd done it. From the way his eyes darkened, she knew he was reliving those same sizzling memories.

"Jillian."

"Aidan."

He drew her closer and closed his mouth over hers. She was lost. For a long while, all she could do was stand there feeling his body plastered to hers, feeling his erection pressed against her, feeling the tips of her nipples poking into his chest while he kissed her. Frissons of fire raced up her spine.

And when she felt herself being maneuvered toward the bed, she was too caught up in desire to do anything about it. The same urgency to mate that had taken hold of him had fused itself to her. As soon as her back touched the mattress she slid from beneath him and pushed him back. She had flipped them and was now on top of him. He stared up at her with surprise in his eyes.

She intended to play out one of her fantasies, one of the ways they'd made love in her dreams—with her on top. But first she needed him to know something. "I take the Pill…to regulate my periods. And I'm safe," she whispered.

"So am I."

She maneuvered her middle over his engorged shaft, which stood straight up. Every hormone inside her body sizzled as she eased down onto him, taking him inside inch by inch. He was big, but like last night her body stretched to accommodate his size.

"Look at me, Jillian." Obeying his command, she held his gaze.

"I love you, whether you want me to or not and it's too late for you to do anything about it."

She drew in a deep breath and continued to ease him inside of her, not wanting to dwell on the problems love could cause. They would talk again later. But for now, this is what she wanted. This is what she needed. And when she had taken him to the hilt, she moved, riding him the way she'd been taught to ride years ago. From the look reflected in the depths of his eyes, she was giving him a ride he would remember for a long time.

She liked the view from up here. Staring down at him, seeing his expression change each time she shoved downward, taking him deeper. His nostrils flared. His breathing was choppy. Was that a little sweat breaking through on his brow?

Riding him felt good. Exhilarating. He definitely had the perfect body to be ridden. Hard, masculine and solid. She had her knees locked on each side of his strong thighs. Her inner muscles clenched, gripping him in a hold that had him groaning deep in his throat.

She loved the sound. Loved being in control. Loved him. The last thought sent her senses spiraling, and when he shouted her named and bucked his entire body upward, she felt his massive explosion. He drenched her insides with thick semen. And she used her muscles to squeeze out more.

Perspiration soaked her head, her face, their bodies… but she kept on riding. When another explosion hit him, she nearly jerked them both off the bed when she screamed in pleasure.

He held her tight and she held him and she wished she never had to let him go.

Aidan pushed a damp curl out of Jillian's eyes. She was sprawled on top of him, breathing deeply. He figured she had earned the right to be exhausted. He'd never experienced anything so invigorating or stimulating in his entire life.

"Don't ask me not to love you, Jillian," he finally found the strength to say softly, and the words came straight from his heart. For the first time in his life, he'd told a woman he loved her and the woman wished that he didn't.

When he felt her tears fall on his arm, he shifted their bodies so he could look at her. "Is me loving you that bad?"

She shook her head. "No. I know it should be what I want but the timing… There is so much I still have to do."

"And you think I'd stop you from doing them?"

"No, but I'd stop myself. I'd lose focus. You would want to be with me and I would want to be with you. In the open. I know you don't understand why I can't do that, but I can't."

She was right, he didn't understand. He believed she was all wrong about how Dillon and Pam, or the entire Westmoreland family, would handle them hooking up. He doubted it would be a big deal. But it didn't matter what he thought. She thought otherwise and that's what mattered.

"What if I agree to do what we're doing now? I mean, keeping things between us a secret."

She lifted her head. "You would agree to that, Aidan? I'm not talking about a few weeks or a few months. I'm talking about until I finish medical school. Could you really wait that long?"

That was a good question. Could he? Could he be around Jillian at family gatherings and pretend nothing was going on between them? And what about the physical distance between them? She wasn't even sure what medical school she would attend. Her two top choices were Florida and New Orleans, both hundreds of miles away from Boston, Maine or North Carolina.

And what about his family and friends? Like Adrian, Aidan had quite a reputation around Harvard. What would his friends think when he suddenly stopped pursuing women? They would think he'd lost his ever-loving mind. But he didn't care what anyone thought.

It didn't matter. Wherever Jillian was, he would get to her, spend time with her and give her the support she needed to be the doctor she wanted to be.

What Jillian needed now more than anything was for him not to place any pressure on her. Her focus should be on completing the MCAT and not on anything else. Somehow he would handle the distance, he would handle his family and friends and their perceptions.

He held her gaze. "Yes, I can wait. No matter how long it takes, Jillian. Because you're worth waiting for."

Then he tugged her mouth down to his for another one of their ultrapassionate, mind-blowing kisses.

Ten

The present

"This is Captain Stewart Marcellus," a deep voice boomed through the intercom in Jillian's cabin. "My crew and I would like to welcome you aboard the Princess Grandeur. For the next fourteen days we'll cruise the Grand Mediterranean for your enjoyment. In an hour we'll depart Barcelona for full days in Monte Carlo and Florence and two days in Rome. From there we'll sail to Greece and Turkey. I invite you to join me tonight at the welcome party, which kicks off two weeks of fun."

Jillian glanced around her cabin. *A suite.* This was something she definitely hadn't paid for. She and Paige had planned to share a standard stateroom, definitely nothing as luxurious and spacious as what she'd been given. When she'd contacted the customer service desk to tell them about the mistake, she was told no mistake had been made and the suite was hers to enjoy.

No sooner had she ended the call than she'd received a delivery—a bouquet of beautiful mixed flowers and a bottle of chilled wine with a card that read, "Congratulations on finishing medical school. We are proud of you. Enjoy the cruise. You deserve it. Your family, The Westmorelands."

Jillian eased down to sit on the side of the bed. *Her family.* She wondered what the Westmorelands would think if they knew the truth about her and Aidan. About the affair the two of them had carried on right under their noses for three years.

As she stood to shower and get dressed for tonight's festivities, she couldn't help remembering what that affair had been like after they'd confessed their love for each other. Aidan had understood and agreed that it was to be their secret. No one else was supposed to know— unless the two of them thought it was absolutely necessary.

The first year had been wonderful, in spite of how hard it had been to engage in a long-distance love affair. Even with Aidan's busy schedule juggling dual residencies, he'd managed to fly to Laramie whenever he had a free weekend. And because their time together was scarce, he'd make it special. They would go out to dinner, see a movie, or if it was a weekend she needed to study, they would do that, too. There was no way she would have passed the MCAT the first time around without his help. She had applied to various medical schools and when she was notified of her acceptance into the one she wanted in New Orleans, Aidan had been the first person with whom she'd shared her good news. They had celebrated the next time he'd come to Laramie.

It was during that first year that they agreed to bring Ivy in on their secret. Otherwise, her roommate would have been worried when Jillian went missing because she was staying with Aidan at the hotel.

Jillian had fallen more and more in love with Aidan

during that time. Although she'd had a lot to keep her busy, she missed him when they were apart. But he'd made up for it when he came to town. And even though they'd spent a lot of time in bed making love, their relationship wasn't just about sex. However, she would have to say that the sex was off the chain, and the sexual tension between them was still so thick you could cut it with a knife. Ivy could attest to that and had teased Jillian about it all the time.

It was also during that first year that their control had been tested whenever they went home for holidays, weddings or baby christenings. She would be the first to admit she had felt jealous more than a few times when Aidan's single male cousins, who assumed he was still a player on the prowl, would try setting him up with other women.

Everything had gone well between them as they moved into their second year together. Aidan had helped her relocate to New Orleans after she bid a teary goodbye to Ivy. Jillian leased a one-bedroom efficiency apartment not far from the hospital where she would be working. It was perfect for her needs, but lonely.

It was during the third year that it became harder for Aidan to get away. The hospitals demanded more of his time. And her telephone conversations with him had been reduced from nightly to three times a week. She could tell he was frustrated with the situation. More than once he'd commented that he wished she would have applied to a medical school closer to Maine or North Carolina.

Jillian tried to ignore his attitude but found that difficult to do. Although Aidan didn't say so, deep down she knew the secrecy surrounding their affair was getting to him. It had begun to get to her, as well. And when it seemed Aidan was becoming distant, she knew she had to do something.

When Ivy came to visit Jillian in New Orleans one weekend, she talked to her best friend about the situation. Even now Jillian could remember that time as if it was yesterday…

"So, how is Aidan?" Ivy asked, after placing her order with their waitress.

Jillian had to fight back tears. "Not sure. We haven't talked in a few days and the last time we did, we had an argument."

Ivy raised a brow. "Another one?"

"Yes." She'd told Ivy about their last argument. He'd wanted her to fly to Maine for the weekend for his birthday. She had been excited about doing so until she'd checked her calendar and discovered that was the same weekend of her clinicals. Something she could not miss. Instead of understanding, he'd gotten upset with her and because of his lack of understanding, she'd gotten upset with him. Their most recent argument had started because he told her his twin now knew about them. He'd gotten angry when she'd accused him of breaking his promise and telling Adrian. He'd explained that he didn't have to tell his brother anything. He and his twin could detect each other's moods and feelings sometimes.

"I'm tired of arguing with him, Ivy, and a part of me knows the reason our relationship is getting so strained."

Ivy nodded. "Long-distance romances are hard to maintain, Jillian, and I'm sure the secrecy surrounding your affair isn't helping."

"Yes, I know, which is why I've made a few decisions."

Ivy lifted a brow. "About what?"

Jillian drew in a deep breath. "I've decided to tell Pam about us. The secrecy has gone on long enough. I believe my sister will accept the fact that I'm now an adult and old enough to decide what I want to do in my life and the person I want in it."

"Good for you."

"Thanks. I know she's been concerned about Aidan's womanizing reputation, but once she realizes that I love him and he loves me, I believe she will give us her blessing."

Jillian took a sip of her drink and continued, "But before I tell Pam, I'm flying to Maine to see Aidan. Next weekend is his birthday and I've decided to be there to help him celebrate."

"What about your clinicals?"

Jillian smiled. "I went to my professor and told her I desperately needed that weekend off. She agreed to work with me and arrange for me to do a makeup the following weekend."

"That was nice of her."

"Yes, it was. She said I was a good student, the first to volunteer for projects and my overall attendance is great. So now I'm set to go."

Ivy grinned. "Did you tell Aidan?"

"No. I'm going to surprise him. He mentioned that since I wouldn't be there to celebrate with him that he would sign up to work that day and then hang around his place, watch TV and go to bed early."

"On his birthday? That's a bummer."

"Yes, and that's why I plan to fly there to help him celebrate."

"You're doing the right thing by being there. I think it's wonderful that you're finally letting your sister know about you and Aidan. When she sees how much he adores you she will be happy for the two of you."

A huge smile touched Jillian's lips. "I believe so, too."

Jillian stepped out on the balcony to look at the ocean as she recalled what happened after that. She had been excited when she'd boarded the plane for Portland, Maine. She couldn't wait to tell Aidan of her decision to end the secrecy surrounding their affair and to celebrate his birthday with him.

Due to stormy weather in Atlanta, her connecting flight had been delayed five solid hours and she didn't arrive in Portland until six that evening. It had been another hour before she'd arrived at his apartment complex, anxious to use the door key he'd given her a year ago for the first time.

The moment she'd stepped off the elevator onto his floor she knew a party was going on in one of the apartments. Loud music blasted and boisterous voices made her ears ache. She hadn't known all the noise was coming from Aidan's apartment until she'd reached the door, which she didn't have to unlock since it was slightly ajar.

Jillian walked in and looked around. The place was crowded and there were more women in attendance than men. The women were wearing outfits that probably wouldn't be allowed out on the streets.

Jillian wondered what had happened to Aidan's decision to come home from work, watch TV and go to bed. It seemed he'd decided to throw a party instead and it was in full swing. In the center of the room Aidan sat in a recliner while some scantily dressed woman gave him a lap dance. And from the look on his face, he was enjoying every single minute of it. Some of the guys on the sidelines, who she figured must be Aidan's friends, were egging on both him and the woman, which prompted the woman to make the dance even more erotic.

When the woman began stripping off her clothes, starting with the barely-there strap of material covering her breasts, Jillian was shocked. She knew she'd seen enough when the woman's breasts all but smothered Aidan's face while she wiggled out of her panties.

Not able to watch any longer, a shaken Jillian had left, grateful Aidan hadn't even noticed her presence. What hurt more than anything was that he'd appeared to be enjoying every single minute of the dance. Aidan Westmoreland had seemed in his element. She couldn't help wondering if they had stopped with the dance or if he and the woman had ended up doing other things later.

When he'd called her a few days later he hadn't mentioned anything about the party at his apartment and she hadn't said anything about being there to witness what had gone on. And when she asked how he'd spent his birthday, he angered her even more when he gave her a smart aleck answer, asking, "Why do you care when you didn't care enough to spend it with me?"

He was wrong. She had cared enough. But he hadn't cared enough to tell her the truth. It was then that she'd made the decision to end things between them, since it was apparent that he missed his life as a womanizer. When he called later in the week and made another excuse for not flying to New Orleans to see her as he'd planned, she decided that would be a good time to break things off with him. She would give him his freedom, let him go back to the life he missed.

Deciding the less drama the better, she told him the secrecy of their affair was weighing her down, making her lose focus and she couldn't handle it any longer. She didn't tell him the true reason she'd wanted to end things.

Her declaration led to a huge argument between them. When he told her he was flying to New Orleans to talk to her, she told him she didn't want to see him. Then she ended the conversation.

He had called several times to talk to her but she'd refused to answer and eventually blocked his number. She knew that was the reason for the angry looks he'd given her when she'd attended the last couple of Westmoreland weddings. The last time she'd seen him was a few months ago at Stern's ceremony.

There had been no reason to tell Pam about the affair that had been a secret for so long, so she hadn't. The last thing Jillian needed was for her sister to remind her that just like a tiger couldn't change its stripes neither could a womanizer change his ways.

It had been a year since their breakup. At times she felt she had moved on, but other times she felt she had not. It was so disappointing and painful to think about the future they could have been planning together now that she'd finished medical school, if only things had worked out the way she'd hoped they would.

Jillian wiped the tears from her eyes, refusing to shed any more for Aidan. She was on this cruise to have fun and enjoy herself, and she intended to do just that.

"Yes, Adrian?"

"I'm glad I was able to reach you before ship left port.

I just want to wish you the best. I hope everything works out the way you want with Jill."

Aidan hoped things worked out the way he wanted, as well. "Thanks."

Like Paige, Adrian and Aidan's cousin Stern had figured out something was going on between him and Jillian a couple of years ago. "I will do whatever I have to do to get her back. When this ship returns to port, my goal is to have convinced Jillian to give me another chance."

"Well, Trinity and I are cheering for you."

"Thanks, bro." Trinity was Adrian's fiancée and the two would be getting married in a couple of months.

After ending his phone call with Adrian, Aidan crossed the suite to step out on the balcony. Barcelona was beautiful. He had arrived three days ago and taken a tour of what was considered one of the busiest ports in the Mediterranean. He had eaten at the finest restaurants, some in magnificent buildings etched deep with history. He had walked through the crowded streets wishing Jillian had been by his side. Hopefully when they returned to this port in fourteen days she would be.

He could just imagine what Jillian had assumed when she'd seen that woman giving him a lap dance last year. He had worked that day, as he'd told her he would, but he hadn't known about the surprise birthday party a few of his fraternity brothers had thrown for him.

And he definitely hadn't known about the lap dancer or the other strippers they'd invited until the women arrived. He couldn't get mad at his frat brothers for wanting to make his birthday kind of wild. All they knew was that for the past few years, the man who'd once been one of the biggest womanizers in Boston had taken a sabbatical from women. They'd had no idea that the reason for his seemingly boring lifestyle was because he was involved in a secret affair with Jillian.

So, thinking he'd been working too hard for too long and hadn't gotten in any play time, they thought they were doing him a favor. He would admit that after a few drinks he'd loosened up. But at no time had he forgotten he was in love with Jillian. The lap dance had been just for fun, and after the party all the women had left.

Yes, he'd made a mistake by not mentioning the party to Jillian. And he would be the first to admit his attitude had been less than desirable for the last year of their relationship. But he knew why. He'd had the best of intentions when he thought he could keep their secret without any problems, but as time went on, he'd become impatient. While she hadn't wanted anyone to know about them, he had wanted to shout the truth from the highest mountain.

It hadn't helped matters when some of his siblings and cousins began falling in love and getting married. It seemed as if an epidemic had hit Westmoreland Country when five of his relatives got married in a two-year period. And some had been relatives he'd thought would never marry. It had been hard being around his happily married kinfolk without wanting to have some of that happiness for himself. He would admit he'd spent too many months angry with himself, with Jillian, with the world. But at no time did he doubt his love for her.

Nothing had changed his feelings. He was still in love with her, which was why he was here. To right a wrong and convince her that she was the only woman he wanted.

He knew he had his work cut out for him. But he

intended to stay the course and not fail in his task. She wouldn't appreciate seeing him and she probably wouldn't like it when she found out about Paige's involvement. Or Ivy's for that matter. If Ivy hadn't told Paige the truth, he would still be angry, thinking the reason Jillian had broken up with him was because they were at odds regarding the secret of their affair.

He went back inside when he heard the cabin phone ring. He picked it up. "Yes?"

"I hope you find your quarters satisfactory."

Aidan smiled. That was an understatement. "It's more than satisfactory, Dominic."

This ship was just one of many in a fleet owned by Dominic Saxon. Dominic was married to the former Taylor Steele, whose sister Cheyenne was married to Aidan's cousin, Quade Westmoreland. Once Aidan discovered Jillian had booked her cruise on one of Dominic's ships, his friend had been all too eager to assist Aidan in getting back the woman he loved. Years ago Dominic had found himself in a similar situation.

"Taylor sends her love and we're all rooting for you. I know how misunderstandings can threaten even the most solid relationships, and I think you're doing the right thing by going after her," Dominic said. "I'm going to give you the same advice a very smart woman—my mother—gave me when I was going through my troubles with Taylor. *Let love guide you to do the right thing.* I hope the two of you enjoy the cruise."

"Thanks for the advice, and as for enjoying the cruise, I intend to make sure that we do."

After ending his call with Dominic, Aidan glanced around the cabin. Thanks to Dominic, Aidan had been given the owner's suite. It was spacious with a double balcony. There were also separate sleeping quarters with a king-size bed and a seventy-inch flat-screen television and a second wall-to-wall balcony. The sitting area contained a sofa that could convert into a double bed, another wall television and a dining area that overlooked yet another balcony. Other amenities he appreciated were the refrigerator, wet bar and huge walk-in closet. The bathroom was bigger than the one he had in his apartment, with both a Jacuzzi tub and a walk-in shower. He could just imagine him and Jillian using that shower together.

He walked back out on the balcony to see that people had gathered on the docks to watch the ship sail, waving flags that represented all the countries they would visit on the cruise. He expected Jillian to attend the welcome party tonight and so would he. Aidan couldn't wait to see Jillian's face when she discovered he was on board with her and would be for the next fourteen days.

He headed for the bathroom to shower.

Tonight couldn't get here fast enough.

"Welcome, senorita, may we assist with your mask?"

Jillian lifted a brow. "Mask?"

The tall crewman dressed in a crisp white uniform smiled down at her. "*Si.* Tonight's theme is a Spanish masquerade ball," he said, offering a red feathered mask to her.

She took it and slid it across her face. It was a perfect fit. "Thanks."

"Your name?" he asked.

"Jillian Novak."

"Senorita Novak, dinner will be served in a half hour

in the Madrid Room; someone will come escort you to your table."

"Thanks."

She entered the huge lounge that had beautiful rosettes hanging from the ceiling and several masquerade props in the corners of the room for picture taking. Flamenco dancers encouraged participation in the middle of the floor and several men dressed as dashing bullfighters walked around as servers. When a woman wearing a gorgeous *quinceañera* gown offered her a beautiful lace fan, Jillian smiled and took it.

"Would the senorita like a glass of rioja?"

"Yes, thanks," she responded to one of the servers.

Jillian took a sip and immediately liked the taste. It wasn't too tart or tangy but was an excellent blend of fruits. As she sipped her wine she looked around the room. It was crowded and most of the individuals were coupled off. Immediately, she felt like a loner crashing a party, but forced the feeling away. So what if there were a lot of couples and she had no one? She'd known it would be like this but had made the decision to come anyway.

"Excuse me, senorita, but someone asked me to give you this," the woman wearing the *quinceañera* gown said, while handing her a single red rose.

"Who?" Jillian asked, curiously glancing around.

The woman smiled. "A *very* handsome man." And then she walked off.

Jillian felt uneasy. What kind of *very* handsome man would come cruising alone? She'd seen a movie once where a serial killer had come on a cruise ship and stalked single women. No one had known just how many women he'd killed and thrown overboard until the end of the cruise. For crying out loud, why was she re-membering that particular movie now?

She drew in a deep breath knowing she was letting her imagination get the best of her. The man was prob-ably someone who'd seen her alone and wanted to state his interest by giving her a rose. Romantic but a total waste of his time. Even the woman's claim that he was *very* handsome did nothing for Jillian since she wasn't ready to get involved with anyone. Even after a full year, she compared every man to Aidan. That was the main reason she hadn't dated anyone since him. On the other hand, she would bet any amount of money Aidan was dating someone and probably hadn't wasted any time doing so.

She drew in a deep breath, refusing to let her mind go there. Why should she care in the least what Aidan was doing or who he was doing it with? Deciding not to think of an answer for that one, she glanced around the room, curiosity getting the best of her. She tried to find any single men but all she saw were the bullfight-ers serving drinks.

Jillian glanced at her watch. She'd deliberately ar-rived a little late so she wouldn't have long to wait for dinner. She'd grabbed breakfast on the run to catch her plane and because she'd come straight from the Barce-lona airport to the ship, she had missed lunch altogether.

After taking another sip of her wine, she was about to check her watch again when suddenly her skin heated. Was that desire floating in her stomach. Why? And for who? This was definitely odd.

Jillian searched the room in earnest as a quiver inched up her spine. Declining a server's offer of another drink, she nearly dismissed what was happening as a figment of her imagination when she saw him. A man wearing a teal feathered mask stood alone on the other side of the room, watching her. So she watched back, letting her gaze roam over him. Was he the one who'd given her the rose? Who was he? Why was she reacting to him this way?

As she studied him she found him oddly familiar. Was she comparing the man to Aidan to the point where everything about him reminded her of her ex? His height? His build? The low cut of his hair?

She shook her head. She was losing it. She needed another drink after all. That's when the man began walking toward her. She wasn't going crazy. She didn't know the when, how or why of it, but there was no doubt in her mind that the man walking toward her—mask or no mask—was Aidan. No other man had a walk like he did. And those broad shoulders...

He was sex appeal on legs and he walked the part. It was a stroll of self-confidence and sinful eroticism. How could he have this effect on her after a full year? She drew in a deep breath. That's not the question she should be asking. What she wanted to know was why he was on the same cruise with her? She refused to believe it was a coincidence.

Her spine stiffened when he came to a stop in front of her. Her nostrils had picked up his scent from five feet away and now her entire body was responding. Sharp, crackling energy stirred to life between them. And from the look in his eyes he felt it, as well. Hot. Raw. Primal.

She didn't want it. Nor did she need that sort of sexual attraction to him again. She blew out a frustrated breath. "Aidan, what are you doing here?"

* * *

Aidan wasn't surprised that she had recognized him with the mask on. After all, they'd shared a bed for three solid years so she should know him inside out, clothes or not…just like he knew her. Case in point, he knew exactly what she was wearing beneath that clingy black dress. As little as possible, which meant only a bra and thong. And more than likely both were made of lace. She had the figure to handle just about anything she put on—or nothing at all. Frankly, he preferred nothing at all.

"I asked you what you're doing here."

He noted her voice had tightened in anger and he figured it best to answer. "I've always wanted to take a Mediterranean cruise."

She rolled her eyes. "And you want me to believe you being here is a coincidence? That you had no idea I was here on this cruise ship?"

"That's not what I'm saying."

"Then what *are* you saying, Aidan?"

He placed his half-empty wineglass on the tray of a passing waiter, just in case Jillian was tempted to douse him with it. "I'll tell you after dinner."

"After dinner? No, you will tell me *now*."

Her voice had risen and several people glanced over at them. "I think we need to step outside to finish our discussion."

She frowned. "I think not. You can tell me what I want to know right here."

In anger, she walked into the scant space separating them and leaned in close, her lips almost brushing his. That was too close. His bottom lip tingled and his heart beat like crazy when he remembered her taste. A taste he'd become addicted to. A taste he'd gone a year without.

"I wouldn't bring my mouth any closer if I were you," he warned in a rough whisper.

She blinked as if realizing how close they were. Heeding his warning, she quickly took a step back. "I still want answers, Aidan. What are you doing here?"

He decided to be totally honest with her. Give her the naked truth and let her deal with it. "I came on this cruise, Jillian, with the full intention of winning you back."

Eleven

Jillian stared at Aidan as his words sank in. That's when she decided it would be best for them to take this discussion to a more private area after all. She removed her mask. "I think we need to step outside the room, Aidan."

When they stepped into a vacant hallway, she turned to him. "How dare you assume all you had to do was follow me on this cruise to win me back?"

He pulled off his mask and she fought back a jolt of desire when she looked into his face. How could any man get more handsome in a year's time? Yes, she'd seen him a couple of times since their break-up, but she had avoided getting this close to him. He appeared to have gotten an inch or so taller, his frame was even more muscular and his looks were twice as gorgeous.

"I have given it some thought," he said, leaning back against a railing.

"Evidently, not enough," she countered, not liking how her gaze, with a mind of its own, was traveling over him. He was wearing a dark suit, and he looked like a male model getting ready for a photo shoot—immaculate with nothing out of place.

"Evidently, you've forgotten one major thing about me," she said.

"What? Just how stubborn you are?" he asked, smiling, as if trying to make light of her anger, which irritated her even more.

"That, too, but also that once I make up my mind about something, that's it. And I made up my mind that my life can sail a lot more calmly without you." She watched his expression to see if her words had any effect, but she couldn't tell if they had.

He studied her in silence before saying, "Sorry you feel that way, Jillian. But I intend to prove you wrong."

She lifted a brow. "Excuse me?"

"Over the next fourteen days I intend to prove that your life can't sail more calmly without me. In fact, I intend to show you that you don't even like calm. You need turbulence, furor and even a little mayhem."

She shook her head. "If you believe that then you truly don't know me at all."

"I know you. I also know the real reason you broke things off with me. Why didn't you tell me what you *thought* you saw in my apartment the night of my birthday party?"

She wondered how he'd found out about that. It really didn't matter at this point. "It's not what I *thought* I saw, Aidan. It's what I saw. A woman giving you a lap dance, which you seemed to enjoy, before she began stripping off her clothes." Saying it made the memory flash in her mind and roused her anger that much more.

"She was a paid entertainer, Jillian. All the ladies there that night were. Several of my frat brothers thought I'd been living a boring and dull life and decided to add some excitement into it. I admit they might have gone a little overboard."

"And you enjoyed every minute of it."

He shrugged. "I had a few drinks and—"

"You don't know what all you did, do you?"

He frowned. "I remember fine. Other than the lap dance and her strip act…and a couple other women stripping…nothing else happened."

"Wasn't that enough?" she asked, irritated that he thought several naked women on display in his apartment were of little significance. "And why didn't you tell me about the party? You led me to believe you'd done just as you said you were going to do—watch TV and go to bed."

He released a deep breath. "Okay, I admit I should have told you and I was wrong for not doing so. But I was angry with you. It was my birthday and I wanted to spend it with you. I felt you could have sacrificed a little that weekend to be with me. I hadn't known you changed your mind and flew to Portland."

He paused a moment and then continued, "I realized after we'd broken up just how unpleasant my attitude had been and I do apologize for that. I was getting frustrated with the secrecy surrounding our affair, with my work and how little time I could get off to fly to New Orleans to spend with you."

As far as Jillian was concerned, his attitude had been more than unpleasant; it had become downright unacceptable. He wasn't the only one who'd been frustrated with their situation. She had, too, which was the reason she had decided to confess all to Pam.

"Now that you're finished with medical school, there's no reason to keep our secret any longer anyway," he said, interrupting her thoughts.

She frowned. "And I see no reason to reveal it. Ever," she said. "Especially in light of one very important fact."

"And what fact is that?"

"The fact that we aren't together and we won't ever be together again."

If she figured that then she was wrong.

They *would* be together again. He was counting on it. It was the reason he'd come on the cruise. The one thing she had not said was that she no longer loved him. And as long as she had feelings for him then he could accomplish anything. At this point, even if she claimed she didn't love him, he would have to prove her wrong because he believed she loved him just as much as he loved her. Their relationship was just going through a few hiccups, which he felt they could resolve.

"If you truly believe that then you have nothing to worry about," he said.

She frowned. "Meaning what?"

"Meaning my presence on this ship shouldn't bother you."

She lifted her chin. "It won't unless you become a nuisance."

A smile spread across his face. "Nuisance? I think not. But I do intend to win you back, like I said. Then we can move on with our lives. I see marriage and babies in our future."

She laughed. "You've got to be kidding. Didn't you hear what I said? We won't be getting back together, so we don't have a future."

"And you're willing to throw away the last three years?"

"What I've done is make it easy for you."

He lifted a brow. "To do what?"

"Go back to your womanizing ways. You seemed to

be enjoying yourself so much at your birthday party I wouldn't think of denying you the opportunity."

He crossed his arms over his chest. "I gave up my so-called womanizing ways when I fell in love with you."

"Could have fooled me with your lap dancer and all those strippers waiting their turn."

"Like I said, I didn't invite them."

"But you could have asked them to leave."

He shrugged. "Yes, I could have. But you're going to have to learn to trust me, Jillian. I can see where my attitude leading up to that night might have been less than desirable, but at no time have I betrayed you with another woman. Do you intend to punish me forever for one night of a little fun?"

"I'm not punishing you, Aidan. I'm not doing anything to you. I didn't invite you on this cruise. You took it upon yourself to…"

Her words trailed off and she gazed at him suspiciously before saying, "Paige and I were supposed to go on this cruise together and she had to back out when she had a conflict, which is why I came alone. Please tell me you had nothing to do with that."

He'd known she would eventually figure things out but he had hoped it wouldn't be this soon. "Okay, I won't tell you."

She was back in his face again. "You told Paige about us? Now she knows I was duped by a womanizer."

Her lips were mere inches from his again. Evidently, she'd forgotten his earlier warning. "I am not a womanizer, and I didn't tell her anything about us. She figured things out on her own. Ivy told Paige about the lap dance and Paige told me. And I appreciate her doing so."

From Jill's expression he could tell that although he

might appreciate it, she didn't. "I am so upset with you, right now, Aidan. You are—"

Suddenly he pulled her into his arms. "You were warned."

Then he captured her mouth with his.

Push him away. Push him away. Push him away, a voice inside of Jillian's head chanted.

But her body would not obey. Instead of pushing him away, she leaned in closer, wrapping her arms around his neck.

Had it been a year since she had enjoyed this? A year since she'd had the taste of his tongue inside her mouth? Doing all those crazy things in every nook and cranny? Making liquid heat she'd held at bay shoot straight to the area between her legs?

How could any woman deal with a master kisser like him? She would admit that during the past year she had gone to bed dreaming of this but the real thing surpassed any dream she'd ever had.

The sound of voices made them pull apart. She drew in a deep breath, turning her back to him so she could lick her lips without him seeing her do so. That had been one hell of a kiss. Her lips were still electrified.

She turned back around and caught him tracing his tongue across his own lips. Her stomach clenched. "I think you have it all wrong, Aidan," she managed to say.

"After that kiss, I'd say I got it all right."

"Think whatever you like," she said, walking away.

"Hey, where're you going? The Madrid Room is this way."

She stopped and turned. "I'll order room service."

Jillian continued walking, feeling the heat of his gaze on her back.

Aidan watched her walk away, appreciating the sway of her hips. He drew in a deep breath. He loved the woman. If there was any doubt in her mind of that—which there seemed to be—he would wipe it out.

Turning, he headed toward his own cabin, thinking room service sounded pretty good. Besides, he had shocked Jillian's senses enough for today. Tomorrow he planned to lay it on even thicker. She had warned him not to be a nuisance. He smiled at the thought. He wouldn't be a nuisance, just totally effective.

Tonight they had talked, although he seemed to annoy her and he'd found her somewhat infuriating. But at least they knew where they both stood. She knew he was aware of the real reason she'd ended things between them. He had to convince her that his life as a womanizer was definitely behind him, that he had no desire to return to that life again.

He would admit getting rid of the lap dancer that night hadn't been easy. Somehow she'd figured it would be okay to hang around after the party was over. She'd been quick to let him know there wouldn't be an overtime charge. He had countered, letting her know he wasn't interested.

When Aidan reached his suite, he saw the elephant made of hand towels on his bed. Cute. But not as cute as the woman he intended to have back in his arms.

Jillian checked the time as she made a call to Paige. It was around ten in the morning in L.A., so there was no reason her sister shouldn't answer the phone. Paige was definitely going to get an earful from her.

"Why are you calling me? Aren't rates higher on the high seas?" Paige asked, answering on the fourth ring.

Jillian frowned. "Don't worry about the cost of the rates. Why didn't you tell me you knew about me and Aidan?"

"Why hadn't you told *me* so I wouldn't have to tell you? And don't say because it was supposed to be a secret."

"Well, it was. How did you figure it out?"

"Wasn't hard to do. Both of you started getting sloppy with it. Aidan slipped and called you Jilly a couple of times, and I caught you almost drooling whenever he walked into the room."

"I did not."

"You did, too. Besides, I knew you had a crush on him that first time we met the Westmoreland family at Pam's engagement party. You kept me up all night asking, 'Isn't Aidan cute, Paige? Isn't he cute?'"

Jillian smiled as she remembered. She had been so taken with Aidan. Although he and Adrian were identical twins it had been Aidan who pushed her buttons. "Well, no thanks to you he's here and he wants me back."

"Do you want him to get you back?"

"No. You didn't see that lap dance. I did."

"Didn't have to see it because I've seen one before. I know they can get rather raunchy. But it was a birthday party. His. Thrown by his friends and the lap dancer and the strippers were entertainment."

"Some entertainment," she mumbled. "He enjoyed it. You should have seen the look on his face when the woman shoved her girls at him."

"Pleeze. He's a man. They enjoy seeing a pair of

breasts. Anytime or anyplace. Will it make you feel better if I get the Chippendales dancers for your next birthday party?"

"This isn't funny, Paige."

"You don't hear me laughing. If anything, you should hear me moaning. Can you imagine a lap dance from one of those guys? If you can't, I can. And my imagination is running pretty wild right now."

Jillian shook her head. "Before I let you go, there's one more thing. Did you really get a part in a Spielberg movie?"

"No."

"So you lied."

"I was acting, and I evidently did a great job. It sounds like you have some serious decisions to make about Aidan. But don't rush. You have fourteen days. In the meantime, enjoy the cruise. Enjoy life. Enjoy Aidan. He plans on getting you back. I'd like to be there to watch him try. I've got my money on him, by the way."

"Sounds like you have money to lose. Goodbye, Paige." Jillian clicked off the phone, refusing to let her sister get in the last word, especially if it would be a word she really didn't want to hear.

Regardless of what Paige said, her sister hadn't been there to witness that lap dance. She hadn't seen that salacious grin on Aidan's face while looking up at the half-naked woman sprawled all over him. There was no doubt in Jillian's mind that he'd enjoyed every minute of it. He had wanted those women there; otherwise, he would have asked them and his friends to leave. And although he claimed otherwise, how could she be certain one of those women didn't spend the night with him; especially since he didn't tell Jillian anything about the party, even when she had asked? She of all people knew what a healthy sexual appetite Aidan had, and they hadn't seen each other in more than three months. And at the time, that had been the longest amount of time they'd been apart.

Before getting in bed later that night, Jillian checked the ship's agenda. Tomorrow was a full day at sea and she refused to stay locked in her cabin. This was a big ship and chances were she might not run into Aidan. She knew the odds of that were slim; especially when he admitted his only reason for coming on the cruise was to win her back. Well, he could certainly try.

She could not deny it had felt good to be kissed by him tonight. Pretty damn good. But there was more to any relationship than kisses. Even the hot, raw, carnal kind that Aidan gave. And when he took a mind to kiss her all over…

She drew in a deep breath, refusing to let her thoughts go there. He would probably try using his sexual wiles to win her back. And she intended to be ready to disappoint him.

Twelve

"Good morning, Jillian."

Jillian glanced up from the book she was reading to watch Aidan slide onto the lounger beside her. She was on the upper deck near the pool. Why had she thought he would never find her here?

"Good morning," she grumbled and went back to her reading. Although she had gone to bed fairly early, she hadn't gotten a good night's sleep. The man stretched on the lounger beside her had invaded her dreams not once or twice, but all through the night.

"Had breakfast yet?"

She glanced away from her book to look over at him. "Yes." She remembered the pancakes and syrup she'd enjoyed. "It was tasty."

"Um, bet it wasn't tasty as you. Want to go back to my cabin and be my breakfast?"

His question caused a spark of heat to settle between her thighs. Something she definitely didn't need after all those erotic dreams she'd had. "You shouldn't say something like that to me."

"You prefer I say it to someone else?"

She narrowed her gaze. "Do whatever you want. At breakfast I happened to notice a group of women on the cruise. All appeared single. I think I overheard one say they're part of some book club."

"You want me to go check out other women?"

"Won't matter to me. Need I remind you that we aren't together?"

"And need I remind you that I'm working on that? And by the way, I have a proposition for you."

"Whatever it is, the answer is no."

He chuckled. "You haven't heard it."

"Doesn't matter."

"You certain?"

"Positive."

He smiled over at her. "Okay then. I'm glad. In fact, you've made my day by not accepting it. I'm happy that you turned it down."

She stared over at him and frowned. "Really? And just what was this proposition?"

In a warm, teasing tone, he said. "I thought you didn't want to hear it."

"I've changed my mind."

He nodded. "I guess I can allow you to do that." He shifted and sat up. She tried not to notice the khaki shorts he wore and how well they fit the lower half of his body. Or how his muscle shirt covered perfect abs.

He took her hand, easing her into the same sitting position he was in, as if what he had to say was something he didn't want others around them to overhear.

"Well?" she asked, trying to ignore the tingling sensation in the hand he touched.

"You're aware the only reason I came on this cruise was to get you back, right?"

She shrugged. "So you say."

A smile touched the corners of his lips. "Well, I

thought about a few of the things you said last night and I wanted to offer you a chance to make some decisions."

She lifted a brow. "Like what?"

"Like whether or not I should even pursue you at all. I don't want to be that nuisance you insinuated I could be. So my proposition was that I just leave you alone and wait patiently for you to come to me. I hope you know what that means since you just turned it down."

She would not have turned it down had she heard him out, and he knew it. Unfortunately, she could guess what the consequences would be and she had a feeling she wasn't going to like it. "What does that mean, Aidan?"

He leaned in closer to whisper in her ear. His warm breath felt like a soft, sensuous lick across her skin. "I want you so bad, Jillian, that I ache. And that means I'm not giving up until you're back in my bed."

She immediately felt a pounding pulse at the tips of her breasts. She leaned back to stare at him and the razor-sharp sensuality openly displayed in his gaze almost made her moan.

"And before you ask, Jillian, the answer is no. It isn't just about sex with me," he murmured in a low, husky tone. "It's about me wanting the woman I love both mentally and physically. You're constantly in my mind but physically, it's been over a year."

She drew in a deep breath and felt the essence of what he'd said in every single nerve ending in her body. It had been over a year. With Aidan she'd had a pretty active sex life, and although there were periods of time when they were apart, they always made up for any time lost whenever they were together.

"Your needing sex is not my problem," she finally said.

"Isn't it?" he countered. "Can you look me in the eyes

and say that you don't want me as much as I want you? That you didn't dream about us making love last night? Me being inside you. You riding me? Hard. My tongue inside your mouth…and inside a lot of other places on your body?"

She silently stared at him but her entire body flared in response to the vivid pictures he'd painted in her mind. Unlike Paige, Jillian wasn't an actress and couldn't lie worth a damn. But on that same note she would never admit anything to him. That would give him too much power. "I won't admit to anything, Aidan."

"You don't have to," he said, with a serious smile on his face. "And it's not about me needing sex but me needing you." He paused a moment as if giving his words time to sink in. "But this leads to another proposition I'd like to make."

She'd set herself up for this one. "And what is the proposition this time?"

He leaned in closer. "That for the remainder of the cruise you let your guard down. Believe in me. Believe in yourself. And believe in us. I want you to see I'm still the man who loves you. The man who will always love you. But that's something you have to believe, Jillian. However, at the end of the cruise, if for whatever reason, you still don't believe it or feel that the two of us can make a lifetime commitment, then when we dock back in Barcelona, we'll agree to go our separate ways."

She broke eye contact with him to glance out at the ocean. Today was a rather calm day outside but inside she was in a state of turmoil. He was asking a lot of her and he knew it. His proposition meant forgetting the very reason she broke up with him. That would definitely be easy on him if she did. Was that why he'd come up with this latest proposition?

Jillian turned her gaze back to him. "You want me to just forget everything that's happened, Aidan? Especially the incident that caused our breakup?"

"No, I don't want you to forget a single thing."

His answer surprised her. "Why?"

"Because it's important that the two of us learn from any mistakes we've made, and we can't do that if we safely tuck them away just because doing so will be convenient. We should talk about them openly and honestly. Hopefully, we'll be able to build something positive out of the discussions. You're always harping a lot on the things I did. What about you, Jillian? Do you think you were completely blameless?"

"No, but—"

"I don't want to get into all that now, but have you ever noticed that with you there's always a *but* in there somewhere?"

She frowned at him. "No, I never noticed but obviously you have." Was it really that way with her? As far as sharing the blame, she could do that. But she hadn't been the one getting a lap dance.

"My proposition is still on the table," he said. "I've been completely honest with you on this cruise, Jillian. I've been up-front with my intentions, my wants and my desires."

Yes, he had. Every opportunity he got. And she knew that he would have her on her back in a flash if she were to let him. Jillian inclined her head to look deeper into his eyes. "And you promise that at the end of the cruise if things don't work out the way we think they should that you will go your way and I'll go mine?"

He nodded slowly. "It would be difficult, but yes. I want you to be happy and if being happy for you means not having me in your life then that's the way it will be. It will be your decision and I would like to have that decision the night before we return to Barcelona."

She digested what Aidan said. He'd laid things out, with no fluff. She knew what, and who, she would be dealing with. But she also knew that even if she decided she didn't want him in her life romantically, he could never be fully out of it; their families were connected. How could they manage that?

"What about the family?" she asked. "Paige, Stern and Adrian know our secret. If things don't work out between us it might have an effect on them."

"We will deal with that if it happens. Together. Even if we're no longer lovers, there's no reason we can't remain friends. Besides, are you sure there aren't others in the family besides those three who know? It's my guess others might suspect something even if they haven't said anything."

She shrugged. "Doesn't matter who knows now. I had planned on telling Pam anyway."

Surprise flashed in his eyes. "You had?"

"Yes."

"When?"

"After I talked to you about it, which I had planned to do when I flew into Portland for your birthday."

"Oh."

She released a sigh. Evidently the one thing he hadn't found out was that she'd intended to release him from their secret. "Afterward, when things didn't work out between us, I saw no need for me to tell Pam anything.

In fact, I felt the less she knew about the situation, the better."

Aidan didn't say anything for a moment and neither did Jillian. She figured he was thinking how that one weekend had changed things for them. He finally broke the silence by asking, "So, what's your answer to my proposition?"

Jillian nibbled at her bottom lip. Why couldn't she just turn him down, walk away and keep walking? She knew one of the reasons was that her mind was filled with fond memories of the good times they'd shared. It hadn't been all bad.

Would it be so dreadful if she were to give his proposition a try? What did she have to lose? She'd already experienced heartbreak with him. And a year of separation hadn't been easy. Besides, she couldn't deny that it would feel good to be with him out in the open, without any kind of secrecy shrouding them. Whenever he'd come to Laramie, she'd always been on guard, looking over her shoulder in case she ran into someone who knew Pam. And he did have a good point about the remaining days on the cruise testing the strength of a relationship between them.

She met his gaze. "Yes. I accept your proposition and I will hold you to your word, Aidan."

Later that night, as Aidan changed for dinner, he couldn't help remembering Jillian's words.

"Fine, baby, hold me to my word," he murmured to himself as he tucked his white dress shirt into his pants. "That's the way it should be. And that's the way it will be."

Today had gone just the way he'd wanted. After she'd

agreed to his proposition he'd been able to talk her into going with him to the Terelle Deck so he could grab breakfast. She'd sat across from him while he ate a hefty portion of the pancakes and syrup she'd recommended. They had chosen a table with a beautiful view of the ocean, and he liked the way the cool morning breeze stirred her hair. More than once he'd been tempted to reach across the table and run his fingers through it.

After breakfast he had talked her into joining him in the Venus Lounge where a massive bingo game was under way. They had found a table in the back and she'd worked five bingo cards while he worked three. In the end, neither of them had won anything but the game had been fun.

Later they had gone to the art gallery to check out the paintings on display and after that they'd enjoyed a delicious lunch in the Coppeneria Room. After she mentioned her plans to visit the spa, he'd taken a stroll around the ship. The layout was awesome and the entire ship was gorgeous. Tomorrow morning before daybreak they would arrive in Monte Carlo, France, and from there, Florence, Italy. He'd never been to France or Italy before but Adrian had, and according to his twin both countries were beautiful. Aidan couldn't wait to see them for himself.

He smiled as he put on his cuff links. Being around Jillian today had reminded him of how much she liked having her way. In the past he had indulged her. But not this time. While on this cruise he had no intention of letting her have her way. In fact, he planned to teach her the art of compromising. That was the main reason he had suggested she drop by his cabin to grab him for dinner instead of the other way around. Although she hadn't said anything, he could tell she hadn't liked the idea.

He turned from the mirror at the sound of a knock on his door. She was a little early but he had no problem with that. Moving across the suite, he opened the door, and then stood there, finding it impossible to speak. All he could do was stare at Jillian. Dressed in a red floor-length gown that hugged every curve, her hair wrapped on top of her head with a few curls dangling toward her beautiful face, she looked breathtaking. His gaze scanned the length of her—head to toe.

Pulling himself together, he stepped aside. "Come in. You look very nice."

"Thank you," she said, entering his suite. "I'm a little early. The cabin steward arrived and I didn't want to get in his way."

"No problem. I just need to put on my tie."

"This suite is fantastic. I thought my suite was large but this one is triple mine in size."

He smiled over at her. "It's the owner's personal suite whenever he cruises."

"Really? And how did you get so lucky?"

"He's a friend. You remember my cousin Quade who lives in North Carolina, right?"

"The one who has the triplets?"

"Yes, he's the one. Quade and the ship's owner, Dominic Saxon, are brothers-in-law, married to sisters—the former Steeles, Cheyenne and Taylor.

Jillian nodded. "I remember meeting Cheyenne at Dillon and Pam's wedding. The triplets were adorable. I don't recall ever meeting Taylor."

"I'll make sure you meet Taylor and Dominic if you ever come to visit me in Charlotte." He'd deliberately chosen his words to make sure she understood that if a meeting took place, it would be her decision.

After putting on his tie, he turned to her, trying not to stare again. "I'm all set. Ready?"

"Whenever you are."

He was tempted to kiss her but held back. Knowing him like she did, she would probably expect such a move. But tonight he planned to keep her on her toes. In other words, he would be full of surprises.

"Hi, Aidan!"

Jillian figured it would be one of those nights when the group of women sharing their table chorused the greeting to Aidan. It was the book-club group. She should have known they would find him. Or, for all she knew, he'd found them.

"I take it you've met them," she whispered when he pulled out her chair.

"Yes, earlier today, while taking my stroll when you were at the spa."

"Evening, ladies. How's everyone doing?" Aidan asked the group with familiarity, taking his seat.

"Fine," they responded simultaneously. Jillian noticed some were smiling so hard it made her wonder how any-one's lips could stretch that wide.

"I want you all to meet someone," Aidan was saying. "This is Jillian Novak. My significant other."

"Oh."

Was that disappointment she heard in the voices of the six women? And what happened to those huge smiles? Well, she would just have to show them how it was done. She smiled brightly and then said, "Hello, everyone."

Only a few returned her greeting, but she didn't care because she was reflecting on Aidan's introduction.

My significant other.

Before their breakup they had been together for three years and this was the first time he'd introduced her to anyone because of their secret. It made her realize that, other than Ivy, she'd never introduced him to anyone, either.

The waiter came to take their order but not before giving them a run-down of all the delectable meals on the menu tonight. Jillian chose a seafood dinner and Aidan selected steak.

She discreetly checked out the six women engaging in conversation with Aidan. All beautiful. Gorgeously dressed. Articulate. Professional. Single.

"So, how long have the two of you been together?" asked one of the women who'd introduced herself earlier as Wanda.

Since it appeared the woman had directed the question to Aidan, Jillian let him answer. "Four years," he said, spreading butter on his bread. Jillian decided not to remind him that one of those years they hadn't been together.

"Four years? Really?" a woman by the name of Sandra asked, extending her lips into what Jillian could tell was a plastered-on smile.

"Yes, *really,*" Jillian responded, knowing just what the chick was getting at. After four years Jillian should have a ring on her finger. In other words, she should be a wife and not a significant other.

"Then I guess the two of you will probably be tying the knot pretty soon." It was obvious Wanda was digging for information. The others' ears were perked up as if they, too, couldn't wait to hear the response.

Jillian tried not to show her surprise when Aidan reached across the table and placed his hand over hers. "Sooner rather than later, if I had my way. But I'll be joining the Cardiology Department at Johns Hopkins in the fall, and Jillian's just finished medical school, so we haven't set dates yet."

"You're both doctors?" Sandra asked, smiling.

"Yes," both Aidan and Jillian answered at the same time.

"That's great. So are we," Sandra said, pointing to herself and the others. "Faye and Sherri and I just finished Meharry Medical School a couple of months ago, and Wanda, Joy and Virginia just completed pharmacy school at Florida A&M."

"Congratulations, everyone," Jillian said, giving all six women a genuine smile. After having completed medical school she knew the hard work and dedication that was required for any medical field. And the six had definitely attended excellent schools.

"And congratulations to you, too," the women said simultaneously.

Jillian's smile widened. "Thanks."

Aidan glanced down at the woman walking beside him as they left the jazz lounge where several musicians had performed. Jillian had been pretty quiet since dinner. He couldn't help wondering what she was thinking.

"Did you enjoy dinner?" he asked.

She glanced up at him. "Yes, what about you?"

He shrugged. "It was nice."

"Just nice? You were the only male seated at a table

with several females, all gorgeous, so how was it just nice?"

"Because it was," he said, wondering if this conversation would start a discussion he'd rather not have with her. But then, maybe they should have it now. They *had* agreed to talk things out. "So what did you think of the ladies at our table tonight?"

She stopped walking to lean against a rail and look at him. "Maybe I should be asking what you thought of them."

He joined her at the rail, standing a scant foot in front of her. "Pretty. All seven of them. But the prettiest of them all was the one wearing the red dress. The one named Jillian Novak. Now, she was a total knockout. She put the *s* in sexy."

Jillian smiled and shook her head, sending those dangling curls swinging. "Laying it on rather thick, aren't you, Aidan?"

"Not as long as you get the picture."

"And what picture is that?"

"That you're the only woman I want. The only one who can get blood rushing through my veins."

She chuckled. "Sounds serious, Dr. Westmoreland."

"It is." He didn't say anything for a minute as he stared at her. "Do you realize that this is the first time you've ever referred to me as Dr. Westmoreland?"

She nodded. "Yes, I know. Just like I realized tonight at dinner that it was the first time you'd ever introduced me during the time we were together."

"Yes. There were times when I wished I could have."

But you couldn't, she thought. *Because of the secret I made you keep.*

"But I did tonight."

"Yes, you did fib a little. Twice in fact," she pointed out.

He lifted a brow. "When?"

"When you said I was your significant other."

"I didn't fib. You are. There's no one more significant in my life than you," he said softly.

Jillian couldn't say anything after that. How could she? And when the silence between them lengthened, she wondered if he was expecting her to respond. What *could* she say? That she believed him? Did she really?

"And what was the other?" he asked, finally breaking the silence.

"What other?" she asked him.

"Fib. You said there were two."

"Oh. The one about the amount of time we've been together. You said four years and it was three," she said as they began walking again.

"No, it was four. Although we spent a year apart it meant nothing to me, other than frustration and anger. Nevertheless, you were still here," he said, touching his heart. "During every waking moment and in all my dreams."

She glanced away from him as they continued walking only to glance back moments later. "That sounds unfair to the others."

"What others?"

"Any woman you dated that year."

He stopped walking, took her hand and pulled her to the side, back over to the rail. He frowned down at her. "What are you talking about? I didn't date any women last year."

She searched his face and somehow saw the truth

in his words. "But why? I thought you would. Figured you had."

"Why?" Before she could respond he went on in a mocking tone, "Ah, that's right. Because I'm a womanizer."

Jillian heard the anger in his voice, but yes, that was the reason she'd thought he'd dated. Wasn't that the reason she had ended things between them as well, so he would have the freedom to return to his old ways? She drew in a deep breath. "Aidan, I—"

"No, don't say it." He stiffened his chin. "Whatever it is you're going to say, Jillian, don't." He glanced down at his watch and then his gaze moved back to her face. "I know you prefer turning in early, so I'll see you back to your cabin. I think I'll hang out a while in one of the bars."

She didn't say anything for a moment. "Want some company?"

"No," he said softly. "Not right now."

Suddenly, she felt a deep ache in her chest. "Okay. Don't worry about seeing me to my cabin. You can go on."

"You sure?"

She forced a smile. "Yes, I'm sure. I know the way."

"All right. I'll come get you for breakfast around eight."

If you can still stand my company, she thought. "Okay. I'll see you in the morning at eight."

He nodded and, with the hurt she'd brought on herself eating away at her, she watched Aidan walk away.

Thirteen

Aidan forced his eyes open when he heard banging coming from the sitting area.

"What the hell?" He closed his eyes as sharp pain slammed through his head. It was then that he remembered last night. Every single detail.

He had stopped at the bar, noticed it was extremely crowded and had gone to his room instead. He'd ordered room service, a bottle of his favorite Scotch. He'd sat on the balcony, looking out over the ocean beneath the night sky and drinking alone, nursing a bruised heart. He didn't finish off the entire bottle but he'd downed enough to give him the mother of all headaches this morning. What time was it anyway?

He forced his eyes back open to look at the clock on the nightstand. Ten? It was ten in the morning? Crap! He'd promised Jillian to take her to breakfast at eight. He could only imagine what she'd thought when he was a no-show. Pulling himself up on the side of the bed he drew in a deep breath. Honestly, did he care anymore? She had him pegged as a player in that untrusting mind of hers, so what did the truth matter?

"Mr. Aidan," called the cabin steward, "do you want me to clean your bedroom now or come back later?"

"Come back later, Rowan."

When Aidan heard the door close, he dropped back in bed. He knew he should call Jillian, but chances were she'd gotten tired of waiting around and had gone to breakfast without him. He could imagine her sitting there eating pancakes while all kinds of insane ideas flowed through her head. All about him. Hell, he might as well get up, get dressed and search the ship for her to put those crazy ideas to rest.

He was about to get out of bed when he heard a knock at the door. He figured it was probably the guy coming around to pick up laundry, so he slipped into his pajama bottoms to tell the person to come back later.

He snatched open the door but instead of the laundry guy, Jillian stood there carrying a tray of food. "Jillian? What are you doing here?"

She stared at him for a moment. "You look like crap."

"I feel like crap," he muttered, moving aside to let her in. She placed the tray on his dining table. His head still pounded somewhat, but not as hard as the way his erection throbbed while staring at her. She was wearing a cute and sexy shorts set that showed what a gorgeous pair of legs she had. And her hair, which had been pinned atop her head last night, flowed down her shoulders while gold hoop earrings dangled from her ears. Damn, he couldn't handle this much sexiness in the morning.

She turned around. "To answer your question as to why I'm here, you missed breakfast so I thought I'd bring you something to eat."

He closed the door and leaned against it. "And what else?"

She lifted a brow. "And what else?"

"Yes. What other reason do you have for coming here? Let me guess. You figured I brought a woman here last night and you wanted to catch me in the act? Right? Go ahead, Jillian, search my bedroom if you like. The bathroom, too, if that suits your fancy. Oh, and don't forget to check the balconies in case I've hidden her out there until after you leave."

Jillian didn't say anything for a long minute. "I guess I deserved that. But—"

He held his hand to interrupt her. "Please. No buts, Jillian. I'm tired of them coming from you. Let me ask you something. How many men did you sleep with during the year we weren't together since you think I didn't leave a single woman standing?"

She narrowed her gaze at him. "Not a single one."

He crossed his arms over his chest. "Why?"

She lifted a chin. "Because I didn't want to."

"Why didn't you want to? You had broken things off with me and we weren't together. Why didn't you sleep with another man?"

Jillian knew she'd screwed up badly last night and she could hardly wait until morning to see Aidan so she could apologize. When he didn't show up at eight as he'd promised, she would admit that for a quick second she'd thought he might have been mad enough to spend the night with someone else. But all it had taken to erase that thought was for her to remember how he'd looked last night when he told her the reason why he'd introduced her as his significant other.

There's no one more significant in my life than you.
And she believed him. His reason for not sleeping

with another woman during the year they'd been apart was the same reason she hadn't slept with another man.

"Jillian?"

She met his gaze. He wanted an answer and she would give him one. The truth and nothing but the truth.

"Sleeping with another man never crossed my mind, Aidan," she said softly. "Because I still loved you. And no matter what I saw or imagined you did with that lap dancer, I still loved you. My body has your imprint all over it and the thought of another man touching it sickens me."

She paused and then added, "You're wrong. I didn't come here thinking I'd find another woman. I came to apologize. I figured the reason you didn't come take me to breakfast was because you were still mad at me. And after last night I knew that I deserved your anger."

"Why do you think you deserve my anger?"

"Because everything is my fault. You only kept our affair a secret because I asked you to, begged you to. Last night when I got to my room, I sat out on the balcony and thought about everything. I forced myself to see the situation through someone else's eyes other than my own. And you know what I saw, Aidan?"

"No, what did you see, Jillian?"

She fought back tears. "I saw a man who loved me enough to take a lot of crap. I never thought about what all the secrecy would mean. And then the long distance and the sacrifices you made to come see me whenever you could. The money you spent for airplane fare, your time. I wasn't the only one with the goal of becoming a doctor. It's not like you didn't have a life, trying to handle the pressure of your dual residency."

She paused. "And I can just imagine what your

friends thought when all of a sudden you became a saint for no reason. You couldn't tell them about me, so I can understand them wanting to help get your life back on track with those women. That was the Aidan they knew. And unfortunately that was the Aidan I wanted to think you missed being. That night I showed up at the party, I should have realized that you were just having the fun you deserved. Fun you'd denied yourself since your involvement with me. I should have loved you enough and trusted you enough to believe that no matter what, you wouldn't betray me. That I meant more to you than any lap dancer with silicone boobs."

He uncrossed his arms. "You're right. You do mean more to me than any lap dancer, stripper, book-club member or any other woman out there, Jillian," he said in a soft tone. "And you were wrong to think I missed my old life. What I miss is being with you. I think we handled things okay that first year, but during those second and third years, because of trying to make that dual residency program work and still keep you at the top of the list, things became difficult for me. Then in the third year, I was the one with focusing issues. It became harder and harder to keep our long-distance affair afloat and stay focused at work. And the secrecy only added more stress. But I knew if I complained to you about it, that it would only stress you out and make you lose focus on what you needed to do.

"You were young when we started our affair. Only twenty-one. And you hadn't dated much. In all honesty, probably not at all, because I refuse to count that dude you dated in high school. So deep down I knew you weren't quite ready for the type of relationship I wanted. But I loved you and I wanted you and I figured everything would work out. I knew how challenging medical school could be and I wanted to make your life as calm as possible. I didn't want to be the one to add to your stress."

He paused. "But it looks like I did anyway. I tried to make the best of it, but unfortunately sometimes when we talked, I was in one of my foul moods because of stress. I would get an attitude with you instead of talking to you about it. At no time should I have made you feel that you deserved my anger. I apologize. I regret doing that."

"It's okay," Jillian said, pulling out a chair. "Come sit down and eat. Your food is getting cold."

She watched him move away from the door. When he reached the table, she skirted back so he could sit down. When he sat, he reached out, grabbed her around the waist and brought her down to his lap.

"Aidan! What do you think you're doing?"

He wrapped both arms around her so she wouldn't go anywhere. "What I should have done last night. Brought you back here and put you in my lap, wrapped my arms around you and convinced you that I meant everything I said about your value to me. Instead I got upset and walked away."

She pressed her forehead to his and whispered, "Sorry I made you upset with me last night."

"I love you so much, Jillian, and when I think you don't believe just how much I love you, how much you mean to me, I get frustrated and wonder just what else I have to do. I'm not a perfect man. I'm human. I'm going to make mistakes. We both are. But the one thing I won't do is betray your love with another woman. Those days are over for me. You're all the woman I'll ever need."

She leaned back from him to look in his eyes. "I believe you, Aidan. I won't lie and say I'll never get jealous, but I can say it'll be because I'm questioning the woman's motives, not yours."

And she really meant that. When he hadn't come down for breakfast she had gone into the Terelle Dining Room to eat alone. She ran into the book-club ladies and ended up eating breakfast with them and enjoying herself. Once Aidan had made it clear last night that he was not available, they had put a lid on their man-hunter instincts. Jillian and the six women had a lot in common, since they were all recent medical-school graduates, and they enjoyed sharing their experiences over breakfast. They invited her to join them for shopping at some point during their two days in Rome and she agreed to do that.

She shifted in Aidan's lap to find a more comfortable position.

"I wouldn't do that too many times if I were you," he warned in a husky whisper.

A hot wave of desire washed over her. He was looking at her with those dark, penetrating eyes of eyes. The same ones that could arouse her as no man ever had… or would. "Why not?"

If he was going to give her a warning, she wanted him to explain himself, although she knew what he meant.

"Because if you keep it up, *you* might become my breakfast."

The thought of that happening had the muscles between her legs tightening, and she was aware that every hormone in her body was downright sizzling. "But you like pancakes and syrup," she said innocently.

A smile spread across his lips. "But I like your taste better."

"Do you?" she asked, intentionally shifting again to lean forward so that she could bury her face in the hollow of his throat. He was shirtless and she loved getting close to him, drinking in his scent.

"You did it again."

She leaned back and met his gaze. "Did I?"

"Yes."

She intentionally shifted in his lap when she lowered her head to lick the upper part of his chest. She loved the salty taste of his flesh and loved even more the moan she heard from his lips.

"It's been a year, Jillian. If I get you in my bed today it will be a long time before I let you out."

"And miss touring Monte Carlo? The ship has already docked."

"We have time." He suddenly stood, with her in his arms, and she quickly grabbed him around the neck and held on. He chuckled. "Trust me. I'm not going to let you fall." He headed for the bedroom.

"Now to enjoy breakfast, the Aidan Westmoreland way," he said, easing her down on the bed. He stood back and stared at her for a long moment. "I want you so much I ache. I desire you so much I throb. And I will always love you, even after drawing my last breath."

For the second time that day, she fought back tears. "Oh, Aidan. I want, desire and love you, too. Just as much."

He leaned down and removed her shoes before removing every stitch of her clothing with a skill only he had perfected. When she lay there naked before him, he slid his pj's down his legs. "Lie still for a minute. There's something I want to do," he instructed in a throaty tone.

That's when Jillian saw the bottle of syrup he'd

brought into the bedroom with them. She looked at the bottle and then looked up at him. "You are kidding, right?"

"Do I look like I'm kidding?" he asked, removing the top.

She swallowed. No, he definitely didn't look as if he was kidding. In fact he looked totally serious. Too serious. "But I'm going to be all sticky," she reasoned. All she could think about was how glad she was for the bikini wax she'd gotten at the spa yesterday.

"You won't be sticky for long. I plan to lick it all off you and then we'll shower together."

"Aidan!" She squealed when she felt the thick liquid touch her skin. Aidan made good on his word. He dripped it all over her chest, making sure there was a lot covering her breasts, around her navel and lower still. He laid it on thick between her legs, drenching her womanly core.

And then he used his tongue to drive her insane with pleasure while taking his time to lick off all the syrup. The flick of his tongue sent sensuous shivers down her spine, and all she could do was lie there and moan while encased in a cloud of sensations.

He used his mouth as a bearer of pleasure as he laved her breasts, drawing the nipples between his lips and sucking on the turgid buds with a greed that made her womb contract. She wasn't sure how much more she could take when his mouth lowered to her stomach. She reached down and buried her fingers in his scalp as his mouth traced a hungry path around her navel.

Moments later he lifted his head to stare at her, deliberately licking his lips. They both knew where he was headed next. The look on his face said he wanted her to know he intended to go for the gusto.

And he did.

Jillian screamed his name the moment his tongue entered her, sending shockwaves of a gigantic orgasm through her body. His hot and greedy tongue had desire clawing at her insides, heightening her pulse. And when she felt another orgasm coming on the heels of the first, she knew it was time she took control. Otherwise, Aidan would lick her crazy.

With all the strength she could muster she tried to shift their bodies, which was hard to do since his mouth was on her while his hands held tight to her hips. When she saw there was no way she could make Aidan budge until he got his fill, she gave in to another scream when a second orgasm hit.

He finally lifted his head, smiled at her while licking his lips and then eased his body over hers. "I told you I was going to lick it all off you, baby."

Yes, he had. Then his engorged erection slid inside of her. All she recalled after that was her brain taking a holiday as passion overtook her, driving her over the edge, bringing her back, then driving her to the edge again.

He thrust hard, all the way to the hilt and then some. He lifted her hips and set the pace. The bed springs were tested to their maximum and so was she. She released a deep moan when he pounded into her, making her use muscles she hadn't used in a year. And then he slowed and without disconnecting their bodies, eased to his knees. He lifted her legs all the way to his shoulders and continued thrusting.

"Aidan!"

He answered with a deep growl when the same explosion that tore through her ripped through him, as well. She could feel his hot, molten liquid rush through her body, bathing her womb. But he didn't stop. He kept going, enlarging inside her all over again.

She saw arousal coiling in the depth of his eyes. They were in it for the long haul, right now and forever. And when his wet, slick body finally eased down, he pulled her into his arms, wrapped the strength of his legs over hers and held her close. She breathed in his scent. This was where she wanted to be. Always.

Hours later, Jillian stirred in Aidan's arms and eased over to whisper in his ear. "Remind me never to let you go without me for a full year again."

He grinned as he opened his eyes. "One year, two months and four days. But I wasn't counting or anything, mind you."

She smiled. "I'll take your word for it." She eased up to glance over at the clock. Had they been in bed five hours already? "We need to shower."

"Again?"

She laughed out. "The last time doesn't count."

"Why?"

She playfully glared over at him. "You know why."

He'd taken her into the shower to wash off any lingering stickiness from the syrup. Instead he ended up making love to her again. Then he'd dried them both off and had taken her to the bed and made love to her again several times, before they'd both drifted off to sleep.

"I guess we do need to get up, shower and dress if we want to see any of Monte Carlo."

"Yes, and I want to see Monte Carlo."

"I want to see you," he said, easing back and raking

his gaze over her naked body. "Do you know how much I missed this? Missed you?"

"The same way I missed you?"

"More," he said, running his hand over her body.

She couldn't ignore the delicious heat of the fingers touching her. "I doubt that, Dr. Westmoreland."

"Trust me."

She did trust him. And she loved him so much she wanted everyone to know it. "I can't wait until we return to Denver for Adrian's wedding."

He looked down at her. "Why?"

"So we can tell Pam and Dillon."

He studied her expression. "Are you ready for that?"

"More than ready. Do you think they already know?"

"It wouldn't surprise me if they did. Dillon isn't a dummy. Neither is Pam."

"Then why haven't they said anything?"

He shrugged. "Probably waiting for us to tell them."

She thought about what he'd said and figured he might be right. "Doesn't matter now. They will find out soon enough. Are you ready?"

"For another round?"

"No, not for another round. Are you ready to take a shower so we can get off this ship for a while?"

He pulled her into his arms. "Um, maybe. After another round." And then he lowered his mouth to hers.

Fourteen

"I hope you're not punishing me for what happened the last two days, Jillian."

Jillian glanced up at Aidan and smiled. "Why would I do that?" she asked as they walked the streets of Rome, Italy. She'd never visited a city more drenched in history. They would be here for two days and she doubted she could visit all the places she wanted to see in that time. She would have to make plans to come back one day.

"Because it was late when we finally got off the ship to tour Monte Carlo, and the same thing happened yesterday when we toured Florence. I have a feeling you blame me for both."

She chuckled. "Who else should I blame? Every time I mentioned it was time for us to get up, shower and get off the ship, you had other ideas."

He smiled as if remembering several of those ideas. "But we did do the tours. We just got a late start."

Yes, they had done the tours. For barely three hours in Monte Carlo. They had seen all they could in a cab ride around the city. Then yesterday, at least they had ridden up the most scenic road in Florence to reach Piazzale Michelangelo. From there they toured several palaces and museums before it was time to get back to the ship.

She had made sure they had gotten up, dressed and were off the ship at a reasonable time this morning for their tour of Rome. Already they had walked a lot, which was probably the reason Aidan was whining.

"What's the complaint, Aidan? You're in great shape." She of all people should know. He hadn't wasted time having her belongings moved into his suite where she had spent the night…and got very little sleep until dawn. But somehow she still felt energized.

"You think I'm punishing you by suggesting that we walk instead of taking a taxi-tour?" she asked as they crossed one of the busy streets.

"No. I think you're punishing me because you talked me out of renting that red Ferrari. Just think of all the places I could have taken you while driving it."

She chuckled. "Yes, but I would have wanted to get there in one piece and without an accelerated heart rate."

He placed his arms around her shoulders. "Have you forgotten that one day I intend to be one of the most sought-after cardiologists in the world?"

"How could I forget?" she said, smiling. She was really proud of him and his accomplishments. Going through that dual residency program was what had opened the door for him to continue his specialty training at Johns Hopkins, one of the most renowned research hospitals in the country.

Last night, in between making love, they had talked about their future goals. He knew she would start her residency at a hospital in Orlando, Florida, in the fall. The good thing was that after a year of internship, she could transfer to another hospital. Because he would be working for at least three years at John Hopkins, she would try to relocate to the Washington, D.C., or Maryland area.

A few hours later they had toured a number of places, including the Colosseum, St. Peter's Basilica, the Trevi Fountain and the Catacombs. While standing in front of the Spanish Steps, waiting for Aidan to return from retrieving the lace fan she'd left behind in the church of Trinità dei Monti, she blinked when she saw a familiar man pass by.

Riley Westmoreland? What was Aidan's cousin doing in Rome?

"Riley!" she yelled out. When the man didn't look her way, she figured he must not have heard her. Taking the steps almost two at a time, she hurriedly raced after him.

When she caught up with him she grabbed his arm. "Riley, wait up! I didn't know you—"

She stopped in midsentence when the man turned around. It wasn't Riley. But he looked enough like him to be a twin. "I'm so sorry. I thought you were some-one else."

The man smiled and she blinked. He even had Riley's smile. Or more specifically, one of those Westmoreland smiles. All the men in the family had dimples. And like all the Westmoreland men, he was extremely handsome.

"No problem, signorina."

She smiled. "You're Italian?" she asked.

"No. American. I'm here on business. And you?"

"American. Here vacationing." She extended her hand. "I'm Jillian Novak."

He nodded as he took her hand. "Garth Outlaw."

"Nice meeting you, Garth, and again I'm sorry that I mistook you for someone else, but you and Riley West-moreland could almost be twins."

He chuckled. "A woman as beautiful as you can do whatever you like, signorina. No need to apologize." He grasped her hand and lifted it to his lips. "Have a good day, beautiful Jillian Novak, and enjoy the rest of your time in Rome."

"And you do the same."

He turned and walked away. She stood there for a minute, thinking. He was even a flirt like those Westmorelands before they'd married. And the man even had that Westmoreland sexy walk. How crazy was that?

"Jillian?" She turned when she heard Aidan call her name.

"I thought you were going to wait for me on the steps," he said when he reached her.

"I did but then I thought I saw Riley and—"

"Riley? Trust me, Riley would not be in Rome, especially not with Alpha expecting their baby any day now."

"I know, but this guy looked so much like Riley that I raced after him. He could have been Riley's twin. I apologized for my mistake and he was nice about it. He was an American, here on business. Said his name was Garth Outlaw. And he really did favor Riley."

Aidan frowned. "Outlaw?"

"Yes."

"Um, that's interesting. The last time we had our family meeting about the investigation Rico is handling, I think he said something about tracing a branch of the Westmoreland roots to a family who goes by the last name of Outlaw."

"Really?"

"That's what I recall, but Dillon would know for sure. I'll mention it to him when we return home. That information might help Rico," Aidan said as they walked back toward the Spanish Steps.

Rico Claiborne, a private investigator, was married

to Aidan's sister Megan. Jillian was aware that Rico's PI firm had been investigating the connection of four women to Aidan's great-grandfather, Raphel Westmoreland. It had been discovered during a genealogy search that before marrying Aidan's great-grandmother Gemma, Raphel had been connected to four other women who'd been listed as former wives. Rico's investigation had confirmed that Raphel hadn't married any of the women, but that one of them had given birth to a son that Raphel had never known about. Evidently, Jillian thought, at some point Rico had traced that son to the Outlaw family.

"Ready to head back to the ship?" Aidan asked, interrupting her thoughts.

She glanced back at her watch. "Yes, it's getting kind of late. You can join me and the book-club ladies when we go shopping tomorrow if you'd like."

He shook his head. "No thanks. Although it's a beautiful city, I've seen enough of Rome for now. But I will bring you back."

She lifted a brow. "You will?"

"Yes."

"When?"

"For our honeymoon. I hope." Aidan then got down on one knee and took her hand in his. "I love you, Jillian. Will you marry me?"

Jillian stared at him in shock. It was only when he tugged at her hand did she notice the ring he'd placed there. Her eyes widened. "Oh, my God!" Never had she seen anything so beautiful.

"Well?" Aidan asked, grinning. "People are standing around. We've gotten their attention. Are you going to embarrass me or what?"

She saw that people had stopped to stare. They had heard his proposal and, like Aidan, they were waiting for her answer. She could not believe that here in the beautiful city of Rome, on the Spanish Steps, Aidan had asked her to marry him. She would remember this day for as long as she lived.

"Yes. Yes!" she said, filled with happiness. "Yes, I will marry you."

"Thank you," he said, getting back to his feet and pulling her into his arms. "For a minute there you had me worried."

The people around them cheered and clapped while a smiling Aidan pulled Jillian into his arms and kissed her.

Aidan walked down the long corridor to his suite. Jillian had sent him away an hour ago with instructions not to return until now because she would have a surprise waiting for him when he got back. He smiled thinking she had probably planned a candlelit dinner for their last day on the cruise.

It was hard to believe their two weeks were up. Tomorrow they would return to Barcelona. After two days in Rome they had spent two days at sea before touring Athens, Greece. While there they had taken part in a wine-tasting excursion and visited several museums. From there they had toured Turkey, Mykonos and Malta. Now they were headed back to Barcelona and would arrive before daybreak.

He couldn't help the feeling of happiness that puffed out his chest when he thought of being an engaged man. Although they hadn't set a date, the most important thing was that he had asked and she had said yes. They talked every day about their future, and although they still had at least another year before she could join him in Maryland, they were okay with it because they knew the day would come when they would be together.

They decided not to wait until they went home for Adrian's wedding to tell the family their news. Some would be shocked, while others who knew about their affair would be relieved that their secret wasn't a secret any longer. They would head straight to Denver tomorrow when the ship docked.

He chuckled when he thought about Jillian's excitement over her engagement ring. The book-club ladies had definitely been impressed as well, ahhing and ooing every night at dinner. Jewelry by Zion was the rave since Zion was the First Lady's personal jeweler. Jillian hadn't known that he knew Zion personally because of Aidan's friendship with the Steele family, who were close personal friends of Zion. Zion had designed most of his signature custom jewelry collection while living in Rome for the past ten years. Thanks to Dominic, Aidan had met with Zion privately on board the ship in the wee hours of the morning while Jillian slept, when they first docked in a port near Rome. Zion had brought an attaché case filled with beautiful rings—all originals hand-crafted by Zion. When Aidan had seen this one particular ring, he'd known it was the one he wanted to put on Jillian's finger.

When Aidan reached his suite's door, he knocked, to let her know he had returned.

"Come in."

Using his passkey, he opened the door and smiled upon seeing the lit candles around the room. His bride-to-be had set the mood for a romantic dinner, he thought, when he saw how beautifully the table was set.

Closing the door behind him he glanced around the dimly lit suite but didn't see Jillian anywhere. Was she in the bedroom waiting on him? He moved in that direction and then felt a hand on his shoulder. He turned around and his breath caught. Jillian wore a provocative black lace teddy that showed a lot of flesh. Attached to the teddy were matching lace garters and she wore a pair of stilettoes on her feet. He thought he hadn't seen anyone as sexy in his entire life and he couldn't help groaning in appreciation.

She leaned close, swirled the tip of her tongue around his ear and whispered, "I'm about to give you the lap dance of your life, Aidan Westmoreland."

The next thing he knew he was gently shoved in a chair. "And remember no touching, so put your hands behind your back."

He followed her instructions, mesmerized beyond belief. Her sensual persona stirred his desire. His pulse kicked up a notch, followed immediately by a deep throbbing in his erection. "And just what do you want me to do?" he asked in a low voice.

She smiled at him. "Just enjoy. I plan to do all the work. But by the time I finish, you will be too exhausted to move."

Really? Him? Too exhausted to move? And she would be the one doing all the work? He couldn't wait for that experience. "Now will you keep your hands to yourself or do I need to handcuff you?" she asked him.

He couldn't help smiling at the thought of that. Did she really have handcuffs? Would she be that daring? He decided to find out. "I can't make any promises, so you might want to handcuff me."

"No problem."

The next thing he knew she'd whipped out a pair of handcuffs slapped them on his wrists and locked them with a click to the chair. *Damn.* While he was taking all this in, he suddenly heard music coming from the sound system in the room. He didn't recognize the artist, but the song had a sensual beat.

While sitting there handcuffed to the chair, he watched as Jillian responded to the music, her movements slow, graceful and seductive. She rolled her stomach and then shimmied her hips and backside in a sinfully erotic way. He sat there awestruck, fascinated, staring at her as she moved in front of him. He felt the rapid beat of his heart and the sweet pull of desire as his erection continued to pulsate.

Although he couldn't touch her, she was definitely touching him—rubbing her hands over his shirt, underneath it, through the hair on his chest, before taking her time unbuttoning his shirt and easing it from his shoulders.

"Have I ever told you how much I love your chest, Aidan?" she asked him in a sultry tone.

"No," he answered huskily. "You never have."

"Well, I'm telling you now. In fact, I want to show you just how much I like it."

Then she crouched over him and used her tongue to lick his shoulder blades before moving slowly across the span of his chest. He would have come out of his chair had he not been handcuffed to it. She used her tongue in ways she hadn't before and he heard himself groaning out loud.

"You like that?" she asked, leaning close to his mouth, and licking there, as well. "Want more? Want to see what else you've taught me to do with my tongue?"

He swallowed. Oh, yes, he wanted more. He wanted to see just what he'd taught her. Instead of answering, he nodded.

She smiled as she bent down to remove his shoes. Reaching up, she unzipped his pants and he raised his hips as she slid both his pants and briefs down his legs. She smiled at him again.

"You once licked me all over, Aidan, and you seemed to have enjoyed it. Now I'm going to do the same to you and I intend to enjoy myself, as well."

Moistening her lips with a delicious-looking sweep of her tongue, she got down on her knees before him and spread his legs. Then she lowered her head between his thighs and took him into her mouth.

As soon as she touched him, blood rushed through his veins, sexual hunger curled his stomach and desire stroked his gut. Her mouth widened to accommodate his size and she used her tongue to show that with this, she was definitely in control. He watched in a sensual daze as her head bobbed up and down while she fanned the blaze of his desire.

He wanted to grab hold of her hair, stroke her back, caress her shoulders but he couldn't. He felt defenseless, totally under her control but he loved every single minute of it. When he couldn't take any more, his body jerked in one hell of an explosion and she still wouldn't let go.

"Jillian!"

He wanted her with an intensity that terrified him. And when she lifted her head and smiled at him, he knew what it meant to love someone with every part of your heart, your entire being and your soul.

While the music continued to play, she straightened and began stripping for him, removing each piece of clothing slowly, and teasing his nostrils before tossing it aside. Sexual excitement filled his inner core as he inhaled her scent. When she was totally naked, she began dancing again, touching herself and touching him. He'd never seen anything so erotic in his entire life.

When she curled into his lap and continued to dance, the feel of her soft curves had him growling, had his erection throbbing again, harder. "Set me free," he begged. He needed to touch her now. He wanted his hands in her hair and his fingers inside her.

"Not yet," she whispered in a purr that made even more need wash over him. Then she twisted her body around so her back was plastered to his chest then she eased down onto his manhood and rode him.

Never had she ridden him this hard and when she shifted so they faced each other, the feel of her breasts hitting his chest sent all kinds of sensations through him.

"Jillian!"

He screamed her name as an orgasm hit him again, deep, and he pulled the scent of her sex through his nostrils. He leaned forward. Although he couldn't touch her, he could lick her. He used his tongue to touch her earlobe and her face. "Uncuff me baby. Please. Uncuff me now."

She reached behind him and he heard the click that released him. When his hands were free he stood, with her in his arms, and quickly moved toward the bedroom.

"You're the one who was supposed to be exhausted," she mumbled into his chest.

"Sorry, it doesn't quite work that way, baby." And then he stretched her out on the bed.

He straddled her, eased inside her and thrust, stroking her, wanting her to feel his love in every movement. This was erotic pleasure beyond compare and her inner muscles clenched him, held him tight and tempted him to beg again.

His thrusts became harder, her moans louder and the desire he felt for her more relentless than ever. And when he finally exploded, he took her along with him as an earth-shattering climax claimed them both. They were blasted into the heavens. Jillian Novak had delivered the kind of mindless pleasure every man should experience at least once in his lifetime. And he was glad that he had.

Moments later, he eased off her and pulled her into his arms, entwining her legs with his. He kissed the side of her face while she fell into a deep sleep.

Their secret affair was not a secret any longer and he couldn't wait to tell the world that he'd found his mate for life. And he would cherish her forever.

Epilogue

"So, you thought you were keeping a secret from us," Pam said, smiling, sitting beside her husband on the sofa as they met with Aidan and Jillian.

"But we didn't?" Jillian asked, grinning and holding Aidan's hand.

"For a little while, maybe," Dillon replied. But when you fall in love with someone, it's hard to keep something like that hidden, especially in *this* family."

Jillian knew exactly what Dillon meant. It seemed the bigger secret had been that she and Aidan had wanted to keep their relationship a secret. No one in the family knew who else knew, so everyone kept their suspicions to themselves.

"Well, I'm glad we don't have to hide things anymore," Aidan said, standing, pulling Jillian up with him and then wrapping his arms around her shoulders.

"You mean you don't have to *try* and hide things," Pam corrected. "Neither of you were doing such a good job of pretending. And when the two of you had that rift, Dillon and I were tempted to intervene. But we figured if it was meant for the two of you to be together, you would be, without our help."

Jillian looked down at her ring. "Yes, we were able to get our act together, although I will have to give Paige some credit for bailing out of the cruise. Aidan and I needed that time together to work things out."

"And I guess from that ring on your finger, the two of you managed to do that," Dillon said.

Aidan nodded as he smiled down at Jillian. "Yes, we did. The thought of a year-long engagement doesn't bother us. After Jillian's first year at that hospital in Orlando, Florida, she'll be able to transfer to one near me. That's when we plan to tie the knot."

"Besides," Pam said, smiling. "The year gives me plenty of time to plan for the wedding without feeling rushed. These Westmoreland weddings are coming around fast, but trust me, I'm not complaining."

Dillon reached out and hugged his wife. "Please don't complain. I'm elated with each one. After Adrian gets hitched next month and Aidan is married in a year, all we'll have to be concerned with is Bailey and Bane."

The room got quiet as everyone thought about that. Only two Westmorelands were left single, and those two were known to be the most headstrong of them all.

"Bay says she's never getting married," Aidan said, grinning.

"So did you and Adrian," Dillon reminded him. "In fact, I don't think there's a single Westmoreland who hasn't made that claim at some point in time, including me. But all it takes is for one of us to find that special person who's our soul mate, and we start singing a different tune."

"But can you see Bay singing a different tune?" Aidan asked.

Dillon thought about the question for a minute, drew in a deep breath and then shook his head. "No."

Everyone laughed. When their laughter subsided Pam smiled and said, "There's someone for everyone, including Bailey. She just hasn't met him yet. In other words, Bailey hasn't met her match. But one day, I believe that she will."

The following month

"Adrian Westmoreland, you may kiss your bride."

Aidan, serving as best man, smiled as he watched his twin brother take the woman he loved, Dr. Trinity Matthews Westmoreland, into his arms to seal their marriage vows with one hell of a kiss. Aidan spotted Jillian in the audience sitting with her sisters and winked at her. Their day would be coming and he couldn't wait.

A short while later, Aidan stole his twin away for a few minutes. The wedding had been held in Trinity's hometown of Bunnell, Florida, at the same church where their cousin Thorn had married Trinity's sister Tara. The weather had been beautiful and it seemed everyone in the little town had been invited to the wedding, which accounted for the packed church of more than eight hundred guests. The reception was held in the ballroom of a beautiful hotel overlooking the Atlantic Ocean.

"Great job, Dr. Westmoreland," he said, grinning at Adrian.

Adrian chuckled. "I intend to say the same to you

a year from now, Dr. Westmoreland, when you tie the knot. I'm glad the cruise helped, and that you and Jillian were able to work things out."

"So am I. That had to be the worst year of my life when we were apart."

Adrian nodded. "I know. Remember I felt your pain whenever you let out any strong emotions."

Yes, Aidan did remember. "So where are you headed for your honeymoon?"

"Sydney, Australia. I've always wanted to go back, and I look forward to taking Trinity there with me."

"Well, the two of you deserve a lifetime of happiness," Aidan said, taking a sip of his champagne.

"You and Jillian do, as well. I'm so glad the secret is a secret no longer."

Aidan's smile widened. "So am I. And on that note, I'm going to go claim my fiancée so you can go claim your bride."

Aidan crossed the span of the ball room to where Jillian stood with her sisters Paige and Nadia, and his sister Bailey. He and Jillian would leave Bunnell in the morning and take the hour-long drive to Orlando. Together they would look for an apartment for her close to the hospital where she would be working as an intern. He had checked and discovered that flights from the D.C. area into Orlando were pretty frequent. He was glad about that because he intended to pay his woman plenty of visits.

Aidan had told Dillon about Jillian's chance meeting with a man by the name of Garth Outlaw while in Rome and how she'd originally thought he was Riley.

Dillon wasn't surprised that any kin out there would have the Westmoreland look due to dominant genes. He had passed the information on to Rico. The family was hoping something resulted from Jillian's encounter.

"Sorry, ladies, I need to grab Jillian for a minute," he said, snagging her hand.

"Where are we going?" Jillian asked as he led her toward the exit.

"To walk on the beach."

"Okay."

Holding hands, they crossed the boardwalk and went down the steps. Pausing briefly, they removed their shoes. Jillian moaned when her feet touched the sand.

"What are you thinking about, baby?" Aidan asked her.

"I'm thinking about how wonderful I feel right now. Walking in the sand, being around the people I love, not having to hide my feelings for you. And what a lucky woman I am to have such a loving family and such a gorgeous and loving fiancé."

He glanced down at her. "You think I'm gorgeous?"

"Yes."

"You think I'm loving?"

"Definitely."

"Will that qualify me for another lap dance tonight?"

Jillian threw her head back and laughed, causing the wind to send hair flying across her face. Aidan pushed her hair back and she smiled up at him.

"Dr. Westmoreland, you can get a lap dance out of me anytime. Just say the word."

"Lap dance."

She leaned up on tip toes. "You got it."

Aidan then pulled her into his arms and kissed her. Life couldn't get any better than this.

* * * * *

HER PREGNANCY SECRET

ANN MAJOR

To Ted,
I love you more.

One

Michael North awakened with a violent start in the middle of the night.

His first thought was for the safety of the exquisite woman curled trustingly against him. She was warm and soft, beguilingly beautiful in the moonlight with her dark golden hair spilling across his pillow. He wanted to touch that hair and kiss her lips again, wanted it so much he had to clench his hands.

Ironically, he'd enjoyed his evening with her more than he'd enjoyed being with anyone in a very long time.

Maybe that was why his gut twisted as he experienced an uncustomary pang of conscience. After all, he'd seduced her for very deliberate, self-serving reasons.

Careful not to disturb her, he sat up and brushed a lock of thick black hair out of his eyes. Everything he'd done tonight—the seductive dinner at her failing bistro, the lovemaking in his penthouse, all the shared laughter and smiles—had been a lie.

He'd set her up so he could protect his naive younger brother.

But at some point Michael had forgotten about Will. His dinner date with Bree had begun with champagne served in sparkling flutes at Chez Z, the intimate French bistro she'd inherited from her famous brother, Johnny Z. She loved to cook and to eat, and Michael had loved watching her indulge.

She'd blushed when she'd drunk champagne. She'd sighed when she'd licked chocolate off her fingertips, and his. The wet, warm tip of her tongue against his flesh had almost been as good as having sex with her. *Almost*.

He'd loved the sound of her laughter, the glow of her cheeks when she teased him, the flash of intelligence in her slanting eyes when she'd made him feel clever and her wildness in bed. When had he had such a good time with anybody?

Surprisingly, Bree had given him more pleasure and tenderness and amusement during their evening than he'd ever imagined possible.

Because, first, she wasn't his usual type. He went for cool, sophisticated glamour, for sleek, slim blondes who made heads turn and other men envy him. Bree was lush and earthy and wanton. She loved color and baubles and cheap scarves and probably didn't bother to carry a comb in her purse.

And second, Bree Oliver, for all her seeming innocence and charms, was a gold digger. She'd targeted his foolish brother, thinking Will was the chump she needed to keep Chez Z from going into bankruptcy.

For Will's sake, Michael had to finish her off. No matter how much he'd enjoyed being with her or how fabulous she'd been in bed, she deserved it.

If only Michael had been as smart five years ago when he'd fallen for Anya Parris. But, no, like a fool, when Anya had lied about being pregnant, he'd married her. He'd suffered through a hellish marriage that had included infidelity, scandal and a very public divorce.

Never again would Michael forget the cynical truth about the North wealth. It attracted women who pretended a genuine interest in him when all they wanted was the use of his penthouse, his ranch, his helicopters, his private jets, his invitations to the right clubs, the best restaurants and the A-list parties. Unlike his brother, Michael wasn't above enjoying the women his money lured, but only for brief intervals.

Never again would he believe any woman wanted more from him than his luxurious lifestyle. Never again would he make the mistake of forming a serious attachment. Unfortunately Will, who'd had a more indulged childhood than Michael, was too trusting for his own good. It was up to Michael to save Will from Bree.

Soft summer moonlight turned the high ceilings of his loft and his large bed to shades of silver and gray. Bree's body felt warm; treacherously so as she nestled closer against him. Her cheap silver bangles and necklaces on the bedside table glittered. Her colorful, filmy clothes and scarves lay in tangles on the floor beside her sandals where he'd stripped her while she'd swayed to music, laughing.

The cozy heat of her satin-soft body lured him. He wanted to stay beside her, to see the shy warmth of her sweetly crooked smile and the flirtatious glow that lit her amber eyes every time he kissed her.

No, he had to finish her off—now—even if her sweet strawberry scent filled his nostrils and made him weak with the craving to bury his lips in her thick, satiny hair, to kiss her throat, to taste her mouth and other parts of her sexy, feminine anatomy just one more time.

Intoxicated by her soft, sensual allure, he lingered in

the bed beside her, torturing himself as he savored her warmth and remembered all the ways they'd made love.

She'd been so silky and tight the first time, like a velvet glove. When he'd pushed eagerly inside, holding her against the wall, she'd cried out. But when he'd stopped out of concern for her, she'd pressed her palms into the small of his spine and pleaded with him to stay—to stay forever if that was possible. Slowly her small body had accommodated itself to him. Driving into her, the pleasure of each stroke had been so total in its visceral thrill that fierce pleasure unlike any he had ever known had saturated every cell in his body.

She'd been a damn good actress, playing at virginal innocence, enticing him, then surrendering like a wanton. She'd nearly undone him. She'd almost made him believe that he alone, not his fortune, was special to her.

"Who knew?" she'd whispered with him sheathed inside her. "I like it. No, I love it." Then she'd stroked his cheek lovingly, her eyes shining with wonder. "I'm glad it's you. I never thought it would be half so nice. I always wanted to date someone as handsome and smart as you. I…I just never thought anybody like you…would look at a girl like me."

It had been nice for him, too, being with her. More than nice.

Special.

His world could be so cold, and she seemed so sweet. For one forbidden moment, when she'd kissed him as if she'd wanted to consume him, he'd lost himself in the searing hot, torrid welcome of her body. He'd almost forgotten to protect himself.

Every time he'd made love to her, even with a condom, the sex had gotten better. And each time afterward when she'd clung to him, she'd seemed sweeter. Whatever this thing was between them, it had shaken him to the core.

Hell, just thinking about her and what she'd done to him made him hard again, even as he lay beside her icily plotting his next step.

"Will said you were cold and uptight," she'd whispered.

He hadn't liked her comparing him to Will, but with every kiss and unassuming glance her power over him had increased. A connection to her built deep inside him and morphed into something that felt more than physical.

What had been going on?

Her mysterious white-hot appeal had fueled a compulsion that no other woman had ever aroused in him. She'd made him ravenous. Together their writhing bodies had burned and soared. His out-of-control excitement had felt addictive, tempting him to forget everything he knew about women like her. She'd provided some deeply needed comfort he hadn't known he'd craved until he'd experienced it in her arms. He had never known a real home, or felt at home with anyone, not even with the Norths, who'd given him their name and had claimed him as family. Not until tonight…with her.

She was dangerous. He had to rid himself of her quickly.

If he stalled for even one more night, she might have him totally in her power. He might even sink his own money into her bistro.

If he invested enough, would she favor him over Will?

Hell, he had the money. A part of him wanted her to prefer him to all others.

He swore. Such thoughts could derail him from his purpose. Just as he was about to throw off the covers and escape her so he could get his head straight, she whimpered. Clutching at his arms, she seemed to expect him to protect her from some mysterious terror.

"Michael…"

His heart throbbed. Oh, God.

Her voice was feminine, helpless. When her feather-light fingertips brushed his skin, he burned, aching for her all over again. No way could he resist her plea.

How old was she? Twenty-five? Ten years younger than he was? Or even younger? Whatever her age, with her thick, dark gold hair tumbling about her face and bare shoulders, her wild beauty dazzled him. She had a classic brow, a long, thin nose, high cheekbones, an incandescent complexion and full, voluptuous lips.

Not that she had the money or sense of style to dress properly. Her baggy, overlarge clothes had concealed and distracted more than they'd enhanced her beauty. But naked—with her tiny waist, curvy hips, soft breasts and those pert nipples exposed—she was perfect.

More than anything he wanted to roll her over, take her in his arms, hold her and pet her hair, and whisper that everything was all right. But nothing was all right. Not when he knew what she was—and what he had to do—and yet still felt so powerfully attracted to her.

Careful not to disturb her, he arose. He had to get a grip. But the minute he broke their physical connection, she sensed it and seemed to miss his presence as much as he missed hers.

"Michael," she purred in a sexy, sleep-blurred tone. "Darling, come back to bed."

"I'm not your darling," he growled, hating that on some level he wanted to be.

"Michael, I… Have I done something…?" At his harsh tone, her voice grew shy and uncertain before it died in the silvery darkness.

The powerful need to comfort her from the hurt he was determined to inflict wrapped around him.

Hell. He had to finish this—or he would go crazy.

"I'm not your darling," he repeated ruthlessly. "To-night, everything, all of it—it was all lies."

"Lies?"

"I seduced you to protect Will. From you. When you came on to me while I was with him at the fund-raiser, I knew what you were and saw how you intended to use him. You made my job easy when you made a play for me, too."

"What are you saying?"

"I'm saying I sought you out tonight and slept with you so I could use it as leverage to make you stop seeing my brother. Tonight was all about Will."

"Will?" She sounded confused. "Wait a minute. You think Will and I…that we're a couple? That we're dating? You…you don't like me?"

"How could I like you, knowing what you are?"

Having been poor himself, he knew all about wanting more, about using people to get what he wanted. He'd worked damned hard. Still, he'd done a few things he wasn't proud of to get where he was.

"You were after him, and then after me, because you needed our money for your failing restaurant."

"No," she whispered.

"Do you deny Will is one of your investors?"

"No." But her beautiful mouth trembled just a little, and her eyes were now glistening with unshed tears. "You… deceived me? You didn't really want me?"

He shook his head.

"Why? How could you do that? I would never use Will…or anybody. Will's a friend, and yes, he's an investor. He's been an investor right from the beginning. But I'm not after his money! I'm not!"

"Then why did you hit on me so blatantly the night we met at the fund-raiser when you were with Will?"

"Maybe I flirted. But only because I thought you liked

me...." She sucked in a breath. "Will is just a friend. He was a friend of Johnny's first, and an investor in Chez Z when my brother first opened it. That's how Will and I became friends."

"Friends? That's all you were?"

The night of the fund-raiser she'd worn a silver back-less gown and a transparent shawl that had left very little of her sensuous shape to his imagination.

Her family history hadn't helped his opinion of her. Six months ago, Johnny Z, her celebrity-chef brother, had been found dead in bed with a prominent plastic surgeon's wife, another of the bistro's investors. Everyone presumed the surgeon had shot Johnny, but the husband, who'd hired lawyers, wasn't talking to the police, and his wife had vanished. Thus, the investigation had stalled. Still, the scandal, coupled with Z's absence in the kitchen, had been devastating to Chez Z's bottom line.

"Will asked me to go with him to the fund-raiser, so he could introduce me to some people who might be in-terested in investing. When he introduced me to you, I thought you might be one of those people."

Her eyes were so brilliant with innocence and outrage he almost believed her. Then he remembered Anya and how gullible he'd been. He'd wanted to believe her. Ca-pable as he might be in the business world, apparently he was an easy mark when it came to women he wanted in his bed.

"Bottle the performance! If you think I'm as big a fool as my little brother, you're wrong. I want you to dress and leave. If you stay away from Will, I won't tell him I slept with you tonight. If you don't leave him alone, I'll tell him about us."

"Tell him for all I care. Better—maybe I'll tell him my-self. He needs to know how far you'll go to control his life. Maybe he'll resent you even more than he already does."

Her reaction caught him off guard. He'd expected her to care more, to bargain, and what she'd said about Will hurt.

"He can't afford to resent me," Michael bluffed. "I write his allowance checks."

"So everything's just about money and control to you? And you think I'm like you—"

"I know you are! So, leave my brother alone, and I won't make him think the worst of you by telling him about us. You bet on the wrong horse this time. Pick another. Someone who isn't naive. Someone more like you and me."

"Tell him. I'm not like you, and you can't blackmail me, either."

"You are like me. Greed isn't the only thing we have in common," he replied coldly. "If Will didn't desire you, I'd be willing to set you up as my mistress. I'd keep you and your bistro afloat for as long you excited me."

"*Do you ever listen?* For the last time, your brother and I are just friends. That's why he won't care if you slept with me. He was just an investor in the bistro. He already has someone in his life."

"Really—who?"

Michael knew she was lying when she faltered and said, "Maybe you should ask him."

If only Will did have someone, then Michael could have Bree for himself. He could afford her a helluva lot more easily than Will, couldn't he?

Suddenly Michael reconsidered the situation. Where was the harm in keeping her, if she wasn't serious about Will? As long as he understood what she was and was willing to be generous to her?

"Okay, then, *if* Will doesn't want you because he has someone else, there's nothing to stop me from having you. Here's a new deal for you. If you cut Will loose as an investor and become my mistress, I'll keep your bistro afloat for as long as you please me in bed."

"What?" She stared at him as if she was having a hard time comprehending him.

"You heard me. Be my mistress, and your money problems will go away for as long as you keep me happy. Like you did tonight."

"I can't believe this. First you sleep with me to destroy an imagined relationship with your brother. And now you want to buy me for yourself? I'm sorry I ever met you."

"I'm sure you'll feel differently after you shop for the right apartment in the neighborhood of your choice and we settle on your generous allowance."

"Now you wait a minute!"

"You want to save the bistro, don't you? We enjoy each other, so why not?"

She pushed herself up from the bed. "You can't just buy people!"

"You'd be surprised what money buys."

"Well, I'm not for sale."

"I doubt that. I just haven't made you the right offer. Tell me what you want, and we'll negotiate."

"I can't believe I ever thought for one second that you were a decent human being." Her expression twisted in utter misery. "And I did. I really did. I can't believe I've been such a fool…again." She sighed. "This just proves what I told you earlier—I don't have very good instincts about men. I think you're the worst of them all…and I have to tell you, that's pretty low."

Her rejection stunned him. Too late Michael saw that he should have flattered her, that he should have seduced her into the deal as he had seduced her into his bed. Obviously she was like all the criminals in prison who proclaimed their innocence; she really didn't see that she had done anything wrong. That's where they were different.

At least he knew when he'd crossed the line and was willing to accept the inevitable consequences.

"I'll call my chauffeur," he said coldly, hiding his disappointment. "He'll be at the front door downstairs in five minutes to escort you out of the building. He'll drive you anywhere you wish to go. After tonight I don't ever want to see you with my brother again. Do you understand?"

"You can't order me around…or your brother, who is an adult, and who is, whether you like it or not, one of my key investors. I fully intend to see him as often as I like! He has every right to invest *his* money where he chooses."

"You're very wrong."

Michael turned his back and strode out of the room because the sight of her shimmering, pain-filled eyes, her quivering lips and her bare breasts were more than he could bear. Damn it, in spite of her rejection, in spite of what she was and how she was using Will, he still wanted her.

Only when he heard her rushing down his spiral staircase to the lower floor—she never used an elevator unless she had to because she was afraid of them—only when he heard his front door slam downstairs, did Michael return to his bedroom.

For a long moment he stood in the dark and stared out at the city that sparkled beneath a full moon and a starless sky. It was a beautiful night, he supposed, a night made for romance, if one believed in such things. He wondered if his failure to do so was due to the many flaws in his soul.

Growing bored with the view he left the window and turned on every light. Never had the vast marble bedroom in his penthouse apartment blazed with such cold and terrible brightness.

Only when he saw the bright splashes of red staining

his sheet did he realize that maybe he'd been wrong about at least one thing.

Had she been a virgin? His heart, which usually felt so solid behind its frozen walls, began to beat with vicious, guilty pain. Surely no virgin would have shown such a wild, uninhibited response. And yet...

When he remembered her little cry when he'd first entered her, and her sweetness, and the admiration in her eyes when he'd discussed some of his projects with her, he recoiled. What if she had been an innocent? What if he, who'd been raised so roughly, had failed to see goodness because it had been such a rarity in his life?

"If I could succeed at even one thing, I'd feel so proud of myself," she had confided. "And look at you—you turned the family investment firm around right after the last global financial meltdown. Now you're opening banks and hotels in China and power plants in Malaysia. You conquer worlds—and accept such feats as your due. Your family must be so proud of you." Her shining eyes had warmed him through.

If he'd been wrong about her virginity, had he been wrong about other things? Had she truly admired his accomplishments? Had she liked him, at least a little? Had he wounded her? And what was she really to Will?

No.

Damn it. He was sure of her ulterior motives. With her famous brother dead, his image trashed and their once popular bistro on the Upper West Side in trouble, she'd been after Will for his money. Then she had zeroed in on Michael at the fund-raiser when she'd seen a better mark. The only reason she'd turned down Michael's second offer was because he'd wounded her pride.

As he yanked the sheets off his bed, he remembered her radiant complexion and the wonder in her eyes and his own intense pleasure. Sheathed to the hilt, he'd felt all male and powerful and yet happy in a bone-melting way he'd never known before.

If she was what he believed, why had she turned him down? Why?

Michael tried and failed to push his gnawing doubts aside. Damn it, he had to know why. But he couldn't face her tonight.

They both deserved a few hours to recover from his brutal offer and her rejection. Tomorrow morning would be soon enough to confront her again.

But by morning she was gone.

After he bribed the doorman to let him in to her empty apartment, he stomped about flinging her cupboards open while he dialed her cell phone, which went to voice mail. For more than an hour he searched for some clue as to where she'd gone and found none. His texts were ignored. When he went to Chez Z, her steely-eyed French mother, Bijou, had been in a meeting with the waitstaff.

"She said she had to go somewhere," her mother said coolly, when he'd insisted upon interrupting her. "She said it was an emergency. She looked upset. I didn't pry. Now, I wish I'd asked more questions. Are you the problem? Is she in trouble because of you?"

"No."

"Well! She is no good with men. In fact, that's an understatement. She's *pathetic*. She took after me, you see. Her father did everything he could to ruin my life. If you aren't going to treat her right, stay away from her, yes?"

What could he say to that? Despite the circumstances, he envied Bree for having such a mother. He hadn't been so lucky.

When Michael went to his brother's to warn him about Bree, Will refused to let Michael into his apartment.

"She already told me what you accused her of," Will said, standing with the door half-closed to keep Michael in the hall. "I don't know where she is, and frankly, I wouldn't tell you if I did. You've overstepped the line."

"She said you were seeing another woman? Are you?"

Will, who usually had an easy nature, scowled. "Right now, maybe you can guess why I don't choose to discuss my personal life with you."

Then he shut the door in Michael's face.

Michael felt guilty and uneasy. What was Will hiding? Not only had Bree rejected him, she'd turned his brother against him. Will wouldn't even confirm he was dating someone else, so did that mean he was still interested in Bree? If Will was involved with another woman, what the hell had Michael accomplished by bedding Bree other than becoming obsessed with her himself?

The odds were he was right about her character. Maybe she was gone, but what good was that if Will felt more protective of her than ever? Instead of turning his brother against her, all he'd done was make his brother angry with him.

Despite everything, Michael burned for her. No matter how hard he tried to bury himself in his work during the weeks that followed, no matter where he traveled or how many glamorous women he publicly dated in the attempt to prove to himself and to her how little she mattered, he couldn't forget her.

Even when he left on what proved to be a month-long business trip to Shanghai to solve a crisis at one of his hotels, memories of her sweetness and outraged innocence lingered, haunting him.

The perfection of their night together drove him mad—especially after he learned that the same day he'd left New York, she'd returned to her bistro and had lunched with Will.

Had she deliberately remained hidden until he was gone? Was she that afraid of him?

What was her game? How could he stop her and save Will?

Two

Eight weeks later

Will has to be okay. He has to be.

As his heart beat in panic, Michael slammed through the heavy steel emergency-room doors with his dripping briefcase. When Pedro, his assistant who'd notified him about the accident, wasn't at the entrance, Michael had rushed inside and hurried down a crowded hall that was a blur of nondescript floor tiles and pale green walls, beds, patients and visitors.

Michael had been trying to call Bree from his limo on the drive through thick rain from JFK airport into the city. When all he could get was her voice mail, he'd decided to stop by Chez Z on the way to his office to confront her again. He'd just pulled up at the curb outside the bistro when Pedro had called him to tell him Will had been in an accident.

"Where's Will North?" Michael demanded of the

nurses in dark scrubs at the nurses' station. "I'm his brother. I got a call a while ago that he was in an accident and that he'd been brought here by EMTs."

"North?" Nurses looked up from their papers and stilled. When they didn't answer him, maybe because they had to choose their words carefully, he sensed the gravity of his brother's condition.

Oh, God. It was bad.

"Where is he?" Michael demanded in a hoarse voice he didn't recognize as his own. "What happened?"

Ask a tough question....

An older nurse with a kindly face gave him the bare facts.

A head-on collision in the heavy rain. Tony Ferrar, who was apparently his brother's friend and the driver, died at the scene. The driver of the SUV that struck them, a twenty-four-year-old woman who'd possibly been drunk or texting, had flown across the median of the interstate and collided head-on with Will's Mercedes. She'd died at the scene. Will had removed his seat belt and thrown himself in front of his wife. As a result he'd suffered back injuries, head injuries and multiple fractures. He needed immediate surgery.

The nurse's words buzzed in Michael's head.

"Wife?"

Was that what Will had wanted to tell him over lunch today? Had he married his secret girlfriend?

On some level Michael's numbed brain faced the harsh reality of his brother's injuries. On another, he refused to accept that his younger brother could be so seriously injured.

Not Will. Michael had called him from Shanghai last night. When Michael had asked him about Bree, Will had refused to discuss her.

"I have some big news. I'll give you an update over lunch tomorrow," was all he'd said.

"Can I see my brother…before his surgery?" Michael demanded of the nurse.

"Of course. But don't say much or you'll tire him."

Only when he saw Will's gray face washed of all color, and Will's body shrunken and as still as death did the gravity of Will's injuries finally hit Michael.

"Will. Can you hear me? It's me. Michael," he said gently.

Tubes hissed and gurgled. His brother, whose bruised face was swathed in bloodstained bandages, stirred faintly. His mouth quivered, and he seemed to struggle to focus on Michael's face.

"Don't talk," Michael commanded.

"Have to… No time… You know, they're wrong about your life passing before your eyes." Will's voice was so thready Michael had to lean close to his brother's lips to hear it. "It's the future you'll never have…that matters."

"Don't waste your strength trying to talk. You're young. You're going to be okay. I swear it."

"Not even you can fix this. But you can do one thing for me…."

"Anything."

"Take care of Bree."

"What?"

"Bree… She's…my wife," Will gasped.

"Bree? You married Bree?"

"She's pregnant. No time to explain. We didn't want to tell you like this. Just promise me…that you'll take care of her and…the baby."

"The baby?"

"She's pregnant and hurt. I don't know how badly. We were in the backseat. Tony was driving. Tony's dead…. Tried…to save her…for you."

"For me…"

"You care about her."

Sweat broke out on Michael's forehead. His hands opened and closed in fists as fury and concern for her and grief for his brother tore at him.

One thing was very clear. She'd lied about her relationship to Will. They had been involved. After she'd slept with Michael, she'd gone back to Will as easy as you please, gotten herself pregnant by him so he'd marry her. They'd kept it all a secret from Michael until he'd gotten back from Shanghai.

Will had been so dazzled by Bree he'd removed his own seat belt to protect her.

Then Michael remembered that Will would receive a million dollars from the North trust when he married, as well as a sizable increase in his allowance. He would receive even more once the child was born.

Had Will informed Bree about all those benefits? Probably.

Her treachery didn't matter right now. Only Will mattered.

His brother's glazed eyes read Michael like a book. "I know you don't think you like her. And I knew you wouldn't approve of our marriage, but she's been through a rough time. She's a wonderful girl. Not a gold digger like you think."

Michael swore silently. His brother was so hopelessly naive.

"What you did to her…was all my fault."

"Whatever I did, I did it for you," Michael said.

"Understood. So, promise me…you'll take care of her. If you'll do this one thing for me, we'll be square."

No way could Michael promise that.

"Promise me," Will insisted.

The room felt stale and airless. His brother looked so

pale—Michael couldn't say no to him. He yanked at his collar and tore at his tie that was damp from the rain. He wanted to run out of the room, to get outside, to breathe fresh air.

Through gritted teeth he said, "I promise I'll take care of your wife." Carefully Michael took his brother's limp hand and pressed it lightly. "I'll even shake on it."

"And her restaurant. Help her save it."

Michael nodded.

Satisfied, Will's heavy eyelids drooped shut.

A few seconds later an older male nurse in blue scrubs rushed up to the gurney and flipped through Will's chart. Without a word, he bent over his patient.

Michael stood in the doorway and watched the man wheel his brother away, watched until they vanished down the long hall. The sounds of people rushing past him died. All he could hear was his own heart. Would he ever see his brother alive again?

Suddenly he felt very cold, and very much alone, as alone as he'd been as a kid. Since he couldn't stand forever in an empty hall staring at waxed floor tiles and feeling sorry for himself, he turned and headed back to the nurse's station where he found Pedro, who took Michael to Bree.

Two women, probably family, hovered over Bree. She lay on a narrow bed that had been curtained off from the other beds in the large room.

Michael held out his hand. "I'm Michael North, Will's brother. Her brother-in-law."

The older woman took his hand. "I'm Bijou, her mother. Wait! I never forget a face. You're that handsome rich guy that came to the restaurant looking for her, yes? I thought maybe you gave her some trouble, yes?"

Heat washed through him. "Yes."

"I'm Marcie," the pretty blonde beside Bijou said. "I wait tables for Bree and Bijou. Bree's just the sweetest person in the whole world. So is Will. I can't believe that two such super people…"

"Marcie! You need to be strong, *oui!*" Bijou turned to Michael. "We'll give you a minute with her," she said. "But only a minute."

When they left, Michael moved closer to Bree's bed. Her thick lashes were still against her bloodless cheeks, so she didn't see him at first. Dark circles ringed her eyes. More than a dozen bruises and livid cuts covered her arms and cheeks. At the sight of her injuries, he choked on a breath.

She looked so slim and fragile in her hospital gown, he felt a stab of fear. She was carrying his brother's child, and Michael had sworn he'd take care of her.

Despite the money she must have been after when she'd married Will, Michael's resentment toward her faded. If Will died, her child would be Michael's last link to his brother.

"Bree? Can you hear me? It's Michael. When I got in from Shanghai I heard about the accident. I came at once."

"Michael…" Her lashes fluttered weakly, and for an instant her face lit up with pleasure…and with some other more luminous emotion that thrilled him. Her eyes had shone like that when he'd first entered her.

In the next second she must have remembered what he'd done because her gaze went flat and cold. "Where's Bijou? What are you doing here? I want my mother back."

"Your mother's right outside. Will asked me to check on you, so I'm here," Michael said softly.

"Will asked you…" She let out a harsh sob and turned her face to the wall. "I don't believe you! He's as fed up with you as I am! Go away!"

Michael felt conscience-stricken and confused, which wasn't like him.

"I don't need you here," she said to the wall, her tone so

low he could barely hear her. "Will knows that, so you're lying if you say he sent you."

"He did. He was facing surgery, and I think he was afraid."

She sucked in a breath. "Oh, God… I'm being so selfish. Tony's dead and maybe Will won't…and he's in there scared and alone…and thinking of me. He's so good."

"Yes, he is." Michael's voice was hard and condemning.

When she jerked her head around to stare at him again, he noted how the soft blue fabric of her hospital gown molded against her breasts. "They told me how badly Will was hurt. They didn't want to. But I made them. If he dies, it will be all my fault. He took off his seat belt…right before that SUV shot across the median and rammed us. Will saw it coming and threw himself in front of me…to protect me and the baby. Poor Tony never had a chance."

"Who's Tony?"

An odd, almost sorrowful expression passed swiftly over her bruised face. Clutching her sheet, she looked away. "Will's best friend. He was driving."

"Funny. I've never met him."

She chewed her bottom lip. "I imagine you were too wrapped up in money matters to really involve yourself in your brother's personal life—except when it came to me—because you saw me as a financial threat."

Her words hurt more than they should have. "Will said you and he were expecting a baby."

Her face went even whiter, if that were possible.

"H-he had no right to talk to you about the baby. He swore to me he wouldn't."

"He asked me to take care of you…and the baby…in case…"

She shuddered. "It just gets worse, doesn't it? You and me—stuck together…maybe without Will?"

"It's probably just a precaution. I promised him I would. If…if the worst happens. I intend to keep my word."

"Really? Your word?" She tipped her head back and frowned, studying him. "As if that means something." She took a deep, stabilizing breath. "Just go away."

"I intend to honor my promise—whether or not you want me to," he said.

"You deliberately deceived me, to get me to do things I find truly humiliating now. How could I have been so foolish?"

Sensual, erotic things he'd dreamed of her doing to him again.

"I thought I'd found the one person—never mind!" she snapped. "You made it very clear how you really felt about me at a moment when I was most tender and open and vulnerable to you. I don't know how all those other women feel, the ones you date for a night or two, but let me be very clear. You are the last person I would ever want in my life, even casually. I don't care if you're Will's brother and my baby's…uncle, or that you feel a duty to keep your promise. I do not want to see you. I do not want my child to know you. Do you understand?"

Her words cut Michael deeply. Curiously, he felt guilt, as well. Why should he feel that when he'd been trying to protect his tenderhearted brother who had proven time and again he was too trusting when it came to people who were after his money?

Not that Michael showed his pain at her words by even the flicker of his dark eyelashes. Having grown up poor, in a rough Houston neighborhood near the ship channel, he'd learned to put on a tough mask whenever he felt the slightest weakness. His mother had barely eked out a living as a masseuse before Jacob North had married her and adopted him.

Until Jacob, his mother had gone from man to man,

taking whatever they offered to survive. Michael had worked on the docks so he wouldn't be dependent on such handouts. He'd hated having nothing and being treated like nothing and feeling ashamed of how they'd lived. He'd learned early on that when you didn't have it, money was everything.

Will, on the other hand, had grown up a rich man's adored only son. Will had loved everybody, especially his older adopted brother, whom he'd accepted right from the first. Maybe Will was the only person who'd ever loved Michael. He'd promised Jacob, to whom he owed everything, that he would look out for Will. Those feelings of profound responsibility carried over to Will's unborn child, even if that child's mother was someone he could never trust.

"If Will dies, Will's child—your child—will be a North heir. Then there's the promise I made to my brother. Whether or not you want me in your life, I intend to take a very active interest in that little person from now on."

"So this is about money and control? My child is nothing more to you than the possible heir to the North fortune."

Why should he let her know what Will's child meant to him when she would only use such knowledge against him?

"A fortune does carry a huge responsibility."

"I'll bet you're used to getting your way."

She was right about that.

Her eyes darkened. "Well, you won't. Not with me. Never again."

"We'll see," he said. Then he let it drop. He fully intended to win this battle, but he wouldn't bully the pregnant wife of his injured brother.

"I want you to go," she said.

"Too bad."

When he sank down into the chair beside her bed, she glared at him. At his thin smile, she shut her eyes and twisted her face away. As he stared at her stiff back, he knew she couldn't force him out of her thoughts any more than he could force her out of his. Just being in the same room with her, even when she was injured, disturbed him.

An hour later, she was still rigid and seething when Will's grim, hollow-eyed surgeon found them.

"Mr. North? Mrs. North?"

When she opened her eyes and met Michael's, she blushed.

"I'm Will North's wife," she said. "Michael North is my brother-in-law."

"I see. Sorry about the confusion."

Michael had only to look into the surgeon's shadowed eyes to know the worst. Will was gone. Slowly Michael stood and shook the man's hand, listening, asking the appropriate questions, thanking him even as ice closed around his heart.

Bree let out a hoarse sob midway through the surgeon's detailed explanation.

"Your brother lost a lot of blood at the scene...."

Michael's vision blurred. He felt himself near some fatal edge. Maybe to steel his own nerves, he concentrated on Bree, whose face had gone as white as her sheets. Leaning over her hospital bed, he took her trembling hand. At his touch, she stiffened. Then, to his surprise, her fingers tightened around his, and she tugged him closer. Grabbing fistfuls of his jacket, she threw her wet face against his broad shoulder and burrowed into it. Clinging to him, she wept soundlessly.

His suit would be a mess tomorrow, but he needed to hold her, needed it more than he had ever imagined needing anything. Despite his own hideous sorrow and the profound gulf that separated them, he was glad Bree was here, glad not to be completely alone with his grief.

"Bree," he murmured. Careful not to hurt her, his arms closed around her. "It's going to be okay."

"You don't know, so how can you say that?"

"Time has a way—" He broke off, unable to repeat the usual trite phrases people offered one another for comfort.

Strangely, holding her seemed to be enough. Never had he felt more powerfully connected to another human being as her tears rained down his cheek.

After a long time she said, "Tell my mother and Marcie… about Will. Please…" Her voice was choked. "I just can't."

"Anything," he murmured as he let her go. "I'll do anything you want."

"Really? Excuse me if I find it hard to believe that the man with no heart is now willing to do anything for me."

"You're pregnant with Will's child, and he's gone. Everything's different between us now."

"Yes. Will's child," she repeated softly.

"There's nothing I wouldn't do for Will's baby, and, therefore, for you."

Three

The pain meds must have made her daft. Why else would she have agreed to spend the night—no, seven nights—at Will's loft with Michael?

Because your Victorian brownstone has stairs—three tall flights of them—and no elevator, remember?

The fact that her building had no elevator had never been a problem before. Okay, so she didn't like elevators or any small, boxy room. With her history, who would?

When she'd been a kid, an older cousin had locked her in a closet and left her there while he'd gone out to play. She'd been hysterical by the time her mother, who'd been busy in the kitchen downstairs, had found her. Every time the doors of an elevator closed Bree remembered Jeremy's gloating smile right before he'd shut the door and turned out the light.

Bree chewed a nail as Michael jammed the key into the door of Will's loft apartment in the Village. Maybe if she deliberately goaded Michael, he'd decide looking after her wasn't worth it.

"I can't believe, that as frequently as you saw your brother, you've never been inside his place before now," she said.

Michael's mouth tightened. "What do you know about it?"

She smiled. "Oh—did I hit a nerve?"

"He used to have me to his place on the Upper East Side all the time," Michael snapped, "but for some reason he didn't want me dropping by anymore when he moved here. Usually we met at my penthouse or somewhere in the city. I did stop by a couple of times, but he was either just going out or his roommate was home and they were busy. I didn't understand why he needed a roommate when he could have easily afforded to live alone. When I asked him about it, he said the guy was a good friend who needed a place to stay."

"R-right," she said uneasily, deciding to back up Will's lie. "He…he was still living here when we married."

"Must have been crowded, you two being newlyweds and all."

She didn't like his tone but refused to comment.

When Michael finished unlocking the door, he caught her elbow to usher her inside.

Startled by the fire in even that brief touch, Bree jumped back. How could she feel anything for a man who'd used her and had lied to her? He was the last person she wanted helping her. But he *was* Will's brother.

"This really isn't necessary," she said, hoping she didn't sound as nervous as she felt. "You don't want to be stuck with me any more than I want you here. Why don't you make it easy on us both and just leave?"

"I'm staying," he said in a tone that was raw and intense. "You can fight about it. Or you can make the best of it. Your choice."

The carved lines of his face looked powerful and strong—implacable. She was much too weak, exhausted and woozy from the pain meds to fight him. When he nudged her inside, she let him.

"Whoa!" Michael said, obviously taken aback by the dramatic design of the apartment and its furnishings. "This is truly amazing, totally different than his other place. I didn't know Will had something like this in him."

There's a lot you didn't know about him.

Strangely, the thought made her feel sorry for Michael.

Tony, who was a top designer and world-famous in certain circles, had put the apartment together. Not Will. The airy rooms with their skylights and soaring ceilings, and dramatic art collection and colorful, minimalistic furnishings screamed Tony.

Not Will, and not her. It wouldn't be long before Michael picked up on the fact that she hadn't really lived here.

Maybe there was a piece of paper from city hall that said she and Will were married, but there was very little of her here. A chipped coffee mug or two, a pair of her jeans and panties and a favorite sweater with a cat on it in the single drawer Will had emptied for her.

She'd slept on their couch for a couple of weeks wondering how she'd ever forget Michael and get clear of the mess she'd made of her life because of him. The only two things she'd been sure about were that she wanted her baby and she wanted to get Z's bistro back on its financial feet. Will had promised to help in every way he could, both personally and financially.

"I really think I'll be fine on my own here."

"Hey, we've been over that. You heard what the doctor said," Michael murmured in the same gentle, mesmerizing tone he'd used to seduce her. "You're pregnant. You have a nasty bump on the head. Your blood pressure is a little low, and you shouldn't be alone for the next week."

He *almost* sounded concerned.

Reminding herself that he didn't care about her, she also reminded herself that she was okay with that. She refused to care about anybody as cold and unfeeling as him. She stepped farther inside, only to feel truly trapped when he slammed the door, stripped off his expensive jacket and flung it toward the sofa.

"I don't want you here. You are the last person I want to be with tonight when I feel so utterly miserable."

"Understood. Ditto."

"Underline ditto," she cried.

"But here we are—together." Grimly, he bolted the various locks from the inside. "It might be dangerous for your baby, my niece or nephew, if I don't stay. Like you said, your mother has cats, and you're allergic to them."

Why was he acting as though he cared?

"From what the papers have said lately, I'd think you'd surely have some gorgeous supermodel waiting in your bed to welcome you home from China," she muttered, dragging her gaze from his wide shoulders.

After the fund-raiser when she'd been so dazzled by him, she'd researched him online. She'd been dismayed to learn about all the glamorous women he dated. After her one night with him, he'd gone right back to dating those women. How could she have thought he was interested in her that night? The eagerness she'd felt for him and the things she'd done in his bed still mortified her.

His jet brows winged upward in cynical surprise. "Jealous?"

Despite her grief and exhaustion, hot indignation that he'd hit a nerve flared inside her. "Only you, who are so arrogant and sure of yourself, would take it like that."

"Yeah, only me—the number one ogre in your sweet, innocent life." His grin was savagely ironic. "You didn't answer my question, sweetheart. Are you jealous?"

"Don't be insane! It's just that I couldn't help noticing an item or two about you and several models in the gossip columns. Did you go out with them to destroy them, too?"

When a muscle jerked in his jawline, she almost wondered if she'd hurt him. Then she remembered he didn't have a heart.

After an ominous pause, he said, "There's no supermodel…if you must know. Hell, there's nobody waiting, which is pretty normal. So, tell me about you and Will. I was shocked when he told me you were married, especially after you'd told me you weren't interested in him that way. How did it happen? And when?"

She turned away to hide her eyes, lest she give something away. "He asked me. I said yes. Unlike you, he's a really nice guy."

"Which made him perfect prey for a woman like you."

"You're wrong. About him and me." She stopped. There was no way she could defend herself without getting into deeper trouble.

"Forget it," she said. "I don't care what you think."

But she did.

Frowning, Michael paced the length of Will's dazzling white room with its grand piano and splashes of paintings and sculptures. He stopped abruptly to look at the photographs of Will and Tony on Tony's piano.

Panic surged through her when he lifted one.

"Who's the big guy in leather?"

She moved toward the shiny black piano. Not that she had to see the picture up close to know that it was Tony in his trademark black biker attire with rings in his ears. In the photograph, he and Will were toasting Johnny and her at a party at Chez Z. It had been only a few months ago, to celebrate the restaurant's success. Will had been ecstatic to be part of a successful venture and to share his happiness with Tony.

Tears misted her eyes. How could so much change so fast? How could they both be gone?

"It's Tony," she said

"The driver? He was Will's best friend who died at the scene? He was Will's roommate, too?"

"And our best man," she said.

And so much more.

Michael slowly set the picture back on the piano beside the others of Tony and Will with different friends. "Tell me again why you married Will."

She backed away. "Do we have to talk about this?"

"You asked me about *my* love life." A dangerous edge had crept into his soft voice. "Did you want him, my brother, as much as you wanted me?"

It made her sick to remember how much she'd wanted Michael; sick to think that even now he wasn't entirely unattractive to her. She wanted to believe he wasn't the man she knew he was, wanted to believe he cared, at least a little. But he'd told her in no uncertain terms how he felt about her, so she steeled herself.

"I married him, didn't I?"

"Why?"

Because of what you did to me. Because your wonderful, caring brother wanted to help me and take care of me, which was something he knew you'd never do. Because I didn't know what else to do.

He seemed to sense her vulnerability. Her heart skittered as his large, tanned hand closed over hers, making escape impossible. His dark eyes flashed with alarming passion as he drew her to him.

She averted her gaze from his handsome face. He'd been so cruel, and she'd fought so hard to forget him.

Why couldn't she? He'd only had to walk into her hospital room this afternoon to make her remember how he'd dazzled her.

Then he'd accused her of being a gold digger and worse.

"I've thought about you," he muttered. "Thought about that night, about everything we did and said, even though all I wanted was to forget you. Even now—when I know you were lying about your relationship with Will all along, you still get under my skin."

Ditto.

Feeling on the verge of a meltdown, she tried to wrench free. It was clear that he'd hated his involvement with her, that he wanted nothing to do with her. And it still hurt— more than it should have, even now when she knew how cold and cruel he was.

When his burning eyes stared into hers, she began to shake because she was terrified he would see her pain and understand how gullible she still was.

He held on to her and drew her closer. "How the hell could you marry my brother?"

Her pulse thrummed. As always when she was in his arms, he aroused forbidden needs.

She had to remember he'd deliberately used her, not caring how he hurt her. He still despised her. She couldn't trust anything he said or did.

Michael certainly did not deserve the truth.

"Why did you marry him?" he asked again.

"It's complicated."

"I'm good at complicated, so tell me. Or better yet, show me," he whispered.

"I don't know what you mean."

"Don't you?"

Suddenly his hands were in her hair, stroking the dark silken gold that fell against her nape. His fingertips followed the sensuous curve of her neck before he cupped her chin and lifted her slender face to his, his touch as gentle and seductive as it had been that night.

Frantically, because it would be so easy to lose herself to the emotions that blazed in his eyes, she fought to resist him.

If only he had a real heart. If only she could truly depend on him and didn't have to be afraid of how she felt. But she knew, and even so, he aroused her.

Her skin burned and her knees went weak. He had only to touch her to make her yearn for his tenderness. Had there been a night since she'd seen him last that she hadn't ached to have him hold her like this and make her feel loved again? To look at her as he was looking at her now, with eyes that devoured her, adored her?

The craving for all the things only he could make her feel became too much to resist. Without thinking, she arched her back and opened her lips, inviting his mouth to claim hers. His tongue entered her. In an instant, the rightness of his searing kiss, and her hunger, were a thousand times stronger than what she'd experienced before.

She had to fight him. She knew what he was about. But the room was spinning and she was clinging, melting, falling. As he pulled her closer, every feminine cell pulsed with the desire to surrender to him in the hope he felt something deeper than he could admit.

All that mattered was that she'd longed for him, and he'd returned. She felt him, erect with a fierce masculine need he couldn't hide as he pressed against her. No matter how he'd denied his feelings, there was a raw, elemental truth in his kisses. In that moment she believed he was as helpless as she to fight the explosive chemistry between them.

Again and again he kissed her, leaving her shaken from the bittersweet joy of being with him again. His tongue dipped deeply inside her mouth and sent a tremor through her. When his grip tightened around her waist, she realized he was trembling even more than she was.

Time seemed to slow as he made love to her with his mouth and tongue, as his hands moved down her curves. She'd missed him, though she'd denied it.

She couldn't deny it now as his hands slid downward to cup her bottom and bring her closer to the powerful, masculine heat of his arousal.

Throwing caution aside, her hands traced over his hard body before sliding inside his waistband. In her desperation she ripped his shirt out of his slacks. But when she caressed his hard abs, he shuddered, let out a savage cry and then tore his lips from hers.

Cursing her softly, he took a step backward, even as he retained a grip on her arm to steady her when she began to sway.

"What's wrong?" she whispered, aching for more.

"You answered my question," he said, his cold, flat voice reducing the tenderness and warmth that burned inside her to ashes. "You still want me—which means you married Will for cold, calculating reasons. You are every bit as low as I thought. I'll never forgive you for using my brother like that. You didn't care how you were going to hurt him, did you? Not as long as you got what you wanted."

"What?" In shock, her wild eyes met his icy ones.

Who was using who? How could Michael kiss her like that and then shut her out again just when she felt so passionately aroused and open to him? Just when she believed there might be feelings beneath his passion. Had he really kissed her like that only to prove a point?

She swallowed and fought to find some control within herself, but she was too close to the edge, too vulnerable. She had been through too much today. She wanted Michael, and he despised her.

"I don't want you. My resistance must be low because they gave me painkillers. I—I didn't know what I was doing."

"Well, you can believe that if it makes you feel better," he began with a calm disdain that chilled her to the marrow. "But you want me, all right."

Because I'm a human being, and I thought you cared.

"So, do you need help undressing or running a bath?"

"What?" His curt, dismissive change of subject hurt.

Surely she would lose all self-respect if he stripped her and touched her and made her even more aware of him as a man while he regarded her with such cool contempt.

Never again would she let him arouse her deepest feelings and play her for a fool. *Never again.*

"I can take care of myself," she snapped, furious. She was weak and injured tonight and that had made her highly susceptible. He'd taken advantage of her.

"Then I suggest you get started," he said.

"I don't want to bathe with you here."

"Then pretend I'm not here."

"Impossible."

"The only reason I'm looking after you is because I made a promise to my brother. Trust me, I'll leave you alone. I didn't kiss you because I wanted to. I kissed you to find out if you wanted my brother, the poor bastard. You didn't. So, go in the bedroom, shut the door and get ready for bed."

How could she stay here with him? How could she pretend he wasn't here while she undressed, when awareness of him still buzzed in her blood despite his icy disdain?

"While I'm waiting for my turn to shower, I'll see what there is to eat and make some business calls."

"Right—the all-important CEO who's always so busy looking after the North fortune he doesn't have time to be human."

"Damn you, I've got other things to do besides baby-sit you. I've got work," he growled. "Lots of it." Turning his back on her, he pulled out his phone and sank down on the couch.

Infuriating man.

Whoever answered on the other end must have begun by offering his or her condolences immediately because Michael lowered his voice and hunched over the phone, his expression haggard as he talked about Will. So, he wasn't totally unfeeling. He just didn't care for her.

Her heart constricted as she heard him going over some checklist about funeral arrangements, and Bree imagined he'd forgotten her. Surrendering to his will, partly because she couldn't bear to listen as he finalized the details of Will's memorial service, she padded softly toward Will and Tony's bedroom.

As she entered it, Michael cupped the receiver. "Don't lock the door," he ordered. "If you faint, I'll need to get in. If I can't open the door, I'll break it down. Do we understand each other?"

Exhaustion and frayed nerves and what was left her desire had her so close to the edge she felt like screaming. Or weeping hysterically. "You're such a brute! I don't want you here. And I don't have to do what you say. I don't! I can't stand you!"

"We've already had this discussion. The doctor released you on the condition you'd remain under my care until your checkup next week because you were spotting. You agreed."

As if he cares about the baby, she thought dismally.

"*Next week!*" she moaned aloud. "I was in so much pain, I was out of my mind to agree to a week with you."

"Bottom line—you agreed," he said. "So, you'll damn well do what I say, or I'll make you!"

She shut the door. Then, thinking about the way he'd

kissed her and rejected her—as if she was nothing—she opened the door and then slammed it so hard its frame shook. Not that the childish action gave her any satisfaction.

Her gaze ran over the guys' bright, modern bedroom. Being in Will and Tony's private space brought the loss she felt for them to the surface again. They'd been so sweet to her. Feeling confused, grief-stricken and concerned about her unborn baby, she went into their bathroom where she stared at her white, bruised face in the huge, carved mirror they'd told her they'd bought on a recent trip to Oaxaca.

Cuts and purple bruises covered her gray skin. Blood stiffened several locks of her hair. How could she have imagined Michael desired her?

He didn't want her. He never had, and he certainly didn't care about her. No, he disliked her. He'd seduced her to drive a wedge between her and Will. Tonight he'd kissed her and used his expertise at lovemaking merely to prove that he had her where he wanted her. His only interest in her had always been using her to protect the North fortune. For that same reason, he was interested in the baby. The baby was his heir.

If only she hadn't agreed to Will's plan. Then Michael wouldn't be here, and she wouldn't have kissed him again and relearned how powerfully she still felt about him. Nor would she have had to endure realizing how much he despised her.

Choking back a sob, she began to strip.

Michael couldn't stop thinking about Bree alone in Will's bedroom.

Had she and his brother been happy in that bed together? Even though a part of Michael hoped she'd made his brother happy, another more selfish part resented any connubial bliss, however short-lived, she might have shared with Will. Because the idea of her in any other man's bed, even his brother's, felt like sacrilege.

She was Michael's. He wanted her. Kissing her again had taught him how much.

Why was he always attracted to users like her? God, what a mess.

How many endless, bleak hours had passed since she'd slammed the door? With his arms pillowed under his head, he felt restless on this couch from hell that was too short for him. He stared up at the bar of moonlight shifting on the ceiling.

Michael had promised his brother he'd look after Bree. He'd come here intending to honor his promise. What had he done instead? He'd mauled her just because he'd had to know if she still desired him.

She did. Her molten response had almost brought him to his knees.

He had no right to touch her. No matter what else she was, she was his brother's widow. She'd been injured in a car wreck that had claimed three lives. She was pregnant, and her condition was precarious. For her protection and the baby's, he had to keep his hands off her.

His eyes grew heavy, but just as he was about to shut them, she screamed. His heart racing with fear, Michael bolted to his feet and raced across the shadowy apartment.

He pushed the door open. "Bree?"

She'd kicked her sheets and blankets aside and was shivering. When she neither cried out nor answered him, he realized she was having a nightmare. His fault, no doubt. She'd been through a lot, and he hadn't made things easier for her.

His anger forgotten, he rushed to her. The masculine, long-sleeved dress shirt she'd chosen to wear had ridden up to her knees. When he saw the paleness of her bruised face and the dark shadows under her eyes, his concern and the self-loathing for his callous treatment of her grew.

Instead of awakening her, he pulled the covers over her gently. When she continued to tremble, he went to the living room and grabbed his jacket. He draped it over her shoulders. Then, unable to leave her, he sank down onto the bed beside her. After a long moment he began to stroke her hair.

Asleep, she looked young and innocent and completely incapable of deceit. He remembered the blood on his sheets that first night and how virginal she'd seemed when he'd made love to her. He'd never been with anyone who'd seemed so young and fresh and eager for him. Although he'd told himself she'd been a clever actress, he'd been enchanted. He'd almost forgotten that he'd ever considered her opportunistic and out to deceive his naive brother.

When she cried out again and then, drawn by his warmth, cuddled against him, he hardly dared to breathe for fear he'd startle her.

Then her hand slid across his thigh and a flame went through him. In an instant he was as hard as granite.

With her soft body lying against him, it was much too easy to forget why he should dislike her, much too easy to remember the heat of her response.

"Michael," she whispered. "Michael."

"I'm here," he said, worried that he'd awakened her somehow.

"I'm…baby…I'm having a baby. Wanted to tell you… but didn't know how."

"It's okay." He looked down at her.

Her lashes were shut. He relaxed when he realized she was only talking in her sleep.

"I know about the baby," he said. "It's all right."

"I wanted you to be happy about it."

"I am happy about it."

He was happy his brother had left something of himself behind. At the same time, illogically, he wished she'd never been involved with Will.

Unable to resist the temptation to touch her and reassure her, he placed his hand on her shoulder. Then very gently he brushed his lips to her forehead.

"Don't be afraid," he whispered. "I won't let anybody hurt you…or your baby. I swear."

In her sleep, she smiled. "I know. You just pretend… to be mean and awful and greedy."

The wistful tenderness in her voice touched his heart. As before, she smelled of strawberries, making him remember how slick and tight she'd been, how she'd cried out at his first stroke—just as a virgin would have—but then had refused to let him stop. She'd felt so perfect. She'd been so sweet.

The memories had him burning up. His every muscle felt tight. The blood on his sheets had been real. He'd been her first. She hadn't been lying about that as he'd tried to make himself believe. No matter what she was, that had to mean something.

He wanted to pull her closer, to hold her, to ask her why she'd never slept with anyone before him. But more than that, damn it, he wanted to make love to her again.

What was he thinking? Why did he care so deeply for this woman who'd only wanted his brother's money?

He had to get up and separate himself from her before he lost all control and kissed her and woke her…and risked jeopardizing her health and the baby's.

Gritting his teeth against the pain of leaving her, he eased himself to the other side of the big bed. Then he got up and went to the window where he stood for a long time, staring down at the glittering rooftops of the Village. Not that he really saw the sparkling lights or the buildings in the moonlight.

He couldn't let himself feel so much for this woman.

When his breathing eased, he walked over to Will's easy chair beside the bed and sat down. He intended to stay only a minute or two, but Bree's sweet nearness eased the savage demons that rode him.

No matter what she was, no way could he leave her alone to deal with her nightmares.

Before he knew it he was fast asleep.

An alarm buzzed in her ear. When she moaned and rolled over onto soft, downy pillows, her throbbing head felt foggy. Every bone in her body, indeed every muscle she had, screamed in pain. Where had this headache from hell come from?

She let out a smothered cry and sat up. What was wrong with her? Why did everything hurt?

"You okay?" growled a deep, protective voice from above her.

In confusion she blinked up at the tall, broad-shouldered man towering over her. "Michael?"

What was he doing in her bedroom?

Confused, she scanned the bright paintings on the walls. No, she was in Will and Tony's bedroom.

As Michael's black eyes continued their blazing appraisal, she blushed at the intimacy of awakening in yet another bedroom with him.

How long had he been watching her? What was she doing here with him?

In the next instant his tense, brooding expression had her flashing back to him sitting beside her in the hospital. She remembered the SUV careening across the median straight at me. Tony had been unable to maneuver into another lane. They'd been hit and had rolled. Will's limp body had crushed hers.

He hadn't made it.

The loss of Will, as fresh as yesterday, slammed into her anew. Sinking into Will's pillow with a shudder, she groaned and buried her face in her hands. Dear, dear Will, who'd become her best friend after Johnny's death, was gone.

Will had been closer to her than most brothers were to their sisters. And now, because desperate circumstances had forced her to agree to marry him, she was stuck with his brother.

"It was so nice before I saw you and remembered... about Will and Tony and everything that's happened," she said. "Reality sucks," she said mournfully.

Michael's black eyes darkened, if that were possible. "I know. There's always that first moment when you wake up...before you remember. Before the horror hits you."

"I don't want to get up and face a day without them," she said. "I don't want to be in their apartment."

"*Their* apartment?"

"I...I mean Will's apartment," she corrected quickly. "*Ours*. I don't want to remember...any of it or try to go on. It's too hard."

"Tell me about it. But we don't have any choice. We have responsibilities."

He sounded nice, almost human. But he wasn't. She had to remember that.

Michael must have grabbed her phone from the night-stand and shut off her alarm because the noise suddenly stopped.

"Do you want coffee?" he asked abruptly.

When she nodded, he vanished.

She was rubbing her eyes when he returned a few minutes later with a steaming mug. "What time is it anyway?"

When he held out the mug, she sat up straighter, causing something to fall from her shoulders.

His jacket. What was his jacket doing wrapped around her? The thought of him worrying about her and watching over her was oddly unsettling.

"It's 9:00 a.m.," he said, picking up his badly wrinkled jacket and folding it under his arm.

On a normal day she would be at the bistro, preparing for the day, but because of her injuries and the spotting, she wasn't supposed to work for a whole week. Her mother had volunteered to take over for her. So, here she was, stuck with Michael.

"I never thought I'd sleep till nine. But since I've been pregnant, it happens fairly often." How could she be talking to him in this normal way?

"You're growing a baby. I don't know much about pregnancy, but I think it wears you out." His deep voice was oddly gentle. "Think how tired little kids get. You've got to take care of yourself."

His desire to protect her for her baby's sake made her soften toward him, which was a dangerous reaction. If she wasn't careful, she'd start believing he was capable of treating her decently.

But that wasn't going to happen, and she couldn't allow herself to wish he could be different.

Last night she'd actually dreamed Michael was a nice guy. In her dream she'd been afraid, and he'd come running to comfort her.

Ridiculous fantasy. He was a ruthlessly cold money machine who believed the worst of her. He'd bedded her solely to protect his brother—and the North fortune. When she'd said she wasn't interested in Will, he'd offered to set her up as his mistress—but for a price. He saw her only as a threat or as a sexual commodity for his own pleasure.

"I've been thinking," he said. "This place is too small for the two of us."

She nodded. "And I hate it here because it reminds me of Will and Tony so much."

"Since we're stuck with each other for the next week," he said, "I think we'd both be more comfortable at my penthouse."

Her heart skittered in fear as she remembered their first wanton night together in his glamorous apartment where he'd seduced her and then broken her heart.

The last thing she wanted was to spend a week in the place where she'd experienced such devastation.

"I can't go back there. Your penthouse isn't exactly neutral ground. Besides don't tony Fifth Avenue buildings like yours have dictatorial boards? Would they approve of a woman, a nobody like me from the West Side just moving in?"

"Leave the board to me. If they exact a price, I'll pay…"

"You think you can buy anything you want."

"I can—most of the time." He stared into her eyes. "I have three floors and five bedrooms. Believe me, you'd be able to avoid me there much more easily than you would here. And vice versa."

"I suppose that does have its appeal," she agreed gloomily, hoping to wound him. For some infuriatingly illogical reason the thought that he wanted to avoid her as much as she wanted to avoid him stung.

He smiled. "For once you see reason. So, pack your bag, and we'll get the hell out of here."

She stared at the single drawer where she kept her things. "I…I can't."

"What is it now?"

"My stuff is still at my old apartment," she confessed.

When one black brow arched quizzically, she had to think fast.

"We…we got married so fast, Will was still in the process of moving things out to clear space for me." Flushing, she looked away.

The trouble with lies was that if you told one, you had to keep stacking more on top of the first. How long would it be before he discovered her secret and her house of cards came tumbling down?

"Okay, then," he said. "What do you say we do breakfast, and then we go to your place? We have to feed the baby, don't we?"

She couldn't believe she was nodding and almost smiling, or that she was agreeing so easily to move in with him, when he'd behaved so terribly last night, and would probably do so again. She should be furious. If only she could hold on to her anger and stay on her guard around him.

"Can we eat at Chez Z, so I can see how Bijou is holding up?" she asked.

He nodded much too agreeably. How would she stand a whole week with this man? She didn't trust herself to be around him when his every nice gesture made her want to trust him again.

What if he caught her in a weak moment? What if she stupidly confided her secret? What would he force her to do then?

Four

No sooner had Bree led Michael through the doors of Chez Z than she regretted it. Not that anything particularly worrisome was going on in the intimate dining room jammed with yellow chairs and tables, and paintings of sunflowers cheerfully aflame on fire-engine red walls. It was simply that being here with Michael brought back *that* night—the one that had changed her life so irrevocably and compelled her to marry Will.

Marcie looked up from setting the tables, smiled and then went back to her work as if having her battered boss show up on the arm of a devastatingly handsome man the morning after she'd survived a fatal car wreck was nothing unusual.

Bijou rushed over to ask how Bree was feeling. After giving her a concerned once-over, her mother must have felt reassured because she thanked Michael for looking after her. Then Bijou left to check the online reservations for the day, the availability of staff and the status of a delivery that was late.

Bree didn't want to think about the first night Michael had come to Chez Z, but with his strong hand gripping her wrist, it was impossible not to. His mere touch made the bright walls squeeze closer and her breath come faster.

Again she saw him striding through the doors alone on that warm summer evening, his black eyes purposeful as he looked for her. She knew now his sole intent had been to seduce her so he could neutralize her importance to Will. But that night, fool that she'd been, she'd felt flattered that he'd sought her out and had rushed up to him with pleasure.

Will had warned her about Michael, of course, saying that he was a real bastard when it came to business and could be rude and overbearing in his dealings with family and his lovers.

"He's a coldhearted genius who ruthlessly annihilates our foes. He'll do or say anything to win. Dad said he's what our family needs in this competitive world—so he put him in charge. Even though he's adopted, we all have to answer to him. Believe me, Michael interferes in everything. He says it's because he cares, and it is. But he can be rough and difficult."

"And you don't mind?"

"I mind, but he grew up hard. He once told me he was raised by wolves, so I sort of understand. He thinks he's protecting me. He really does, and he'll destroy anybody he sees as a threat to me. He worries about any woman I get close to, so stay away from him."

"But that's ridiculous. We're just friends."

"Believe me—he won't see it that way."

Had she listened?

Despite Will's warning, when his darkly handsome brother had flirted with her at the fund-raiser, she'd fallen fast and hard, maybe because he'd exuded way too much masculine power, confidence and charm for an innocent like her to resist.

And, oh, how foolishly she'd exulted when he'd walked into Chez Z looking for her. *For her,* when he could have had a gorgeous supermodel.

Tall and fit in his perfectly cut gray silk suit, his brilliant gaze and quick smile had dazzled her.

Mark, the maître d', had bowed and stepped aside when she'd rushed up to Michael, saying she'd lead him to his table.

"Hello again," he'd whispered against her ear as she picked up a menu and a wine list for him. "I wasn't sure you'd remember me."

As if any woman could forget…least of all her, who had zero experience with men like him.

"Will's brother? Even if you weren't my dearest friend's brother, how could I possibly forget *you?*" Realizing how eager she must have sounded, she'd blushed. "I—I didn't mean," she'd stammered. But she had. He was gorgeous. "Welcome to Chez Z."

His hard, sensual mouth had curved in amusement as if he considered her blushes and stammering his due. "I want a table in your section."

"I'm afraid I'm off tonight. I was just about to leave." She felt a pang of acute disappointment at this admission. "I'm going to see a movie with a friend."

"Too bad," he said with such genuine regret her tummy flipped. "Perhaps I can tempt you into joining me for a glass of champagne." He grinned down at her gently. "If I promise to select a very good year, maybe you'll decide to go to a later show."

Bree knew she was in over her head and that she should say no and leave to meet her friend, but when he looked at her in that intimate way, she wanted to be with him too badly to deny herself. Never in her whole life had she felt so excited. Cathy would have to understand.

"I guess I could stay for one glass…if it's a very good year."

He took her hand and squeezed it. As his thumb casually stroked the inside of her palm, thrilling warmth flooded her. He laughed at her blushes. Heads turned to regard them. The feminine gazes lingered on him before resting quizzically on her.

When she called Cathy, her friend suggested they postpone the outing until later in the week, which suited Bree even better.

She'd never been with anyone like Michael. Truthfully, she hadn't dated much at all. Oh, she'd loved a boy in college, but he'd broken her heart when he'd fallen for her best friend. Others had been interested in her, but she would have been settling if she'd let any of them make love to her. So, here she was, a virgin in her twenties, flirting with a man she should have run from.

Champagne, coupled with the aromas of garlic, duck and foie gras, had heightened her senses until she'd become giddy with conceit at finding herself the companion of such a virile and attractive man.

The heady pleasure of his company, of eating and drinking with him, had quickly proved too much. Food was like an aphrodisiac to her, and she wasn't much of a drinker. One glass of champagne had led to another because she hadn't wanted him to think her an ingenue.

She couldn't get enough of the cool pale liquid that tasted so bubbly and sweet. She'd basked in Michael's teasing and flirting. Suddenly there had been only him filling the dining room. The murmur of the other diners' voices and the clatter of their plates and silverware had soon died to nothing.

Soon she'd forgotten her shyness and her amazement

that such a stunning man was interested in her. With such chemistry between them, of course he was interested, she'd told herself, as she'd allowed him to draw her out.

When he leaned across the table, questioning her as if he found her fascinating, she'd told him all about her brother, Z, and about the strong-minded Bijou, who had adored Z more than anyone or anything in the world. Next Bree told him about the rest of her colorful family who had supported Z in his efforts to garner fame and respect with his cooking skills.

When their frogs' legs came, Michael picked one up with his fingers, and she watched him eat it. She picked up her own frog leg and nibbled at the rich, succulent flesh as gracefully as she could. He smiled when she sucked at the juice dripping down one of her fingertips. At the same moment they both dipped their fingers into the bowl of warm water tartly scented with lemon. When their fingers accidentally touched, a hot dart of excitement made her tummy turn over.

"I wanted to go into publishing," she said, quickly yanking her hand from the bowl. "To be an editor, but the family needed me here to help Z, who was bringing us all such glory. I couldn't resist them even if I always felt a little lost and colorless around all of them. They are all people of such grand passions and ambitions."

"Don't sell yourself short," he murmured.

When he looked at her, she felt alive, special—every bit as exciting as her relatives. It was a new and heady experience.

"I'm a book person. They love being center stage. They love the television shows shot in the bistro's kitchen. But Z left me the bistro, maybe because I shared his passion for food and was the most faithful about showing up whenever he had an emergency. Ironically, my exciting family works for dull me now."

"You are not dull. Far from it. Z must have realized you cared for the bistro."

Maybe she hadn't known how much she loved it until Z was gone and he'd left it to her. Michael had a point. She did care. She didn't want to lose the bistro and all Z and her family had worked for.

"Well, I'm not doing well in business, so dull or not, I'm in trouble with them for failing Z."

Michael picked up another frog leg. "Can't you quit? This wasn't your dream."

"But it is now," she said, realizing for the first time it was true. "The bistro means so much to all of them... and yes, to me. Investors, family, friends—they've sunk money into the restaurant. It's not just about a livelihood. It's about respect and family honor. It's for Z...and all the people I love. I'll do anything to save it. *Anything.*"

His eyes had darkened. "But what about you? Are you sure this is what you want?"

"It wasn't at first, but it is now."

"I envy you, having a family, a real family, and the goal to help them."

She paused. "I'm sorry. I shouldn't have gone on like that. I've done all the talking. You know, I don't normally do this."

"Do what?"

Once more he took her hand and turned it over in his, and again she felt the sharp sizzle of sensual excitement.

"*This.* I don't date much. I don't have the time right now. I'm sure you'd have more fun with some other girl... I mean, some other woman."

"You're very wrong." When he ran his thumb over her wrist, she gasped.

His eyes lit up, and she wondered if he sensed the intensity of her response.

"Don't apologize for being who you are," he whispered. "I like you. I came here because I wanted to get to know you better."

"Why?"

"I think you know why."

Did he feel something, too?

As he continued to run his thumb over her wrist and the inside of her palm, the hot current of desire throbbed with an ever greater force.

"Will said you're adopted."

A shadow passed over his face and his eyes grew bleak before he looked down.

She felt so stupid. Why, oh, why had she said that?

"Yes. I'm adopted." Then he was silent so long she grew uncomfortable.

"I'm sorry. I shouldn't have pried."

"No, it's okay. It's not something I talk about often, but I want to talk to you. I grew up poor. Poor enough to know what it feels like to be nothing."

"I'm sure you were never nothing."

"Well, I felt like I was. My father, who worked in a refinery in Baytown, died when I was a baby. So, I never knew him. My mother was a masseuse and earned just enough for us to scrape by. She had boyfriends. Too many boyfriends. I didn't like them or the gifts they gave me to bribe me into accepting them. I was in the third grade when I got my first job—on the docks. Not long after that I bought a used lawn mower and started mowing lawns. I had to put myself through junior college and the University of Houston. My life was tough until my mother married Jacob North."

"How in the world did she meet him?"

"He was a client. I was nineteen and just out of college when they married. I asked him for a job, and he hired me as a stockbroker. I didn't know much back then, but I guess he saw something in me because he took me under his wing.

"With his help I advanced rapidly, which a lot of people resented, including most of his family who disliked my mother. Right before my mother died, perhaps to please her, Jacob adopted me legally—because he said he needed somebody strong he could trust to run his businesses and look after the family interests. He said Will, his only son, was too weak because he'd been spoiled. Strangely, Will, who had no interest in the business, took to me in a brotherly way, and I took to him.

"When Jacob died, Will was all I had. The rest of the Norths tried to get rid of me. They sued, tried to break Jacob's will—but they lost—big-time." His grim expression should have warned her.

"At least they're not blood kin, so there's a reason you don't fit in."

He'd smiled and pressed her slim fingers tightly. "Except for Will, I feel like I've been alone my whole life."

"That's sad."

"It's just the way things are."

When he'd drawn her closer, she'd felt powerfully connected to him when he'd said, "It's a little hard for me to trust anyone."

Why hadn't she *listened?* Too late she'd learned the man annihilated those he didn't trust.

The waiter had come, and they'd elected to share crème brûlée and raspberries. The combined flavors of caramelized sugar, crème and tart berries had proved to be sheer perfection. Looking back, she couldn't believe she'd let Michael spoon-feed her. The memory of how warmly she'd felt toward him that night, of how deftly he'd used the sensual delight of food to seduce her, chilled her. Now she knew his interest in her had been based solely on his desire to destroy his brother's feelings for her.

Pushing back from the excruciating memories, she stiffened and marched ahead of him toward the kitchen. Even though it was still too early for lunch, her mother had already done most of the prep work, so the rich aroma of sautéed onions and garlic and other herbs flown in from Provence lingered in the air.

"I'll make you a soufflé," she said.

"You don't have to."

"Cooking relaxes me." Better than that, it would distract her from him and the reality that she was moving in with him.

She put on her apron and took four eggs out of the refrigerator while he wandered about, opening her drawers and investigating her cupboards. Just when she was about to object to his nosiness and tell him not to touch anything, his phone rang. Instantly, he was all business as he left the kitchen to discuss stock trades and a real-estate project in Mumbai.

He didn't return until she told him the soufflé was done. Then they sat down together to enjoy it with warm, buttery croissants thick with fresh, homemade raspberry jam and rich black coffee.

As always the lush flavors of even such simple fare put her in a better humor—which meant, she'd better be on her guard. She was eating with him again.

"Thanks for letting me come here," Bree said as he sank his fork into her luscious soufflé. "I needed to see that Marcie and Bijou have everything under control."

"Where's your chef and waitstaff?"

"Bijou's here. Mark's running late because he has some family issues, but he'll be here in a few minutes to cook. We do a lot of takeout orders, and we don't need waiters for that."

"Your mother can cook?"

"Yes…and no. She loves to cook, so she cooks. But…

no! Z and I were lucky to survive her cooking. Some of her guests were once hauled away from our house in ambulances after a family dinner when I was a child. We used to watch her in the kitchen, so we'd know what dishes to avoid."

"You're kidding."

"I wish. She used to throw anything that was about to spoil into a casserole or soup and then invite people over."

He laughed.

"We only let her start working here when she promised not to cook. Since Z died, she says she feels his spirit here. We need her, and when she's busy helping us hold Z's dream together, she feels better. Z was her favorite, you see."

"And you know this how?"

She wasn't about to tell him *she* was the reason her parents had felt obliged to marry, or that her mother had blamed Bree for the loss of her career as a concert pianist as well for her unhappy marriage.

Instead Bree said, "Z was their long-awaited son. The only thing my parents agreed on was how perfect Z was and how much they loved him. After he was born, I sort of ceased to exist."

There was a bread crumb on his lower lip. She clenched her fingers to resist the impulse to brush it away.

"Did you hate him for that?" Michael licked his lips, and the tempting bread crumb vanished.

Just the opposite. She'd felt relieved. "Z was just always so gifted, so charming and confident. He looked up to me and adored me, so how could I hate him?"

"So, when you were younger, you wanted to be an editor."

She wished she hadn't told him that, wished that he hadn't asked her so many personal questions. Her secret longings were none of his business. But talking to him like this touched her somehow, made her think that if they tried, they could have a normal relationship.

Unable to resist opening up to him, she began to babble. "I loved reading. Stories offered a safe escape from our family dramas. I wanted to do my own thing, though I hadn't figured out what that was. But when Z became famous and had to go shoot shows in foreign lands or do book tours, he needed someone to run the restaurant, and he asked me. None of us could ever say no to Z. Mother would have helped, too, but she broke her hip and was down for six months.

"The busier Z became, the more he needed me here. And I liked being needed. Unfortunately, he died at a very bad time for the business. He'd just expanded and taken on a lot of new investors."

"Like Will," Michael said in a grim tone that made her wish she'd avoided that topic.

"Will was already an investor." She took a bite of soufflé before continuing. "The restaurant is saddled with debt. If I fail, my family will never forgive me any more than I could forgive myself. To them, closing Chez Z would be the end of Z's dream. For them, he's still alive here, you see. I feel the same way."

"I know a thing or two about dealing with family issues and business," Michael muttered as he sank his fork into the airy perfection of her soufflé again. "It's rarely easy."

"But I've got to make it work, now more than ever, and not just for my family. I need to pay off the debt and earn a decent income so I can support my baby."

"Your baby's a North. You must know you won't have to worry about money. You're Will's widow. I'll take care of you."

"Do you think that, knowing what you think of me, I want to be dependent on you or the illustrious North money?"

His eyes hardened. "Will's dead and you're his pregnant widow. We're stuck with each other whether we like it or not."

With a coldly withering glance, he shut down on her.

He was impossibly controlling. How would she endure living with him for a week? He was an arrogant beast who thought awful things about her and was determined to control her life and her child's. Why the hell had she cooked anything for him? Why had she talked to him, told him about her family, shared her dreams?

Steamed, more at herself than at him, she stood up. Just as he was about to sink his fork into her soufflé again, she grabbed his plate.

"Hey!" he cried.

At his yelp of dismay, she grinned wickedly. When he leaped to his feet, she whirled and scraped the last of his soufflé into the sink. While he sulked, she turned on the faucet to wash it down the drain.

"That was cold," he said.

"You deserved it. We've wasted enough time on idle chitchat. I have a bistro to run. Why don't I pack, so I can get back here?"

"The doctor said you're to take the week off."

"I will. I'll just sit around here and supervise, juggle a few bills."

"The hell you will. If you think I'm going to let you stress yourself and endanger your baby just because you're stubborn, you don't know me at all."

"Look—you stress me out more than anyone or anything here ever could. I need a break from you. Okay? The last thing I need is a bullying babysitter. Don't you have an empire to run, or someone else to boss around?"

"I have quite a lot to do—as a matter of fact—but nothing matters to me more than Will's child."

"The North heir."

"*My* heir."

"Exactly," she whispered. She felt her stomach twist. "The only reason your heir matters is because he stands to inherit your precious fortune. Money is all you care about."

"You know me so well."

As Michael's gaze followed the steep, Victorian staircase up several stories into the gloom, he heard Bree struggling to get her key out of the heavy interior door that had closed behind them.

When she caught up with him, he whirled on her. "You are not climbing these stairs."

"I promise, I'll take it very slowly."

"Not in your condition! Your doctor said no to subways because of all the stairs, remember?"

"I don't remember all that."

"Well, I do, so you're to sit down on the stairs and make me an itemized list of everything you'll need for next week."

"Michael, it will be so much easier if I just go upstairs and grab—"

"You're going to give me your key, and wait here while I go up and pack for you."

"You couldn't possibly find—"

"I run an empire, remember."

"Hey, maybe I don't want you going through my things."

"You prefer to risk the baby?"

"You're making me feel like a child."

"The sooner you stop acting like one and start writing that list, the sooner we get out of here." He pulled a pen and a pad out of his pocket.

Sulkily she sat down and scribbled out a list. Then she told him that she hid her key outside her door in the bowl of potpourri. As he climbed the stairs, she dutifully stayed where she was.

Three Victorian flights were more like five modern flights, he thought as he let himself into her apartment. It was tinier, messier and much shabbier than he'd imagined for someone who had such a flair for color. He had to call her cell to ask her where her duffel bag might be when it wasn't in its proper place. Once he found it, he charged into her bathroom and pulled panties and bras and a transparent nightgown off hooks where they'd been drying. Next he scooped up toiletries and a large bottle of prenatal vitamins. Then he made his way to her bedroom so he could rummage in her chest of drawers and closet.

With an eye for what he thought would look best on her, he chose several outfits and pairs of shoes. When he was through packing he even watered her plants, a task she'd forgotten to put on her list.

"You're very bossy," she said after he'd rejoined her at the bottom of the stairs and she'd checked the contents of her duffel bag.

"I get that a lot. Mind if I take that as a compliment?"

"No. And you're fast. What you picked out…will do."

"That last's definitely a compliment."

"You're grasping at straws."

"With you, I have to. So—how come you didn't have a single picture of Will in your apartment?"

She paled. "They…they're all on my computer. I needed to print one and frame it. I just hadn't gotten around to it, I guess."

When she lowered her eyes, he sensed there was more, way more.

But what? What was she hiding?

Michael stared at his lawyer before flipping another page of the legal document in disgust. What had he expected?

Feeling acute betrayal on behalf of his trusting brother, Michael flung the papers down onto his desk.

Nothing like a legal contract in black-and-white to spell out the truth.

No doubt about it, just like his own ex-wife Anya, Bree's sole motive for marrying Will had been getting her hands on his money.

"You're saying the day Will married Bree, *on his wedding day,* he signed documents to set up a million-dollar trust fund to care for her baby? And his new bride was with him in this office when he did it? She cosigned?"

His attorney ran a hand through his shock of silver hair and then nodded. "I wasn't there when they came in, but that's her notarized signature. They had new wills drawn up, as well."

When inspired, a conniver like her sure worked fast.

"You knew about all this, and you didn't tell me?"

"I didn't draft the documents myself. You were still dealing with that mess in Shanghai when Will told me he'd hired an independent attorney who would be sending the documents over for me to review before Will and his bride signed them."

"Can we break them?"

"You can take anything to court, but if she puts up a fight, which she probably will, it will cost you more than it's worth," Roger said. "I don't have to tell you that family lawsuits are very unpleasant emotionally as well as financially. When I expressed my concerns about these documents, Will made it very clear that this was what he wanted. In fact, he insisted that I promise to tell you that very thing if anything should happen to him. He seemed very anxious to take care of his child."

"He mentioned me, did he?"

"He did. As for the new will, he left the bulk of his estate to his friend Tony. But in the event of Tony predeceasing him, which is what has happened, you still get everything as in his old will."

Now that was odd. Michael would have thought a man anxious enough to sign his will on his wedding day would have left his brand-new wife everything.

"Except Bree gets her million dollars," Michael said.

"Not exactly. He left her nothing. She's merely the trustee of her baby's fund."

"Which means," Michael said, "that she can do exactly what she wants with the money."

"There will be a second million deposited into the trust when the baby's a month old."

"Thanks for clarifying where things stand," Michael said coldly.

"Anytime. Is there anything else I can do for you?"

"Do you know how much my brother had sunk into Chez Z?"

"I have it here." Roger handed him another document. "My best guess is, he'd given her close to a quarter of a million dollars."

Michael whistled as he studied the document.

"Anything else?"

Michael shook his head. "I can't thank you enough for coming by."

When the other man stood, Michael arose and extended his hand. He didn't sit down again until the older man shut the door behind him.

Bree made Will sign the documents on their wedding day. *On their wedding day.* And she'd called Michael cold.

On top of the will, his brother had given her bistro nearly a quarter of a million dollars.

Michael found the whole situation oddly disturbing. Why had his brother left everything to Tony, a man he'd never even bothered to introduce to Michael or to the rest of his family, instead of to his new wife? And how had Bree felt about that?

Still puzzled by the documents, Michael buzzed Eden, his secretary, who filled him in on his various meetings for the day. Before ending their conference, she reminded him that he was having drinks at a midtown bar with a Mr. Todd Chase at 6:00 p.m.

"Oh, that's right. Todd."

"Who's Todd?" she asked.

"An old friend from the University of Houston," Michael said. "I completely forgot he was in town." Todd had taken a job as the CEO of a huge investment-banking firm that needed a genius at the helm, and Michael had invited him for drinks to celebrate.

"You had me make a notation that he's bringing his wife, and you're taking a date. Someone named Natalia."

Damn. The last person he felt like dealing with was Natalia. Although she was beautiful, she was extremely high-maintenance. A model, she always made sure the media knew her every move. He'd seen her a couple of times before he'd left for Shanghai, mostly to send Bree a message that he was through with her.

He'd forgotten all about his "date" with Natalia tonight. Knowing her, she'd have a media event planned.

"Do you want me to call and remind her for you?" Eden asked.

"No." There'd be hell to pay with the needy, supersensitive Natalia if he didn't make the call himself—especially since he hadn't been in touch with her for nearly a month.

Even though she was one of the world's most beautiful and celebrated women, she was riddled with self-doubt. A perfectionist, she saw only her imperfections and needed vast amounts of reassurance. Strangely, disillusioned as he was with what he'd discovered today, he would have much preferred to go home early to Bree.

* * *

Bree didn't do helpless well, so she felt guilty doing nothing as she sat in her tiny office amid piles of paper she very badly needed to organize, one eye on the nightly news and the other on Bijou and their undermanned kitchen staff. Several people had begged to be off tonight, so Bijou was dashing about shouting orders and screaming ineffectively at the waiters and prep cooks.

The closer it got to the dinner hour, the more pressured Bree felt to help. But she had promised Michael she'd go to his place at 6:30 sharp. She knew that was the bistro's busiest time, and didn't want to be tempted to pitch in. Glancing at her watch, she realized she'd be late if she didn't leave immediately.

Just as she was about to grab her purse and turn off the television, Michael's tall, dark image blazed on the screen. He strode out of one of the city's flashiest hotels with a beautiful blonde dressed in a sheath of skintight silver who smiled as reporters swarmed them.

While the newscaster babbled excitedly about Natalia's seven-figure contract with a major cosmetics company and Michael's multigazillion-dollar project in Shanghai, Bree couldn't take her eyes off the sexy supermodel, whose hands were all over Michael.

Bree turned the television off and flung the remote aside so roughly it smashed against her desk, causing its back to pop open and its batteries to spill out.

She caught them before they hit the floor. With shaking fingers she grabbed the remote and stuffed the little suckers back inside.

She didn't care who Michael dated…or how damn beautiful the woman was. He was nothing to her, nothing other than her bossy brother-in-law who'd used her doctors to bully her into moving in with him so he could run her life for the rest of this week.

He was nothing to her.

He's the father of my unborn child.

That was an unfortunate fact she would have preferred to forget.

No way was she going back to Michael's stuffy building and endure the snooty stares of his doorman and then sit in her suite behind his kitchen all alone while he was with the incredibly beautiful, immensely successful Natalia. No way. She'd stay where she was, with people who loved her and approved of her.

Just because he was her brother-in-law and a North, just because he was immensely wealthy and lived in a palatial building on Fifth Avenue, just because he was the father of her baby didn't mean he had the right to dictate to her.

He would have to earn that right.

It was well after 8:00 p.m. when Michael let himself into his dark penthouse. He'd worked with a vengeance at the office and had been five minutes late to pick up Natalia. Then she'd embarrassed him by sulking in front of Todd at the bar because he hadn't called or texted or sent flowers during the past month. When he hadn't invited her to dinner after they'd said goodbye to Todd and his wife, she'd thrown a fit.

Unfortunately, Michael had been so exhausted from his sleepless night in that chair beside Bree's bed and his long day at work, he'd exploded.

Forgetting how sensitive she was to even the slightest criticism, he'd said something about beauty, even hers, being impermanent and had advised her to let him or someone like him invest her money for her.

"My money! Is that all you care about? You don't think my beauty will last. Are you saying you don't love me, either?"

When he hadn't argued that point, she'd puffed up in hurt and indignation and slapped him. "You don't love me!"

"You don't love me, either."

"Why, oh, why does everybody hate me?"

Then Natalia had broken up with him.

She was such a child. He'd hurt her, and he hadn't meant to. Tomorrow he'd send her a note apologizing and proclaiming her beauty along with roses and a parting gift.

Okay—so he was buying her off.

But the only good thing that had come out of their unpleasant night together was that she'd taken his mind off Bree and Will for a little while.

Still, no matter what had happened today or what he'd found out about Bree, she was injured and pregnant and he'd sworn he'd take care of her and the baby.

So here he was, home early to check on a houseguest he would have preferred to strangle.

He removed his jacket and threw it on a chair. Crossing his great room, he went to the bar where he poured himself a single shot of vodka. As he bolted it, the silence of the immense room ate at him.

Earlier, before he'd left for the office, Bree had his stereo going as well as her television because she said his penthouse felt like a tomb.

Where the hell was she?

He needed a night's sleep to calm down from the attorney's news. The last thing he wanted to do was deal with Bree and risk more feminine drama, but he strode across the living room, down the hall and past his vast kitchen until he reached the guest suite.

The space was on the lower floor and had originally been designed as a maid's quarters. Since he didn't have a live-in maid, and since Bree had a thing against elevators and he had a thing against her climbing stairs in her delicate condition, he'd suggested she use the suite.

He was about to raise his hand to knock when he realized her door was ajar. Slightly alarmed, he pushed it open.

Her suite was dark. Flipping on the lights, he tore through the rooms, calling her name, first in anger, then in mounting concern.

Her duffel bag was open. Colorful, silky clothes and sparkly costume jewelry that she hadn't bothered to put away spilled onto the floor. Lacy bras and panties littered the top of the dresser. It didn't take long to determine she was out or to figure out where she probably was—Chez Z.

Damn it. She had a baby to think about. What didn't she get about her condition and the gravity of her injuries?

Did she want to lose Will's baby?

Slamming his glass down, he spun on his heel and tore out of his penthouse.

Five

When Michael didn't see Bree in the noisy, crowded dining room of Chez Z, he found Bijou, who was pouring ice water into stemmed glasses.

"Is she still here?"

Bijou's brows shot upward. "I told her to go home an hour ago, but she's in a mood."

"In a mood?"

"Everybody says she's super-dedicated to saving Z's restaurant for the family and the investors, but I call it stubborn. Still, she did take it easy all day...until this evening...around 6:30. I don't know what set her off. I told her to go home. When she was obstinate, I thought about calling you, but I misplaced your business card. And then things got busy."

He gave Bijou another business card for future reference. "Where is she now?"

"We had several plates returned to the kitchen because the scallops were soggy, so she's in the back teaching

Mark how to dry scallops properly before he sautés them so they won't taste as if they've been steamed. The poor thing's nearly dead on her feet, but will she listen?"

Dead on her feet.

A pang of sympathy shot through him. Then he grew angrier. Whose fault was it, if she was tired?

Irritated, he swept past Bijou, banging through the kitchen doors in his impatience to find her.

When a startled Bree looked up, her eyes blank and shadowed with exhaustion, another wave of concern hit him.

"You're coming home with me now," Michael said.

"Your penthouse in that stuffy building is so not home."

"I'm not here to play word games," Michael said firmly.

She turned her back on him and faced the line of people in white behind her. "Ignore him. Don't let him break your concentration."

"If you don't get your purse and whatever else you think you need tonight in two seconds flat and come with me, I swear I'm going to pick you up and carry you out of here."

She whirled. "Just because you think you rule the world, and you practically do, you aren't the only one who has a job to do, you know. I have one, too."

"This isn't about our work. You're pregnant. You're the only survivor from a wreck that killed three people yesterday. You were injured."

"Minimally. I'm young and strong."

"Young and strong? You're exhausted and grieving. A corpse has more color and life than you do."

"Your heir is perfectly safe," she said.

"Step away from that stove," he ordered.

"He's right. Go on home, darlin'," Mark said behind her. "We've got your back. I swear. We won't let you down."

With Mark's betrayal, the last spark of resistance in her eyes dulled. "Okay," she whispered wearily to Mark, and then to Michael she said, "You win. I'm coming. Just don't touch me. Don't you dare put a hand on me or try to pick me up."

Although she was trying to stand up to him, she looked like she was about to shatter.

"Wouldn't dream of it," he drawled softly.

He felt close to some edge himself, dangerously out of control. Why was it that only she affected him like this?

It was a beautiful night. The moon was big, the air crisp. Not that either of them was enjoying the loveliness of the black velvet sky lit by starlight.

No, the air in the dark interior of his silver Mercedes fairly crackled with white-hot tension as Michael whipped through the crowded streets. He hadn't spoken to her since they'd left the restaurant, and he was driving so fast, Bree was almost afraid to say anything for fear of distracting him. His hands clenched the wheel. His eyes narrowed as he focused on the flying vehicles on all sides of them and the changing traffic signals ahead.

Suddenly the silence felt so thick and smothering she couldn't breathe. Reaching forward, she turned on his radio, moving the dial instinctively until she found hard rock, hoping the heavy beat would make it impossible for her to think about Michael's pulsing fury.

With a hard jerk of his wrist, he switched the radio off.

"So—do you want to talk to me or not?" she said after a long interval of unendurable, hostile silence.

"No. I just prefer silence to your insane music."

"Well, I find your bullying and your rage oppressive."

"Deal with it—since you're the cause of it."

"You didn't need to drive all this way to get me, you know. You could have called me or something."

"Right," he growled. "And just like that, you would have come running."

Glad she'd goaded him, she fought not to smile.

The big silver car shot through the dark like a missile, narrowly missing a biker, who shot the finger at them.

When she heaved in a breath and clenched her door, she realized how shaken she must still be from the accident.

"Hey, shouldn't you slow down before you kill us or some innocent courier?"

"You're so self-destructive I'm surprised you care," he said, but after glancing at her, he lifted his foot off the accelerator fractionally.

"Oh, because if I don't do exactly what you say, I'm self-destructive?" she persisted, trying to ignore her fear of the other cars.

"How long were you at the bistro?"

"All day."

"Exactly." His single word punched the air with such force it took all her courage to dare a shocked glance at his broad-shouldered profile.

"Quit sulking. Everybody works better if I'm there," she said. "I owe a lot of people a lot of money. I don't want to let them down."

"Right—you're so *dedicated*."

His scowl told her he was still furious.

"What's the matter with you? I thought you were on a date, enjoying yourself with that model. Having the time of your life."

"*What?*" The single word ripped into her like an explosion.

Before she knew what he was doing, he'd jerked the car across two lanes, to the curb, amid a barrage of blaring horns. Once they stopped, he engaged his warning lights.

"What's wrong with you?" she cried.

"*You!* Do you think I want you in my life? Want you

haunting my every thought? I drove myself all day at the office in the hope I could forget about you and the way you used your charm to blindside my brother. The poor fool took off his seat belt to save you. *He's dead because of you!*"

His cruel words hit their intended mark. She'd tormented herself with the same thought, but she swallowed tightly and held her head high.

"Hey," she said, "while I was in my office—resting *obediently*—who should I see but you? On TV. With one of the world's most beautiful women. Natalia Somebody Or Other."

"I had a late business meeting. She was my date."

"Right. Well, you didn't look the least bit haunted to me. You weren't going to be at your penthouse, so why should I go over there and sit around all by myself dwelling on Will and Tony when you were out having fun?"

"Fun? You think you know everything about me, do you?"

"I know you want to be seen with women like her, that you date them or collect them…probably just to enhance your image because you don't have a heart."

"Collect them? No heart? So—now I'm inhuman, too?"

"I know that the only reason you slept with me was to make Will hate me because you were protecting his precious money…and your own."

When he thought about the trust fund she'd acquired the day of her marriage, her holier-than-thou attitude grew intolerable.

"With sharks like you out there, someone had to protect it."

"See—you don't care about me at all! Why are you so concerned about what I'm doing?"

"*I don't care?* You think I don't care?" He felt out of

control, on dangerous ground, but he couldn't back down. *He cared too much.* That was the problem.

"I felt lost and miserable. The restaurant took my mind off things. So what if I didn't go to your penthouse? You had Natalia to distract you, didn't you?"

"Shut up. Forget Natalia. She means nothing to me."

"Well, she had her hands all over you, and you seemed to be eating it up."

"You don't know anything about me. About what I feel."

"What do you feel then?"

"Disappointment. Disillusionment…that you're as bad as I believed you to be."

"Oh…." She *so* didn't like him.

Then why did his assessment crush her?

Unsnapping his seat belt and then hers, he yanked her toward him roughly.

"Quit it! I don't want to be manhandled by someone who dislikes me."

"I wish I disliked you," he muttered. "Even though I know what you are, on some level I fell for the sweet innocent you pretended to be that first night and can't get her out my head."

"The last thing I want to think about is that night!" When she balled her hands and pushed against his massive chest, his mouth closed over hers.

"I don't want to kiss you when you're angry like this, when you say such awful things," she whispered as his hard, determined lips took hers again. "Don't do this."

His breath came in harsh rasps. "I don't want Natalia, you little fool," he said. His tongue pushed inside her mouth. "I want you," he said. "In spite of everything that's hard and cold about you, I want you." He kissed her again.

Beneath his anger, Bree felt the fierce desire inside

him. Natalia or no Natalia, he was as lonely as Bree was and driven by needs he fought but couldn't deny.

It was as if they were both two lost creatures hemmed in by this crowded city where neither could find a haven anywhere but with each other. Which was ridiculous. She wasn't lost; she had a family. And he hated her. He was a heartless money machine who dated gorgeous supermodels for show. She didn't even like him.

So why was his mouth fused to hers, and why had she stopped fighting?

Why was he kissing her like a man who would die if he couldn't have her?

Her hurt over his poor opinion of her, her hurt over Natalia, was forgotten. Dazed, her arms closed around his neck, and she pulled him closer, communicating with her seeking lips and tongue that she wanted him as desperately as he wanted her.

He kissed her until she couldn't breathe. Until his anger dissolved, and his kisses grew sweeter. Then his lips moved lingeringly down her throat.

After an infinite time of shared kisses and feverishly whispered love words passed between them, he dragged his mouth from hers and stared at her in the dark. Again, the intensity in his gaze communicated his need. The same wildness that pulsed in his blood, pulsed in hers. Confused, she didn't think she'd ever seen so much misery, shock or passion in anyone's eyes as she saw in his.

How could he, of all people, blow away everything she knew to be sensible and logical and make her want him with every fiber of her being?

What if he's not as bad as I thought or as bad as he thinks he is? He came after me tonight, didn't he? He came after me because he cares.

If you think that, you're a fool—you never want to see the truth about people when your heart's involved.

But my heart's not involved. I won't let it be.

She didn't know what to say or do. Apparently neither did he. Without offering an apology or explanation, he turned off the warning lights, snapped on his seat belt and ordered her to fasten hers. Too shaken by what had happened to protest, she obeyed him.

They drove through a tangle of Manhattan traffic, most of it jostling taxicabs, in tense silence until they reached Fifth Avenue. Then, even as he was racing around the front of his Mercedes to open her door, she jumped out. Slamming it, she stalked silently past him and his uniformed doorman, although she did blush when the man's eyebrows rose in what she imagined to be disapproval.

She'd forgotten how impossibly stuffy Michael's building was with its rules that had been dreamed up for decades—to keep out the wrong *elements*.

Michael caught up to her at the elevator. "Behave," he whispered, "at least, while we're in the lobby."

Ignoring the splendor of marble and chandeliers, she shut her eyes and swallowed a deep breath. When she opened her eyes she focused on the bronze elevator doors.

Wrong move.

Elevators! Why did he *have* to live in a penthouse? Why had she ever agreed to stay here? Even for one night?

Her wild eyes must have betrayed her fear because he said, "You ever going to tell me why you're scared of elevators?"

"Maybe someday," she said trying to make her voice light.

After her cousin Jeremy had locked her in that dark closet for hours, she'd disliked all closed spaces, but a second childhood experience had further refined her phobia so that elevators had become her number one terror.

When her mother had taken Bree along to sign a paper at her attorney's office, Bijou had gotten off on the attorney's floor while talking to another woman. Bree had dropped a bunny and rushed back inside the elevator for it. Unfortunately, the doors had closed and the elevator had whooshed upward. She'd become too hysterical to punch the buttons, and the thing hadn't stopped until she'd reached the top floor. By then she'd been lost and alone and terrified she'd never find her mother.

Michael must have sensed her desire to bolt when the elevator doors opened because his hand closed gently over her elbow and he nudged her inside. When the bronze doors shut them inside, she clenched her hands and shut her eyes and tried not to think that they were shooting up dozens and dozens of stories in a closed box at rocket speed.

Sensing her growing panic as the elevator ascended, he muttered something that might have been meant to reassure her, but she felt too on edge to comprehend anything.

She didn't realize she'd begun to shake until his arms closed around her, and he drew her close to steady her. She should have fought him, but instead she clung gratefully.

Then the doors opened, and she came back to herself. Pushing free of him, she all but jumped out into his elegant hall. When he caught up with her at his door and unlocked it, she raced toward her suite and shut herself inside. Sagging against the door, she waited for her heart to slow down.

No sooner could she breathe normally than she heard him in the kitchen, slamming cabinet doors. When the rich aroma of bacon and eggs frying and bread toasting wafted into her room, she realized that even though she'd been at the bistro, she hadn't eaten in hours.

Her stomach growled. Why couldn't he have gone upstairs so she wouldn't have to think about him out there enjoying eggs and bacon while she was trapped in here?

When he kept stomping about, she removed her phone

from her purse and attached it to a set of external speakers. Soon the suite was flooded with pulsating rock. She'd shower. By then maybe he would have finished his meal and gone upstairs and she could safely raid his kitchen.

Hearing the roar of her rock music, Michael's thoughts turned to the woman in his guest suite.

Hell, why couldn't he forget the taste of her sweet mouth in the car? Forget the sharp bite of her nails digging into his back?

He wanted her, his brother's pregnant widow, this woman he'd sworn he'd protect.

But she was injured, and a gold digger, so he fought not to think of her stripping in her bathroom, showering and then slipping into her bed wearing the transparent nightgown he'd selected. Or maybe she'd wear nothing.

It drove him crazy to remember how warm and soft she'd felt curled against him that night after they'd made love. He'd wanted to hate her, but he hadn't been able to. The truth was, he'd give anything to hold her close like that again.

Who was she? The gold digger or the sweet voluptuous siren who'd enchanted him with her innocence?

Who had seduced who? He still didn't know.

Had Michael really been her first? *Had he?* Why did he care? She'd wasted no time getting herself pregnant so Will would marry her.

But Michael's questions wouldn't stop. Something was wrong with his picture of her. The pieces to the puzzle didn't fit.

Was she dedicated to the bistro for noble reasons? Or was she as low and conniving and greedy as he kept telling himself? She'd damned sure signed those documents on her wedding day. Did she kiss him in the car merely because he was rich?

Hell, she'd damn sure responded when he came on to her.

Michael's mind and emotions raged as he tore his hand through his hair. He had to get a grip.

When he finished his dinner, he rinsed his dishes and left them in the sink for Betsy Lou, his cleaning lady, who came every morning to tidy up.

Long after he'd climbed the stairs and endured a long, icy shower, he thought about Bree. Only in sleep did he have what he craved, when she came to him in his dreams and lowered her naked body over his and did everything that he desired.

Just as he was about to find his release, he heard a scream from two floors below.

Six

One minute Bree was sound asleep and happily dreaming that she was back in Michael's Mercedes wrapped in his arms as he whispered such sweet words.

Then her dream twisted, and she was shut out of his Mercedes. Standing on the sidewalk. Feeling lost and abandoned, she watched him inside his car kissing the beautiful Natalia whose slanting eyes glittered in triumph as she stared at Bree over Michael's shoulder.

Hurt washed over Bree. Thrashing against her sheets and pillows, she came awake in Michael's moonlit guest suite.

Sitting up amid tangled covers, she gave herself a minute to settle. Then she forced herself to think about her dream because she believed that dreams were a form of truthful self-talk. If she didn't think about it immediately the most telling details would recede.

She chewed on her bottom lip. The dream was worrisome. It told her that she wanted Michael even though she couldn't believe he really wanted her.

So what else was new?

As she lay there feeling frustrated and unable to sleep, a fierce craving for sardines—for anything salty and fishy—compelled her to arise, shrug into the enormous man's robe she'd found earlier in her closet and pad into his kitchen.

Remembering seeing a can of sardines sitting right by a big jar of peanut butter in the pantry, she found them easily. Smiling, she grabbed the can.

A sandwich would be good. A sandwich with mayo and pickles and maybe mustard and onions. Now that she thought about it, a white creamy cheese…Camembert. Almost tasting the rich, gooey French cheese, she headed toward his refrigerator. Her head buzzing with food fantasies, she wondered if Michael had chips, as well.

Disappointed when she found only an old onion, some cheddar and a jar of mayo but no pickles—she could never be with a man who could live without pickles—she grabbed the mayo. But as she turned to close the door the overlong sleeve of her borrowed robe snagged on the handle. The mayo jar along with the cheddar cheese and onion slipped out of her hand and smashed to jagged bits on the granite floor. Off balance, she grabbed for the counter and dropped everything else into the mess. When she moved to start picking up after herself, a shard of glass sliced into her heel and she screamed.

She froze when she saw the pool of scarlet oozing out of her torn heel. Just when she spotted his paper towels on the far side of the kitchen, a bare-chested Michael, wearing only blue pajama bottoms, stepped into the kitchen.

Why did he have to be so heart-stoppingly sexy? "Stay where you are," he ordered in that tone that made her feel gauche and then bristle defensively. His black eyes darkened dangerously at the sight of her blood as he strode toward her.

"I don't want to be a bother. I can take care of myself," she protested.

"Right," he grumbled testily as he stared at her bloody foot. "I can see that."

"I was just about to get the paper towels—"

"Do think I would risk you cutting yourself again before we even know how bad it already is?"

"I'll be fine."

"I intend to make sure of that."

Lifting her into his arms as if her weight was nothing, he crushed her against his chest as he carried her out of the kitchen and then down the hall.

Pressed so close to his hard bare flesh, she couldn't help but inhale his clean male scent. The smell brought back the night she'd spent in his arms when they'd made love. He was too virile and too sexy when he was being so nice, and she was a sucker for nice.

"Put me down," she whispered even as he headed for the stairs. "Blood is dripping behind us."

"Good thing I have stone floors and a maid coming in the morning."

"Only one maid for this place?"

"I'm not nearly as messy as you are."

Stung, maybe because she could see that about him, she rushed to her own defense. "My apartment isn't always the way it was when you saw it. I…was sort of… preoccupied last month."

"I wasn't criticizing you. I was stating a fact. Do you think I care about your apartment?"

"Put me down. Where do you think you're going? What are you doing?"

"I need to clean up your foot, and the nearest bathtub

is on the second floor. Since you don't like elevators, I'm carrying you up."

"But I can handle elevators," she said testily, perversely annoyed at his thoughtfulness.

"Right." He grinned down at her. "You do them so well."

"I practice."

"How? Like one would a piano?"

Her lips twitched. She fought not to smile. "Sort of."

He wasn't nice. She didn't like him. She didn't find him amusing. He was making fun of her neurotic fear, a fear that was perfectly logical considering what had happened to her. She should be furious.

But it felt much too marvelous to be in his arms, much too nice to have him pretending that he cared.

Be careful. He's tricky. He was nice the night he seduced you. And here you are—pregnant.

As he climbed the stairs, he went more slowly at the top, and she noted with satisfaction that his breath came a little harder.

She smiled. So he was human after all.

When he reached the lovely white marble bathroom accented with gold, he helped her sit down on the edge of the tub. Kneeling, he ran his hands over her ankle before he lifted her foot and examined it.

"It's not too deep," he said as he gently removed a couple of pieces of glass. "I think I got them all. Don't watch, or this will hurt more," he said.

"What?"

"Shut your eyes. I need to make sure I got all the glass."

"Ouch," she cried when he yanked out a third sliver.

"Sorry about that. It was a little deeper than the others. But I think that's it. I'll just wash your foot now and bandage it."

She'd never imagined a man stroking her foot could

make her feel so sexy, especially when she was bleeding, but apparently he could make any activity sexy.

"If you give me your first-aid kit, then I can take it from here."

"No," he snapped in that forceful tone that could so annoy her. Only it didn't annoy her now.

Turning on the water, he held his hand under the stream until it was cool enough to suit him.

"That's too cold," she cried when he stuck her foot into the flow.

But his grip on her ankle remained firm. "Hold still. Cold water helps blood clot."

"I think you just enjoy torturing me—Dr. North."

"That, too," he teased. Ignoring her, he let the icy water stream over her heel for another minute. Then he found towels. After drying her foot, he deftly applied ointment, butterfly stitches, and a bandage.

"There," he said, after he'd finished. "I don't think we need to go to the E.R."

Feeling a little chagrined, she studied her expertly bandaged foot and then the wreck they'd made of the lovely bathroom. But after the car accident, she felt truly grateful that he'd taken care of her. The last place she wanted to visit was an E.R.

"Thank you," she whispered.

"You're welcome. Now what exactly were you doing in my kitchen in the middle of the night?"

It started with a dream about you kissing Natalia, she thought. Aloud she said, "It couldn't possibly matter."

"Tell me."

For no reason at all she found herself staring at the black hair on his bare chest in fascination. "I woke up with this…er…craving."

When he turned, she couldn't resist watching the play of his muscles as he folded the towels.

Brilliance flashed in his black eyes when he glanced at her lips. "For what?"

Heat crept up her throat before she could avert her eyes. "If I tell you, you'd better not laugh at me."

With some effort he made his handsome face severe. "I won't—I promise."

"A sardine sandwich."

He struggled not to laugh, he really did, but he couldn't help himself. The rich rumble of amusement made him seem slightly less formidable.

"You promised," she whispered.

"Well, since I broke my promise—I owe you. After all that you've gone through tonight and now my sin of laughter, you damn sure can't go back to bed without your sardine sandwich."

"It's okay. The cheese and onion are ruined, and you don't have anything else in your refrigerator. And I really have to have cheese and onions with sardines…"

"Trust me. There's more onions and cheese in Manhattan."

"It's late. I don't want to be a bother. I should let you go to bed."

"I'm making you a sardine sandwich, the sardine sandwich slathered in cheese and onions of your dreams… whether you agree to eat it or not."

She considered before she said yes. "I'm agreeing to this only because you are too obstinate to argue with. But—I'm taking the elevator down."

"You sure about that?" When he grinned, she nodded fervently. "It's only one floor. What could possibly go wrong?"

"Famous last words. So, do we go down together? Or one by one?" he asked, humoring her.

"One by one. That way if either of us gets trapped, the other can call for help."

"Right," he said. "Just for the record, there's a phone in my elevator, if you're ever caught in it alone."

"But the phone could malfunction."

"Are you always a worst-case-scenario thinker?"

"Always when it comes to elevators."

In the kitchen he cleaned up the mess, salvaging what he could, which was the can of sardines. The rest he threw in the garbage while she sat at his table and watched.

"Tell me exactly what you want on your sandwich, and I'll call my doorman."

"Can you do that? Will he do that? In the middle of the night?"

"Just tell me what you want."

"You must be impossibly spoiled."

"I pride myself on it."

When she told him the ingredients, he wrinkled his nose.

"Don't laugh at me again."

He smiled. "I believe you *are* pregnant."

He picked up his phone and made the call. When he hung up, he said, "One sardine sandwich will appear as if by magic in fifteen minutes."

Her opinion of his stuffy building and his uptight staff went up a notch.

"I've been thinking about your restaurant," he said while they waited for her sandwich. "I could help you turn it around."

She remembered he'd said that before—if she became his mistress.

"But why would you? I mean…" She frowned. "What would you want in return?"

"Nothing. You're my brother's widow. My brother sunk a quarter of a million dollars into it."

Her eyes widened. "That much? No wonder you're—"

"Didn't you know?" His voice was grim. "Really, you should know these things."

"You're right. I should have known. It was just that Z handled all that."

As he studied her, she would have given anything to be able to read his mind.

"Okay, then," she said, knowing she'd be a fool not to let him help her. "What exactly do you have in mind?"

"For starters, I'd send over an expert in the restaurant business to evaluate what's going on. Have you ever heard of Luke Coulter?"

"The genius with seafood on TV? Who hasn't?"

Not only was Luke Coulter a successful restaurateur, he was one of New York's most renowned celebrity chefs. Z had resented that she'd been hooked on one of Luke's cooking shows.

"Z considered him a fierce rival. Bijou knows how he felt about Luke."

"Well, you're not Z, and you're in serious trouble. From what I've read, Z was not only creative, he was practical. I'm sure he'd want you to do whatever it takes to succeed. Look, I recently helped Luke restructure the financing of his latest restaurant, which, as you know, is another big hit. So he owes me a favor or two. Why don't I ask him to come over? He'll take a look at your books and your costs, watch your staff, observe how you handle them, sample your food and then give you advice. You don't have to take it—if you don't think it applies to your bistro."

Had Will really invested a quarter of a million dollars in Chez Z? No wonder Michael thought she was out for all she could get. How much did she owe her other investors? He was right. She *should* know these things.

Fresh tension ate at her. The only thing she knew for sure was how much she didn't know.

Z had been in charge of the numbers. She had only a

vague idea about her food costs and the specifics of her financial situation. She felt a bit defensive at the thought of Michael sending in an expert who might humiliate her. But what was a little humiliation? The bistro was in trouble, and things were getting worse under her management, not better. If she kept on her same path, wouldn't she keep getting the same results?

In the end she decided she owed too much money to too many people to say no. What if Luke could give her a crash course that would help her turn things around?

"Okay," she whispered, her voice low and tight. "Thanks. I'd be happy to hear what he has to say."

Not that she was happy. No, she felt scared and nervy. Fortunately, the doorbell rang.

"Great! Your sardine sandwich is here, and it's right on time."

After Michael brought it to her, they sat down again at his kitchen table. She grew increasingly self-conscious when he smiled as she unwrapped her huge sandwich.

"Don't you want some? This really is much too big for me," she said.

He shook his head. "You're eating for two."

"I could cut it in two and share."

"That's very generous of you. But no."

"I'm absolutely ravenous."

"Enjoy."

When he didn't talk about business anymore, she began to relax. She studied her magnificent sandwich. Appetite and sensuality flooded her as she bit into the crusty bread and sardines.

"Careful," he whispered, handing her a napkin.

She munched happily, savoring the combination of tart mustard, cream cheese and fish.

A few minutes later she'd eaten all she could and was

feeling sick with pleasure when she set her huge sandwich aside.

He smiled. "Had enough? Okay, then. Run along to bed. I'll tidy up."

"Why are you being so nice to me all of a sudden?" she said, feeling suspicious again.

"Maybe because you were hurt in my home. Suddenly I've been thinking maybe we should call a truce. What are we accomplishing by being so rude to each other?"

She stared at him blankly. "You started it."

"I won't argue. So, will you let me end it? What do you think—can we have a truce?"

When she hesitated, his quick, easy grin made her blood heat, made her remember the kisses in the car and the wonderful sandwich he'd ordered for her.

"Come on," he coaxed. "You're always acting like you're the one who's all heart. Show me that you're a tolerant, liberal denizen of the West Side for real."

Knowing she shouldn't let her guard down, she nodded warily as she backed out of the kitchen.

Funny, she'd felt so much safer when he'd acted as though he was dead set against her than she felt when he was helpful and friendly. Was he trying to lower her defenses so he could move in for the kill?

With some effort she recalled his ruthless reputation in business and with women, and how ruthlessly he'd treated her to protect his brother.

His feelings for her hadn't changed. If she were smart, she wouldn't let her defenses down.

Seven

"Have you got those food costs for me yet?"

Luke Coulter smiled down at her as he stepped into her office.

"Not quite. But almost. Like you said, I haven't been keeping very good records, so it's taking me a while."

"It's essential that you know what they are. You can't be fuzzy about numbers or they'll kill you."

When she handed him her notebook, which bulged with dog-eared receipts, he took the jumble and sat down.

Bree couldn't believe how easy it was to work with Luke once Bijou and everybody had warmed up to him. With his shaggy blond hair and affable smile, he seemed like a huge blond bear, albeit a friendly one—most of the time. His quick temper could be formidable.

Michael had brought Luke to the bistro three days ago. After he'd gone over her books and sampled their menu, he'd been fairly brutal with his criticism about everybody, especially her. She and her staff had been doing their best to improve so they could please him.

He'd told her she had to take control of everything—the staff and every creative and financial detail. "You can't please everybody," he'd said. "This is a job—more than a job, it's your career. Your future."

And her baby's future. Who knew if the trust fund Will had so generously set up would be enough?

Besides, Bree didn't come from a family who sat around.

"You have to account for everything you buy and sell, and to know what everything costs so you can price your menu correctly. You can't keep advancing money to all your employees the way you've been doing. Marcie's in to you for five hundred dollars."

"Her little girl's been sick."

"You can't afford to be everybody's lifeboat when the mother ship is sinking. Will you let me talk to your staff about this and establish a new policy?"

"Yes."

He'd managed to squeeze in two more tables in their back dining room, he'd revised their menu and taught her cooks several new, delicious dishes that would be easier and less costly to serve.

"This place can make it," he said as he skimmed her receipts and slashed through several marks she'd made in her notebook with his red pencil. "You have a devoted staff and a loyal clientele. You were doing fine until you lost Z, who kept a firm rein on the finances. Nobody's stealing money. Things haven't slid that far. We don't have that much to tweak."

"You have been incredibly generous with your time. I can't believe you came over right after Michael called you."

Luke's intense blue eyes met hers. "Michael let me know just how important you are to him."

New hope sent hot blood rushing to her cheeks, but she was embarrassed that Luke might read her too accurately.

"It's not what you think. He was just trying to be helpful," she said.

"Michael is never helpful without some motive. I wouldn't underestimate his interest if I were you," Luke said. "Be careful. He's extremely focused, calculating and very, very dangerous. You're not exactly his type."

She looked away. "Right, he prefers models."

"That's not what I meant. Being a man, maybe I read him a little more clearly than you do."

"I'd rather not talk about Michael, if you don't mind."

Luke held up his hands. "Okay. We could go back and forth all day. Michael is not as fierce as he sometimes seems. He was different…before he married Anya. She made him feel as if he was worthless, made him believe no woman would want him for anything other than his wealth. Because of his past, when he felt he was nothing— he can't let those feelings go. Since he divorced her, he has concentrated single-mindedly on business and he's grown harder."

"I don't know why you're telling me this."

He laughed. "Don't you? Michael's unhappy, and you have a soft spot for people who are in trouble. Look at the way you've tolerated Mark's repeated absences even on nights when the bistro is packed or the way you've let Marcie take advantage of your generosity. Michael's like a wounded wild creature, and you want to heal him and tame him. If you aren't careful, he'll gobble you alive."

She felt her cheeks flame. He already had.

"I'm sorry." His voice was kind. "I've said too much. I've got you blushing and upset again. It's just so obvious that the two of you—"

"I'm not upset." But she was.

"Why don't we get back to these fascinating numbers before you are," he murmured drily. He pointed to a number. "Did you know you were spending this much on toothpicks?"

As Michael deftly whipped his silver Mercedes past a honking cab, he parked at the curb just in time to see Bree laughing as she walked out of Chez Z on Luke's arm.

She wore a brightly flowered pink blouse and a flounced lavender skirt. Bright beaded necklaces dangled from her neck, and her waist was sashed with a fringed orange scarf. He remembered how his doorman had smiled and then refused to meet Michael's eyes when he'd left the building with her this morning.

Michael had never seen her looking so lighthearted and happy. He frowned. Yes, he had. She'd been like that the first night he'd flirted with her at the fund-raiser, and then again *that* night at the bistro when he'd seduced her... before he'd told her the truth.

She had a beautiful smile, and he liked the way her golden eyes sparkled and her bright curls tumbled. What he didn't like was thinking that Luke had caused her special radiance.

Michael wanted Bree to look at him like that, to feel that relaxed and happy around him.

When he called out to her, she blushed and gave Luke a quick goodbye hug. Luke's broad, tanned face broke into a grin, too, as he waved at Michael before lumbering off down the crowded sidewalk.

Her eyes wary now, Bree came over to the Mercedes. When Michael opened his passenger window, she leaned down and he caught the fragrance of strawberries mingling with the rich aroma of onions a vendor was grilling on a cart.

"Ready?" he growled.

"I'll just be a minute," she said, smiling. "I need to get my purse."

A few seconds later, purple clutch in hand, she slid breathlessly into his Mercedes.

"How did it go today?" he asked as he'd asked her every day after work. He liked the way it was beginning to feel like a pleasant habit.

"Better and better. Luke's wonderful, like you said."

He knew how things were going because he talked to Luke every night. Luke liked her.

"Great," Michael replied.

"Thanks so much for asking Luke to take a look at the bistro. He's made me see all sorts of things I never saw before."

"I'm glad it's working out." He was, but at the same time, he envied her easy friendship with his friend.

"Yes. But it's been a stressful three days."

"Change is never easy."

"I'm lousy with money, but I'm determined to improve."

When he pulled into the traffic she fell silent and stared out the window.

"How did it go at the doctor's?" he asked.

"Wonderful. He cleared me. The baby's doing great. I'll be fine on my own now."

"He released you a day early, did he?"

He was relieved she was out of danger. Even so, her bright smile and quick nod darkened his mood.

"What did he say about your foot?"

"That you missed your calling, that you would have given him a run for his money if you'd gone into medicine. If we go to your place now, I can pack and be out of your hair in no time. I'm sure you think that's wonderful because you won't have to explain me to your super or your board or come down to breakfast every morning and be bombarded by hard rock anymore."

"Right."

Funny, how little the thought of peace and quiet and indulgent luxury or the approval of a bunch of nosy, up-tight neighbors mattered to him.

He wanted Bree with him in his penthouse. He enjoyed her. He wanted...

What he wanted was dangerous as hell.

"Hey," he said, "I've been making the arrangements for Will's memorial, so there are a few last-minute details we need to go over together."

"Sure. We'll talk while I pack."

That would mean she'd be gone in less than an hour.

He shook his head. "I worked through lunch. Since we both have to eat, why don't I take you somewhere nearby for a quick dinner?"

It annoyed him when she argued, but he easily over-rode her complaints and drove them to one of his favorite restaurants with a magical view of Central Park.

"I thought you said a quick dinner," she said as he let her out at the five-star hotel.

"I know how you love really good food."

"But you shouldn't bring me here," she protested even as they followed the maître d' into an elegant dining room accented with soft, muted colors and the glow of warm candlelight.

"Why not?"

"You said we were going to discuss the memorial ar-rangements."

"All the more reason we should choose an enjoyable place, don't you think?"

"But I'm not dressed properly."

"Nonsense. You look lovely."

"Like a gypsy with too many scarves and bangles."

"A truly lovely gypsy," he replied in a husky tone that was meant to coax and seduce.

This time, he knew her vivid blush, which said *don't you dare try to seduce me over a meal again,* was meant for him instead of Luke.

The waiter seated them by a window with a magnificent view. As soft music tinkled in the background, he watched her as she admired the park and the city. Why did he feel so at home in her presence and so uneasy at the thought of her moving out?

The sky was dark, and the sommelier pointed out the lightning in the far distance.

"Looks like it's going to rain," Michael said. "It may get a little chilly."

"It's that time of year," she replied.

With a smile, Michael ordered the tasting menu and asked the sommelier to bring appropriate wines for each course.

"You know I can't drink right now," she said.

"Wine looks so nice on the table."

"It's extravagant to use wine to decorate."

"You've already told me I'm spoiled. Indulge me. After all, you did agree to that truce, and it is our last night together."

He made quick work of the memorial details and settled down to enjoy her, a pleasure that began even before the waiter brought them a tiny plate with a minuscule porcini tart and other delicacies, including slim slices of lamb tucked into crisp greenery.

"An amuse-bouche, mademoiselle," the waiter said in his perfectly accented French. "*Un petit* gift from the chef."

"This is too exquisite, Michael," she said as soon as the waiter vanished. "I can't believe what I'm tasting. Lamb sorrel, chickweed and dandelion. What an imaginative combination of flavors. So rich…and yet subtle. How do they do this? I feel like I'm in a romantic forest glade."

What the hell was chickweed? He didn't care. All that mattered was that his lovely gypsy was running her tongue over her lips and shutting her eyes in pure, sensual bliss and looking so aroused it was all he could do not to reach across the table and touch her. Too bad they were in a public restaurant instead of her imaginary forest glade.

He caught himself. He knew what she was, so why did he continue to want her in his life?

Next, they had soup. Again, she noted her surprise at its originality. She couldn't stop rhapsodizing about the sharp mint of the chives mingled with the sweetness of the garlic.

"I've never had such an elegant soup made from such basic ingredients," she said in pleasure and awe. "How does he get the flavors to run so deep?"

And so it went, her attitude toward him improving with each marvel that she tasted, each course delighting her more than the last. All around them the rich fragrances of roasted ducks being carved at nearby tables and caramel sauces being drizzled over poached foie gras swirled around them.

The festive and voluptuous richness of the food seemed to make her forget her fear of him. It definitely made him forget his doubts about her.

He was so mesmerized by her sparkling eyes and quick blushes, he scarcely noted the clinks of silverware or the sounds of the other diners' muted laughter. It was as if they were the only two people in the universe.

For dessert he ordered a chocolate napoleon and she ordered warm raspberries followed by vanilla cream, which she ate with the relish of a true gourmet.

"That was all so delicious," she said dreamily as she licked the last of the cream off her spoon with the pink tip of that tongue of hers that he knew could be so wickedly clever at other erotic things.

A hot frisson of desire shot through him. God, he wanted her—wanted her to continue living with him indefinitely, wanted to sleep with her again.

Not that he gave her any indication of his feelings or intentions as he caught the waiter's eye, held up his hand and signaled for their bill.

When it was time to leave, she arose reluctantly, as if she'd enjoyed dining with him as much as he'd enjoyed her.

"That was nice. Really, really nice," she gushed. "You shouldn't have done it, but thank you so much."

He nodded. "I assure you. It was my pleasure."

She was still blushing when the valet brought his car around and Michael helped her slide into the cocoon of the plush, black leather interior.

Her heart beat much too fast as they stepped outside into the damp coolness of the rainy night.

She shouldn't trust him. The meal, which had been too fantastic for words, combined with his attentive, amusing companionship, had her in a dangerously aroused mood. Had he remembered how their first shared meal had primed her senses in the same way? All night his gaze had been so dark and intense, she burned. Had he planned tonight's dinner tonight for some underhanded reason?

She, who never wanted to believe the worst of anyone—not even him—didn't want to think that. He'd been nicer since she'd injured her foot, treating her almost as if he was her friend. He was helping her with the bistro, wasn't he? Maybe he was beginning to like her a little. She felt a dangerous hunger to finish this night of sensual delights in his bed.

Stupid idea. She couldn't let him know.

He helped her into his sleek Mercedes and then slid behind the wheel. When she dared a glance at him, their eyes met and she felt the familiar sizzle. Then her gaze fell to his tight mouth and lingered as she remembered the erotic pleasures those lips were capable of giving her.

Realizing how desperately she longed for him to kiss her, she tore her gaze away and forced herself to focus on the pedestrians that streamed past them on the sidewalks in an endless, colorful flood.

Closing her eyes, she tried to settle down as the big silver car—its tires hissing, its windshield wipers slashing—raced through the rain.

Why had she told him the doctor had released her early? If she hadn't told him, she could have stayed another night. Then maybe she wouldn't feel this perverse urgency, this sense that it might be her last chance to be with him....

When she nervously began to chew on a fingernail, he seized her hand, brought it to his lips and blew a warm breath over her skin.

"Don't!" he admonished. "Your hands are too pretty to ruin."

She yanked the offending hand free and sat on it as stubbornly as a guilty child. All the while, savage, inexplicable desire for him pulsed inside her like a jungle drum. He didn't look at her or speak again, but she was afraid he read her mind because suddenly the air between them grew so tense it sparked.

She wanted him—this impossible, difficult man, who was the secret father of her precious, unborn child. Despite his critical opinion of her and all the other reasons she shouldn't want him, what she wanted, more than anything, was another taste of the forbidden in his bed.

She did *not* have to surrender to temptation.

She *would not* surrender to it. After spending the past

few days with him, her feelings now ran deeper. She was pregnant with his child. If he insulted her this time, the hurt would be even more unbearable than before.

What she *would* do was throw her belongings in her duffel bag and march out of his penthouse with her head held high.

Geography, if not willpower, would save her from herself and this much-too-sexy man.

But she'd forgotten about his elevator.

Eight

Even before the doors of the elevator trapped her inside a tiny box with Michael, her heart was drumming madly in her throat. Then the cage jerked, throwing her against him. She let out a shriek before they shot upward. Her heart spiked to rocket speed, and her wide eyes lifted beseechingly to his.

He put his lips softly against her ear. "Don't be so afraid. You're perfectly safe. This stuffy building, as you call it, is state of the art. I'm on a committee that oversees maintenance issues." His deep voice was a comforting rumble.

"You're right," she said. "I'm fine."

"Let's make sure, why don't we?"

When he caught her closer, her breath hitched.

"Oh, my God. You're as cold as ice and shaking. Don't tell me I'm going to have to give up my penthouse view and move to a lower floor."

She was too foolishly pleased that he'd said he'd move

just for her, too pleased he was holding her close. She pressed herself against his powerful body and gasped when she found him rock hard and fully aroused.

"See, you make me even crazier than this elevator makes you," he whispered. "I can't help myself where you're concerned. I don't care who you are or what you've done."

His words cut. "But I care what you think. If you don't see me as I really am, how can we ever have a real connection? I'm not the bad person you think I am. I'm not your ex-wife, you know," she murmured.

"Why did you bring her up?"

"Luke told me she married you for your money."

"Leave her out of this."

"Did you love her?"

"I don't want to talk about her."

"Well, FYI—*I'm not her*."

His jaw tightened, but he didn't argue.

"I'm just a dull working girl."

"A very attractive one."

"You prefer glamorous."

"Maybe we should concentrate on the present," he muttered bitterly. "You have plenty of charm."

His hard arms tightened around her, and he drew her closer—so close she forgot to be afraid, so close she forgot to be logical or sensible. All that mattered was his fierce power and the raw desire she saw in his eyes.

Her hands wound into his silky black hair. In the restaurant, she'd barely been able to think because of his intense gaze and dominating presence. He'd been so nice for the past three days, and then tonight he'd swept her away with the meal and his sexiness.

He bestowed a soft kiss on her forehead. His gentleness and unexpected kindness lessened her doubts.

Maybe he'd loved his wife and had been hurt. Maybe

if he moved past that he would be able to see Bree more clearly.

"Hold me," she whispered. "Hold me forever."

Standing on her tiptoes, she pressed her lips gently to his chin, tempting him to kiss her for real.

"Now who's seducing who?" he teased in a triumphant tone.

"Don't be so impossibly conceited. As soon as we're off this elevator, I'll remember how terrible you've been to me because you're determined to think me a horrible person, and I'll want to avoid you all over again."

"In that case, I'd better seize the advantage while I still have it."

Pushing her back against the wall, his lips found hers. He kissed her hard and long, plunging his tongue into her mouth again and again. Glorious heat rushed through her veins as she kissed him back. Her heart still knocked, but no longer with fear. Reading her response, he lowered his mouth and kissed her nipple through her shirt.

He lifted his head. Dazed, her heart racing, her mouth open, her eyes met the wildness in his gaze. He was the father of her unborn baby. In spite of all the walls she'd tried to erect against him, she still felt connected to him.

What she really wanted was for him to love their child and maybe someday love her, too. And when he kissed her like this, some idiotic part of her believed that could happen, that he might change some day, that he might see her as she was and be capable of respecting her…of loving her.

When the doors opened, he took her hand and tugged her into his dimly lit hall. He pulled her to his door, which he unlocked. In the entry, he slammed his door and locked it. Then he scooped her into his arms and carried her to her bedroom behind his kitchen, all the while kissing her as if he'd been driven mad by forced abstinence.

"I've been a fool," he whispered, "to deny myself when

you make me feel like this. When no other woman, not ever, has come close to affecting me the way you do. The last few days with you have been hell because I've wanted you so much. I don't care how you manipulated my brother."

She wished he'd quit saying that. Will had demanded she marry him—for the baby's sake.

"I...didn't manipulate Will."

"Shh. I don't care."

"But you don't believe me—"

"I don't care."

But she did. Why couldn't Michael wrap his mind around that?

He was the one who had manipulated her and gotten her pregnant. Will had felt so horrible that his brother had abandoned her that he'd insisted she marry him.

Gently Michael laid her on the bed and then followed her down. She opened her eyes and met the heat of his gaze as he smoothed her hair from her fevered brow and kissed her lips, nose and throat.

"I don't believe in happily ever after," he whispered as his mouth moved lower.

"I know." He didn't listen to her or believe her or even *see* her. "Believe me—I get all the bad stuff about you."

"But I'll give you everything else...if only you'll live here and become my mistress."

"No."

"I want you. Never again will you have to worry about money or losing your bistro. I'll take care of you...and Will's baby. No matter what you say, I know those things matter to you."

Money, she thought but with only the faintest irritation. He wanted her, and he still thought she was so low that he could buy her. Their relationship was just another ne-

gotiation, a deal to him, terms to be established, services
to be rendered for money that would be owed.

She got him, but he didn't get her. Did anything other
than money and closing deals really matter to him?

Money wasn't the most important thing to her. Far
from it. She was going to have his child. To her, *that* was
all-important. Would that even matter to him if he knew?
And if it did, what kind of deal would he propose?

She could not be with a man like him on a permanent
basis.

But being with him tonight was a different matter. Tonight his passionate ardor had stirred her past caring that
he was incapable of giving her what she really wanted for
herself and their child—a lifetime of commitment and
happiness, tenderness, trust and love.

Deliciously pinned beneath his massive body, knowing
he would soon strip her and fill her, felt so pleasurable
she didn't want to think about all the negatives. Dimly
she remembered her plan to pack and run, to get herself
as far away from him as possible. But she was much too
weak to follow such a wise course that might protect her
heart from a man who didn't seem to have one.

So she smiled up at him and kissed him on the lips.

Tonight she would enjoy him. Tomorrow, and all the
dreary tomorrows after that one, would be soon enough
to deny herself.

Tonight, she wanted him far too much to walk away.

She seemed so utterly sweet as she lay radiant beneath
him.

His wallet lay facedown on her bedside table, the
packet of condoms he always carried inside ripped open.
They were naked, and he was buried to the hilt in her
slick, satin heat. He inhaled her sweet strawberry scent.
She was warm, silky, tight—perfect, just as he'd remem-

bered. Better than he'd remembered. Knowing her better
had somehow increased his craving for her.

His heart thudded violently. Primal urgency drove him
to withdraw and plunge into her again and again, to rush,
to finish, to make this an animal conquest instead of a
spiritual connection. Instead, as if she was infinitely precious to him in ways he couldn't begin to understand,
he held her close, savoring this first moment of being
joined to her.

Relief that had nothing to do with sex flooded him.

He felt whole.

As a child he'd known the insecurity and the degradation of poverty, known too much about the things his
mother had done for money.

His mother had loved him, he supposed, but he'd never
felt loved. He'd seen other mothers fuss over their kids.
They'd come to games, cheered at competitions, met with
teachers or worked in the classrooms. Not his mother, and
he'd felt the lack of her concern. She hadn't pushed him
to succeed either or even believed that he could.

He, however, had believed that if he became wealthy,
he'd have power, respect and happiness—he'd have everything he'd craved as a child, including love.

But it hadn't worked out like that. He'd made it big in
the financial sector. Somehow his loneliness and sense of
alienation had only increased, until finally he'd let down
his guard and trusted Anya. She'd gutted him, making
him feel as powerless as he'd felt as a neglected child. He'd
vowed never to allow himself to feel that vulnerable again.

Irony of ironies: here he was again, wanting Bree so
much he risked everything for her even though he knew
she'd used his brother. The increasingly powerful need
he felt for her terrified him.

Being with her felt so good, so immensely pleasurable.
Nothing had ever come close to the intensity of his feel-

ings for her. He liked sharing the penthouse with her. All day as he worked, he liked knowing she'd be waiting for him when he came home. He'd enjoyed grocery shopping because he'd known she'd revel in the cheeses and crackers and sweets he'd bought her.

He mustn't let himself feel so much, couldn't let himself want so much. Not with Bree, a woman who'd used his beloved brother.

Money and power were the sources of his strength, not this woman. Maybe money couldn't bring the happiness he'd once believed it could, but it bought some awfully nice substitutes. He had to be content with that.

Bree moved in his arms and whispered his name, bringing him back to the present as she begged him in husky tones to kiss her, to take her, to please, please take her.

His mouth found hers, and her instant response made him want her even more. Where would this end?

Something stronger than he was made a mockery of his best intentions not to yield to his feelings for her. In her thrall, his lips ground against hers; his tongue mated with hers. When she clutched him frantically, he lost all control. Her nails bit into his back as she gasped.

In that timeless moment when she melted and clung, he cried out her name. Shattered, he held her close, and all their differences fell away.

His arms tightened around her as she bathed his face with kisses. She was his, and he was hers, so completely that nothing could ever come between them. Never before had he known such pleasure. Despite his doubts, the experience felt so true and honest happiness filled him.

Slowly the moment of shared bliss ebbed. A few minutes later, when she idly stroked his nape, he tensed. As a small child he'd longed for such a simple caress.

He blinked, terrified that she might sense how much such thoughtless affection meant to him.

She couldn't matter this much. Whatever this was, it had to be controlled, managed, put away.

He could not lose himself completely to her. He would not.

Without a word, he slid away from her burning fingertips and arose, knowing grimly that if he didn't, he would make love to her again and again. And every time they came together, she would increase her hold over him until she was everything to him while only his money would matter to her. He didn't want to feel craven, rejected and alone as he had as a child.

Feeling doomed and miserable at the thought of leaving her, and yet knowing it was a matter of survival to do so, he forced himself to climb the stairs to his own bedroom. He would boot up his computer and work tonight. Work would be his salvation. Surely with work he could drive her out of his heart and mind.

It wasn't her fault that he had not felt enough love as a child or that no woman could ever make him feel loved now that he was a man. But he didn't have to put himself under her power. He would lock this thing away, contain it, forget about it, admit nothing to her.

Though earlier this same evening he'd been looking for ways to keep her here, now he wanted her gone—out of his penthouse.

As for the rest of tonight, he couldn't allow himself to see her again before he had himself firmly mastered. It would take every ounce of discipline and willpower he had, but he was determined not to wreck his life a second time.

Bree felt acute heartache when Michael deliberately rolled away from her and got up, cutting their connection.

She wanted another night like their first. She wanted him to take her in his arms again. She wanted him to say he liked her, respected her. If he did, maybe she could trust him enough to confide the truth about her unborn child.

A compulsion to bare her soul, to reach for him, to seize his hand and pull him back, took possession of her. But instead of begging him to stay as she'd done that first night, she lay still and quiet and watched him walk away. Even when she saw him stop in the doorway and turn, his profile was so stern she refused to call out to him.

Then he walked out and closed the door, and she was left to toss restlessly in the dark, telling herself sorrowfully that his departure was really for the best. She should will herself to sleep. But she was too edgy, and she wanted so much more from him. Counting hundreds of imaginary sheep while she knotted and unknotted the corner of the sheet, she lay frozen in misery for at least an hour.

When he didn't come back to bed, she finally arose and pulled on his overlarge robe. Stealthily, she made her way out of her suite, down the hall and across his vast, opulent living area that was bathed in shadow and moonlight. Avoiding his elevator, she tiptoed up two flights of stairs. His bedroom door stood ajar, a stream of light spilling across the dark hall.

He didn't want her; he'd left her. She should go. But what if something was troubling him? Maybe no one had ever been there for him before. Maybe she could help him in some way.

When she pushed the door open, she saw him hunched over his computer. In the bright glare of the screen his face was haggard and fierce. He was working; he often worked so hard he forgot to eat.

"Michael," she whispered softly as she slid inside the room. "You shouldn't be working at this hour. Is anything wrong?"

He was shirtless, so she saw every muscle in his pow-

erful back swell and harden when he whirled on her. His
strong body was as tough and hard as his brilliant business mind. He clenched his fists, as if he felt the need to
defend himself from her attack.

But she had no intention of attacking him.

"What are you doing here?" he demanded so harshly
he froze her heart.

"I couldn't sleep," she murmured, seeking to soothe him
rather than frighten or anger him. "I was too worried…
about you."

"Worried? Right." He sounded edgy, dubious, angry.

Was he afraid? Of her? No, that couldn't be. Not when
his black eyes were so hard. It was she who felt terrified
that he would reject her or be cruel.

"Have I done something wrong?" she asked. "Tonight
was wonderful for me. Even better than before. I hoped…
I thought that maybe we could start over."

"I'm fine," he ground out. Then as if he couldn't bear
the sight of her, he closed his eyes and turned his back on
her. "Go back to bed. I have an important meeting tomorrow. I need to go over a few things as you can plainly see."

Hurt swamped her. Swaying a little, her nails dug into
the doorframe. She didn't know how she summoned the
nerve to hold her ground.

"You can't work all the time, darling, now can you?"
she said gently. Before she lost her courage, she crossed
the room and slid her arms around him.

He jumped as if her touch and nearness burned him.

"I'm sure your meeting will go better if you get some
sleep," she persisted.

"As if I could sleep with you—downstairs."

"I could stay up here and maybe give you a massage."

"No!"

"Yes! You're much too tense. Your muscles are all
knotted."

"Because I have work to do!"

Beneath her exploring fingertips his warm, bare skin was smooth as she kneaded the deep tissue of his muscles. When he slowly relaxed and then sighed as if in defeat, she sucked in a breath and laid her lips against his wide chest.

"I can't bear it down there without you, darling. Not when tonight's our last night together."

He hesitated briefly before slamming his laptop closed and folding his arms around her. "I left you because I thought it was best for both of us."

"You won't be sorry. I'm really very good at massages," she said. "I even took a course once…at night school during a short-lived self-improvement kick."

"Bree, oh, my darling," he murmured, the tension flowing out of his deep voice. "Like I said, I came up here with the best of intentions."

"Did you now?"

"You have no idea what you do to me."

"You have the rest of the night to tell me…or better yet, show me. Whichever you prefer, my love."

His mouth claimed hers in a long kiss that was the sweetest he'd ever given her. *He did feel something.* She was almost sure of it.

Maybe there was hope, she thought. Maybe…

For a long moment, as she pondered the possibility, she didn't dare breathe.

Pulling her closer, he opened her robe and stroked her body, knowing just where to touch to arouse her.

"Oh, God, I want you too much to say no to you." Frustrated by the thick fabric, he yanked it off and carried her to his bed where he made love to her again and again, each time as fervently and as passionately as she'd dreamed of him doing.

He did everything he could to please her, and he was

everything she had ever wanted or imagined a perfect lover would be.

If only he could be as good for her in other ways, she thought afterward as she lay in the dark beside him. She'd say yes to him, stay with him and tell him about the baby. Maybe their affair would turn into something meaningful.

With an effort she reminded herself that he cared about one thing only—money.

Funny that he should despise her because he thought she was the same.

It was hard to concentrate on packing with him standing over her, his black gaze watching her every movement. He sipped steaming black coffee she'd brewed for him from a porcelain mug.

"I know it's smart for both of us to end it, but I don't want you to go." His tone was that of a command. "I don't want it to be over. You know that."

When she looked up, his eyes were so hot her tummy turned over. The long night of sex had left her tender both physically and emotionally. She couldn't look at him without feeling too much.

As always he was devastatingly handsome in an impeccably tailored three-piece suit he'd put on for his important meeting this morning. He was dazzling. Would their child be equally so?

"I'll miss you, too." Her voice was choked.

Last night in his arms, she'd been so happy, felt so cherished.

She *would* miss him. Too much. More than was sensible. So what else was new? Angrily she threw a blouse toward her duffel bag.

She had to do this.

Had he ever once told her she could matter as a person to him? No. If she thought there was any hope—any hope at all—that he could ever see her for who she was or really care about her, maybe she would have agreed to the abysmal, degrading terms of his affair on the slight possibility she could make him so happy he would change his mind about her over time.

But he was absolutely incapable of being the kind of man she needed in her life, and he could never trust her to be the right woman for him. So why prolong a relationship that wouldn't work?

Because it works in bed, said a sneaky little voice inside her. *Be fair. Not just in bed. Remember how he was last night at dinner? He deliberately took you somewhere special. He was kind when he tended your foot, too, and protective when he slept all night in that awful chair watching over you.*

Remembering everything he'd done to her last night and how she'd reveled in the expertise of his mouth and tongue on all her intimate body parts, she colored.

They'd had last night. Nobody could ever take that away from her.

"Why won't you move in with me permanently?"

"I need my own place where I can be *me* and have *my* friends over."

"You can have whoever the hell you want here."

"Are you kidding? In this stuffy co-op on Fifth Avenue? Your doorman rolls his eyes every time I walk into the building. I value my independence. And you value yours."

"To hell with my independence. I want you."

"For sex."

"I don't deny it."

"That's not enough. If I stayed, I wouldn't respect myself."

"Why the hell not? This is the twenty-first century."

"Because to you, our relationship would just be another business arrangement. Everything is a deal to you. You pay—I continue to sleep over, only in your bed. It's as simple as that."

"No. That's not how it would be." But he spoke sheepishly.

"Isn't it? You don't want a real relationship with me based on respect and trust, and I don't want to be with a man who doesn't really *like* me."

He changed tack. "But you do admit that you enjoy me…as much as I enjoy you?"

Again she blushed. "That's hardly the point. You think all I've ever wanted from you and your family is money."

"Well, I know you like me in bed, so maybe not *all*."

"See!"

"What do you mean, *see?* Okay, I didn't want to mention this, but since you're forcing the issue, I know that you had my brother set up a million-dollar trust fund for you and your baby. And that you got him to sign it over to you on the day he married you."

"*I* got him to sign it over to me?"

"You heard me! Do you deny you signed documents to claim those monies on your wedding day?"

"Get out! Go to work! Go to your precious meeting! This is what you've been thinking about me all week… and last night when we were making love? A hibernating snake in a frozen hole in the dead of winter has a warmer heart than you do."

"I'd be a fool if I refused to face facts."

"I don't want to sleep with a man who always thinks the worst of me. What can't you understand about that? You'll never change. I'm glad you brought this up because now I can leave here without caring if I ever see you again!"

Tears stung her eyes, but she didn't want to cry. She couldn't give him the satisfaction of knowing how much he was hurting her. Why couldn't he have just asked her about the documents? Why did he always assume the worst?

"Did you or did you not sign them the day you married my brother?" he demanded.

"Yes! Yes! Yes!" Her voice dropped to a whisper. "You've got that part right. I signed them."

When a single tear tracked down her cheek she scrubbed at it furiously with her fist and turned away.

"But it didn't happen like you said, Michael!" she blurted out through strangled sobs. "Or for the reasons you think. I swear it didn't! But did you ask me for the truth? Ever? No!"

"I'm asking now, and you're telling me not to believe what I've seen with my own eyes—which is your damn signature on a dated document. On your wedding day!"

It had all been Will's idea. Not hers. He'd feared his brother wouldn't do the right thing for her or his child.

But would Michael believe that?

"I'm not what you think, but I'm past caring about your opinion of me. I'm through talking to you, through trying to explain myself. It's hopeless to try to change your mind because you *want* to believe the worst. I wish I'd never met you, wish I'd never slept with you. I don't want to ever see you again! Not for as long as I live! I don't want you in my baby's life either—because I want him to grow up with a trusting heart, which is something you'll never have!"

He went white, absolutely white.

"If you change your mind, call me," he said in a voice that was like ice. "Because I want you, no matter who you are, no matter what you've done."

Every time he said that, he carved out a little piece of her.

When he turned and strode out of the room, she lunged at her duffel on the bed and heaved it onto the floor, spilling her clothes everywhere.

Nine

Michael looked so lost, haunted and alone as he stood by his brother's urn. She couldn't take her eyes off him. It was all she could do not to rush to him and put her arms around him.

She was such a wuss. Was it only two days ago that she'd told Michael she never wanted to see him again?

For the past forty-eight hours she'd missed him horribly. The raw agony in his face when his eyes sought hers compelled her for an interminable second or two. He'd loved his brother deeply.

In that long moment when neither could tear their eyes from the other, she shared his all-consuming grief. Maybe that was all they could ever share.

Besides the baby she was too afraid to tell him about.

Whatever faults Michael had, he'd loved Will and was grieving now. She wanted to go to him, to thread her fingers through his, to pull him close and say comforting words in the hope that she could ease that pain.

What if she told him they were going to have a child, that Will had only married her to protect Michael's future child? Would that ease some of his conflict and grief? Or would it add fresh torment since he despised her and believed the baby to be a part of Will?

He was so alone. Maybe Michael had money, but he'd lacked love when he'd needed it most. And the lack had hardened him. Only Will had seen Michael's faults and loved him anyway. Now Michael had to say goodbye to the one person who'd loved him.

When the preacher introduced Michael, he stepped up to the podium and began to speak, his deep voice filling the sanctuary. The words he chose to celebrate his brother's life were so eloquent, they resonated inside her. Hot tears filled her eyes. Her heart ached for him. Soon everybody around her was sniffing and sobbing, too.

Funny that such a heartless man knew exactly what to say to touch so many. If he could speak like that and love that deeply, why couldn't he love her and their child?

When her tears threatened to fall, she brushed them away. Will was dead. Michael was who he was. She couldn't help him or change him. She had to say goodbye to both brothers, keep her secret and move on.

After the service, when the family stood beside the urn receiving mourners, a middle-aged woman with hard gray eyes and a thin, pursed mouth pointed her silver-handled cane at Bree.

"*You!* I've been wanting to have my say," the woman said. "Michael told me that you were pregnant and injured. But here you are—looking fit as a fiddle."

Suddenly Michael, his face grim, materialized beside Bree. Not that he greeted her by word or smile. He was just there, shielding her from the older woman like a protective force field.

When the woman's brows knitted, Michael's hand touched Bree's elbow

"I saw her watching you during the service, so don't think I don't see how it is between you two," the woman said. "She didn't love Will. If either of you think I believe for one minute she had a real marriage with my nephew or that her baby is his…"

Bree reeled.

"Not here, Alice," Michael warned in a voice of steel.

"You can't stop me, Michael. You're as greedy as she is. It wouldn't surprise me to learn you set some sort of trap for Will and used her for bait."

"Don't be absurd," Michael said. "Leave her alone."

"You can't tell me what to do, and I'll sue you again if you try."

His fingers tightened protectively on Bree's elbow. Drawing her closer, he gave Alice a warning look that was so fierce the woman squinted and backed away.

"Thank you," Bree said stiffly as Alice fled down the aisle.

"I told you…the family can be difficult," he murmured. "She was equally cruel to my mother."

Thankfully the next person to approach them was a lovely older woman with silver hair who was dressed in soft grays and blues.

She clasped Bree's hand. "I've wanted to call you and tell you how sorry I am about Will, but I just couldn't work up the strength…until now. I'm Mrs. Ferrar, Tony's mother."

"I'm so sorry for your loss, Mrs. Ferrar. So very sorry," Bree said.

"I know you are. Tony told me how much you and your child meant to Will." Her kind, sympathetic blue eyes shifted to Michael. "He told me how much you meant to

Will, too, Mr. North. I know you will take good care of Bree and her precious baby. Will would want that."

Mrs. Ferrar opened her arms, and Bree stepped into them. "There…there… That's right. Give me a big hug. Tony's service will be tomorrow. I sure hope you'll come. I don't know how I'll get through it if people like you, people who knew Tony, aren't with me."

"I will be there," Bree promised. "Again, I'm so sorry."

"I've been cleaning out their apartment, sorting through Tony's things. You two will have to do that for Will. The landlord told me he already has a new tenant, so he's willing to forgive their lease. So, the sooner, the better."

"We'll take care of it, Mrs. Ferrar," Michael said. *We'll…*

"I'll miss them both," Mrs. Ferrar said, "and so will you. Some days are going to be hard for you…really, really hard. But when that happens, you think about your precious baby. I have young grandchildren. And they're so full of life, just their pictures on my fridge are enough to cheer me up. I'll do all right."

Despite the sorrowful occasion, Mrs. Ferrar's warmth cheered Bree. In the future, whenever she became sad or confused, she needed to focus on her baby.

"Mr. North, I want a hug from you, too. Such a shame you never got to meet my Tony. I told Will, and more than once, I was sure you'd like him."

"I'm sure of it, too," Michael said, but the new questions in his eyes when he regarded Bree made her swallow hard.

How long would it be before he figured out the truth? The whole truth?

Michael locked his Mercedes, crossed the street and strode to his brother's building. After an endless week of bleak days and nights grieving for Will without seeing or talking to Bree, he couldn't believe she'd actually taken a phone call from him and agreed to meet him at Will's apartment today. He had Bijou to thank for that, he supposed—Bijou, whom he'd bribed with flattery and with dozens of red roses.

Unsure about the reception he'd receive from her daughter, he felt on edge riding up to Will's floor in the tiny elevator.

If the past seven days without Bree had felt like an eternity, what would a lifetime without her be like?

He had it bad. He couldn't sleep, and food, no matter how expensive or how beautifully presented, tasted like cardboard. Even work failed to distract him.

He wanted her. And not just in his bed.

He wanted to talk to her, to look forward to her company at night when he came home. He wanted to make love to her. But he wanted more than all that—so much more. He wanted her companionship and affection, her adoration. She'd adored him that first night—before he'd come clean and ripped her heart open. He wanted her eyes to shine when she looked at him again.

Last week he'd screwed up a major deal because his mind had been on Bree. Since he hadn't pushed ruthlessly enough, he would have to look for new financing for the deal. He needed to go to Shanghai to sort out a mess over there, but he couldn't make himself get on a plane because he didn't want to leave New York with their relationship unresolved.

Why did he feel so lost and alienated with her out of his life?

Because of his illogical need for her, he felt resentment toward her. Had she suffered at all?

Probably not, he thought. Then his heart leaped when he unlocked his brother's door, stepped into the apartment and heard her singing an aria from *Carmen*. She was a little off-key maybe, but not too bad. Hell—off-key or not, the music was charming. She sounded happy.

She was probably thriving without him. And who could blame her?

"Hello!" he yelled, not wanting to follow that train of thought.

She continued to sing. No reply. Either she didn't hear him or she was deliberately ignoring him.

"Hello, damn it!"

The singing stopped, but she didn't call out to him. Annoyed, he stomped into Will's bedroom and found her kneeling over a box of thick wool sweaters.

"What's with the opera? I thought you were into rock music."

Her quick blush made his gut tighten and his body harden.

"Apparently, Mrs. Ferrar took Tony's player and speakers. So I was singing something Luke was humming earlier at the bistro."

"Luke? I thought he finished his assessment of Chez Z. Doesn't he have his own empire to run?"

"I'm sure he does, but he came by because he's so sweet."

Sweet, my ass.

"He took me to dinner at one of his restaurants last night to show me a few more tricks."

Dinner? *Sweet* had nothing to do with it. He was hitting on her.

"Sorry. I know I can't carry a tune. Luke has the most beautiful voice."

Luke, again. Damn. "You sounded okay. Not bad," he said, grumpily, his mind on Luke.

"What can I do to help around here?" Michael muttered.

She refused to look at him. "Just pack everything, I guess."

"Okay. I can do that."

"Maybe you could work in the living room, that way—"

"Right. That way you can avoid me."

"Did I say that?"

"I was rough on you last week, so you think maybe I should apologize."

"Why? You meant what you said. I'm glad I know what you think of me. Now I can move on."

Her cutting words made him feel bleak as hell. But she was right. He didn't trust her. Why should he? Unfortunately, he still wanted her in his life.

He let out a long, frustrated breath and shoved a hand through his hair. Not knowing what else to do, he grabbed a box off the floor and went into the living room where he began slinging books into it with a fury. Consumed with her, he worked, banging about in the living room for more than an hour. After he finished unloading the bookshelf, he started on the desk and then the computer.

The drawers were slower going because he couldn't pack papers and files without going through them in an effort to figure out if they were important. After an hour, he'd finished two drawers and filled two boxes. Then he opened the bottom drawer and found it stuffed with discs and flash drives that were labeled as photos and videos.

Curious, he loaded a disk that Will had titled *Our First Night Together and Honeymoon* into the computer, because Michael had to prove to himself once and for all that she'd been lying about her relationship.

But the pictures weren't of Will and Bree; they were of Will and Tony.

In the first series of shots, Will and Tony were holding hands. In the next, they were hugging. Then the pictures got racier.

In each shot, the two of them wore less. Hell, was this some kind of strip session? When they were down to their briefs, Michael decided he'd seen enough and tore the disc from the machine.

Will and Tony?

He stared into space blankly. Why hadn't he seen what had been right before his eyes? Will had always been so sensitive, so sweet and caring. So damned perfect in all the ways Michael wasn't. Michael remembered how Jacob used to beg Will to bring a girl home. *Any girl,* he'd say. Had he suspected?

I will, Dad. I just have to meet the right girl.

But just after Jacob's death, Will had moved here and become nearly impossible to reach.

Had Will been nervous about introducing Michael to Tony? Afraid Michael wouldn't accept their partnership?

But he would have. He did accept it. Realities were realities. People were what they were. He'd loved Will. Period.

The reason Bree hadn't displayed a single photograph of Will in her apartment was because they'd been friends, not lovers.

Just like she'd said.

She'd been telling the truth about that at least.

So why the hell had Will married her?

Michael remembered his brother's glazed eyes in the E.R. and his final words.

"She's a wonderful girl. Not what you think. In a way, what you did to her was all my fault. So, if you'll just promise me…you'll take care of her, that you'll do this one thing for me, we'll be square."

What you did to her…

What had Will meant? What was Michael missing?

When Michael got up and walked into the bedroom again, Bree looked up absently from the growing mountain of packed boxes.

"What? What is it, Michael?"

"Will was gay."

She drew a breath and quickly averted her eyes. "Okay."

"You knew!"

She swallowed.

"So—apparently everybody knew but me…even Aunt Alice. This puts everything in a new light."

Her face was flushed and her lips trembled.

"Who got you pregnant? Why the hell did he marry you?"

"It's complicated."

Her answer drove him over some edge. "You've said that before. My work is complicated. I bet this is simple. If he was in love with Tony, if he lived here with Tony, if he was never your lover as you claimed all along, how the hell did you manipulate him into marrying you? Who's the father of your baby? Some other guy I don't know about? Tell me his name!"

"Damn you," she lashed out at him. "I was a virgin when I slept with you. You have to know that!"

On some rational level, maybe he did. But women had been tricking men about their virginity for centuries, and he was too angry for logic to work.

She stood up, her eyes aflame, her cheeks dark with rage. "This from you right now…is too much!"

She was angry, angrier than he'd ever seen her. Fighting for control, she shut her eyes. Not that she calmed down any. When she opened her eyes again they were so bright they shot sparks at him. "I don't want to talk about this with you. Not even now."

"Well, I do. You had some sordid affair and made my brother feel sorry for you—"

"Used him? Had a sordid affair? This is the final straw! I've had it with you! You always think I'm some cheap hustler! You always think everything is my fault! It's *my* fault we got married! It's *my* fault because I'm greedy and manipulative!"

Eyes aflame, she stared at him for a long moment.

"Well, it's not my fault! It's yours!"

"What are you saying?"

"When you slept with me to drive a wedge between me and Will, I *was* a virgin, and *you* got me pregnant!"

He'd gotten her pregnant? Her accusation jolted him like a blow. He reeled backward.

He'd taken every precaution; he always took every precaution.

"I couldn't have gotten you pregnant. That's not possible." Then why did his chest feel heavy as he stared into her eyes that blazed with outrage and hurt? It was as if her eyes were a fist she'd rammed inside him.

"Apparently it *is* possible because I *am* pregnant. This mess is your fault as much as it is mine! But unlike you, I take part of the blame because I was the simpleminded idiot who slept with you."

"You're claiming I'm the father, and that's *why* Will married you?" Michael's voice was hoarse.

"Yes! I didn't know who to turn to. Like a fool, I cried on his shoulder. He said you were so set against me, it was up to him to do the right thing. He felt someone in the family had to help me get on my feet. He said you'd had a grudge against all women ever since Anya lied about being pregnant and you married her. He said you wouldn't change your mind about me easily. And, oh boy, how right he was! Your brother had a sense of honor—which you don't."

Her words were sinking in, making sense. Horrible sense.

Pregnant. She was pregnant.

"You're sure it's mine?" he rasped.

"Damn you!"

"Sorry," he growled, hanging his head with genuine repentance.

"Look, I've never been with another man. How many times do I have to tell you that? Not that I'm proud of that fact. I wish I'd been with ten other men before you, men who had hearts. Maybe if I'd been the gold-digging slut you thought I was, I would have seen through you. I wish I was pregnant by somebody else!"

He was going to be a father.

Michael felt too shocked to say anything for what felt like an interminably long interval.

She was pregnant with his child and she'd been doing her damnedest to hide that fact from him. And he didn't blame her for that.

He felt sick with regret. What could he say to her now? What could he do? His thoughts were a painful jumble.

He'd gotten a virgin pregnant and had run off to Shanghai to try to forget her. He had a lot to answer for.

"I did my best to protect you—you have to know that. I did everything in my power to prevent this."

"I know. I remember. *Because I was the last person you wanted to have a baby with*. I'm sure there's a lot of collateral damage with every deal you close."

Her voice cut like an ice shard.

"So," she continued, "here we are. You and I are going to have a baby. What now? How are you going to spin it so I'm the evil one? Do you still think I'm trying to manipulate you the way Anya did?"

"No. You're not like her."

"Wow! I can't believe you said that."

What he couldn't believe was that he'd been so blind to the truth where she was concerned. But so many people lied to him, not only in his relationships but in the business world. Too often the men he negotiated with would say or do anything to make a deal.

Bree was not like Anya or the sharks in Shanghai.

The reality hit him hard as he considered how badly he'd behaved toward her.

She was so different from the women he usually dated that he hadn't understood that she might be genuine.

"Were you ever going to tell me about the baby?" he asked softly.

"Maybe…in time."

"You mean in a year or so? Or maybe in twenty years?"

"Maybe."

After the way he'd treated her, he knew he deserved that answer or worse. "Which was it going to be?"

"I don't know. Maybe I wasn't ever going to tell you."

He raked a hand through his hair. His heart was hammering violently.

God, what had he done? Had he thrown away the best thing that had ever happened to him?

"Damn it, Bree."

"You made your feelings for me very, very clear, Michael, on that first night. And on all the nights since."

His gut twisted. Yes, he'd sweet-talked her and made love to her until she'd become radiant every time he looked at her. He'd caressed her so seductively she'd trembled when he barely touched her. Her every nerve had leaped in response to him, but he'd thought she'd been faking.

She hadn't been. While she'd been sincere with him, he'd treated her as deceitfully as Anya had treated him. He was guilty of everything he'd accused Bree of. Afterward he'd told her he hadn't wanted her, that he'd been lying all along and had only pretended he'd cared about her. While she'd been sweet and authentic, he'd been a blind, brutal, rampaging fool. Now, as he remembered the despair in her eyes that night, he knew her virginal pain would haunt him for as long as he lived.

"Everything's different now," he said.

"Not for me, Michael," she said quietly. "You hurt me. You've expressed your poor opinion of me too many times for me not to believe that's how you really feel."

He couldn't blame her. "I know. I'm truly sorry."

"Michael—"

When she looked up at him, distress and confusion showing in her damp eyes, the suffering he'd caused her tore him apart.

"What I did to you that night was wrong. The things I accused you of, even after the accident, were wrong. I see that now. I did something I'd never do in a business deal. Because it involved Will, I rushed into the situation, thinking I had all the facts, but I was clueless. I'm sorry for what I did to you, what I said to you then, and ever since."

She lowered her eyes and bit her lip. Then she lifted her chin. Her eyes were cool, passionless. "I accept your apology. But none of this really matters anymore."

Because he didn't matter to her anymore.

He took a deep breath. "I want to make this right," he said, "but I don't know how."

"It's too late for us."

"We're going to have a baby," he said. "We need to do what's right for our child…maybe get married, maybe—"

"What? Maybe get married? You're willing to marry me because you feel guilty right now? Or because you want control of your precious North heir? Are you out of your mind? You haven't thought this through. You don't want to marry me, and I certainly don't want to marry you. We'd make each other miserable."

"Hear me out. You're going to have my son or daughter."

"Right. Like I said—your precious North heir."

"Listen to me—"

"No! You hear *me* out for a change! I want to marry a

man who loves me for me, who wants to conceive a child with me, who thinks well of me, and you're not capable of that. All you're good at is making money."

When he moved toward her, she went white and shrank against the wall to avoid his touch.

"It wouldn't be about your child being my heir."

"I don't believe you, Michael."

"I still want you," he muttered thickly. "I want you so much, and I don't want to hurt you ever again."

"But you would hurt me. Because you can't love me. You can't love anyone. Money is all you really care about because that's what saved you from poverty. I'm sorry for you, but I've accepted the fact that you are how you are…and that no amount of wishful thinking on my part can change you. I won't change my mind. We come from very different worlds and we are very different people."

The undiluted pain in her eyes pierced his heart. "I can change," he said. "We'll make it work. Somehow. I swear to you."

"I don't think so." She didn't fight him when he lifted her chin and tried to convince her with a kiss. She trembled when his mouth covered hers, but she didn't move into him or pull him close. Her taste intoxicated him even though she simply waited stiffly until he ended the kiss.

"I want you too much to let you go, Bree. The past few days have been hell for me."

"For me, too. But what we feel about each other doesn't really matter. We don't have the same values. You instantly accused me of sleeping around, and I'm not like that. You care only about money and deal-making…we're not right for each other."

"I lost Will. And now I'm losing you. And our child."

"You didn't lose us. You can't lose what you never had. At least, I keep telling myself that. I can't lose you for the same reason—because I never had you."

"Damn it, Bree—"

"Go back to the living room and pack. I don't want to talk to you any longer."

There was a roar in his ears, a fire in his blood as he caught her roughly to him again. "You're pregnant with my child, and I want to do what's right."

"Then stay out of my life!"

His mouth was hard when it met hers. He was determined to claim every part of her, to make her see that love wasn't necessary when two people belonged together. She was like the air he breathed, the water he drank, the food he ate and the earth he walked on. He couldn't live without such essentials. He didn't love the air or water or food, did he? He just had to have them, or he would cease to exist.

"Kiss me back, damn it." His command was crisp and impatient. "You know you want to."

Her heart pulsed erratically and her skin warmed with fiery need, but she didn't put her arms around him or lift her face to his or give him any indication that she was tempted.

"No—let me go," she whispered raggedly. "Please, just let me go."

The warmth of her breath against his cheek alone was enough to drive him crazy. "Why? You know the sex would be great."

"I told you," she whispered huskily. "I want to be valued as a person. Not bought. Or kept. This is just another deal to you. I'm the mother of your child. You enjoy me in bed. I'm not quite as bad as you thought. All in all, I'm a better deal than Anya. In order to get control of your heir, you're willing to marry me."

"Damn it, no." He lifted her dark golden hair and pushed it back from her neck. "I do value you. Or…or, damn it, I'll learn to value you."

"You're just saying that to get what you want. But I know what you really feel and think about me. You've always thought I'm greedy and unscrupulous and can be bought. That's simply your viewpoint."

He lowered his lips to the base of her throat where her pulse pounded. "Because before you, that's all I knew."

"Well, that's not who I am, and I don't want to be with a man who lusts after me but can't respect me. Nothing's different except now you know the baby I'm carrying is yours."

"That's a helluva big difference."

When his hand cupped her breast, and he kissed her again, she shuddered. But she didn't kiss him back.

"I can change. I can learn," he said. "I will try to see you as you are. I will."

"It's too late. Because now it's me who doesn't believe you, Michael. How can I believe anything you say? I'm through. Finished. The suspicions you feel toward others are ingrained so deeply into your character, you'll never rid yourself of them."

"I'm the father of your baby."

"If you insist, I'll inform you about anything that has to do with your child."

"I insist."

"Okay. I'll keep you informed. Other than that, we're through." She picked up her purse and slung it over her shoulder. "I can't even pack up Will's apartment with you. I thought I could, but I can't. You'll have to finish on your own. Or use your precious North money to hire movers. Frankly, I don't care how you handle it."

She turned on her heel and walked past him, out of the apartment, leaving him for good.

Feeling hollow at the core, he stared after her, the tomb-like silence of Will's apartment closing in around him.

He needed a drink, so he began to ransack the shelves and open the closets.

Where the hell was Tony and Will's liquor cabinet?

Ten

It was amazing what money could buy. And what it couldn't.

Not personal happiness. Not love.

Not the one woman he wanted in his life.

For two months, she'd avoided him.

Michael, who had jet lag from hell, was staying in one of the world's most opulent hotels while on business in Abu Dhabi. Gold glittered from the walls. The drapes and upholstery were decorated in an Arabian theme without restraint. Many floors beneath him, waves lapped gently at the building's foundation and caused a faint and constant hum no matter where one stood in the hotel.

And still he couldn't stop thinking about Bree.

"May I run your bath, sir?" The butler appointed to Michael's lavish hotel suite spoke politely in an upper-class British accent.

Rubbing his temple, Michael switched off the giant plasma-screen TV and went to the floor-to-ceiling windows that overlooked the sparkling blue waters of the Persian Gulf. "No. You can go. I'm expecting an important business call."

The hotel was otherworldly, over-the-top. Michael had a meeting with the sheikh who owned it. He aspired to build another that would be even more ostentatious, more luxurious and more expensive than this one. It was the deal of the decade.

Normally Michael would have been excited to be here, excited to be asked to be part of such an ambitious project.

But he missed Bree.

She'd sounded so cool over the phone when she'd told him they were having a little boy.

A little boy they'd agreed to name Will.

She'd refused to talk about anything other than her doctor's visit. When she'd finished, she'd hung up.

"I'll call you when I have something else to tell you about our child," she'd said right before she'd ended the call.

Michael missed her so much. More than anything. She didn't answer when he phoned her. She didn't reply when he texted. He sent her roses every day, and every day she sent them back to the florist.

Before he'd left for Abu Dhabi, he'd gone to Chez Z to check on her, but she'd made it plain she didn't like seeing him in person. She'd answered his questions in unenthusiastic, monosyllabic tones before she'd asked him to leave.

When he'd told her his agent had found her a two-bedroom, second-floor apartment in her neighborhood in a building that had an elevator, she'd shaken her head. "Leave me alone, Michael. I don't want to discuss anything other than our child."

"But this is about our child. It's about you avoiding stairs until he's safely born. I'll pay for it."

"This is about your money."

"No. It's about the baby. After he's born, I don't want you carrying him down five flights of stairs. What if you fell?"

"I'll figure something out on my own."

"You're carrying my son. Why won't you let me do this for you?"

"I know what apartments cost in this city," she'd whispered in a shattered tone that had cut him. "A favor like that would give you financial power over me. I don't want to be dependent on you for anything."

"No way will I let you stay in that apartment and risk our baby on those stairs," he'd said. "Why won't you let me help?"

"You know why. Because you use your money to get what you want. Because you think I'm out for anything I can get from you."

"I don't think that anymore!"

"This isn't a deal. I'm not for sale. Neither is our baby. You've used your money to control people for so long, you don't know any other way. Remember how you used to treat Will? Well, I'm determined never to take anything from you again."

"This isn't about money!"

"With you, everything's about money. I can't live that way, or think that way. It's too cold."

He'd once believed that if he became rich enough, he'd have everything he wanted. But he'd been wrong.

Too often his money had put him on the defensive. All he'd been able to see was who wanted what from him. Waiters wanted big tips. Women wanted jewels. Socialites wanted him to give to their causes. He'd been catered to by everybody because they'd all wanted his money. And on some level he'd loved it, because he'd felt strong and powerful and in control.

Michael didn't know what to do to win Bree back.

She'd been a virgin and grieving for her brother. Since Michael was her best friend's brother, she'd trusted him and had shyly opened herself to him body and soul. Then he'd deliberately crushed her.

To win her back, he had to become the kind of man she admired. But how?

What if she was right? What if he couldn't change?

Michael, who sat near Chez Z's cash register, looked up from smearing marmalade on a slice of warm, crusty bread and grinned. Bree was storming out of the kitchen toward him. Her cheeks brightened with indignation and that only made her look lovelier in her tight yellow dress and starched white apron that molded to her lush curves.

When he raked his eyes down her shapely body she reddened even more.

"You have to stop this," she said.

"Stop what?" Michael ignored the desperation he heard in her husky voice.

"Coming to Chez Z every single morning you're in town. Constantly embarrassing me like this. Looking at me like that."

His smile broadened. As always, he was so dazzled by her beauty and the immensity of his attraction to her, he felt momentary hope that she might feel a spark of warmth for him if he kept pushing her.

"Embarrassing you? How?" he asked with seeming innocence.

She yanked out a chair and sat down. Leaning across the table so that her staff couldn't hear her, she said, "You know perfectly well how. You send flowers every day."

"I'm the money guy, remember. They look good on the tables. I'm just protecting my investment."

"You drop by every morning on your way to work.

You eat breakfast here. You devour me with those black eyes of yours."

"Devour..." He let the word linger as his gaze traveled to her mouth. "Can I help it if you're the most talented cook in Manhattan as well as the most beautiful?"

"Don't you dare compliment me!"

"Sorry." He bit into his crispy hash browns.

"You call so frequently you've got Bijou feeling sorry for you. Everybody who works here is talking about us and taking sides."

"Who's winning?" he asked flirtatiously.

"Since my vote is the only one that counts—me! So stop! You're supposed to be a powerful CEO. Why can't you fly off to Abu Dhabi or Shanghai or at least hole up in your office and run your empire like a good boy?"

"A man has to eat breakfast."

When his gaze touched her as intimately as a caress, her hand darted to her throat. "We have a rule—I call you when I have something to tell you about the baby, otherwise we stay away from each other. Please, just go."

"That's your rule. I'm playing by my own."

"Which is still another reason we can't be together. Look, I need to get back to the kitchen and supervise the prep work."

"I thought maybe you'd like to see the papers for the foundation I'm setting up in Will's name."

Despite her obvious intention to dismiss him, her annoyance gave way to curiosity. "What foundation?"

"It will provide educational opportunities for disadvantaged boys in this city."

"What's in it for you?"

"Would you believe the pleasure of giving back?"

Her eyebrows lifted. "Your PR guy must have told you that a charitable foundation would improve your image. Am I right?"

Teeth gritted, he swore softly. "That's your unwavering opinion of me? You can't imagine that I might empathize with kids who have it as tough or tougher than I did and want to help them? Or that I might want to honor Will?"

"No. This is probably just camouflage. You're hoping to make yourself look less like the shark you are to your gullible prey."

"I want to take care of you and our baby. You probably don't believe that either."

"Michael, we're having a kid because we both made a huge mistake in judgment. Huge! We have no reason to be together other than the baby."

"That's reason enough for me."

"But not for me! Why can't you just go away and let me run my bistro?"

"Okay, I get it. You think I'm always motivated by greed—even when I try to do good things. We're going to have a baby. I want to take care of you. Why is that bad?"

She just looked at him. "I've told you."

"What if you're wrong?" he demanded. "What if I can change?"

"What if cows could fly over the moon?"

"What if we could get past our mistakes, huge as they are, and become...er...friends?"

"Friends? You and me?" She lifted her chin and stared at him. "Not possible."

"I'll bet our baby would disagree if he had a vote."

"Even for you, that's low."

"There's one more thing." He hesitated. "I found a building in your neighborhood that just happens to have a vacant first-floor apartment that I thought would be perfect for you."

"Please, please don't tell me you've bought it."

"No, but I want you to take a look at it and see what you think. I'm willing to buy the lease on your present apartment and make the owner a very good deal on the one in this building."

"How many times do I have to tell you that you can't buy me?" She pushed her chair back from his table. "You've finished your breakfast, and I've got a full day ahead of me."

"Right," he murmured. "But just so you know, I'm leaving the keys to the apartment with your mother—on the slim chance that she can talk you into looking at it."

"Leave my mother out of this." She whirled and left him.

He watched her until she disappeared. Then he arose and pulled out the envelope containing the photos and information about the building and the necessary keys. Documents in hand, he paid the bill and tracked down Bijou.

"The apartment *is* perfect! I love the garden. I'll try to talk some sense into her," she said after looking at the pictures. She tucked the keys into her purse. "But she's stubborn…especially when it comes to you. This may take a while…and a miracle. I think I'd better go to church tonight and pray. Yes. I think so, yes."

Bree raced ahead of Marcie on the cracked concrete sidewalk that edged the riverbank. She almost passed two joggers, so determined was she to get far enough ahead of Marcie that her friend would be forced to stop nagging Bree about Michael.

The afternoon was cold and sunny, perfect for a walk in the park if only Marcie would change the subject. The humid breeze that gusted off the silvery Hudson River smelled of the sea while gulls laughed and wheeled above them.

"I really think you should reconsider about Michael," Marcie was saying as she caught up to Bree after stooping to hand a dollar to a street musician playing a trumpet.

Bree, who had finally had enough, stopped abruptly, and a guy on Rollerblades nearly slammed into her.

"Hey!" he cried. "Watch where you're going!"

"I mean, if someone rich like Michael was interested in me and wanted to 'buy me' as you put it," Marcie continued, undeterred, "I'd let him."

"Look, Marcie, I love Riverside Park. I come here to exercise and relax and get away from my problems. Right now Michael is a big problem. So please stop talking about him or go home."

Marcie's brows knitted as she watched an immense white yacht pull up to the 79th Street Boat Basin. "But a foundation? How cool is that? How bad can he be if he gives a fortune away for a cause like that?"

"He told you about that to manipulate you. He's using his money to buy your good opinion. It's a trick."

"Well, if he created that foundation to win you over, I think it's sort of romantic…and sweet."

"Believe me, he is *not* sweet. He's a cunning manipulator who uses his money for insidious, calculating reasons that profit him."

"He thought badly about you not so long ago. And he was wrong about you, wasn't he? He sees that now."

"Do not compare me to him."

"I'm just saying he was wrong about you, so maybe you could be wrong about him."

Two bikers whizzed past them.

"Marcie, he seduced me just to make Will dislike me. That's bad. He's not to be trusted. Not ever."

"But he's so-o-o cute…and rich. And…and even if he did seduce you for the reasons you say he seems genuinely interested in you now. You should see the way he looks at you. He's got the major hots for you."

Bree's heart constricted. She knew he wanted the baby, and he wanted her in his bed, but she knew as well that he didn't love her. Her mother had married her father because he'd gotten her pregnant, then she'd complained about it so often, Bree had felt guilty for being the baby in question.

"And, God, all those flowers! I wish somebody half as handsome and half as rich would try to seduce me."

"Did he put you on his payroll or something?"

"Hey, I'm not the only one. Everybody else at the bistro thinks you should forgive and forget."

The only reason Michael wanted her was because she was pregnant with his child, and he wanted control over his heir. His attitude hadn't changed until he'd realized Will was gay and had proof that she'd been telling the truth about only being Will's friend.

"You want to know something—sometimes it's very hard to forgive."

A light must have gone out somewhere in the stairwell because the second-floor landing of Bree's steep Victorian staircase was as dark as a cave.

Bree, who was tired and weighted down by two bulging grocery sacks and her purse, grumbled as she readjusted her load before tackling the final, shadowy flight to her apartment. It was only four in the afternoon, but she'd left Chez Z earlier than usual because she'd been too tired to stay. She was looking forward to a cup of tea and a long, hot bath and maybe a nap when her cell phone buzzed inside her purse.

Don't answer it. Not now.

But after it stopped for a short interval it began ringing again. She set her bags on the dark stair above her and began to dig in her purse.

When she saw Michael's name, her heart beat a little faster. He'd been in Asia for the past five days, and so hadn't been by Chez Z to pester her while he ate his breakfast. Was he back? Was he okay?

Even though she knew she shouldn't take his call since she had no news about the baby, she couldn't resist picking up to find out where he was and to make sure he was okay. But just as she touched the phone and his husky voice wrapped around her, something in the bags on the stair shifted. The sack ripped open and shot a barrage of cascading apples and oranges straight at her.

"No!" she cried as she jumped to catch them before they rolled down the stairs.

"What is it?" Michael demanded. "What's wrong?"

Caught off-balance as she stupidly grabbed for an apple, she lurched to one side. Frantically, she reached for the balustrade and missed, falling backward, tumbling along with her fruit back down to the second-floor landing. At least, she had the presence of mind to throw out her hands defensively. Even so, she rammed the wall so hard a white-hot burning sensation shot through her abdomen.

"The baby," she whispered. "Please let him be okay."

For a long time she lay in a crumpled heap, too dazed and winded to move. As the unpleasant burning in her belly subsided, she thought she heard Michael shouting.

"Where are you? Tell me what happened? What's wrong? Bree? Bree! Are you there?"

The phone, she thought. Her phone had to be somewhere nearby. Michael had been talking to her before she'd fallen? Was he back? Oh, how she hoped he was in the city!

Where was her phone?

With a supreme effort, she sat up and discovered her phone blinking madly in a dark corner.

"I'm…on my staircase," she said shakily after she'd managed to inch her way to the phone. "I fell."

"Damn it, Bree. I told you those stairs were dangerous."

"I think I'm okay. I have to be okay."

"Stay where you are," he ordered. "I'm not far. I'm coming over. I'll be there in five minutes—max."

Good. He was nearby. She'd never felt more thankful about anything in her life.

"No hurry.... I'm fine," she whispered. But he couldn't have heard her feeble protests because her phone had dropped his call.

Realizing she was in one of the building's dead spots so there was no use calling him back, she forced herself to her knees. The last thing she wanted was for him to find her on the stairs and panic.

Pushing up to her feet, she stood. For a second or two, she swayed dizzily. When her head cleared, she grabbed the railing and began climbing, grateful that she hadn't sprained an ankle, or worse.

It was slow going, but once she was safely inside her apartment, she collapsed on her couch and willed the cramping in her belly to stop.

She had to be all right. The baby had to be all right.

Four minutes later she heard her buzzer in the foyer downstairs. Then Michael rang her on her intercom. "It's me."

"Michael!" Unabashed joy filled her as she hit the button and buzzed him inside.

She heard the thunder of his heavy footsteps as he ran up her stairs, taking them two at a time, never slowing even when he neared the top. He ran through the door that she'd left ajar and rushed to her side.

For the first time since their quarrel at Will's apartment, she didn't try to push him away when he pulled her close. She was much too thankful to be wrapped in his powerful arms while he quizzed her about her delicate condition.

He was breathing hard, and his heart was pounding.

He was as scared for her and the baby's safety as she was.

"How far did you fall?" His unsteady tone told her that he'd feared the worst, that he still feared it.

Did that mean he wanted their baby as much as she did? That maybe his interest in her wasn't just about controlling the North heir?

"Not so very far."

"How are you feeling now?"

"I was shaken at first. But I feel better now." Especially now that he was here. "And lucky. I feel very, very lucky." With a deep sigh, she laid her head against his heaving chest and listened to the violent thudding of his heart. "It's going to be okay. Don't worry so much."

"Your doctor's agreed to meet us at the emergency room just to make sure."

"Michael, that really isn't necessary."

"Shh," he whispered. His eyes met hers. "It is for me, so let me take care of you. Just this once…for the baby's sake."

Upon hearing the very real concern in his husky voice, the lump in her throat grew larger.

"I'm glad you're here," she admitted as she pulled him closer. "So glad."

His powerful arms tightened around her. "Well, that's a first."

She was so happy she didn't object, at least not very much, when the team of paramedics he'd summoned arrived, checked her vitals, strapped her to a stretcher and carried her back down the stairs.

Thankfully, her doctor, who beat them to the hospital, confirmed her opinion that although she'd been shaken up a bit, essentially she was fine. "I would suggest that you climb as few stairs as possible for a while. And as for resuming intimate relations, I advise you two to take a break for a couple of days. After that, just be careful."

"I like your doctor," Michael said after the man left.

"Because he agreed with you about the stair thing."

"No—because he said we can have sex in two days."

She felt her cheeks heat. She glanced around to make sure they were alone. "Michael! We don't have that kind of relationship anymore."

"I miss it. He just reminded me of how much I miss it." He leaned into her and cupped her chin with his fingers. "I want you all the time, and it's been too long. Way too long," he murmured right before he slanted his hard mouth over hers.

"Don't," she whispered, but when he didn't stop, she didn't push against his chest as she should have.

She was thinking about how frantic he'd been when he'd arrived at her apartment, how capable and truly caring. Maybe he wasn't so bad; maybe he truly was trying to change.

Or maybe her pregnancy had her feeling more vulnerable and, therefore, more forgiving. Whatever the reasons, she was glad he'd come over and so obviously wanted to take care of her.

When his arms wound around her waist, her pulse quickened. Then he pressed her against his muscular length and her hips arched against him.

At her response, he slid his hands over her bottom. "I missed you, missed this."

Desire licked through her like a hot tide. Unbidden came the realization that she still hoped he could care for her. She still hoped that maybe him wanting her in his life because of the baby could be a fresh beginning.

Suddenly all the emotions she'd been fighting exploded, and she rubbed herself against the bulge in his slacks.

"Too bad we have to hold off…for a couple of nights," he whispered grimly.

She pressed herself against him again and then smiled. "You're killing me. We've got to stop."

His expression was so tender and his eyes were so warm, they melted the ice around her heart.

Eleven

The city sparkled in the night like a million jewels.

Michael lay in his bed counting his blessings for the first time in a while. Thank God he'd been in town two days ago and had been able to get to her apartment so fast.

Two days! For two whole days, ever since her fall, she'd been nice to him. When he'd come into the bistro every morning for breakfast, she'd joined him willingly. She'd even laughed at some of his jokes. When he'd called to check up on her during the day, she sometimes answered her phone.

He was feeling lucky about sex tonight, too.

Her pregnancy was showing—just a little—but that only made her more beautiful to him. Her tummy, which had been a smooth, flat plane when they'd met, was slightly rounded. The bump fascinated him and made him feel protective.

She was carrying his son. He was going to be a father. Maybe after the baby came, he wouldn't feel so alone.

"This doesn't mean anything," she murmured as she lay down on his bed and eased out of her black lacy bra.

"Right." He attempted to suppress his excitement as his eyes feasted on the silky skin and voluptuously soft curves she revealed. "Of course not."

She was still wearing her pants and he his jeans.

They'd eaten Chinese earlier in the evening because he'd wanted Peking duck, and she'd indulged him by accompanying him to a favorite restaurant that wasn't far from his penthouse.

In a corner booth of a glossy black dining room accented with white marble monkeys dangling from the ceiling and golden dragons encircling the walls, she'd eaten jellyfish and oxtails with increasing rapture. He'd feasted on Peking duck presented with scallions, julienned cucumber, delicate crepes and amber-colored hoisin sauce.

Of course they'd shared, nibbling off each other's plates and feeding each other—although she'd been much fonder of his duck than he'd been of her jellyfish. His glass of plum wine had glittered on their table like an enormous jewel. On their walk home they'd stopped at a chocolate shop for plump, chocolate-covered strawberries. Now they lay in his penthouse bedroom lit with silver moonlight.

They'd talked for hours about themselves. He'd told her more than he'd ever told anyone. At one point, when he'd confessed how ashamed he'd felt of the homes he'd lived in with his mother, Bree had placed her hand on his.

"My mother was a little like Anya. She chose her men for what they could give her. I thought all women were like that."

The soft shining light in Bree's eyes had eased the tension caused by the memories and confessions. Normally he never told such stories because they made him feel weak and powerless, but sharing them with Bree had made him feel closer to her, and less alone.

It was a beautiful night. Not that he had the slightest interest in the sweeping panorama of gilded buildings or the immense park beneath them, all of which had been selling points before he'd signed a contract and applied to the board to purchase the apartment.

No, his body's terrible longings had taken him over; it was she alone who compelled him. But unlike the first night they'd been together, his feelings for her now were honest. He liked her as a human being, and he wanted her to like him, too. He knew it would take a while, but he intended to show her he would never again treat her with anything less than the respect she deserved.

Her breasts were fuller than they'd been that first night, their tips dark and tight. He wanted to pull her close, lick her nipples and revel in her fecundity. But he knew better than to rush her. What they had was still too fragile.

"It's just sex," she said.

Not to him, not anymore.

"Whatever you say…as long as you'll keep getting naked for me," he murmured.

She laughed.

Nothing like a good meal to ease her anxieties and turn her on, he thought.

Finding out that she was carrying his child had made him feel far more closely connected to her. She had never slept with another man. She'd chosen him.

Her justifiable fury and their separation combined with his fear for her and the baby after the fall had taught him that she meant even more to him than he'd imagined. Not that he was comfortable with the depth of his feelings for her.

After her fall, with the help of her mother, he'd convinced Bree to move into his penthouse for a few days. So once again, she was installed in his downstairs guest suite behind his kitchen. He was in the process of acquiring the first-floor apartment he'd mentioned to her earlier, but he hadn't told her yet because he didn't want to argue about it.

For the past two evenings they'd spent the early hours after work together, and in an effort to gain her trust he'd deliberately kept things light and friendly. He hadn't touched her.

After meeting her doctor at the E.R., he'd brought Bree straight home and put her to bed. When she'd said she was ravenously hungry, he'd ordered pizza and served it to her on a tray in her room. Afterward, he'd sat on her bed and they'd talked. He'd been pleased that she'd wanted to know everything he'd done while he'd been away. He'd loved telling her of his adventures and business problems. Then he'd caught up on her activities in New York. He, too, had been thrilled that the bistro was doing better.

He'd stayed in her room for a long time even after she'd shut her eyes and fallen asleep. He'd liked listening to her gentle breathing, liked knowing she was safe in his home…and that their baby was out of danger.

"Kiss me," she whispered now, bringing him back to the present. "I want you to undress me. Then I'll undress you."

A sizzle of heat shot straight through him. With a long sigh, he reached for her and pulled her close.

Coiled around him, with her breasts nestled against his chest, she fitted him perfectly, like the vital piece of a missing puzzle. Holding her, he felt good, safe, on fire. He would feel even better when he was inside her.

With deft expertise they began to undress. Then with a silent moan, she slid her fingers along his nape.

"Oh, how you turn me on," she said.

"You could have fooled me," he said with a smile.

"I'm probably being a fool again, but I can't help myself." Brushing her parted lips along his jawline, she kissed her way down to the base of his throat.

He made a silent, secret vow to be good to her, to believe in her, no matter what. Maybe in time, he would win her.

He threw his head back so that her mouth and tongue could have easier access. She was warm and soft, everything he needed and desired in a woman but hadn't known he had to have.

He'd missed her so much while he'd been away. Every night he'd lain in his lonely hotel bed thinking about her hair, craving her body and that oh-so-intoxicating scent of strawberries.

Now that she was in his arms, the time he'd spent without her in those lavish surroundings seemed drab and empty. If he'd never met her, he would have gone on seeing and being seen with the world's most beautiful women, but feeling restless and empty because he felt no emotional involvement. He would have gone on closing deal after deal all the while longing for something more. He would have had no idea what "more" he wanted, other than more of what left him feeling so empty.

"Kiss me back," she begged.

Their mouths met, open and equally needy. Once he started kissing her, he couldn't seem to stop.

The tips of their tongues flicked against each other and then mated. Heat flooded him, pulsing between his legs. He wanted her, all of her, especially her heart and soul.

For a long time they necked like teenagers, teasing each other mercilessly by remaining partially dressed until their need grew to such a fever pitch they tore each other's clothes off, their bodies contorting so their mouths wouldn't have to part.

When they were both naked, he gently eased her onto her back, spread her legs apart and positioned himself so that his sex touched hers. She gasped in breathless delight at the liberty.

He rubbed himself against her. "I want to be with you like this all the time. When I kiss you, I feel you here. Even on the first kiss, I felt you here." His voice was so raw and intimate she blushed.

"I feel the same way."

He stroked her hair and stared into her shining eyes that finally dared to meet his. He savored the shy warmth in her gaze as well as the heat of her body underneath him. Then slowly, oh-so-slowly, she arched upward, inviting him, and he slid inside her. Holding on to his wide shoulders, she let out a shudder and tugged him closer.

"Why do I want you so much?" she whispered as she began to writhe. "Why?"

"Just accept it like I have."

"So, I'm doomed…just like my mother before me."

"Don't say that," he muttered fiercely, hating that she felt that way. She'd become so important to him.

He withdrew and then pushed deeper. She cried out and pulled him back. Then he lost all control and carried her over the flaming edge.

Afterward as he lay sated in the moonlit dark with his arms looped around her perspiring body, she turned to him. "You've had a lot of women and I haven't had anyone else. Since there's a lot lacking in my sexual education, there's something I have to know—"

"Don't," he muttered in a low, hoarse tone, feeling awkward. "Don't ask me about other women. They don't matter to me—do you understand?"

She tensed. "I don't mind about them so very much."

He knew better than to believe that, but he said nothing.

"I mean…sometimes I do mind, just not so much at this moment. I'm the odd duck, you see, who never would…

maybe because I was too shy or too busy or maybe because my mother was always telling me that the minute I had sex with a guy, he would have all the power."

"What did she mean by that?"

"The reason she married my father was because she was already pregnant with me. She wanted to have this big career, but she felt she had no say in her life after she got pregnant with me."

He tensed, wondering where she was going with this. "Oh."

"You wouldn't believe how guilty she made me feel."

"What they did before you were born isn't your fault."

"Bijou is not a logical person. She said sex can ruin a woman's life if she lets it, that more good women have been brought down by bad men than she could count, that it's women who always pay the price for mistakes in love. And she paid dearly."

"It's not always just the women who pay," he muttered gloomily, thinking of Anya.

"Bijou didn't want me to ruin my life the way she did."

"Then why has she been okay to me?"

"That doesn't make sense. When I told her I'd made this huge mistake and had gotten myself pregnant with your child, she didn't have much to say at first. She's impressed with you, with who you are, with what you've achieved. I don't know. Maybe she just likes it that you're rich."

"Ouch."

"Well, you asked. She must approve of you for some reason."

He smiled, glad that her mother seemed more or less on his side, whatever the reason.

"So, about those other women," she persisted. "Is the sex always this good?"

"No," he muttered fiercely. "How can you ask that?"

"Curiosity." She ran her fingertip down his nose. "You see, I researched you. I saw who you dated. They're all so beautiful. So much more beautiful than I am."

"Bree, baby, you have to understand—they were just going out with me to get things they wanted. Models are into enhancing their image, their brand. I was sort of using them, too. Sex like that, when it's between two people who are out for what they can get, is like…well, it's like a sport or a commodity that you both enjoy but neither of you feel all that deeply about. I was a single man, in need of an escort to parties and feminine companionship. Don't worry about those women because they don't matter at all."

"I don't matter either," she murmured. "Not really. You're only with me because of the baby."

Was she right? Then why did he enjoy doing things with her so much, like eating dinner, talking and laughing? He'd liked her in bed from the first. From the beginning he'd felt connected to her—even when he'd thought she was after the North money, even *then,* he'd liked her.

She was beginning to matter to him so much it scared him.

Instead of reassuring her, he kissed her.

Spiked high heels clicked impatiently on the wooden floor as the Realtor pointed out the many charms of the truly lovely apartment Michael wanted her to move into.

"Original, wide-plank floors!" Lisa Morris gushed. "Can you believe it? Well, what do you think?"

"I don't know."

"You already live in the neighborhood, so you know how wonderful the Upper West Side is. The people in this building are all young, hardworking professionals like yourself. Michael wants you to have the apartment so badly he's willing to meet the seller's first price. Believe

me, sweetie, Michael never goes to contract without nego-
tiating. You have no idea how utterly ruthless he can be."

"Oh, I have an idea." A very good idea. That's why she
still felt wary about their relationship even though he'd
been so nice of late.

"For a lower floor, the apartment is amazingly sunny."
Lisa's voice was as rapid as gunfire. She walked to a window and impatiently snapped open the blinds.

If Michael's high-powered Realtor was small in stat-
ure, she made up for it in presence. She was in her forties,
fit and sexy in her own brash way. She had big orange
hair and bright red lipstick. Nail polish of the same color
matched her bright stilettos and the huge leather designer
bag. Her short black skirt showed off great legs.

"It's modern," she said. "And cheerful. And totally updated. The garden makes it so special."

If only the woman would stop pressuring her, maybe
Bree could think.

"You wouldn't have to spend a dime. Not that Michael
would be against remodeling it for you—if that's what
you want. He's made it clear he's willing to do *anything*
to please you."

"I already owe him a lot because of an investment his
brother made in my business, so I don't want be obligated
to him for this, too."

"I'm beginning to see why he's so taken with you. Unlike the women I've seen him with before, you have principles. But trust me, principles will only carry a girl so far.
If I were you, I'd snap this place up in a heartbeat. Then
I'd snap him up, too. He's a prize catch, sweetie. Nail the
deal and the man before they slip through your fingers
and you spend the rest of your life regretting it. This is
New York. Beautiful women are throwing themselves at
him all the time."

"He's just trying to buy me."

"So, let him. He's gorgeous and he can give you the kind of fairy-tale life girls dream of."

"He doesn't care about anything but money."

"So? Sweetie, what do you think drives this city and everybody who lives here? What do you think buys all the goodies…like this apartment with its lovely garden and historic floors? Money. Always has. Trust me, you're lucky if a chance like Michael North comes once in a lifetime."

"Okay, I'll think about it," Bree said.

"You have my card," Lisa said. Her phone rang as she headed for the door. "We'll be in touch." She smiled, lifted her phone to her ear and was gone.

Giving the apartment a final look, Bree couldn't shake the feeling that Michael was trying to buy her by offering what he'd offered every other woman in his life.

Why say no to the apartment when you no longer say no to the flowers he sends, when you're sleeping with him?

Because I don't want to give in to all his demands until I am sure of what I really want. I don't like being pressured.

Michael was nothing if not relentless.

He could take care of her financially. She understood that. But could he love her?

Bree's heart knocked as she followed Michael's beautiful secretary down the marble hall to his office. She felt tense and defensive about her reason for visiting him on such short notice. The girl, a gorgeous brunette who had introduced herself as Eden, had told Bree in pleasant, hushed tones that Michael had canceled an important conference call to make time to see her.

"I'm sorry to interrupt you without giving you more warning," Bree said to him as soon as Michael opened the door and dismissed Eden. "I understand you postponed an important call."

"It'll wait." He looked deeply into her eyes. "You look upset. Are you okay?"

When she nodded, he pulled her to him and kissed her gently. Then he let her go. "What is it? What's wrong?"

Putting his hand against her waist, he led her to a guest chair and then sat down across from her.

She felt nervous, so she stared at his office. Compared to the glamorous marble lobby of his building and the waiting rooms and secretary's office outside, Michael's office was Spartan. Other than his sunny corner view of the city, no luxuries adorned his personal working space.

His immense, sleekly modern desk was flanked by equally minimalistic tables with monitors. Floor-to-ceiling bookshelves and cabinets were stacked with documents and file folders. Here, there were no photographs, no evidence he had a personal life at all.

"You have a nice view," she said, feeling the need to say something.

"Do I?" he replied, turning to look at it absently. Then he swiveled so that he faced her again. "I prefer this view," he said, his intense gaze causing her to blush. She'd put on a black dress, dangly silver earrings and a red pashmina just to please him. "So—why the visit?"

Feeling a mixture of pride and anxiety, she pulled an envelope out of her purse and pushed it across his desk.

Watching her, he grabbed it, tore it open with his bare hands, pulled out her check and then whistled. "What is this?" he demanded almost angrily.

"I made out a schedule," she said in her most business-like tone. "I intend to start repaying you on Will's investment in Chez Z."

"That is not necessary."

"You're saying that because I'm pregnant with your child, and you feel obligated to me now."

His black eyes narrowed. "I am obligated."

"I know how everything's a deal to you...." Her cheeks turned red and her voice faltered.

He flushed darkly. "Our relationship is not a deal."

"I'm pregnant, and you feel you have to take care of me. I want you to understand that even though I am pregnant, I can take care of myself. And from now on, I'm going to do so."

"We're sleeping together. Did it occur to you I might want to be generous to you?"

"I don't want our relationship to revolve around money."

"Then why are you here with this check?"

"It's a matter of principle. A time or two, you proposed that if I slept with you, you'd keep Chez Z afloat. Well, I refused that deal then, didn't I? So, I don't want you to think that because we're sleeping together I don't owe you that money."

"Damn it, Bree. You're having my child. Everything's different now."

"I don't want you to think I'm greedy or that I'm only involved with you because of your money. That's not the case."

"I don't think that. The money's a dead issue to me. So, can we not do this?"

"But I don't quite believe you. You've always bought your women, paid them off—"

"You're not like them, okay? How many times do I have to tell you that I was wrong about you before you'll believe me?"

"I...I don't know."

Sometimes she did believe him. Other times she remembered how he'd crushed her.

He must have seen her face fall because he said, "I guess I deserve that. I know I hurt you badly."

"Let's just say the way you made me feel is burned into me like a brand. I'm having a hard time letting it go."

He cursed softly. "I want to make that up to you. I don't want to hurt you like that ever again. As you know, I had a rough start and got knocked around a lot as a kid, so I'm not always an easy guy—and that's when I'm not deliberately being a jerk. Not that my history is an excuse, but I was prejudiced against your sex after Anya. Now, though…everything's different. I only hope that someday I'll be able to prove to you I've changed my attitude."

"For now—just take the money," she whispered. "It's important to me…in ways I can't explain. I'm going to start repaying you in two-week intervals."

"Okay. Whatever you want. However you want." His cynical tone was low and biting.

When she stood up, he led her to the door.

"One more thing," he said. "Since we're discussing finances maybe now would be a good time to inform you that I signed a contract on that building in your neighborhood."

"Oh, no. I wish you hadn't."

"I know, more proof you're nothing but a financial obligation to me, but hey, why don't you look at this a different way? My purchasing the building gives you choices. You can continue to stay with me at the penthouse. I told you last night how much I look forward to coming home to you. Or if you need more independence you can move into the apartment and be on your own."

"I would not be on my own, if you own the apartment."

"Then you can pay rent."

"I have a lease where I am."

"I'm sure I could work out a deal with your landlord.

I don't want to force you to be with me. I just want you and the baby to be safe."

"Okay," she said. "I'll think about it."

"So—do we have any more finances to discuss?"

She shook her head.

"Good." His gaze warmed as he took her hand and drew her to him. Realizing that he wanted her to kiss him goodbye in spite of their disagreement, she softened, too.

Standing on her tiptoes, she closed her eyes and slid her arms around his neck. Against all logic, her resistance melted when his lips claimed hers. Why did she always feel that something was very right in her world when he held her like this?

"See you tonight?" he whispered, sweeping the back of his hand across her cheek.

She nodded. "I'll cook. What are you in the mood for?"

"Not food." His hot glance and quick grin made her knees go weak.

"We were discussing supper," she whispered primly.

"We were?" He arched his dark brows.

She nodded.

"How about steak and potatoes?"

"Okay, then," she said, her eyes aglow as she envisioned juicy slabs of beef topped with mushroom sauce, baked potatoes oozing with crunchy bits of bacon, chives and sour cream. She would buy a deep red wine for him, a burgundy maybe, and crisp garden-grown greens to make a salad for herself.

"Followed by you for dessert," he whispered with a sexy smile right before he kissed her again.

Twelve

Four weeks had passed, and in that time Michael had grown relaxed in his relationship with Bree. She'd allowed him to help her get out of her old lease and move into the apartment he'd bought for her. She'd agreed to pay him the same rent she'd paid her previous landlord.

Tonight, Michael felt heavy and sated after an hour or so of deeply satisfying sex that had followed the lamb dinner she'd cooked for him. Funny how the more times he had her, the more his need for her grew.

Utterly content, he pulled her closer.

The doors to her garden were open. City sounds and moonlight crept over the walls and filled her bedroom. He was glad she'd relented about the apartment. Before she could change her mind, he'd sent a team of movers and packers to her old place.

Maybe it was time he pushed on a much more important issue.

"I want to marry you. I want you in my life forever,"

he said, speaking softly as his hand caressed her arm. "We've had a month together. I think we work."

He felt her tense, but she stayed where she was.

"We've been over this," she said tightly.

"Not lately."

"You only want to marry me because of the baby— *your heir.*"

Damn it, he thought. Ever since her fall, he'd spent as much time as he could with her because he cared about her. Why couldn't she see that?

He'd taken her to the theater, to movies and out shopping. He'd joined her on her afternoon walks in Riverside Park. They'd picnicked in Central Park, enjoyed dozens of fabulous dinners in New York's top restaurants. Then there were the countless rounds of mutually satisfying sex.

They got along. More than got along. He looked forward to every moment he had with her. They enjoyed friendship as well as sex. Weren't those things they could build on?

"As soon as I found out you were carrying my child I wanted to take care of you. I asked you to marry me then, remember?"

"Because you felt obligated."

"You said no, and because you felt that way, I've worked hard to develop a relationship with you."

"Because you just see this as the best solution, the best deal. Or you feel you *have* to do this, maybe for the baby—"

"What if I said that maybe I do feel obligated because of the baby, but I want *you* in my life, and that maybe I do...love you."

Hissing in a breath, she pushed away from him, plumped her pillows and sat up straighter. "Well, I wouldn't believe you, Michael." She crossed her arms over her breasts. "So don't do this."

"Why the hell not?"

"Because loving me has never been part of your agenda. You'll say or promise anything to close this deal."

"I admire you. I like hanging out with you. I can't keep my hands off you. I miss you when we're not together. I miss you so much it consumes me. If what I feel isn't love, it'll do until love comes along."

"Marriage demands a total commitment. For me, it demands love. Even then, there's a fifty percent divorce rate."

"Love is just a four-letter word for a complex emotion that means different things to different people."

"Look, Michael, Will told me you would say anything to get what you want. Look at this apartment. Look at the way you've been sending flowers to the bistro for months. You got my mother and everybody who works for me to badger me until I agreed to move in here. They're all on your side. You've totally won them over."

"So, I've been vetted. Maybe you should take that as a sign we belong together."

"No, I take that as a sign you'll do anything to close the deal. I can't believe that even you would stoop so low as to try to trick me into letting myself believe you could love me. Do you think I'm such an illogical romantic that I'll do what you want if you just toss out the word *love?*"

"You think that my reasons for proposing to you have to do solely with a pragmatic concern for gaining more control over my heir?"

"I didn't at first. In the beginning I was starry-eyed about you. But the way you treated me that first night and right after Will died burned away my romantic illusions. I can't help it if I see you plainly now. I don't dislike you, Michael. Far from it. You have to know I'm crazy stupid about you in bed. And you're fun to hang out with. But this is an affair. Nothing more. An affair I think I'm stupid to engage in because I'm not sophisticated enough to keep my emotions guarded all the time."

"Guarded?"

"Yes. Guarded. I can't let myself care too much again. You have affairs all the time with women like Natalia."

"What I have with you isn't like that."

"I may be naive, but I know that an affair between people like us, who have different values about life, will end. I don't want ours to end now…so let's not discuss this. And let's not talk about marriage, either. Let's just enjoy each other while we can. Later, we'll part, and when we do, we'll work out a way to raise our son, okay?"

"Not okay!" He threw off his sheet, stood up, scooped his clothes off the floor and began to throw them on.

"Oh, so now you're mad at me? This is so unfair, Michael. You're the one who seduced me and got us into this mess. No matter what you say, I know the only reason you'd ever want to marry me is because I'm pregnant with your heir!"

"Well, I don't deny I've been a damned fool when I stupidly thought you were using my brother. If I was prejudiced then it was because I couldn't see who you were. But now you're the one who can't see who I am. For the past month I've tried to show you that I'll be good to you. Maybe I deserve this. I thought we were happy together."

"It has been fun," she agreed.

"It's been way more than fun. But if you don't want this to go any further, then I won't push myself on you any longer. If you think this relationship is all about closing a deal, well, the deal's off."

"Michael, stop this. You've got to see that we could never have a real marriage. My mother married my father because she was pregnant with me and she was miserable. The only thing you and I have in common is the baby. You do international deals. I'm the owner of a bistro. I'd hold you back."

"The hell you would."

"You'd resent me just like she resented him. Why don't we just enjoy our affair until its natural conclusion…and then we'll figure out a way to raise our baby together?"

He felt raw and sick to the core at that prospect—devastated. Bitter pride made him mask the deep wound she'd inflicted.

"If that's the way you really feel, maybe you're right." His voice was cool. "Maybe you are better off without me. I've given it my best shot. I'm through."

"Michael!"

He tore his key to her apartment off his key ring and flung it on her bedside table. "Consider our affair concluded. No deal."

His heart wasn't in what he was saying as he shoved his shirt into his slacks and picked up his cell phone. Why couldn't she see who he was now? Why couldn't she accept that he truly wanted to be with her? That he could come to love her? That he didn't want this half-assed deal she was proposing?

As he strode out of her bedroom blind to any emotion other than his own hurt, he willed her to come after him.

But she didn't see who he was, didn't feel the pain that was choking off his breath and she didn't follow him. When he left the building, he prayed that she would call him on his cell and agree that what he felt for her was enough. Love grew day by day, like a flower, didn't it, if it was real? Hell—what did he know about love?

When his cell phone buzzed, his heart raced. Thinking it was Bree, he grabbed for it, but it was Natalia, of all people, so he declined the call.

As he looked up from the sidewalk, he saw Bree standing in her window wrapped in a tangled bedsheet.

She was as pale as a ghost. Did he only imagine the shimmer of brightness on her cheeks? His heart constricted. Had he made her cry?

He wouldn't let himself care. She'd rejected him.

When she let go of the curtain, and it fell back into place, he tore his gaze from her window and hurried down the sidewalk.

When Natalia called him again a few minutes later, he picked up. Why the hell shouldn't he?

Bree stared up at her bedroom ceiling. Feeling lost and uncertain, she'd been staring at it for hours.

With shocking, devastating suddenness their affair was over.

Bree had known she'd be hurt when he left her, but the pain that pulsed in the center of her being cut like a blade. It was as if all hope for happiness was draining out of her like blood seeping from a fatal wound.

Hours later, when the sun turned the rooftops in her neighborhood bloodred, she got up, dressed and walked out of her apartment, feeling heavy from her long, sleepless night.

Hoping to clear her head, she made her way toward the park. She wanted to be around noisy cars on their way to offices and schools, around people rushing to catch buses or subway trains. Near the park, she bought herself a bagel and coffee from a street vendor and kept walking.

Michael had said he cared about her, that he knew he craved her, missed her…. And because she'd been a fool to believe him before, she'd refused to let herself believe him now.

But what if he'd been telling the truth? She remembered how tenderly he'd treated her when she'd fallen on her stairs. He'd said he'd been happy with her this past month. She'd certainly been happy with him.

What if he *had* come to care for her? What if he *could* love her? What if this relationship wasn't just a deal to him?

What if she was wrong? What if he'd been telling her the truth? What if he didn't feel trapped into marrying her? What if he really was beginning to fall in love with her, and instead of giving him a chance, she'd driven him away? What if she'd hurt him with her rejection exactly as he'd hurt her?

Oh, God. Thinking herself a naive fool, she pulled her phone out of her pocket and called him.

"What do you want?" he said, his tone so harsh he terrified her. "I'm on another line."

"Michael…"

The line went dead.

She wanted to hold on to his voice, but he was already gone.

She caught a slow, agonized breath. Had he deliberately hung up on her?

Motion on the street seemed to stop as she clasped the phone against the violent pounding of her heart. The horns and sirens around her grew silent. The hawker's voice died away. The pedestrians passing her seemed to walk in slow motion. All she could feel was the pain in her heart.

She felt like screaming, like crying out, but of course she did not. Instead, she stumbled back to her apartment where she waited in her living room for over an hour for him to call her back. When he didn't, she set her phone on an end table and picked up her purse.

She took the key to his penthouse off her own key ring. She dug an envelope out of her desk, addressed it and put his key inside. Leaving the package on the table, she walked outside to water the ivy that climbed her garden wall.

While she watched water from her hose rain down on the bricks, she tried to imagine how she would live the rest of her life without him.

"Aren't you sleeping?" Bijou demanded.

"I'm fine," Bree said, annoyed by her mother's constant hovering of late.

"Why the dark glasses then? Afraid I'll see the shadows under your eyes? Why aren't you sleeping?"

Bree yanked off the offending glasses and tossed them into her purse. "I am sleeping!" she lied. "Why wouldn't I be sleeping?"

She hated it when her mother poked her long nose where it didn't belong and kept poking it—which had been happening way too often lately.

"No more flowers?" Bijou persisted.

It was now day two after Michael had walked out on her, day two since he'd stopped sending flowers.

Bijou lifted a vase from a table in the main dining room and removed two withered roses. "Did you have a quarrel? Or is this more serious?"

Bree wasn't ready to talk about Michael. "Why don't you go check on the prep work? Or maybe sweep outside?"

"Why hasn't he been coming by for breakfast anymore? I miss him."

"Bijou! Please!"

"Should I maybe call him, yes? And tell him we miss him, very much, yes?"

"No!"

"So—you did quarrel. Then you foolish, sad girl, you must call him and make up!"

She'd tried, hadn't she? And he hadn't called her back.

"You don't know anything." When Bree's eyes began to sting she went to her purse, grabbed her sunglasses and slammed them back on her face. "Please. Don't ask me about him right now."

"You two are so romantic," Marcie whispered from a table in the back. "Such passion. Such fire."

Not anymore.

Her life felt empty, colorless.

Feeling hollow despair, Bree shut her eyes.

"You're just as unhappy as he is," Luke said as he set his fork down. "I came by because I thought that would be the case."

"It's just an off night," Bree countered defensively as she stood over his table.

"Yes. Everything about this place is off...*you,* the service, the pastries, the soup, even the omelets, which were always perfect, but especially you. Since I know what you're capable of and what your staff is capable of, you can't fool me. A month ago, you were doing so well. This place was fun. Hot."

Since Michael had walked out two weeks ago, she'd had to force herself to go through the motions of living. She knew she hadn't been concentrating at work.

"I'm sorry if your dining experience has been such a disappointment."

"Bull! What's going on between you and Michael?"

"Nothing."

"Funny, he said the same thing when I went to check on him."

"You've seen him?" She tried to keep her face blank but her heart had begun to race.

"Yesterday. Did you know that he's all but withdrawn from the world?"

"We haven't been in contact lately, so—no."

"Really? Well, he's taken the week off—hell, he never takes a week off—he's a ruthless workaholic for God's sake! Right now he's just sitting around his penthouse reading. Or watching his cleaning lady do her tasks. *Watching his cleaning lady!* He's not shaving or showering. She took me aside when I was leaving. She told me she's worried sick about him. He won't answer the phone—especially if it's Eden, his secretary, calling about work.

"I asked him about you. I said if you love her, for God's sake, man, tell her. He looked up at me with eyes that were as dark and dead as death. You know what he said?"

She shook her head.

"He said, 'I tried, Luke. But I guess I don't know what love is. Or at least she doesn't think I do. Or I'm not the man she wants. Do you really think I didn't try?'"

Bree sank into the chair across from Luke. Had Michael really said all that?

"Thank you for caring about him. And thank you for coming by to check on me. It was sweet, really. Thank you."

"So—are you going to call him?"

"I don't know. He broke up with me."

"Call him. He loves you, woman."

Did he? Did she dare believe that she was really more than an obligation or another deal he had to close?

She thought about the way he'd grown up…without ever getting enough love. Maybe he did love her. Maybe love was such a new experience for him, he wasn't sure what it was or how to express it.

She remembered how sweet he'd been after her fall, how committed and determined he'd been to have her in his life ever since.

He could have any woman he wanted, and he'd chosen her.

Maybe he *did* love her. Maybe she'd been wrong.

Whether he truly cared or not, she was worried about

him. Should she go to him? Check on him? After all, he was the father of her child. They would have to talk at some point. Why not now?

But what if he wouldn't let her in?

Her key. Since she'd procrastinated as usual, the envelope with his key was still in her purse, waiting to be mailed.

When the intercom buzzed for the fifth time, Michael got to his feet, swaying slightly. How many shots of scotch had he had? Who cared? He'd lost count.

On unsteady feet he crossed the room that was littered with newspapers and business magazines and answered his intercom.

"It's me, Natalia."

Surrounded by media, she looked gorgeous on his video screen.

"Go the hell away," he said.

"Carlo, I told you about Carlo, he jilted me. He thinks he's this big important producer. But nobody jilts Natalia publicly and gets away with it. I was so wrong about you, wrong to blame you for anything. Carlo—he is the real bastard."

"Well, I'm sorry about Carlo, but I can't talk right now."

"Can I please come up?"

"I said this is a bad time, Natalia. Look, you're a beautiful girl. Sooner or later your luck with men will change."

Platitudes, he thought. Who was he to give advice to the lovelorn when he was in a lot worse shape than Natalia?

He cut the connection and poured himself another scotch. Then he slumped onto his couch again and tortured himself with more memories of Bree—Bree with her cute baby bump climbing on top of him, Bree taking him into her mouth, Bree kissing him everywhere with those little flicks of her tongue that drove him wild.

What the hell was he doing, dreaming of a woman who didn't want him? Luke was right. He couldn't go on like this.

Michael had brought this on himself. She saw him as deal-maker, not as a husband. He'd offered her all he had to give and she'd rejected him.

She was the mother of his child, and he had to establish a workable, familial, brotherly relationship with her so they could raise that child together. That was all that was left, their bond as parents.

With Michael's key clutched tightly in one hand and her purse in the other, Bree walked up to his building just as Natalia emerged with a smile meant to dazzle the paparazzi lying in wait for her.

"Yes, I'm dating Michael North again," she said to a reporter when he thrust a microphone to her lips. "He invited me here." When flashes blazed, she laughed triumphantly and raced for her limo.

An inner voice cried inside Bree. *See how easily he replaced you with someone more beautiful. You were just an obligation, a deal he wanted to close. Go home. Forget him.*

On the walk through the park from her place to his, visions of married life had flooded her mind. She'd imagined Michael beside her when the baby came, Michael beside her at their son's first birthday, Michael beside her at the holidays and dining at home with friends. And all the while that she'd been imagining a shared life with him, he'd been entertaining Natalia.

She flung the key into the bottom of her purse. Lacking the strength to walk home, she went to the curb and asked the doorman to hail a taxi for her.

* * *

Somewhere a bolt turned in a lock. Michael blinked, annoyed at the sound. Dimly he grew aware that someone was outside his front door fumbling with a key. Who the hell could it be?

Natalia? Hadn't he sent her away? Despite the liquor that fogged his brain he was almost sure he had sent her away. He hadn't given her a key, had he?

When his door gave way, he shot to a sitting position in time to see a woman glide gracefully inside.

"Natalia?"

The great room was filled with gloom and long shadows and his vision was blurry from drink, so he couldn't make out her features. Still, something didn't seem right. Natalia was several inches taller, wasn't she?

"Not Natalia. It's me, Michael," said the soft feminine voice he'd dreamed of for days.

A pulse in his gut beat savagely.

"Bree?"

"Yes."

When she turned on the lights, he blinked at the glare and sat up straighter, pushing back his tangled hair. When was the last time he'd showered or shaved? Why did he give a damn? She'd turned him out, hadn't she? She saw him as nothing more than a crass deal-maker.

"Why are you here?" he demanded coldly.

She shut the door and moved cautiously around the newspapers that littered his floor. She moved as if she was approaching a dangerous wild animal.

Aware suddenly that he wore the same T-shirt and pair of jeans he'd put on yesterday, the same ones he'd slept in, he flushed. His eyes burned as he studied her, and his head ached.

Damn it. He didn't want her pity or her tenderness.

"Tell me what you want and go," he growled fiercely.

"Luke came to the bistro and told me…you weren't well."

"The two of you should mind your own damn business. As you can see, there's nothing wrong with me. I'm fine. Having the time of my life! Go home."

She picked up his empty scotch bottle. "Looks like we've got one dead soldier. Why don't I make you some coffee?"

"Because I don't want coffee," he snarled.

"Well, maybe I do. Why don't you freshen up so you can play host while I putter around in the kitchen?"

"What gives you the right to barge into my house and boss me around? We broke up—remember?"

"I'll be happy to tell you why I'm here after you take a shower and make yourself presentable. You really don't look very civilized, darling." Again her voice was maddeningly light and cheery as she disappeared into his kitchen.

He considered going after her, but when he took a step in pursuit, he stumbled. Feeling unsure, he thought better of following her.

One glance in his bathroom mirror had him shuddering in disgust. Who was that man with the narrowed, bloodshot eyes and the greasy, tangled hair?

Ashamed at how low he'd sunk, he stripped and stepped into an icy shower.

The cold water was hellish, but it revived him. Five minutes later, when he returned to the great room, he'd shaved, brushed his teeth and slicked back his damp hair.

She smiled. "You look like a new man."

Except for his headache, he felt a lot better. Not that he was about to admit it.

"Why the hell are you here? If you've come because you pity me, so help me…"

"I don't pity you. I love you. I've missed you. Picnics in

the park. Dinners out. And the passionate things you did to me in bed. I think I'm okay with you thinking maybe you love me."

He looked down at her, unable to comprehend her words.

"What?"

"Drink your coffee," she whispered as she handed him a steaming cup.

His hand shook slightly, but he took a long sip and then another. It was strong and black, just what he needed.

"What are you saying?" he demanded.

"Luke came to see me."

"Oh."

"I was worried about you, so I came over. Then I was so scared when I saw Natalia downstairs in your lobby. She was all but holding a press conference and telling everybody you two were back together."

"We're not back together," he said.

"I know. The doorman told me you hadn't let her up. If he hadn't told me that while he was helping me hail a cab, I would have lost my courage and gone home."

"We haven't been together since I called it off months ago. Her new boyfriend broke up with her and she has such low self-esteem she goes crazy when that happens. She can't stand to feel abandoned or rejected, so she came over here. But I was in no shape to deal with her."

"It's a very difficult feeling…abandonment," Bree whispered.

"Yes, it is," he said.

"That's how I felt that first night when you told me you'd lied and didn't care about me."

"I'm so sorry." He sucked in a breath. Without Bree these past few weeks, he'd felt as if he was a dead man. Now that she was here, he felt alive again. "I missed you," he whispered. "I missed you so much."

She sat down and put her arms around him. "I love you, too. I love you enough for both of us. I'm going to hope that what you feel for me will grow...as you said it would."

"Bree. I do love you. Now. And forever. If I didn't know it before, I know it now. You don't know what I've been through...without you. I couldn't work or think. I was utterly worthless without you. I want you and our baby... more than anything."

He set his coffee cup down as she circled his neck with her arms. Her hands moved gently through his hair, which was still damp from his shower.

"You really love me?" she said.

Their eyes met. "Yes, these past few days I haven't been able to forgive myself for how I treated you. You don't know how I despised myself. You were so sweet and wonderful that first night. And I never gave you a chance. I tried to crush you. And I nearly did. I couldn't blame you for not trusting me."

"We both must forget about that night."

"Never. It's the night I first began to love you...I just didn't know it or couldn't admit it. Forgive me...please."

"I do. Oh, I do."

He took her face between his hands, his thumbs lightly brushing her lips. "I thought I'd lost you, and I didn't know how I'd live without you."

"I felt the same way. Isn't it wonderful we don't have to live without each other?"

It was too wonderful for words.

He kissed her long and hard. He pulled her closer and kissed her again and again, drinking of her deeply, tasting her, reveling in her nearness, her sweetness, until they were both breathless. "I will never get enough of you."

"I love you," she said again.

"Yesterday, I dreaded all the tomorrows of my life," he murmured. "Now I'm looking forward to them. You, dear, sweet Bree, have freed me from myself, from Anya, from all the dark emotions that hardened me."

"If I've helped you even a little I'm very glad."

"You've given me such happiness, a whole new life."

His lips claimed hers, and he didn't let her go for a very long time.

Epilogue

Never had Bree felt so content, so proud of herself, nor so filled with love and affection as she did right now. Lying in her hospital bed she watched Michael pace proudly, his voice soft as he tried to soothe their darling, newborn son.

Michael was such a good husband. Every morning she woke up loving him a little more, and she knew he felt the same. Not only had he stayed with her during labor and stood beside her during the delivery, he'd gone with her to every doctor's visit and to every childbirth class she'd taken.

Baby Will's eyes and hair were as black as ebony. The instant the nurses had laid him in her arms she'd fallen in love. She'd uncurled his fingers and he'd wrapped them around hers and hung on. Maybe she loved him so much because he was a tiny replica of his handsome dad.

Michael walked over to the bed and leaned down to show her their son was sleeping. As she lifted back the blue blanket to stare at her son's wrinkled, red face, a great rush of tenderness swept her.

She was the luckiest woman in the world.

"Michael," she whispered. "Isn't he wonderful?"

"He is, and so are you. I love you," he said in a low tone that shook her to the depths of her soul. "I love you more than anything in the world."

His words shook her because she was sure, so very sure, he meant them. Deep down, he'd always been a family man. Even though he'd been wrong about her in the beginning, love of his younger brother and his fierce desire to protect him was what had brought them together. He'd wanted his brother to experience the kind of love he'd never had himself, but had craved.

She was so glad she saw who he really was now—a man who had found the love he must have been looking for his whole life.

He was a fighter. He would always be there for her; he would always love and protect her.

Yes, she was the luckiest woman in the world to have this man and be loved by him.

* * * * *

CLAIMING HIS
SECRET SON

OLIVIA GATES

To the romance writing community –
editors, authors, reviewers and readers – who
helped me realise not one but two major life goals.
This one is for you. Love you all.

One

Richard Graves adjusted his electric recliner, sipped a mouthful of straight bourbon and hit Pause.

The image on the hundred-plus-inch TV screen stilled, eliminating the unsteadiness of the recording. Murdock, his second-in-command, had taken the footage while following his quarry on foot. The quality was expectedly unsatisfactory, but the frame he'd paused was clear enough to bring a smile to his lips.

The only time a smile touched his lips, or he experienced emotions of any sort, was when he looked at her. At that graceful figure and energetic step, that animated face and streaming raven hair. At least, he guessed they were emotions. He had no frame of reference. Not in the past quarter of a century.

What he remembered feeling in his youth was so distant, it was as if he'd heard about it from someone else. Which was accurate. The boy he'd been before he'd joined The Organization—the criminal cartel that abducted and imprisoned children and turned them into unstoppable mercenaries—though as tough as nails, still held no resemblance to the invulnerable bastard everyone believed him—rightfully so—to be.

From what he remembered before his metamorphosis, and even after it, the most he'd felt had been allegiance, protectiveness, responsibility. For his best-friend-turned-nemesis Numair, for his disciple-turned-ally Rafael and to varying degrees for the Black Castle blokes—his reluctant partners in their globe-spanning business empire, Black Castle Enterprises—and their own. But that was where he drew the line in noble sentiments. What came naturally to him were dark, extreme, vicious ones. Power lust, vengeance, mercilessness.

So it never failed to stun him when beholding her provoked something he'd believed himself incapable of feeling. What he could only diagnose as…tenderness. He'd been feeling it regularly since he'd upgraded his daily ritual of reading surveillance reports on her to watching footage of what Murdock thought were relevant parts of her day.

Anyone, starting with her, would be horrified to learn he'd been keeping her under a microscope for years. And interfering in her life however he saw fit, undetectably changing the dynamics of the world she inhabited. He broke a dozen laws on a daily basis, from breach of privacy to coercion to…far worse, in his ongoing mission of being her guardian demon. Not that this was even a concern. The law existed for him to either break…or wield as a weapon.

But he *was* concerned she'd ever sense his surveillance or suspect his interference. Even if she never suspected it was him behind it all.

After all, she didn't even know he was alive.

As far as she knew he'd been lost since she was six. He doubted she even remembered him. Even if she did, it was best for her to continue thinking him gone, too.

Like the rest of their family.

So he only watched over her. As he had since she was born. At least, he'd tried to. There'd been years when he'd been powerless to protect her. But the moment he could, he'd given her a second chance for a safe and normal existence.

He sighed as he froze another image. He vividly remembered the day his parents had brought her home. Such a tiny, helpless creature. He'd been the one to give her her name. His little Rose.

She wasn't little now and certainly not helpless, but a surgeon, a wife, a mother and a social activist. He might help her here and there, but her achievements had all been ones of merit. He just made sure she got what she worked so hard for and abundantly deserved.

Now she had a successful career, a vocation and a husband who adored her—one he'd thoroughly vetted before letting him near her—and two children. Her family was picture-perfect, and not only on the outside.

Unfreezing the video, he huffed and tossed back the last of the bourbon. If only the Black Castle lads knew that he, aka Cobra, the most lethal operative The Organization had ever known and who was now responsible for their collective security, spent his evenings watching the sister they didn't know existed, who didn't know *he* existed, go about her very normal life. He'd never hear the end of it.

Suddenly he frowned, realizing something.

This footage didn't make sense. Rose was entering her and her husband's new private practice in Lower Manhattan. Murdock always only included new developments, emergencies or anything else that was out of the ordinary.

So watching Rose *was* his only source of enjoyment. But when he'd told Murdock to provide samples of Rose's normal activities, he'd stared emptily at him then continued to provide him only with what he considered worth seeing.

Had Murdock now decided to heed him and start giving him snippets of Rose walking down the street or shopping or picking her children up from school?

He snorted. That Vulcan would never do anything he didn't consider logical or pertinent. Even if he obeyed him blindly otherwise, Murdock wouldn't fulfill a demand he considered to be fueled by pointless sentiment and a waste of both their time.

This meant there was more to what he was watching than Rose entering her workplace.

What was he missing here?

Suddenly his heart seemed to hit Pause itself. Everything inside him followed suit, coming to a juddering standstill.

The person who entered the frame, the one Rose turned to talk to in such delight… Though the image was still from the back with only a hint of a profile apparent, he'd know that shape, that…*being*…blindfolded in a crowd of a million.

Her.

Sitting up, exercising the same caution he'd approached armed bombs with, he reached to the side table, vaguely noting how the glass rattled as he set it down. It wasn't his hand that shook. It was his heart. The heart that never crossed sixty beats per minute even under extreme duress. It now exploded from its momentary cessation in thunderclaps, sending recoil jolting through every artery and nerve.

The once waist-length, golden hair was now a dark, shoulder-length curtain. The body once rife with dangerous curves was svelte and athletic in a prim skirt suit. But there wasn't the slightest doubt in his mind. That *was* her.

Isabella.

The woman he'd once craved with a force that had threatened the fulfillment of his lifelong obsession.

He'd long resolved it according to his meticulous plan. It was *her* issue that hadn't been concluded satisfactorily. Or at all. She'd been his one feebleness, remained his only failure. The only one who'd made him swerve from his course and at times forget all about it. She remained the only woman he'd been unable—*unwilling* to use. But he'd let her use him. After their incendiary fling, when a choice had had to be made, she'd told him he'd never been an option.

Not that the memory of his one lapse was what had set off this detonation of aggression.

It was who she was. *What* she was.

The wife of the man who'd been responsible for the deaths of his family and for orphaning Rose.

He'd gone after her almost nine years ago as her husband's only Achilles' heel. But nothing had gone according to plan.

Her impact had been unprecedented. And it had had nothing to do with her rare beauty. Beauty never turned a hair on his head. Desire was his weapon, never his weakness. He'd been the one The Organization sent when women were involved, to seduce, use, then discard with utmost coldness.

But she'd been an enigma. At once clearly reveling in being the wife of a brute forty years her senior, who doted on her and submerged her in luxuries, while studying to be a doctor and involving herself in many humanitarian activities.

Going in, he'd been convinced her benevolent facade had been designed to launder her husband's image, in which she'd been succeeding, spectacularly.

But after he'd been exposed to her, this twenty-four-year-old who seemed much older than her years, he'd no longer been sure of anything. Seducing her had also proved much harder than he'd anticipated.

Though he'd been certain she'd reciprocated his unstoppable desire, she wouldn't let him near. Thinking she'd been only whetting his appetite until he was ready to do anything for a taste of her, as her husband had been, he'd intensified his pursuit. But it had only been after he'd followed her on a relief mission in Colombia—saving her and her companions during a guerilla attack—that her resistance had finally crumbled. The following four months had been the most delirious experience of his life.

He'd had to force himself to remember who she was to continue his mission. But it had been the hardest thing he'd ever done. When he'd had her in his arms, when he'd been inside her, he'd forgotten who he was.

But he'd finally extracted secrets only she'd known about her husband without her realizing it. Then he'd been ready to make his move. Not that it had been that easy.

Putting his plan into action had meant the end of his mission. The end of them. And he'd been unable to stomach walking away from her. He'd wanted more of her. Limitlessly more.

So he'd done what he'd never thought he'd do. He'd asked her to leave with him.

Though she'd claimed she couldn't think of life without him, her rejection had been instantaneous. And final. She'd never considered leaving her husband for him.

In his fever for a continuation of the affair, he'd convinced himself she'd refused because she feared her husband. So he'd pledged carte blanche of his protection.

But playing the distraught lover seamlessly, she'd still refused, adamant that there was no other way.

It had been only then that the red heat of coveting had hardened into the cold steel of cynicism. And he'd faced the truth.

She'd preferred her protection and luxury from the less-demanding man she'd married when she'd been twenty and had wrapped around her finger. Him, she'd only replace in her bed. There'd never been any reason she'd choose him over her decades-older ogre.

But he was certain she'd long regretted her choice when he'd shortly afterward destroyed her sugar daddy, protractedly, agonizingly, pulverizing her own life of excess with him.

Not that he'd cared what had happened to her. She'd made her bed of thorns thinking it was the lap of eternal luxury. It was only fitting she'd be torn apart lying in it.

But this searing vision from his past looked patently whole. Even in the video's inferior quality, he could sense her sangfroid. None of the hardships she must have suffered had come close to touching her.

Then it was over. The two women entered the building, and the video came to an abrupt end.

He stared at the black screen, questions an erupting geyser.

What was she doing at Rose's practice? This didn't seem to be a first-time meeting. So how had he missed the earlier ones leading to this level of familiarity? How had she come in touch with Rose at all?

This couldn't be a coincidence.

But what else could it be? There was no way she could know of his connection to Rose. His Richard Graves persona—the one he'd adopted after he'd left his Cobra days behind—had been meticulously manufactured. Not even The Organization with its limitless intelligence resources had found a shred of evidence tying him to their vanished agent.

Even if she'd somehow discovered the relationship between him and Rose, their affair had ended in unequivocal finality. No thanks to his own resolve. While he'd sworn he'd never check on her, he'd weakened on another front. He'd left the door ajar for a year afterward, in case she'd wanted to reestablish contact. Which she hadn't. If she'd wanted to do so now, she would have found a way to bring herself to his attention. It didn't make sense she'd target Rose to get to him. Or did it?

He exploded to his feet, snatched his phone out and punched Murdock's speed-dial number.

The moment the line opened, he barked, "Talk to me."

After a moment Murdock's deep voice was at once composed and surprised. "Sir?"

Impatience almost boiled his blood. "The woman with my sister. What was she doing with her?"

"It's all in the report, sir."

"Bloody hell, Murdock, I'm not reading your thirty-page report."

Silence greeted his snarl this time. Murdock must be stunned, since that was exactly what Richard had been doing for the past year. Murdock's documentation of Rose's every breath had been getting more extensive at his own demand. But right now he couldn't focus on a single paragraph.

"Everything I found out about Dr. Anderson's liaison with the woman in question is in the last two pages, sir."

"Did you sustain a serious head injury lately, Murdock? Am I not talking the Queen's English? I'm not reading two damned words. I want your verbal report. *Now.*"

At his barrage the man's chagrin almost crackled down the line, reminding him again that Owen Murdock was a relic of a bygone era.

Richard had always thought he'd be more at home in something like King Arthur's round table. He did treat Richard with the fervor of a knight in the service of his liege.

He'd been the first boy Richard had been given to train when he'd first joined The Organization as a handler…six years old to his own sixteen, making Murdock Rafael's age. He'd had him for six more years before Murdock had been taken from him and Rafael given to him instead.

Murdock had refused to accept anyone else's leadership, until Richard had been summoned to straighten him out. Richard had only told him to play along, that one day he'd get him out. Murdock had unquestioningly obeyed him. And believed him.

Richard had fulfilled his pledge, taking him away with him when he'd left, manufacturing a new identity for him, too. But instead of striking out on his own, Murdock had insisted on remaining in his service, claiming his training hadn't been complete. He'd actually been on par with the rest of the Black Castle chaps from day one, could have become a mogul in his own right, too. But Murdock had only wished to repay what he considered his debt to Richard before he could move on. Knowing how vital that had been to him, Richard had let him.

Now, ten years later, Murdock showed no signs of moving on. He'd have to shove him off the ledge soon, no matter if it would be like losing his right arm for real.

Murdock's current silence made Richard regret his outburst more. His number two prided himself on always anticipating his needs and surpassing his expectations. The last thing he wanted was to abuse such loyalty.

Before he made a retraction, Murdock talked, his tone betraying no resentment or mortification.

"Very well. At first, that woman appeared to be just another colleague of Dr. Anderson's. I ran a check on her, as I always do, and found nothing of note. But a development made me dig deeper. I discovered she'd changed her name legally five years ago, just before she made her first entry into the United States after a six-year hiatus. Her name was…"

"Isabella Burton."

Murdock digested the fact that Richard already knew her. He'd told neither him nor Rafael about the intensely personal mission he'd undertaken, or about her.

Murdock continued, "She's now Dr. Isabella Sandoval."

Sandoval. That wasn't either of her maiden names. Coming from Colombia, she'd had two. She must have been trying to become someone else when she'd adopted the new surname, after what had happened to her husband. That would also explain the changes in her appearance. And she *was* a doctor now.

Murdock went on, "But that wasn't what made me wary—what made me single out her meeting with Dr. Anderson to present to you. It's because I found a gaping thirteen-year hole in her history. From the age of twelve to the age of twenty-five, I couldn't find a shred of information on her."

Of course. She'd wiped clean the time she'd been Burton's wife, and for some reason only known to her, years before that. No doubt to hide more incriminating evidence that would prevent her from being accepted by any respectful society.

"The information trail starts when she was twenty-six, when she started a four-year surgical residency in Colombia, in affiliation with a pediatric surgery program in California. It was a special 'out of the match' residency arrangement with the chief of surgery of a major teaching hospital. She obtained her US credentials and board certification last year. Then a week ago, she arrived in the United States and signed a one-year lease on a six-bedroom house in the Forest Hills Gardens section of Queens. She is here at the behest of doctors Rose and Jeffrey Anderson to start working in their private practice as a full partner, major shareholder and board member."

After that, Richard didn't know when he ended the call.

He only knew he was replaying that video over and over, Murdock's words a revolving loop in his mind.

Isabella. She was going to be his sister's partner.

Swearing under his breath, he almost cracked the remote in two as he pressed the off button.

Like hell she was.

Four hours later Richard felt as if the driver's seat of his Rolls Royce Phantom was sprouting red-hot needles.

It had been more than two hours since he'd parked across the street from his sister's house. He'd driven here immediately when Murdock had called back saying he'd neglected to tell him Isabella was having dinner there tonight. She had yet to make an exit.

What was taking the bloody woman that long? What kind of dinner lasted more than four hours?

This alone told him things were worse than he'd first thought. Isabella seemed to be a close friend of his sister's, not just a prospective partner. And though Murdock hadn't been able to pinpoint the events leading to this bizarre status quo, Richard was certain this wasn't an innocent friendship.

Not on Isabella's side. She always had an angle. And obtained her objectives through deception and manipulation. Her medical qualifications themselves had probably been obtained through some meticulously constructed fraud.

Yet that was all conjecture. He had nothing solid to explain how Rose and her husband had developed such a deep connection with her that they'd invite her to be their equal partner in their life's crowning achievement. She'd made herself so invisible, her past so untraceable she'd fallen off Murdock's radar until now, when she was about to be fully lodged into their lives.

He'd torn over here once Murdock had informed him they'd finished dinner and coffee, expecting to intercept her soon afterward as she left. That had been—he flicked a glance at his watch—two and a half bloody hours ago.

Every minute of those he'd struggled with the urge to storm inside and drag her out.

He hadn't stayed out of his sister's life only to let that siren infect it with the ugliness of her past, the malice of her intentions and the exploitation in her blood.

Suddenly the front door of Rose's two-level, stucco house opened and two figures walked out. Isabella first, then Rose. His every muscle tensing, he strained to decipher the merriness that carried on the summer night air through his open window. Then they kissed and hugged and Isabella descended the stairs. At the bottom she turned to wave to Rose, urging her to go in, before she turned and crossed the street, heading to her car.

The moment Rose closed her door he got down from his car.

In the dim streetlights, Isabella's figure seemed to glow in a light-colored summer coat unbuttoned over a lighter dress beneath, its supple material undulating with her brisk walk. Her hair was a swathe of dark silk swinging over her face, her eyes downcast as she rummaged through her purse.

Then feet before he intercepted her, he stopped.

"Well, well, if it isn't Isabella Burton."

Her momentum came to a startled halt, her alarm a sharp gasp that echoed in the night's still, humid silence. Then her face jerked up and her eyes slammed into his.

A bolt struck him through the heart.

His sudden appearance seemed to have hit her even harder. If a ghost had stopped her to ask her the time, she wouldn't have looked more shocked...or horrified.

"What...where the hell did you...?"

She stopped. As if she found no words. Or breath with which to say them. He was almost as shocked as she was... at his reaction. He'd thought he'd feel nothing at the sight of her. He didn't know what he did feel now. But it was... enormous.

And it wasn't an overwhelming sense of familiarity. It was her impact as she was now.

She'd changed. Almost beyond recognition. It made it that much stranger he'd recognized her in that video so instantaneously. For this woman had very little in common with the younger one he'd known in total, tempestuous intimacy.

Her face had lost all the plumpness of youth, had been chiseled into a masterpiece of refinement and uncompromising character. If she'd been irresistible before, even with shock still seizing her every feature, the influence she'd exuded had matured into something far more formidable.

But her eyes had changed the most. Those eyes that had haunted him, eyes he'd once thought had opened up into a magical realm, that of her being. They *looked* the same, glowing that unique emerald-topaz chameleon color. But apart from the familiar shape and hue, and beneath the shock, they were bottomless. Whatever lay inside her now was dark and fathomless. And far more hard-hitting for it.

Her lids swept down, severing the two-way hypnosis. Gritting his teeth at losing the contact, his own gaze lowered to sweep her body. Even through the loose clothes, it still had his every sense revving. Just being near her had always made him ache.

Then a puff of breeze had her scent inundating him and his body flooded with molten steel. That was the one thing about her that hadn't changed. This distillation of her essence and femininity that had constantly hovered at the edge of his memory, tormenting him with craving the real thing.

And here it was at last. What he'd once thought an aphrodisiac nature had tailored to his senses. That belief was renewed in full force.

Hard all over, he returned his gaze to hers, eager to read her own response. She poured every bit of height and poise into her statuesque figure, made him feel she was looking him in at eye level when even in three-inch heels, she stood seven inches below his six-foot-six frame.

"Richard." She gave a formal nod as if greeting a virtual stranger. Then she just circumvented him and continued walking to her car.

He let her pass him, one eyebrow rising.

So. His opening strike hadn't been as effective as he'd planned. She'd gotten over her shock at seeing him faster than he had and had decided to dismiss him.

Surely she considered anyone who knew her real identity a threat to her carefully constructed new persona. But if there were levels of danger to blasts from the past, she must think his potential damage equivalent to a ballistic missile. She couldn't end this "chance" meeting fast enough.

Which proved she hadn't tied him to Rose, wasn't here because of anything concerning him. But that changed nothing.

Whatever she was here for, she wasn't getting it.

He stared ahead, listening to the steady staccato of her receding heels, a grim smile twisting his lips.

In the past he'd been the one who'd walked away. But it had been her who'd made the decision. It now entertained him to let her think the choice remained hers. He'd let her strike his presence up to coincidence, think it would cause no repercussions for her. Then he'd disabuse her of the notion.

Last time, he hadn't been able to override her will. This time, he'd make her do what he wanted. And right now, all he wanted was to taste her once more. He'd postpone his real purpose until he satisfied the hunger that had roared to life inside him again at the sight of her.

He'd much prefer it if she struggled, though.

The moment he heard her opening her car, he turned and sauntered toward her.

She lurched as he passed behind her and murmured, "I'll drive ahead. Follow me."

He felt her gaze boring into his back as he reached his car two spaces ahead. Opening his door, he turned around smoothly, just in time to witness her reaction.

"What the hell...?" She stopped, as if it hurt to talk.

He sighed. "My patience has already been expended for the night. Follow me. Now."

Her eyes blazed at him as she found her voice again. Not the velvety caress that had echoed in his head for eight endless years but a sharp blade. "I'll do no such thing."

"My demand was actually a courtesy. I was trying to give you a chance to preserve your dignity."

Her mouth dropped open. His own lips tingled.

Then his tongue stung when hers lashed him. "Gee, thanks. I can preserve it very well on my own. I'll drive away now, and if you follow me, I'll call the police."

Hostility was the last thing he'd predicted her reaction would be, considering the last time he'd seen her she'd wept as he'd walked away as if her heart were being dragged out of her body. But it only made his blood hurtle with vicious exhilaration. She was giving him the struggle he'd hoped for, the opportunity to force her to succumb to him this time. And he would make her satisfy his every whim.

He gave her the patented smile that made monsters quiver. "If you drive away, I won't follow you. I'll knock on your friends' door and tell them whom they're really getting into business with. I don't think the Andersons would relish knowing you were—and maybe still are—the wife of a drug lord, slave trader and international terrorist."

Two

Isabella stared up at the juggernaut that blocked out the world, every synapse in her brain short-circuiting.

When he'd materialized in front of her, like a huge chunk of night taking the form of her most hated entity, her heart had almost ruptured.

But she'd survived so many horrors, had always had so much to protect, her survival mechanisms were perpetually on red alert. After the initial brutal blow, they'd kicked in as she'd made an instinctive escape. That didn't mean she hadn't felt about to crumple to the ground with every breath.

Richard. Here. Out of the depths of the dark, sordid past. The man who'd seduced and used…and almost destroyed her.

That he hadn't succeeded hadn't been because he hadn't given it his best shot. Ever since, she'd been trying to mend the rifts he'd created in the very foundations of her being. She'd only succeeded in painting over the deepest ones. Though she now seemed whole and strong, those cracks had been worsening over time, and she was sure they'd fissured right to her soul.

But she'd just reached what would truly be a new start. Then he'd appeared out of thin air.

It had flabbergasted her even more because she'd just been thinking of him. It had been as if she'd conjured him.

Yet when had she ever stopped thinking of him? Her memory of him had been like a pervasive background noise that could never be silenced. A clamor that rose to a crescendo periodically before it settled back to a constant, maddening drone.

But there was one explanation for his reappearance. That it was a fluke. An appalling one, but one nonetheless. What else could it have been after eight years?

Not that time elapsed was even an issue. It could have been eight days and she would have thought the same thing. She'd long realized he'd left her believing he'd never see her again.

After all, he must have known what he'd done would most probably get her killed.

Believing their meeting to be a coincidence, she'd run off, thinking the man who'd once exploited her then left her to a terrible fate would shrug and continue on his way.

But just as she'd thought she'd escaped, that he'd fade into the night like some dreadful apparition, he'd followed her. Before she could deal with the dismay of thinking this ordeal would be prolonged, he'd made his preposterous demand.

Not that it had felt like one. It had felt like an ultimatum. Her instinct had been correct.

She hadn't forgiven him, nor would she ever forgive him, but she'd long rationalized his actions. From what she'd discovered—long after the fact—he obtained his objectives over anyone's dead body, figuratively or literally. She, and everything he'd done to her, had been part of a mission. She only had theories what that had been or why he'd undertaken it, according to the end result.

But what he was doing now, threatening with such patent enjoyment what he must know would destroy everything she'd struggled to build over the past eight years, was for his own entertainment. That man she'd once loved, with everything in her scarred psyche and starving soul, had progressed from a cold-bloodedly pragmatic bastard into a full-fledged monster.

"Don't look so horrified."

His bottomless baritone swamped her again, another thing about him that had become more hard-hitting. The years had turned the thirty-four-year-old demigod of sensuality she'd known into an outright god, if one of malice. He still exuded sex and exerted a compulsion—both now magnified by increased power and maturity. But it was this new malevolence that now seemed to define him. And it made him more overwhelming than ever.

But that must have been his true nature all along. It was she who'd been blinded and under his control. She hadn't even suspected what he'd been capable of long after he'd gotten everything he'd wanted from her, then tossed her to the wolf.

"I'm not interested in exposing you." His voice had her every hair standing on end. "As long as you comply, your secret can remain intact."

Summoning the opaqueness she'd developed as her greatest weapon against bullies such as him, she cocked her head.

"What makes you think I haven't told them everything?"

"I don't think. I know. You resorted to extreme measures to construct this St. Sandoval image. You'd go as far to preserve it. You'll certainly give in to anything I demand so no one, starting with the Andersons, ever finds out what you really are."

"*What* I am? You make it sound as if I'm some monster."

"You're married to one. It makes you the same species."

"I'm not married to Caleb Burton. I haven't been for eight years."

Something…scary slithered in the depths of his cold steel eyes. But when he spoke, he sounded as offhand as before.

"So it's in the past tense. A past full of crimes."

"I never had a criminal record."

"Your crimes remain the same even if you're not caught."

"What about your crimes? Let's talk about those."

"Let's not. It would take months to talk about those, as

they're countless. But they're also untraceable. But yours could be easily proved. You knew exactly how your husband made his mushrooming fortune and you made no effort to expose him, making you an accessory to his every crime. Not to mention that you helped yourself to millions of his blood money. Those two charges could still get you ten to fifteen years in a snug little cell in a maximum-security prison."

"Are you threatening to turn me in to the law, too?"

"Don't be daft. I don't resort to such mundane measures. I don't let the law take care of my enemies or chastise those who don't fall in line with my wishes. I have my own methods. Not that I have to resort to those in your case. Just a little chat with your upstanding friends and they wouldn't consider getting mixed up with someone with your past."

"Contrary to what you believe, from your own twisted self and life, there are ethical, benevolent people in the world. The Andersons don't hold people's pasts against them."

He gave her back her pitying disdain, raised her his own brand of annihilating taunting. "If you believed that, you wouldn't have gone to such painstaking lengths to give your history, and yourself, a total makeover."

"The makeover was only for protection, as I'm sure you, as the world's foremost mogul of security solutions, are in the best position to appreciate."

His lethal lips tugged. "Then, it won't matter if your partners in progress find out the details of your previous marriage to one of the world's most prominent figures in organized crime. Along with the open buffet of unlawful immorality that marriage entailed and that you buried. Refuse to follow me and we get to put your conviction of *their* convictions to the test."

Feeling the world emptying of the last atom of oxygen, she snapped, "What the hell do you want from me?"

"To catch up."

Her mouth dropped open.

It took effort to draw it back up, to hiss her disbelief. "So you see me walking down the street and decide on the spot to blackmail me because the urge to 'catch up' overwhelmed you?"

His painstakingly chiseled lips twisted, making her guts follow suit. "Don't tell me you thought it even a possibility I happened to be taking a stroll in a limbo of suburban domesticity called Pleasantville, of all names?"

"You were following me."

The instant certainty congealed her blood. Realizing his premeditation made it all so much worse. And the possible outcomes unthinkable.

He shrugged. "You took your time in there. I was about to knock on the Andersons' door anyway to see what was taking you so long."

Not putting anything beyond him, she imagined how much worse it would have been if he'd done that. "And you went to all this trouble to 'catch up'?"

"Yes. Among other things."

"What other things?"

"Things you'll find out when you stop wasting time and follow me. I'd tell you to leave your car, but your friend might see it and get all sorts of worrisome ideas."

"None would be as bad as what's really happening."

His expression hardened. She was sure it had brought powerful men to their knees. "Are you afraid of me?"

That possibility clearly hadn't occurred to him before. Now that it did, it seemed to…offend him.

The weirdest part was, though she'd long known he was a merciless terminator, her actual safety wasn't even a concern.

It was in every other way that she feared him.

She wasn't about to tell him that. But she did give him an honest answer to his query. "I'm not."

"Good."

His satisfaction chafed her. The urge to wipe it off his cruelly perfect face surged. "I'm not, because I know if you wanted to harm me, I wouldn't have known what hit me. That you're only coercing me indicates I'm not on your hit list."

"It is heartening that you grasp the situation." That soul-searing smile played on his lips again. "Shall we?"

She stood there, her gaze trapped in his, her thoughts tangling.

They both knew he'd cornered her from the first moment. But succumbing to this devil without resistance would have been too pathetic. She'd at least let loose some of her anger and bitterness toward him first. What she'd thought long extinguished.

It was clear they'd only been suppressed under layers of self-delusion so they wouldn't destroy whatever remained of her stability, what everything—and everyone—in her life depended on.

Now that she'd admitted that, it was easier to admit why she'd succumb to his coercion.

The first reason was that she would have, even without his threat. If he'd turned a consummate fiend like Burton into mincemeat so effortlessly when he'd been a younger and less powerful man, she didn't want to know what he was capable of now. She was nowhere in his league. No one was.

The second was harder to face. But what she'd belatedly learned about his truth and that of what they'd shared and what he'd done to her *had* left a gaping hole inside her.

She wanted that hole filled. She wanted closure.

Holding his hypnotic gaze, she finally nodded.

He just turned and walked away. Before he lowered himself into the gleaming black beast that looked as sleek, powerful and ruthless as he did, he tossed her an imperious glance over his acres-wide shoulders.

"Chivvy along."

At his command to hurry up in his native British English,
she expelled the breath she'd been holding.

Chivvy along, indeed.

Might as well get this over with as quickly as possible.

In minutes she was following him as ordered as he
headed to Manhattan, emotions seething inside her. Fury,
frustration, fear—and something else.

That "something else" felt like…excitement.

How sick would that be? To be excited by the man who'd
decimated her heart and almost her world, who'd just threatened to complete the job and had her following him like
a puppy?

But…maybe not so sick. Excitement could encompass
trepidation, anxiety, uncertainty. And everything with Richard had always contained maximum doses of all that. It was
why he'd been the only one who'd made her feel…alive.
She'd been in suspended animation before she'd met him
and since he'd walked away.

For better, or in his case, for worse, it seemed he'd remain the only one who could reanimate her.

"Get it over with. Catch up."

Isabella threw her purse on the black-and-bronze Roberto
Cavalli leather couch and looked at Richard across his gigantic, forty-foot-ceilinged, marble-floored reception area.

He only continued preparing their drinks at the bar, his
lupine expression deepening.

So. He'd talk when he wished. And he hadn't wished. Yet.
Got it.

Good thing she'd called home during the forty-minute
drive to say she'd be *very* late.

Pretending to shrug away his disregard, she looked around.
And was stunned all over again.

The Fifth Avenue penthouse overlooking the now shrouded
in darkness Central Park and Manhattan's glittering Upper
East Side drove home to her how staggeringly wealthy he

was now. The opulent, technologically futuristic duplex on the sixty-seventh and sixty-eighth floors had to have cost tens of millions.

Among the jaw-dropping features of the fully automatic smart-home was its own elevator, its remote-, voice- and retinal-recognition doors and just about everything else.

It even housed a thirty-by-fifty-foot pool.

As they'd passed the sparkling expanse, he'd told her something she hadn't known about him. That he hated the sun and preferred indoor sports. She'd already worked out that he hated people, too. A pool in his living room at the top of the world away from the nuisance of mere mortals was a no-brainer to someone with his kind of money.

He'd been saying he'd expand the pool to get a decent exercise without having to flip over and over when she'd stopped listening. The image of him shooting through the liquid turquoise like a human torpedo, then rising from the water like an aquatic deity with rivulets weeping down his masterpiece body had tampered with her mental faculties.

Snatching her thoughts away before they slid back into *that* abyss, she examined the L-shaped terrace of at least five-thousand square feet. The city views must be breathtaking from there. They were from every corner in this marvel of a home.

Though *home* sounded so wrong. Anywhere he was could never be a home. This place felt like an ultramodern demon's den.

Avoiding looking at him, she noted the designer furniture and architectural touches that punctuated each zone, couldn't guess at many of the functional features. But it was spectacular how the mezzanine level took advantage of the massive ceiling heights and ingeniously provided extensive library shelves. He'd probably read every book. And archived its contents in that labyrinthine mind of his.

But what made the mezzanine truly unique was its glass floors and balustrade, with the staircase continuing the transparent theme. Looking down wouldn't be for the fainthearted.

But Richard didn't have to worry about that, since he was heartless. A fact this astounding but soulless place clearly underlined.

That he had other residences on the West Coast and in England, as he'd offhandedly informed her as they'd entered this place, no doubt on the same level of luxury and technology, was even more mind-boggling. Burton had been a billionaire and it had been hard to grasp the power such wealth brought. But those had been a fraction of Richard's, who was currently counted among the top one hundred richest men on the planet. The security business was booming, and his empire reigned over that domain.

But money, in his case, was the result of the immense influence of his personality and expertise, not the other way around. And then there were his connections. Black Castle Enterprises, which he'd built from the ground up with six other partners, had a major hand in everything that made the world go round and was one of the most influential businesses in history.

"I just learned of your presence in the country today."

His comment dragged her out of her musings, his deepened voice making the cultured precision of his British accent even more shiver worthy. She'd always thought that killer brogue of his the most evocative music. She used to ask him to speak just so she could revel in listening to him enunciate. It had always aroused the hell out of her, too.

But everything about him always had. During the four months of their affair she'd been in a perpetual fugue of arousal.

She watched him approach like a leisurely tiger stalking his kill, every muscle and sinew flexing and pulling at his fitted black shirt and pants, his stormy sky-hued eyes striking her with a million volts of charisma. The familiar ache she hadn't felt since she'd last seen him, that had been trembling under the suppression of shock, hostility and anxiety since he'd appeared before her, stirred in her deepest recesses.

Time had been criminally indulgent with him, enhancing his every asset—widening his shoulders, hardening his waist and hips, bulking up his torso and thighs. Age had taken a sharper chisel to his face, hewing it to dizzying planes and angles, turning his skin a darker copper, intensifying the luminescence of his eyes. His luxurious raven hair had been brushed with silver at the temples, adding the last touch of allure. He was now the full potential of premium manhood realized.

As he reached for the cocktail glass, his fingertips grazed hers, zapping her with a bolt of exquisite electricity.

Great. His deceit and her ignorance of his true nature and intentions had had nothing to do with his effect on her as she'd long told herself. He'd almost cost her her life, and she knew what he truly was and how she'd been a chess piece he'd played and disposed of…yet it made no difference to her body. It didn't deal in logic, cared nothing about dignity and hadn't learned a thing from the harsh lessons of experience. It only saw and sensed the man who'd once possessed and pleasured it almost beyond endurance.

She sat before he realized he still liquefied her knees… and everything else. When she'd thought she'd irreversibly turned to stone.

But she'd thought that before she'd first met him. It had taken him one glance to get the heart she'd believed long petrified quivering. He remained the one man who could reverse any protective metamorphosis.

Safe on a horizontal surface, she looked way, way up at him as he loomed over her like a mystic knight, or rather a malevolent wizard, from an Arthurian fairy tale.

"So the moment you realized I was on American soil, you decided to track me down and ambush me."

"Precisely."

In a heartbeat he was beside her. She marveled again at the strength and control needed for someone of his height and bulk to move so effortlessly. Even though he didn't come too near, her every nerve fired.

Sipping the amber liquid in his crystal glass, he turned to face her fully. "I've been remembering how we met."

She sipped her drink only to suppress the impulse to hurl it in his face. The moment it slid down her throat she realized how parched she was. And how it hit the spot. Perfect coolness and flavor, light on alcohol, heavy on sweetness.

He remembered. How she took her drinks.

Something suffocating, something similar to regret, swept her.

Suddenly the bitterness that had lain dormant in her depths seethed to the surface again. "We didn't meet, Richard. You tracked me down then, too. And set me up."

Nonchalance tugged a corner of his lips. "True."

She took another sip, channeling her anger into sarcasm. "Thanks for sparing me the aggravation of denial."

His gaze lengthened, becoming more unreadable and disturbing. Then he shrugged. "I don't waste time on pointless pursuits. I already realized you know everything. From the first moment, your hostile attitude made it clear I'm not talking to the woman who cried rivers at my departure."

"Why conclude that was because I *know everything*? That could have been classic feminine bitterness for said departure. Surely you didn't expect even the stupid goose I used to be to throw herself in your arms after eight years?"

"Time is irrelevant." Just what she'd been thinking. "It's what you realized that caused you to change. You clearly worked everything out." His gaze intensified, making her feel he was probing her to her cellular level. "So how did you?"

"You know how."

"I probably do. But I'd still like to know the actual details of how you came to realize the truth."

A mirthless laugh escaped her. "If you're asking so you never repeat whatever clued me in, don't bother. Working it all out wasn't due to any discernment on my side, and I only did over three years after the fact." One formidable eyebrow rose at that particular detail. "Yeah, pathetic, right?"

"Not the adjective I'd use." She waited for him to substitute his own evaluation, but he left her hanging. "I don't want details as a prophylactic measure for future operations. I know I am untraceable. Your deductions couldn't have been backed up by any evidence. Even if they were, I made sure your best interest remained in burying any."

"So you're asking only to marvel at how good you are?"

"I know exactly how good I am." The way he said that… The ache deep inside started to throb. "I don't need validations nor do I indulge in self-congratulations." Eyes narrowing, his focus sliced through her. "Why the reluctance to tell me? We're laying our cards down now that the game is long over."

"You laid down nothing."

"I'll lay down whatever you wish." When she opened her mouth to demand he start, he preempted her. "You first."

Knowing she'd end up giving him what he wanted, she sighed. "When the blows to Burton started coming out of the blue, I just thought he'd slipped in his secrecy measures. One day, when he was finally on his knees, he asserted that the breach hadn't come from his side, that I was the only one who knew everything he did. I thought he was just looking for someone to blame, but that didn't change a thing. I believed he'd soon make up his mind that I betrayed him. So I ran."

Draining his glass, he grimaced, set it down on the coffee table. Then he sat back, his eyes so intense it felt as if he was physically attempting to yank the rest out of her.

Torrents of accusations almost spilled from her. Forcing them down, she skipped over the two worst years of a generally hellish existence, and went on, "I only revisited his accusations *much* later, started to wonder if I'd been some-how indiscreet. That pointed me in the direction of the only one I could have been indiscreet with. You. That led to a reexamination of our time together, and to realizing your ingeniousness in milking me for information."

"And you realized it was I who sent him to hell."

She nodded, mute with the remembered agony of that awareness. She'd felt such utter betrayal, such total loss. Her will to go on, for a while, had been completely spent.

"It dawned on me that you had targeted me only to get my insider info and asked me to leave with you to agonize and humiliate him on every front. Everything made so much sense then I couldn't believe I didn't suspect you for years. Who else but you could have devised such a spectacular downfall for him? It takes a monster to bring down another."

His watchfulness lifted, fiendishness replacing it. "*Monster* wasn't what you screamed all those times in my bed."

"Don't be redundant. I already admitted I was too oblivi-ous to live. But once the fog of my obliviousness cleared, I only wished I could forget ever meeting you."

"Don't hold your breath. Even if our meeting wasn't spontaneous, it wasn't only memorable, it remains indel-ible."

The fateful encounter that had turned her life upside down had been that way for him, too?

His cover story had been arranging security for the hu-manitarian organization she'd been working with. He'd de-manded to meet all volunteers for a dangerous mission in Colombia to judge who should go.

Her first glimpse of him remained branded in her mind.

Nothing and no one had ever overwhelmed her as he had. And not because he'd been the most gorgeous male she'd ever seen. His influence far transcended that. His scrutiny had been denuding, his questions deconstructing. He'd rocked her to her core, making her feel like a swooning moron as she'd sluggishly answered his rapid-fire questions.

After telling her she'd passed his test, she'd exited his office reeling. She hadn't known it possible for a human being to be so beautiful, so overpowering. She hadn't known a man could have her hot and wet just by looking at her across a desk. She hadn't been interested in a man before, so the intensity of her desire for him, for his approval, and her delight at earning it had flung her in chaos. She'd never known such excitement, such joy...

"The changes become you."

She blinked, realized she'd been staring at him all the time. As he'd been staring at her.

"The sculpting of your body and features...the darkening of your hair. An effective disguise, but also an enhancement."

"I wanted to look different for security reasons, but ended up not needing to do anything. Time and what it brought did it all."

"You talk as if you're over the hill."

"I feel it. And that's my real hair color. No longer bleaching my hair was the second best thing I ever did, after getting rid of Burton himself, who insisted I looked better as a blonde."

His lips compressed. "Burton wasn't only a depraved wanker, but a gaudy maggot, too. The feast of caramels and chocolates of your hair pays tribute to your creamy complexion and jeweled eyes far better than any blond shade would, framing them to the best effect possible."

She blinked again. Richard Graves paying her a compliment? And such a flowery one, too?

And he wasn't finished. "Before I approached you, I had photos, knew of your unusual beauty. But when I saw you in the flesh, the total effect punched me in the gut and not just on account of your looks. Time had only scraped away whatever prettiness youth inflicted and brought you profound beauty in its place. I believe it will only keep bestowing more on you. You were stunning, but you've become exquisite. With age, you'll become divine."

She gaped at him. Once, when she'd believed him to be a human being, not a machine that made money and devised plans of annihilation, she'd believed him when he'd praised her beauty. But even then, when he'd been doing everything to keep her under his spell, he'd never done it with such fervor and poetry. That he did so now...offended her beyond words.

Fury tumbled in her blood. "Spare me the nausea. We both know what you really think of me. Is this one of the 'other things' you had in mind? To ply me with preposterous flattery and have some more sick fun at my expense?"

"I was actually trying my hand at sincerity." He turned fully to her. "As for the 'other things' I had in mind, it's... *this.*"

And she found herself flat on her back with Richard on top of her, his chest crushing her breasts, his hips between her splayed thighs.

Before her heart could fire the next fractured beat, he rose over her and stopped it.

This was how a devil must look before he took one's soul.

Inescapable. Ravenous. Dreadfully beautiful.

"Eight years, Isabella. Eight years without this. Now I'll have it all again. I'll consume every last inch and drop of you. That's why I brought you here. And that's why you really came."

Three

Time congealed as she lay beneath Richard, paralyzed. Even her heart seemed afraid it would rupture if it beat.

Then everything that had been gathering inside her since he'd walked away—all the betrayal and despondence and yearning—broke through the cracks and she started to tremble.

A shudder traversed his great body as if her tremors had electrified him, making him crush her harder beneath him, crash his lips on her wide-open ones.

His tongue thrust deeply and his scent and taste flooded her bloodstream, a hit of a drug she'd gone mad for since she'd been forced to give it up cold turkey. Gulping it down, she rode rapids of mindlessness as he filled her, drank her the way she remembered and craved. Richard didn't kiss. He invaded, ravaged.

He didn't only catapult her into a frenzy, but sent her spiraling into a reenactment of that first kiss that had launched her addiction.

That day he'd materialized like an answer to a prayer, cutting down the guerillas who'd been threatening her team with death…or worse. She'd been so shaken thinking she could have died without having the one thing she'd ever wanted—him—had been so grateful, so awed, she'd gone to offer him what he'd seemed to want so relentlessly. Herself.

He'd let her into his room, his gaze consuming her, letting her see what he'd do to her once she gave him consent.

And she had, melting against him, giving him permission to do anything and everything to her.

He'd taken her mouth for the first time then, with that same thorough devouring, that coiled ferocity. From that moment on her body had learned what heart-stopping pleasure his kiss would lead to, had afterward burst into flames at his merest touch, the fire raging higher with each exposure.

The conflagration was fiercer now, with the fuel of anger and animosity, with the accumulation of pain and craving and repression. This was wrong, insane. And it only made her want it—want *him*—more than her next breath.

His roughness as he teased her turgid nipples, his dominance as he ground against her molten core, made her spread her thighs wider, strain to enfold him, her moans rising, blind arousal fracturing the shackles of hostility and memory, drowning them and her.

Suddenly he severed their meld, wrenching a cry of loss from her as he rose above her.

His gaze scalded her, his lips filled with grim sensuality. "I should have listened to my body—and yours—and done this the moment I got you in here."

His arrogance should have made her buck him off. But lust for this memorized yet unknown entity, so deadly and irresistible, seethed its demand for satisfaction.

"Say this is what you wanted all along. *Say* it, Isabella."

A hard thrust and squeeze of her buttocks accompanied his brusque order, melting her further. But it was the harshness on his face that jogged her heart out of its sluggish surrender.

The world spun with too many emotions, after years of stasis. Years when she'd felt him this way only in dreams that had always turned into nightmares. In those visions, he'd always aroused her to desperation before pushing her away and taking off his mask. The merciless face he'd exposed before walking over her sobbing body had always woken her in tears then plunged her into deeper despondence.

Dreading those nightmares had robbed her of the ability to rest. It was the memory of them now that made her struggle to stop her plummet into the abyss of addiction all over again.

"What if I don't say it?" Her voice shook.

At her challenge, his gaze emptied of intensity. He released her trembling flesh and in one of those impossible moves, he separated their bodies and was on his feet.

To her shame, she'd thought his response to her challenge would be to take his onslaught to the next level. She still expected he'd pick her up and carry her off to bed.

He only sat on the coffee table, clearly deciding to end their encounter. The letdown deepened her paralysis.

His brooding gaze made her acutely aware of how pathetic she looked prostrated as she was, sending chagrin surging through her numb limbs. Feeling she'd turned to jelly, she pulled herself up and her dress down.

Once she'd tidied the dishevelment he'd caused, he drawled, "Now that there's no hint of physical coercion... *say* it."

Her heart skidded at his deceptively calm command. "You mean there's no coercion because you're not on top of me anymore? I'm here *purely* by coercion."

"I submit, this is false. I only gave you an excuse to have your cake and eat it, too, a justification you can placate your dignity with. But it's easy to invalidate your self-exonerating assertion. I'll escort you to the door, activate it for you and you can walk right out."

"And then you'll call my friends."

"There *are* things you could do that would make me do that. None of them include choosing to walk out now." He rose to his feet. "Shall we?"

She scrambled to her feet only when she found him striding away for real and had to almost run in his wake.

"That's it? You go to all this trouble to get me here, interrogate me for a bit, then abruptly shift to what seems to be your real objective, and when I refuse to 'say it' you show me the door?"

"I have to. It won't open unless I tell it to."

His derision, and the fact that he'd shrugged off what had happened when it had turned her inside out had her fury sizzling.

Catching up with his endless strides beside the pool, she snatched at his arm. Her fingers only slipped off his rock-hard muscles. It was he who stopped of his own accord, daring to look as if he had no idea what was eating her, but was resigned to putting up with an inexplicably hysterical female.

"Why do you want me to say it?" she seethed. "Is your ego that distorted? You want me to admit how much I want you when you never wanted me in the first place?"

His winged eyebrow arched more. "I didn't?"

"If we're both certain of one thing, it's that."

"And you've come to that conclusion, how?"

"Like I did all the rest. Seduction is no doubt your weapon of choice with women, and pretending to desire me was only to turn me into your willing thrall. The info I had was my only real use to you."

He inclined his head as if examining a creature he'd never known existed. "You think I spent four months in bed with you and didn't desire you?"

"You're a man, and an overendowed one. I bet you could…perform with any reasonably attractive female, especially one in heat."

"That you were." His reminiscent look made her want to smack him across that smug mouth. "I never thought a woman could always be that hot and ready for me." Before she lashed out, he sighed. "I *would* have seduced you even if you'd been a slime-oozing monstrosity. Stomaching a mark was never a prerequisite in my search-and-seduce missions. But even based on my indiscriminate libido, as you presume, I would have still suffered the minimum of physical contact to keep you on the hook. I wouldn't have gone to lengths you can't imagine to create a rendezvous almost daily, and then to have sex with you as many times as could be squeezed into each encounter. Even with my 'endowments' I couldn't have *performed* that repeatedly or that…vigorously if I wasn't even hotter and readier for you than you were for me. And I was. None of that was an act."

Her heart stuttered as she met the gaze that suddenly felt as if it held no barriers. As if he was telling the truth, probably for the first time.

He'd really wanted her?

But… "If you wanted me as much as you claim, and still used and discarded me like any other woman you didn't want, that makes you an even colder bastard."

His gaze grew inscrutable again. "I didn't discard you. You chose Burton."

"Is that what you call what I did? I had no choice."

"You always have a choice."

"Spare me the human-development slogans."

"A choice doesn't have to be an easy one, but it remains one. Every choice has pros and cons. Once you make one, you put up with its consequences. You don't blame others for those."

"I categorically disagree. I certainly blame others, namely Burton and you, for making it impossible for me to have a choice. Leaving him was out of the question."

"You did end up leaving him."

"I didn't leave, I ran for my life."

"You could have done so with me."

"Could I? And where would I have been if you failed to destroy him, then had enough of me, as I'm sure you would have sooner or later, and discarded me *then*, after I made a mortal enemy of him?"

His glance was haughtiness itself. "There was no possibility I wouldn't destroy him." His eyes narrowed with… reproof? "And I promised you protection."

"You dare make it my fault I ended up in mortal danger when you executed your plan? When I couldn't have known your promise would amount to anything, when you didn't tell me anything of your real abilities, let alone purpose?"

"You dare ask why I didn't when you were his accomplice?"

A bitter scoff escaped her. "You promoted me from passive accessory to active accomplice in under an hour? Wonder what you'd make me by the end of this conversation."

"Whatever *you* call what you did, my desire for you didn't blind me to the probability you'd run to him if I confided in you. It would have been an opportunity to entrench yourself further in his favor, adding indebtedness to his already pathological infatuation with you. And I was right."

She closed the mouth that had dropped open at his preposterous interpretations. "Yeah? How so?"

"When a choice was to be made, not knowing my real 'abilities,' you chose the man you thought more powerful. This indicates what you would have done had you thought I was a threat to your billion-dollar meal ticket." He shrugged his massive shoulders. "Not that I blame you. You thought you made the right choice based on available information. That you were grossly misinformed and therefore made a catastrophic mistake doesn't make you a victim."

Protests boiled in her blood. But there was no point in voicing any. She had no proof, as he'd said.

Even if she did, to whom would she submit it? To him? The mastermind of her misery?

Her shoulders slumped as the surge of aggression he'd provoked drained. "You have everything worked out, don't you?"

"Very much so."

She exhaled in resignation. "So you orchestrated everything, got the result you desired, while even Fate indulged you and gave you the bonus of a mark to enjoy sexually, huh? That must have made your mission of patiently milking me for all I had more palatable."

His shrug was indifference incarnate. "More or less." His gaze shifted to an expression that seemed to sear her marrow. "With one amendment. It wasn't palatable. It was phenomenal."

"I—it was?"

"Along with a dozen superlative adjectives. Being with you was the only true and absolute pleasure I ever had."

He'd already said he'd wanted her. But the way he'd spelled it out now... His words fell on her like a punch, jogging her brain in her skull.

It had been what had most mutilated her, had left her feeling desecrated. Thinking she'd wanted him with every fiber of her being while he'd only reviled her even as he'd used her in every way. Learning that he'd wanted her had just begun to ameliorate her humiliation. But now his claim that it had been as unprecedented to him... It felt genuine. If it was, then at least their intimacies, which had been so profound to her, among all the lies and exploitation, had been real. She could at least cleanse those intensely intimate memories and have them back.

"And that's why I want you to say it, Isabella."

The hunger in his voice and eyes had her heart ramming against her ribs as if unable to bear their confinement.

"I want you to say you've craved having again what we had all those years ago. That every time you closed your eyes, I was there, in your mind, on your tongue, all over you and inside you, giving you everything only I could ever give you."

Every word he said, soaked in hunger, seething with demand, brought a wave of wet heat surging in her core, her body readying itself for its master doing all the things she'd never stopped yearning for.

She still had to resist. Because of what he'd done to her.

Past and present. Because of what he thought of her. What he was. For every reason that existed, really.

"What if I don't say it?"

Those incredible eyes crinkled, those lips that made her every inch ache with the memory of what they could do to her twisted.

"You want me to force you to take what you're dying to take, so you'd have it, and the moral high ground, too? No, my exquisite siren. If I take you now, it will be because you'll tell me in no uncertain terms that you want me to. That you're *burning* for me to. It's that…or you can go."

And it turned out every reason under the sun to tell him to go to hell was nothing compared to the one reason she had to give him what he wanted.

That he was right.

Giving in, she reached out, wound his tie around her hand and yanked on it with all her strength.

Which didn't say much right now. Her tug was trembling and weak like the rest of her. She was that aroused. He wouldn't have moved if he hadn't wanted to.

But her action was seemingly enough of an appeasement. He let her drag him down so his face was two inches from hers.

His virility-laden, madness-inducing breath flayed her lips, filled her lungs. "Now say it."

Voice as unsteady as her legs, she did. "I want you."

"Say it *all*, Isabella."

That cruel bastard had to extract her very soul, didn't he? Just as he had in the past.

Knowing she'd regret it when her body stopped clamoring, *if* it ever did—but she'd sooner stop her next breath—she gave him the full capitulation he demanded. "I wanted you with every single breath these past eight years."

His satisfaction was so ferocious it seared her as his hand covered the one spastically pulling on his tie, untangling it in such unhurried smoothness. Then, like the serpent he was, he slinked away from her. Heartbeats shook her as she watched him sit on the huge couch facing the pool.

After sprawling back in utmost comfort, he beckoned. "Show me."

Not knowing whom to curse more viciously, him or herself, she walked toward him as if on the end of a hook.

Once her knees bumped his, she lost all coordination and slumped over him under the weight of eight years' worth of craving. Barely slowing her collapse with shaking hands against his unyielding shoulders, her dress rode up thighs that opened to straddle his hips. His eyes burned into hers with gratification up until her lips crashed down on his.

He opened his mouth to her urgency, let her show him how much she needed everything he had as her hands roamed his formidable body, convulsed in his too-short-for-her-liking wealth of hair and her molten core rode the daunting rock of his manhood through their clothes.

"I want you, Richard…I've gone mad wanting you."

At her feverish moan he took over, his lips stopping her uncoordinated efforts to posses them. Sighing raggedly, she luxuriated in his domination, what he'd so maddeningly interrupted before.

His hands roved her, melting clothes off her burning body with the same virtuosity that had always made her breathless. His every move was loaded with the precise ruthlessness of a starving predator unleashed on a prey long kept out of reach.

Breaking the kiss, he drew back, his pupils flaring, blackness engulfing the silvered steel as he spilled her breasts into his palms. His homage was brief but devastating before he swept her around, had her sitting on the couch and kneeled before her. After dragging her panties off in one sweep, he lunged, buried his lips in her flowing readiness. She shrieked at the long-yearned-for feel of his tongue and teeth, her thighs spreading wider to give him fuller access to her intimate flesh, which had always been his.

Hours ago she'd been going about her new life, certain she'd never see him again. Now he was here, pleasuring her as only he had ever done.

Was she dreaming all this?

He nipped her bud, and the slam of pleasure was too jarring to be anything but real. One more sweep or suckle or graze would finish her. And she didn't want release.

She wanted *him*.

"Richard…you…" she gasped. "I need *you*…inside me… *please*…"

Growling, he heaved up, caught her plea in his savage mouth, letting her taste herself on his tongue as he rose, lifting her in his arms. Then the world moved in hurried thuds before it stopped abruptly with her steaming back against cool glass.

The idea that Richard was about to take her against a window overlooking the city almost made her come right then.

Plastering her to the glass with his bulk, he locked her feet around his buttocks, thrilling her with his effortless strength. Then he leaned back, freeing his erection.

The potency that had possessed her during so many long, hard rides had her mouth watering, her core gushing. And that was before the intimidating weight and length of it thudded against her swollen flesh, squeezing another plea from her depths. He only glided his incredible heat and hardness through the molten lips of her core, sending a million arrows of pleasure to her womb, until she writhed.

He didn't penetrate her until she wailed, *"Fill me."*

Only then did he ram inside her.

The savagery and abruptness of his invasion, the unbearable expansion around his too-thick girth, was a shock so acute the world flickered, darkened.

Her senses sparked again to him growling, "Too long… too damned long…" as his teeth sank into her shoulder like a lion tethering his mate for a jarring ride. Then he withdrew.

It felt as if he was dragging her life force out with him. Her arms tightened around his back, her hands clawing it, begging his return. He complied with a harder, deeper plunge, blacking out her senses again with the beyond-limits fullness. After a few thrusts forced her flesh to yield fully to him, he quickened his tempo.

Every withdrawal brought maddening loss, every plunge excruciating ecstasy. Her cries blurred and her muttered name on his lips became a litany, each thrust accentuated by the carnal sounds of their flesh slapping together. The scents of sex and abandon intensified, the glide and burn of his hard flesh inside her stoked her until she felt she'd combust.

She needed…needed… *Please…please*…please…

He'd always known what she needed, when and how hard and fast. He gave it to her now, hammering his hips between her splayed thighs, his erection pounding inside her with the cadence and force to unleash everything inside her, until he breached her womb and shattered the wound-up coil of need.

Her body detonated from where he was buried deepest outward, currents of release crashing through her, squeezing her around him, choking her shrieks.

Roaring her name, he exploded in his own climax, jetting the fuel of his pleasure over hers, filling her to overflowing, sharpening the throes of release until he wrung her of the last spark of sensation her body was capable of.

She felt him pulse the last of his seed into her depths, and a long-forgotten smile of satisfaction curved her lips as her head slumped in contentment over his chest…

A rumble beneath her ear jogged her back to consciousness. "Not enough, Isabella…never enough…"

Feeling boneless, her head spun as he strode away from the window, still buried within her depths. Knowing he'd carry her to his bedroom now, she drifted off again, wanting to rest so she'd be ready for round two…

She jerked out of her sensual stupor as he laid her down.

His scent rose from dark cotton sheets to cloak her in its hot delight, compensating her for his loss as he left her body to rid himself of his clothes. Her clamoring senses needed him back on top of her, inside her. She held out unsteady arms, begged for him again.

This time he didn't let her beg long. He lunged back over her, had her skidding on the sheets with the force of his impact. Spreading her quivering thighs, he pushed her knees up to her chest, hooking his arms behind them, opening her fully. Then, lowering himself over her to thrust his tongue inside her panting mouth, he reentered her in a long, burning plunge.

A shriek tore out of her as he forged inside her swollen flesh, undulating against her, inside her, churning soreness and ecstasy into an excruciating mixture as he took her in even more primal possession than the first time. He translated every liberty he was taking with her body into raw, explicit words that intensified the pleasure of his every move inside her beyond endurance. She climaxed all over him again, then again, eight years of deprivation exploding into torrents of sensation, each fiercer than the previous one.

At her fourth peak, he rammed her harder, faster, till he lodged into the gates of her womb, held himself there, roaring his release. Her body convulsed as she clutched his straining mass to her, her oversensitized flesh milking him for every drop of satisfaction for both of them.

At last, he gave her his full weight, which she'd always begged him for after the storm was over, his heartbeat a slow thunder against her decelerating one, completing his domination.

Always able to judge accurately when his weight would turn from necessity to burden, he rose off her, swept her enervated mass over his rock-solid one, dragging a crisp sheet over their cooling bodies.

She wanted to cling to this moment, to savor the descent with him...but everything slipped away...

* * *

Her mind a silent, empty scape, she tried to open lids that felt glued together. How strange. There'd never been peace after Richard...

Richard!

Her lids tore open, almost literally, and there he was. Illuminated by the dim daylight seeping in from the window of what she now realized was a hangar-size bedroom. He was propped up on one elbow beside her, looking down at her, his gaze one of supreme male triumph as he coated the body he'd savagely pleasured in languid caresses.

She was in his bed. She'd begged him to take her—repeatedly. If she could find her voice, she'd do it again right now.

"I didn't intend to rush your pleasure the first...or subsequent times. I wanted to keep you hovering on the edge of orgasm so long, when I finally gave it to you, I knocked you out on the first try."

"You did knock me out every single time," she croaked.

"No. Knocked out as in nothing could wake you up for hours afterward. I did that the last time only." He pinched and rolled one delightfully sore nipple, glided his hair-roughened leg between hers and pressed his knee to the soaked junction of her legs, dragging a whimper from her depth. "But no harm done. It's time to savor driving you crazy."

Her body clamored for him harder than ever. This addiction hadn't subsided; it had gotten worse.

She caressed his face, his shoulders, his chest, reveling in the longed-for delight of feeling him this way. "Your efforts would be in vain. I'm already crazy for you."

"I know. But I want you desperate."

Before she could protest, his tongue thrust inside her mouth, claiming, conquering. His hands, lips and teeth sought all her secrets, sparked her ever-simmering insanities until he had her writhing, nothing left inside her but the need for him to finish her, annihilate her, leave nothing of her.

Clawing at him, crushing herself against him, she tried to drag him inside her. "Just take me again, Richard."

He held her filling eyes, as if gauging if she was truly at his required level of desperation. Seemingly satisfied, from the grim twist of his lips and the flare of his nostrils, he rose above her, leveling her beneath him.

Locking her arms above her head, his knees spreading her legs wide-open, he was where she needed him most, penetrating her in one forceful thrust.

This time the expansion of her already swollen and sore tissues around his massive erection sharpened into pleasure so fierce, it was almost unbearable. Darkness danced at the periphery of her vision. She gasped, thrashed, voiceless, breathless. His face clenched with something like agony as she clung to him as she would a raft in a tempestuous sea.

She sobbed into his lips. "I wanted this every minute…"

"*Yes*. Every. Single. Minute." His growls filled her lungs even as he refilled her, the head of his shaft sliding against all her internal triggers, setting off a string of discharges that buried her under layers of sensations. It all felt maddeningly familiar, yet totally new.

Then everything compacted into one unendurable moment before detonating outward. She shattered.

Her flesh pulsed around his so forcefully she couldn't breathe for the first dozen excruciating clenches. He rumbled for her to come all over him, to scream her pleasure at the top of her lungs. His encouragement snapped something inside her, flooded air into her. And she screamed. And screamed and screamed as he pumped her to the last twitches of fulfillment.

Then he rose above her, supernatural in beauty, his muscles bulging, his eyes tempestuous. He threw his head back, roared her name as every muscle in his body locked and surrendered to his own explosive orgasm.

Instead of fainting, she remained fully aware this time throughout the stages of the most blissful aftermath she'd ever experienced with him.

Suddenly he spoke. "I wasn't satisfied with how things ended with you in the past. It felt…incomplete. And I must have everything wrapped up to my satisfaction."

For long moments she couldn't breathe, waiting for a qualification to tell her she'd jumped to the worst conclusions of his words.

He only validated her suspicion. "I got you here to close your case. If I may say so, I reached a spectacular conclusion."

Feeling as if he'd dumped her into freezing water, she fought to rise to the surface and from his arms.

Without one more word or glance she dragged the sheet off his body, wrapped herself in it and teetered out of the bedroom, looking for the clothes she hadn't been able to wait for him to tear off her body earlier.

She felt him following her, heading to the open-plan kitchen. Her numbness deepened.

When she was dressed, and as neat as she could get herself after he'd ravaged her, she turned to him.

He raised a mug. "Coffee? Or will you storm out now?"

"You have every right to do this." Her voice was thick and raw as it always had been when he'd made her scream her heart out in repeated ecstasy. It intensified her shame. "I deserve whatever you say or do. After all you've done to me, I disregarded all the injuries you caused me and fell into your arms again."

"And even now, you'd fall there again if I let you. But I'm no longer interested. I'm done."

Gritting her teeth against the pain digging its talons inside her, she said, "Then, I can look forward to never seeing you again for real this time. And no matter what you'd like to tell yourself you can get me to do, *I'm* beyond done."

"Yes, you are. That's the other thing I got you here to do. To tell you that."

She frowned. "What the hell do you mean by that?"

"You're done *here*. You will tell your new partners you've changed your mind about the partnership. You will terminate your lease, pay whatever early termination penalty your contract states, then pack your bags and leave this city, preferably the States. And this time, you will never return."

Four

In her first twenty-four years, Isabella had suffered so many brutal blows, had endured and survived them all, she'd believed nothing would shake her or knock her down again.

Then Richard had happened to her. Every second with him, and because of him, had been a succession of earthquakes and knockouts. After he'd exited her life, it had been a constant struggle not to fall facedown and stay there. But it hadn't been an option to give up. She'd had no choice but to forge on. But she'd thought even if she saw him again, whatever madness he'd induced in her, her own ability to experience towering passions, had been expended.

Then he'd reappeared and just by dangling himself in front of her, he'd made her relinquish all sanity and beg for his destruction.

Now there he stood, barefoot, in only pants, leaning indolently on the counter of his futuristic kitchen, looking like the god of malice that he was. He sipped painfully aromatic coffee in utmost serenity, clearly savoring its taste and her upheaval.

But what else did she think would happen after she'd committed that act of madness? Hadn't she already known she'd regret it? Or had she been that pathetic she'd hoped it wouldn't end horribly? That she'd have the ecstasy she'd hankered for without the agony that she'd learned would come with it? Had she even thought of the consequences as she'd grabbed for the appeasement only he could provide?

But this… What he'd ordered her to do wasn't only horrific, it was…incomprehensible.

The numbness of humiliation and self-abuse splintered under the blow of indignation. "Just who the hell do you think you are? How dare you presume to tell me what to do?"

Almost groaning at how clichéd and cornered she sounded, she watched in dismay as he gave her a glance she was certain had hardened criminals quaking in their shoes.

"Trust me, you don't want to know who I really am."

"Oh, I know enough to extrapolate the absolute worst."

Another tranquil sip. "From your defiant response I actually gather the worst you can imagine is nothing approaching the truth. But your misconception might be the result of my own faux pas. If I gave you the impression that this is a negotiation, I sincerely apologize. I also apologize for previously stating you always have a choice. You never do with me. Of course, there are *always* catastrophic mistakes, still categorized as choices, open to you. In this situation, the wrong choice is to stall. I strongly advise you don't exercise it."

Even now, his delivery of this load of bullying was so sexy and sophisticated his every enunciation reverberated in her reawakened senses like a shock wave.

Loathing her unwilling response, she gave him a baleful glance. "I assure you I won't stall. I will ignore you and your deranged demands altogether."

"In that case *my* only choice is to force you. So you're now down to one catastrophic choice, and it's how hard you decide to make this for yourself."

"Give it your best shot. Hard is my middle name."

As she kicked herself for how lame and how reeking of innuendo that had come out, his lips twitched his enjoyment of her slipup.

Out loud, he only said, "I can assure you, you wouldn't like it if I resorted to extreme measures."

"What extreme measures? Are you threatening to off me?"

His eyes turned to slits opening into thunderclouds. "Don't be daft."

It again seemed to insult him she'd suggest he'd physically harm her. But she wasn't falling yet again into the trap of seeing any measure of light in his darkness.

She twisted the strap of her purse around her hand until her fingers went numb. "I guess you don't off people if you could at all help it. You don't put people out of their misery. You didn't even kill Burton, just consigned him to a worse hell than even I hoped for him."

"Are you *extrapolating* what I did to him?"

"No, I know." His eyebrows rose in astonishment-tinged curiosity, and she hugged herself against a shudder that took her by surprise. "I wasn't a kingpin's trophy wife for four years without cultivating methods and sources to navigate his world and to execute an escape plan when necessary."

Heat entered his gaze again, this time tinged with… admiration? "Indeed. The way you wiped your history was a work of art. We must discuss said methods and sources at length sometime. It could be mutually beneficial to exchange notes on how we execute our deceptions."

She watched his mesmerizing face, wondering how he made anything he said so…appealing to her on her most fundamental levels, logic, self-respect and even survival be damned.

The only explanation was that she was sick. She'd contracted a disease called Richard Graves. And it was either incurable or would have to be cured at the cost of her life.

She huffed in resignation. "Nothing I developed could be of use to you. Next to yours, my abilities are like an ape's IQ to Einstein's. And I use fraud only to survive. It's a fundamental part of your career, of your character. Deceit is a preference to you, a pleasure. But you are right."

He raised an eyebrow. "In my advice not to stall?"

"In supposing I'm extrapolating Burton's fate at your hands. I know where you sent him, what that place is. But what is being done to him there?" She shook her head, the nausea she'd felt since he'd told her he was done intensifying. "Even after all I've seen in my life, my imagination isn't twisted enough to conceive what your warped mind could devise, or what you're capable of."

His gaze fixed on her with a new kind of intensity as he put down his mug, straightened from the counter and prowled closer.

Feeling more exposed now that daylight gave her no place to hide, she forced herself to stand her ground. "If physical threats aren't among your extreme measures, what then? If you think your previous warning of exposing me to Rose and Jeffrey stands, it doesn't. I'm walking out of here and going straight to the practice to tell them everything."

His ridiculing glance told her he didn't believe her capable of doing that. Out loud he only taunted, "I'd still have dozens of ways to make you comply."

"Why are you even asking me to do this?"

"I'm not asking you. I'm telling you."

She rolled her eyes. "Yeah, yeah...I got that already. You're the man who says 'jump' and everyone hops in the air and freezes there until you say down. Quit marveling at your unstoppable powers. It got old after the first dozen times. So give me a straight answer already. It's not as if you care about going easy on me, or about me at all."

"Bloody hell, who am I kidding." Without seeming to move closer, he was all over her. Before she could even gasp, he buried his face in her neck and groaned, "It was I who made a catastrophic mistake, Isabella. I'm not done. I'll never be."

Suffocating under the feel of him, the hard heat and perfection of him, with the mess of reactions he wrenched from her depths, she started struggling. "Let me go. *Now.*"

He only carried her off the ground. She opened her lips to blast him and he closed them with a mind-melting kiss, tasting her as if he couldn't stop.

It was only when she went limp in his arms that he let her lips go, barely setting her back on her feet, pouring one final groan of enjoyment inside her.

"Got that out of your system?" She glared up at him, wishing her hatred could melt his flawless face off his skull.

"I just told you there is no getting you out of my system. So let's not waste more time in posturing and theatrics. Let's get past what I said to you earlier."

"Just like that, huh?"

He squeezed her tighter. "It would be more time efficient. I already admitted to being a pillock and a tosser."

"What?"

His lips spread wider at her croak. It wasn't right. Nature was such a random, unjust system, to endow him with such an array of assets and abundance of charisma. But then, that was what made him such an exemplary fiend.

"That means *massive idiot* and *supreme jerk* in the tongue of my people."

"And you think calling yourself a couple of fancy British insults exonerates you and compensates me? I'm sure in your universe you consider tossing a half-assed apology at someone will wipe away any injury you've dealt them. Not in mine."

His eyes sobered. "I got you here thinking I could get closure and move past you at last. I went through the motions but not only didn't I get said closure, I no longer want it."

Needing to poke out his eyes and wrap her legs around him at once, she pushed at him, bracing against the feel of his silk-sprinkled steel flesh. Just remembering what that chest had done to her as he'd tormented her breasts and pounded his potency inside her...

She gave a strong enough shove that he let her go at last. Because he'd decided to, she was sure.

Regaining her footing, she steadied herself. "So you're not even apologizing. You just realized you've jumped the gun, that you didn't get enough of me and want a few more rounds."

He stroked his hands over his chest, as if tracing the imprint of her hands against it. "I want unlimited rounds. And I never thought it a possibility to have enough of you. I only wanted to be rid of my need for you. I no longer want that. I want to indulge that need, to wallow in it." He reached for her again, slamming her against him, cupping one of the breasts he'd ravaged with pleasure. "And before I made that bloody blunder of following through with my no-longer-viable intention, you wanted nothing more than to binge on me, too."

She pushed his hands away from her quivering flesh. "I'm actually grateful for said bloody blunder. It gave me the closure *I* needed, in the form of a vicious slap that jogged me out of my pathological tendencies where you're concerned."

He grabbed both her hands and dragged them up to his face. "Slap me back as hard as you like. Or better still…" He pulled her hands down, pressed them nails first over his chest. "Take your pound of flesh, Isabella. Claw it out of me."

Trembling with the need to sink her nails and teeth into his chest, not to hurt but to worship him, she fisted her hands against the urge and stepped back. "Thanks, but no thanks."

Circumventing him, the soreness of his possession and the evidence of their intimacies between her legs making her gait awkward, made her curse him and herself all over again.

His voice dipped another octave, penetrating her between the shoulder blades. "I'm rescinding my ultimatum."

That made her turn, that mixture of rage and swooning warring inside her. "You're no longer threatening unimaginable punishments so I'd leave and never return? How kind of you."

He covered the distance she'd put between them, eyes boring into her as if he wanted to hypnotize her. "You only need to end your partnership."

Before she took him up on his offer of slashing her hands open on those razor-sharp cheekbones, or breaking her nails claiming a handful of those steel pectorals, he went on, "Give the Doctors Anderson a personal excuse. If you'd rather not, I will manufacture an airtight one for you and pay the penalty for unilaterally dissolving the partnership. But you don't have to worry about that. I'll arrange a far more prestigious and lucrative partnership for you. Better still, I'll establish your own private practice or even hospital."

Head spinning at the total turnabout he'd made, but more at the sheer nerve of his standing there orchestrating her life for her, the utter insanities he was spouting, she raised her hands. "Stop. Just stop. What the hell is wrong with you? Were you always a madman and I never noticed it?"

"I *am* definitely mad, with wanting you. And you showed me you're as out of your mind for me. So you'll stay and we'll pick up where we left off, without the restrictions of the past. I'll acquire a new residence for you close to me, so you won't waste time commuting. You can have anything else you want or need. You can work with anyone in the world, have access to all the funds and facilities and personnel you wish for. I will accommodate and fulfill your every desire."

He dragged her back to him, hauling her by the buttocks against his hardness, his other hand twisting in her hair, tilting her head back, exposing her neck to the ravaging of his tongue and teeth. His growl spilled into her blood at her pulse point. "Every single one."

Her traitorous body melting inside and out for him, she felt she was drowning again. "Richard…this is insane…"

"We've already established I am, for you." He punctuated every word with a thrust, and her voracious body soaked up the pleasure of every rough grind. "I discovered I have been all these years, but my training, and everything else, held it all in check. I no longer want to hold back. And I won't." He took her mouth in a compulsive kiss that almost made her orgasm there and then. He ended the kiss, transferred his possession to the rest of her face. "If you ever thought Burton indulged you, that was nothing compared to what I'll do for you."

Lurching, feeling as if he'd slapped her, she punched her way out of his arms this time, her voice rising to a strident shout. "I don't want anything from you, just like I never wanted anything from him. So you can take your promises and offers and shove them."

He caressed his body where her blows had landed, licked his lips as if savoring her taste. "I'm telling you everything on offer, for full disclosure's sake. You're free to make use of whatever you choose." He captured her hands again, pressing his lips in her aching palms. "But I am compensating you for the termination of your partnership. That's the one thing that's not negotiable."

She snatched her hands away. "Are you done?"

"I told you I could never be done with you."

"Okay, I've changed my diagnosis. You're not insane, you're delusional. On top of having multiple personality disorder. I'm terminating nothing. And I already told you what you can do with your 'compensations.'"

He tutted, all indulgence now. "I'm not letting you go until we get this settled. So let's get on with it so I can leave you to get on with the rest of your day. You have new partners you have to let down easy after all."

"'This' is already settled. And you're letting me go *now*, Richard."

Turning, she strode the long way back to the door. Though slower, his impossibly long strides kept him a step behind her.

At the door, he pressed himself into her back, plastering her against it, seeking all her triggers. But she was finally angry enough to resist and desperate enough to leave.

"Tell your damn pet door to open sesame, Richard."

Taking a last suckle of her earlobe, sending fireworks all over her nervous system, he sighed. The sound poured right into her brain as he mercifully ended their body meld. But instead of murmuring the door open, he leaned on outstretched arms, bars of virility on both sides of her body, and pressed his hands against it.

So it also had palm-print sensors.

The moment the door opened, she spilled outside as if from a flooding tunnel.

Once she reached the elevator, he called out, "I've laid all my cards on the table. It's your turn."

Looking over her shoulder, she found him standing on his threshold, long legs planted apart, hands in pockets, the embodiment of magnificence and temptation. And knowing it.

She cursed under her breath. "Yeah, my turn. To tell you what I want. I want you to take your cards and go to a hell even you can't imagine, where crazy monsters like you belong."

He threw his head back and laughed.

She'd never heard him laugh before.

Rushing into the elevator to escape the enervating sound, she was still followed by his amusement-soaked question.

"Want me to pick you up from work, or will you finish your vital errand and come back on your own?"

She almost stomped her foot in frustration. The elevator buttons made as much sense as hieroglyphics in her condition.

She smacked every button. "I'll willingly go to hell first."

His dark chuckle drenched her again. "The hell for irresistible sirens is the same one for crazy monsters?"

She glowered at him in fuming silence as the elevator doors finally swished smoothly closed.

The moment she could no longer see him, she slumped against the brushed-steel wall…then shot up straight again.

The damn snake must have cameras in here. She'd dissolved all over him all night, and even just now, she wasn't about to let him see he still messed her up, albeit remotely. She had to hold it together until she was out of his range.

By the time she was in her car, one realization had emerged from the chaos.

She'd never be out of his range. There was no place on earth he couldn't follow her to if he felt like it. And he'd made it clear that he had nothing else on his mind right now.

There was only one way out of this. To change it for him somehow, before he took one step further into her life. And destroyed everything. Irrevocably this time.

How she would do that, she had absolutely no idea.

Richard closed the door, stood staring at it as if he could still see Isabella through it.

He could monitor her for real until she exited the building. But he preferred imagining her in his mind's eye. As she stood there in the elevator, letting go of the act of defiance. As she walked to his private parking area where her car was, every step impeded by the soreness he'd caused her as he'd given her and taken from her unimaginable pleasure. As she drove home in an uproar, furious at him yet reliving their climactic night, her every inch throbbing, needing an encore.

Dropping his forehead against the door he'd sandwiched her against, he could almost feel her every thought and breath mingling with his, melding, tangling, wrestling. Just as her limbs had with his, as her core had yielded to him, and clasped him in a mindless inferno. His body buzzed with exquisite agony as his hardness turned to burning steel.

Pushing away from the door, he discarded his pants as he headed to the pool, his steps picking up speed until he launched himself into the air, arced down to slice into the cool water like a missile.

It was an hour before he'd expended sufficient incendiary energy and centered his thoughts enough to consider the exercise had served its purpose. Pulling himself out of the pool, he sat on its edge, staring through forty-foot-high windows at the sprawling green expanse of Central Park, seeing nothing but Isabella and everything that had happened between them.

So. For the first time in…ever, nothing had gone according to his plan. And he couldn't be more thrilled about it.

Though he'd known she'd been his only kryptonite, he'd believed she wouldn't retain any power over him. Even after he'd realized he still coveted her, he hadn't thought there'd been the slightest danger she'd breach his impenetrable armor.

But every moment with her had been pleasure beyond imagining. Even more indescribable than anything he remembered sharing with her in the past. He now realized his invulnerability had only been the deep freeze he'd plunged into when he'd walked away from her, thinking he'd never have her again. He'd stored everything inside him, starting with his libido, which he'd kept behind barricades of thorns and ice. But mere re-exposure to her had pulverized them as if they were cobwebs, thawed him out as quickly as New York's summer sun melted an ice cube.

He'd tried to fool himself into thinking he could apply brakes to the desire that had overtaken him. But even as he'd told her he was done, the thought of losing her again had made him want to take it back at once. The utter contempt that had dawned on her face had made him willing to do anything to erase it, to restore the contentment his words had wiped away.

And he *had* offered everything. Again. Without trying, she'd snared him again. It was a trap he'd eagerly been caught in. She remained the only person who had his secret access code. The one, in spite of every reason on earth against it, he gladly relinquished power to.

Satisfaction spread like wildfire, pulling at his lips as he jumped to his feet and headed for the shower.

Once beneath the pummeling water, he closed his eyes and relived his nightlong possession of her and her captivation of him. Next time, this was where he'd end their intimacies, soothing and refreshing her before he let her leave him. He certainly wouldn't end another climactic night together by doing his best to alienate her.

After his contradictory behavior, she'd run away screaming *monster. Crazy monster*, to be exact.

She wouldn't come back on her own. No matter how much she craved him. As he was now beyond certain she did.

So he had to pursue her. But he predicted that the harder he did, the more she'd push him away. He had no problem with that. It would only make the hunt that much more intoxicating.

He *would* have her at his mercy and that of the unstoppable passion they shared. This time, he wouldn't let her go before he was glutted. If he couldn't be, then he wasn't letting her go at all.

Exiting the shower, he stood in front of the floor-length mirror, grimacing his displeasure with his too-short hair.

She'd loved it when it had been longer. He'd woken so many times still feeling her clinging to it as he'd ridden her, or combing through it languorously in blissful aftermaths. It had been why he'd kept it razed, thinking it would abort the phantom sensations. Not that it had.

Deciding to grow it out, he took extra care with his grooming, but didn't shave so he wouldn't have a stubble by the time he saw her again. It had driven her out of her mind when his whiskers had burned her during sex. But she'd always complained afterward that he'd sandpapered her. When he hadn't been able to meet her smooth-shaven as he had last night, he'd learned how to handle his facial hair to keep the pro of pleasuring her without the con of scraping her sensitive skin raw. By tonight, when he had her again, his current stubble would be the perfect length to give her the stimulation without the abrasion.

After dressing in clothes she'd love, he called Murdock. As always, he answered on the second ring. "Sir."

"I need to get into Dr. Sandoval's home."

"Sir?"

Annoyed that Murdock's response wasn't a straight "Yes, sir," he frowned. "I want to prepare a surprise for her."

After a beat, Murdock said, "You didn't read my report."

Suddenly, Richard was at the end of his tether. He was unable to bear a hint of obstacle or delay when it came to Isabella. "What is it with you and your fixation on that bloody report, Murdock? Did you even hear what I said?"

"Indeed, sir. But if you'd read my report, you would have known it wouldn't be wise to break into Dr. Sandoval's home."

"Why the bloody hell not?"

"Because her family is in there."

Two hours later Richard was driving through Isabella's neighborhood, a sense of déjà vu overwhelming him.

He hadn't even known such a place existed in New York. But there it was—Forest Hills Gardens, what looked like a quaint English village transplanted into the heart of Queens.

A private, tucked-away community within the Forest Hills neighborhood, it was based on the model of garden communities in England. Its streets were open to the public, but street parking was reserved for the residents of the elegant Tudor and Colonial single-family homes that flaunted towers, spires, fancy brickwork and red-tiled clay roofs. Wrought iron streetlights inspired by Old English lanterns lined the block, while the curving street grid was lined with London plane and white ash trees.

It felt as though he was back where he'd grown up.

Shaking off the oppressive memories, he parked in front of Isabella's leased residence, a magnificently renovated Tudor.

Glaring at the massive edifice, he exhaled. If he'd been in any condition to think last night, he would have deduced the reason why she'd leased such a big house when Murdock had imparted that information. It was understatement to say he'd been unpleasantly surprised to find out she lived with her mother, a sister and three children.

That put a serious crimp in his plans of relocating her to be near him. Now instead of invading her home to execute the seduction he'd had in mind, he'd come to get the lay of the land and to lie in wait for her.

Exiting his car, he strode across the wide pavement and ran up the steps to her front porch. He rang the bell then stood back as the long-forgotten sounds of children rose from inside.

The last time he'd heard sounds like that had been the day he'd left his family home.

He'd stood outside as he did now, listening to Robert and Rose playing. They'd sounded so carefree with the ominous shadow of Burton lifted, if only temporarily.

Little had his brother and sister known that Burton had only been absent because he was finalizing the deal that would make Richard the indentured slave of The Organization. They wouldn't have been so playful if they'd known it would be the last time they'd ever see their older brother.

Gritting his teeth, he reeled back the bilious recollections as feet approached, too fast and too light to be those of an adult.

Splendid. One of the little people in her stable was the one who'd volunteered to open the door. An obnoxious miniature human to vex him more than he already was.

All of a sudden the door rattled with what sounded like a little body crashing into it. That twerp had used the door to abort his momentum, no doubt not considering slowing down instead. Maybe waiting for Isabella in a home infested with abominations-in-progress who might aggravate him into devouring them wasn't a good idea.

But the door was already opening. It was too late to change his plan. Or maybe he'd pretend he'd knocked on the wrong door and—

He blinked at the boy who'd opened the door and was looking at him with enormous eyes, his mind going blank.

His heart crashed to one side inside his chest as the whole world seemed to tilt on its axis.

Then his mind, his very existence, seemed to explode.

Bloody hell...that's...that's...

Robert.

The bolt of realization almost felled him.

There was only one explanation for finding a duplicate of his dead younger brother in Isabella's home.

This boy was his.

Five

"Who're you?"

The melodious question sank through him, detonated like a depth mine. Observations came flooding in at such an intolerable rate, they buried him under an avalanche of details.

The texture of the boy's raven locks, the azure sky of his eyes, the slant of his eyebrows, the bow of his lips. His height and size and posture and every inch of his sturdy, energy-packed body...

But it was the boundless inquisitiveness and unwavering determination on his face that hit Richard so forcefully it threatened to expel whatever he had inside him that passed for a soul. That expression was imprinted in his mind. He'd seen it on his brother's face so many times when he'd been that same age. Before exposure to Burton had put out his fire and spontaneity and hope, everything that had made him a child.

Even had it not been for the almost identical resemblance, that jolt in his blood would have filled him with certainty. That Isabella had had his child.

This was his son.

"Mauri...don't open the door!"

"Already opened it, Abuela!" the boy yelled, never taking his eyes off Richard. Then he asked again, "Who're you?"

Before Richard considered if he could speak any longer, a woman in her fifties came rushing into the foyer.

Her hurried steps faltered as soon as her eyes fell on him,

becoming as wide as the boy's, the anxiety in them dissipating, a genial smile lighting up her face.

"Can I help you, sir?"

Something tugged at his sleeve. The boy—Mauri—pursuing his prior claim to his attention. And insisting on his all-important question. "Who're you?"

Richard stared down at him, literally having trouble remembering the name he'd invented for himself.

The boy held out his hand in great decorum, taking the initiative, as if to help him with his obvious difficulty in answering that elementary question. "I'm Mauricio Sandoval."

In the chaos his mind had become, he noted that Isabella had given the boy her new invented surname. He stared at the small proffered hand, stunned to find his heart booming with apprehension at the idea of touching him.

So he didn't, but finally answered instead, his voice an alien rasp to his own ears. "I'm Richard Graves."

The boy nodded, lowering his hand, then only said, "Yes, but who are you?"

"Mauri!"

At the woman's gentle reprimand, Richard raised his gaze to her, shaking his head, jogging himself out of the trance he'd fallen in. "Mauricio is right. Telling you my name didn't really tell you who I am."

"You talk funny."

"Mauri!"

The boy shrugged at the woman's embarrassment, undeterred. "I don't mean funny ha-ha, I mean not like us. I like it. You sound so…important. Wish I could speak like that." His gaze grew more penetrating, as if he wanted to drag answers from him. "Why do you speak like that?"

"Because I'm British."

"You mean from Britain?" At Richard's nod he persisted, "That's not the same as English, is it?"

The boy knew things most adults didn't. "Not exactly. I do happen to be English, too, or rather, English first, hav-

ing been born in England. But a lot of people are British—
and that means they're citizens of Great Britain—but not
English. They could be Scottish, Welsh, or some Irish from
Northern Ireland, too. But most of those people hate being
called British, rather insisting on calling themselves English
or Scottish or Welsh or Irish. I say British because the majority of people from the rest of the world don't know the
difference. And most don't care."

"So you say British so they won't ask questions when
they don't care about the answers. I ask questions because
I like to know stuff."

Richard marveled at the boy's articulate, thorough logic,
his insight into what made people tick. He was too well informed and socially developed for his age. Isabella and her
family were clearly doing a superlative job raising him.

After digesting the new information, the boy persisted.
"You still didn't tell us who you are."

At the woman's groan, Richard felt a smile tug at his
lips at the boy's dogged determination. It was clear when
he latched on to something, little Mauricio never let go.

That trait was more like him than Robert.

On his next erratic heartbeat his involuntary smile froze.
He sensed that there was more to Mauricio's insistence than
the drilling curiosity of a young and tenacious mind. Could
it be the boy was that sensitive he felt the blood bond between them?

No. Of course not. That was preposterous.

But what was really ridiculous was him standing there
like a gigantic oaf, unable to carry his end of an introduction with a curious child and a kindly lady.

Forcing himself out of his near stupor, he cocked his
head at the boy, that bolt of recognition striking him all over
again. "In my defense, you told me only your name, too."

That perfect little face, so earnest and involved, tilted
at him in challenge. "You're visiting us, so you know stuff
about us already. We don't know anything about you."

Richard's lips twisted at how absurd the boy's rebuttal made his previous comment. It really hadn't occurred to him to consider that simple fact when he'd made it. His mental faculties had been all but demolished.

While the boy was as sharp and alert as his mother. He got to the point and held his ground. As she always did.

He inhaled a much-needed draft of oxygen. "You're quite right. Knowing your name tells me a lot about you, based on what I already know about your…family, while knowing mine tells you nothing about me. You're also right to insist on knowing who I am. It's the first thing you always need to know about other people, so you can decide what to expect from them. Let me introduce myself better this time."

He held out his hand. The boy didn't give him a chance to brace himself for the contact, eagerly putting his hand in his. And an enervating current zapped through him.

He barely withdrew his hand instead of snatching it away, suppressing the growl that clawed at his throat at the lash of sensations.

"My name is Richard Graves and I'm an old…associate of Dr. Sandoval's."

Mauricio ricocheted a new question. "Are you a doctor?"

"No, I'm not."

"Then, what are you?"

"I'm a security specialist."

"What's that?"

Richard frowned. No one had ever asked him that question. When they probably should have. People assumed they understood what he did when most had no idea. That boy didn't presume. He asked so he'd know exact details, build his knowledge on solid ground. As Robert had.

Realizing his shoulders had slumped under the still-intensifying shock, he straightened. "It's a lot of things, actually, and it's all very important and very much in demand. The world is a dangerous place—and that's why your grandmother was rightfully upset that you opened the door. I'm sure she told you never to do that."

The boy sheepishly looked at the woman who was standing there watching them, her expression arrested. "Yeah, she did. Mamita, too. Sorry, Abuela."

Anxious to drive his point home, make it stick, Richard pressed on. "You must promise never to do that again, to always—*always*—do as your mother and grandmother say. Security is the most important thing in the world. I know, trust me."

The boy only nodded. "I trust you."

The boy's unexpected, earnest response was another blow.

Before he could deal with it, the boy added, "I promise." Then his solemn look was replaced by that burning interest again. "So what do you do?"

"I am the one people come to, to make them safe."

"Are you a bodyguard?"

"I'm the trainer and provider of bodyguards. To banks, companies, individuals, private and public events and transportation, and of course my own business and partners—and many other interests. I also keep people's private lives and businesses safe in other ways, protecting their computers, communications and information against accidental loss or hacking."

With every detail, Mauricio's blue eyes sparkled brighter in the declining sun. "How did you learn to do all that?"

With another groan, the woman intervened again. "Mauri, what did we say about not asking a new question every time someone gives you an answer?" Then she squeezed her dark eyes in mortification. "As if my manners are any better!" She rushed toward him and touched him on the arm. Her smile was exquisite, reminding him so much of Isabella, even though she barely resembled her. "Please come in."

Her gentle invitation agitated him even more. The idea of spending more time with that little boy with the endless questions and enormous eyes that probed his very essence felt as appealing as electrocution. In fact, *that* would have been preferable. He'd suffered it before, and he could say for certain what he was feeling now was worse.

Wishing only to run away, he cleared his throat. "It's all right. I don't want to interrupt your day. I'll connect with Isabella some other time."

The woman's hand tightened on his forearm, aborting his movement away from the threshold. "You wouldn't interrupt anything. I already cooked and updated my website where I do some of my volunteer work. Bella stayed overnight at work, but Saturday is her half day, so she'll be home soon."

So Isabella had explained her night away. But that wasn't the important thing now. The pressing matter was the alien feeling coming over him as he looked into this woman's kind eyes. He could only diagnose it as…helplessness. For the first time in his life he was being exposed to genuine hospitality, and he had no idea how to deal with it.

As if sensing his predicament, she patted his forearm, her eyes and voice gentling. "We'd really love to have you."

Corroborating his grandmother's request, the boy grabbed his other forearm. "Yes, please. You can tell me how you learned everything you do. Your job is as cool as a super-hero!"

The woman looked at her grandson with tender reproof. "Mr. Graves isn't here to entertain you, Mauri."

The boy nodded his acceptance. "I know. He's here to see Mamita." He swerved into negotiation mode seamlessly, fixing Richard with his entreaty. "But you have to do something while we wait for her."

At Richard's hesitation, the boy changed his bargaining tactic on the fly. "If your job is top secret and you can't talk about it, I can show you my drawings."

Richard stared down at the boy. He drew. Like him. Something no one knew about him.

His whole body was going numb with…dread? It was

beyond ludicrous to be feeling this way. But he'd been in shackles, had been tortured within an inch of his sanity, and he'd never felt as trapped and as desperate as he did now with those two transfixing him with gentleness and eagerness.

But there was no escape and he knew it. Those two frail yet overwhelming creatures had him cornered.

Feeling as if he was swallowing red-hot nails, he nodded.

Mauricio's smile blinded him as he whooped his excitement, pulling at Richard. Once he had him over the threshold, he let him go and streaked away, calling over his shoulder, "I'll go get my stuff!"

Watching Mauricio disappear, Richard stepped into Isabella's home as if stepping out from under tons of rubble.

The woman closed the door behind him and guided him inside. "I'm Marta, by the way. Isabella's mother, in case you didn't work that out. I don't know if Bella ever talked about me."

She hadn't. Isabella had never mentioned her family. When he'd tried to investigate them as part of his research into her life, there'd only been basic info until she was thirteen. Anything beyond that age had been blank until she'd married Burton. He now knew she'd later wiped out her years of marriage to him, too. But at the time he hadn't bothered to probe the missing parts, thinking them irrelevant to his mission. But he did remember Marta was her mother's name. She hadn't changed her name, either.

Suddenly something else bothered him. He stopped. Marta stopped, too, her gaze questioning.

"Once your grandson puts that logical mind of his to use, he'll realize you didn't follow your own rule about security. You didn't make sure I know Isabella, or if I do, that we're on the sort of terms that make it safe to let me into your home."

She waved his concern away. "Oh, I'm certain you know her, and well enough. And that it's safe to invite you in."

Warmth spread in his chest at yet another thing he'd never been exposed to. Unquestioning trust. Not even Murdock, Rafael or Isabella had trusted him so completely that quickly.

But such trust was unlikely coming from someone of Marta's age, and one who'd grown up in a country where danger was a part of daily life to so many people.

Was she letting her guard down now that they were in the States and in a secure neighborhood? Or because she judged people by appearances and from his she judged him to be refined and civilized? If she was that trusting with strangers, she could expose them all to untold dangers.

He didn't budge when she urged him onward, needing to make sure she didn't make that mistake again, either. "How did you come by that certainty? Did your daughter ever talk about me?"

"No." She grinned. "And she's going to hear my opinion of that omission later." Her eyes grew serious, but remained the most genial thing he'd ever seen. "But in a long and very eventful life, I've learned to judge people with absolute accuracy. I've yet to be wrong about anyone."

He grimaced. "You think you have an infallible danger radar? That's even worse than having no discretion at all."

She chuckled in response to his groan. "So you first feared I drag in anyone who comes to our door, and now you think I overestimate my judgment?" She tugged at him again, her face alight with merriment. "Don't worry, I'm neither oblivious nor overconfident. I am a happy medium."

He still resisted her, imagining how silly they must look, a slight woman trying to drag a behemoth more than twice her size, with him appearing the one in distress.

"What happy medium? You think I'm harmless."

This made her giggle. "I'd sooner mistake a tiger for a kitten." She sobered, though she continued grinning. "I think you're *extremely* harmful. I know a predator when I see one, and I've never seen anyone I thought as lethal as you. But I'm also sure you don't hunt the innocent or the defenseless. I have a feeling your staple diet is those who prey on them."

His thoughts blipped, stalled. How could this woman who'd just met him read him so accurately?

She wasn't finished. "So yes, I let you in because, beyond the personal details I don't know, I took one look at you and knew who you are. In a disaster, and when everyone else is scared or useless, you're the man I'd depend on to save my family."

He gave up. On trying to predict, or even to brace himself for what the next second would bring in this *Twilight Zone* of a household. He also gave up any preconceptions he'd unconsciously formed about Marta since she'd come rushing after Mauricio. Once he did, he let himself see beyond her apparent simplicity to the world of wisdom, born of untold ordeals, in her gaze. This woman had seen…and survived…too much.

A kindred feeling toward her swept him almost as powerfully as the one he'd felt toward Mauricio, if different in texture.

It seemed his weakness for Isabella extended to those who shared her blood. He might have a genetic predisposition to let anyone with her DNA influence his thoughts and steer his actions.

Marta tugged him again, and this time he let her lead him inside.

As they entered a family room at the center of a home right out of a syrupy family sitcom, she said, "Mauri never opens the door, either. I don't know why he did this time."

He pursed his lips as he sat on a huge floral couch that jarred him with its gaiety, considering the austerity he was used to. "He probably sensed that I'm the one to defend his home against invading alien armies…before he even saw me."

She spluttered, causing his own lips to twitch. He'd already known she wouldn't be offended when he poked fun at her, would relish his caustic humor.

Beaming, the eyes he was learning to read held something he didn't wish to translate. "You can joke about it, but you can actually be right. Mauri is an extremely...sensitive boy. There have been a lot of instances when he realized things he shouldn't or felt things before they happened."

Before he decided what to think, let alone formulate an answer, she clasped hands beneath her chin. "Now let me offer you something to drink. And you'll stay for dinner, yes?"

"Maybe Isabella won't want to have me."

"I want to have you for dinner. Mauri wants that, too. Bella can't say no to either of us. So you're safe."

Admitting that it was easier to decimate a squad of armed-to-the-teeth black ops operatives unarmed than resist this tiny woman, he surrendered. "Tea, please. If you have any."

"Bella has us stocked on every kind of tea on earth. It's the only thing she drinks."

It had been him who'd started her drinking tea, addicted her to it as per her admission. So she hadn't stopped. Just as she hadn't been able to stop her addiction to him.

He inhaled deeply, suppressing the acutely sensory memories that flooded his mind. "Earl Grey. Hot."

Clapping her hands, Marta rushed away. "Coming right up."

As she receded, Richard finally made a conscious comparison between her and her daughter.

She was much shorter and smaller, and her complexion, eyes and hair were darker. There were similarities in their features, but it was clear Isabella had taken after another relative, probably her father or someone from her father's side.

Marta was also different in other ways. Though she'd evidently lived a troubled life, she seemed more carefree, more optimistic than Isabella, even younger in spirit. If he'd ever imagined having an older sister, he would have probably wished for someone exactly like her.

He frowned at the strange idea, shaking it off. And all other distractions fell off with it, releasing his mind, letting it crash in the wreckage-filled abyss of reality.

Isabella had given birth to his son.

She'd been pregnant as she'd run for her life.

When had she found out? Before or after she'd fled?

If before, she would have had to run anyway to hide another betrayal from Burton. Or would she have aborted Mauricio, if he hadn't suspected her, to avoid his wrath?

That was a moot question. She'd had Mauricio, so she'd either discovered her pregnancy just as she'd run or afterward.

But why had she kept him? Had she wanted his child? Or had it all been about Mauricio himself? Had she wanted him?

That she'd had him proved it. Whatever she'd felt when she'd discovered her pregnancy, whatever dangers had been present, her desire to have him had trumped it all.

But she'd been on the run and pregnant, and hadn't considered asking him for help. Even before she'd realized he'd been the cause of her predicament.

So why? If she hadn't hated him then, why hadn't she run from Burton to him? He'd waited for her to, had left all channels open hoping she would. For some reason he couldn't fathom, she hadn't.

But if she had, and had told him about Mauricio, what would he have done? He had no idea.

He still had no idea. What to think, let alone what to do.

And here he was, after an explosive reunion with her that had plunged him right back into the one addiction of his life, sitting in her land of overwhelming domesticity, waiting for her mother to bring him tea and her son his portfolio. Not only had every single plan he'd had coming here been vaporized, every other one in his life had been, too.

What the blistering bloody hell would he do now?

What *could* he do?

Nothing. That was what. Nothing but sit back and observe, and make decisions as he went along. For the first time in a quarter of a century he wasn't steering everything and everyone wherever he wished. All his calculations had gone to hell the moment he'd laid eyes on her again. He expected them to remain there for the foreseeable future.

Making peace with that conclusion, he looked around the place. Murdock had said it had been turnkey, so he couldn't use it to judge anything about her or who she'd become.

Or maybe he could. She had chosen the finished product after all. It indicated this was what she wanted for herself, for her family now. The total opposite of what she'd had when she'd been with Burton, a fifty-bedroom mansion with two ballrooms and an attached garage for thirty cars. The demotion to a six-bedroom house with street parking was quite drastic. At most, he estimated this place to rent for six thousand a month, and to sell for a couple of million. While this neighborhood, though elegant, could as well be a row of hovels next to the outrageous hundred-acre estate of her former residence.

So was this what she wanted? An undistinguished upper-middle-class life? A safe, comfortable neighborhood for her family with good public schools for her child? Had she really changed her life so completely around? It appeared so.

And it appeared it had all been for Mauricio.

Mauricio. A son he hadn't known he had for seven years.

He couldn't get an actual grip on that. The shock of discovering Mauricio's existence would only deepen with time.

Almost as shocking had been Mauricio's and his grandmother's behavior with him. He couldn't rationalize, let alone cope with their instant acceptance. No one had ever reacted to him that way. He scared people on sight. At least awed them. He made the most hardened thugs wary, even before they knew who he really was and what he was capable of. So how had they taken to him so immediately?

Then it all happened at once. The sound of china rattling on a tray heralded Marta's approach. Stampeding feet down the stairs indicated Mauricio's. And the front door was opening.

Isabella.

The others, so focused on him as they rejoined him, missed her arrival until she entered the room. He held her eyes—her glorious, murderous eyes—as Mauricio foisted his precious load in his hands before hurtling himself at her. Her mother greeted her with as much joy. Isabella had eyes only for him.

If looks could kill, he would be a riddled corpse by now.

Mauricio fell over himself to fill her in on their whole meeting, word for word. Marta scolded her lovingly for never bringing Richard up. And though Isabella had brought her deadly displeasure with him under control and gave them a face he'd never seen—one of vivacious delight at being home—they seemed to realize that wasn't what she felt about his presence.

Not about to risk her spoiling their dinner plans, as Richard had intimated she might, Marta preempted her by announcing they'd have dinner at once and have tea later.

He had to give it to Isabella. All through what turned out to be an exceptional dinner, crafted to perfection by Marta, she somehow held back from doing what he could feel her seething to do: hurl a fork into his eye.

Along with discovering what superb home-cooked Colombian food tasted like, he found out the answer to a question he'd fumed over just last night. How a dinner could last four hours.

This one lasted even longer. And not because Isabella's younger sister, Amelia, and her two children arrived mid-dinner and extended the proceedings. That was the usual leisurely rhythm in this household. Something he was amazed to find he couldn't only tolerate, but enjoy. The experience was totally alien, but he still navigated it as if he had dinner with a household of women and children every night.

And like Mauricio and Marta, the newcomers immediately treated him as if they'd known him forever. Minutes after their arrival, he learned that Amelia's husband was finishing a contract in Argentina and would join them in the States next year. Until then, they were staying with big sister Isabella. As they had almost since the children were born.

Having grown up in a subdued household with a military father and a conservative mother, he had no idea how loud and lively a family could be. But it did seem everyone was more gregarious than usual on his account. Probably because an adult male presence was a rarity in their lives. The only other male in the family was Isabella's younger brother who lived abroad. But no matter how many men they'd been exposed to, they'd never seen anything like him. Everyone was so intrigued and awed by him and thrilled to have him.

Everyone but Isabella, of course. But she ignored him with such ingenuity, no one but him realized she hadn't given him one word or look all through dinner, even avoiding answering his direct questions without appearing to snub him.

He ate as much as all of them put together, to Marta's delight, who said she'd finally found someone with an appetite to do her efforts justice. When he said it was only expected, since he could probably house them all in his body, she laughed and was only happy her culinary artwork wouldn't have to be reduced, again, to the status of shunned leftovers.

After dinner they retired to the family room and he was served his promised Earl Grey. Mauricio solemnly told him he'd have to postpone showing him his drawings. He didn't trust the younger children to respect his works of art, and they wouldn't have the peace needed to discuss them anyway.

The evening progressed for another hour with everyone asking him a thousand questions, hanging on every word of his answers, laughing readily at his every witticism.

He sat there feeling like a sprawling lion after a satisfying meal, with a pride of lionesses lounging around him and cubs crawling all over him.

Then Mauricio and the younger children, Diego and Benita, started yawning. Marta and Amelia took them to bed, leaving Richard alone with Isabella for the first time.

Without turning her head toward him, just her baleful gaze, she seethed, "You'll get up now, and you'll get the hell out of here. And you will *never* come back."

Sighing in satisfaction that she'd finally talked to him, even to slash him before evicting him, he only sat forward to pour himself another cup of tea.

He settled back even more comfortably, slanting her a challenging glance. "Are you going to make me?"

"I'll do whatever it takes." Her usually velvety voice was a serrated blade. "I got my family out of a country full of thugs like you, and I am never letting one near them again."

Now, *that* piqued his interest. But direct questioning now wouldn't get her to elaborate. He had to get what he wanted indirectly, by giving her more chances to flog him.

"Thugs like me? What kind do you think I am?"

"I can *extrapolate* well enough."

"Shoot."

"If only I could. Right between your snake eyes."

This took him by such surprise he threw his head back and laughed. "If only you knew."

As if his merriment was the last straw, she turned to him, her body rigid with rage. "What's that supposed to mean?"

"Just that I was once code-named Cobra. So your assessment of my reptilian attributes is quite accurate."

"Of course I'm accurate. As for what kind of snake you are, I think you must have been Burton's rival gangster or you'd been sent by another cartel to destroy the competition.

Though your legitimate image was and remains flawless, I know what you really are. A criminal." At his ridiculing pout, she narrowed her eyes. "Don't bother spouting I'm a criminal, too. Take that to the law or shut up. But I'm telling you here and now, I'll go to any lengths to make certain you never come near my family again."

He sipped his tea, luxuriating in how fury intensified her allure. "You knew all that when you not only let me come near you, but let me be all over you and inside you."

"When it was between us, that was one thing. Now you've involved my family, all rules have changed. You don't want to find out what I'm capable of doing to protect them."

"But I do want to find out. Recount some of the unspeakable things you did in their defense. Who knows, maybe I can be deterred after all."

"Anything I previously did is irrelevant. What I'd do would be tailored to you. I'll keep that a surprise."

"Like you did with Mauricio?"

"Why would my adopted son be a surprise to you?"

That was the story she was going with?

From her immediate retort, she'd prepared that story in case he investigated her. He was sure she'd get her story straight with her mother and sister. She thought he wouldn't be able to find the truth in the void she'd created in her past. She had every reason to believe she'd get away with it since Mauricio looked nothing like him. But he wouldn't contest her claim, not now.

Maybe not ever.

She rose, flaying him with her antagonism. "Why did you come here in the first place?"

He drained his cup, put it on the tray and then rose to his feet. She took a step back, and he knew. She didn't fear him coming closer, but her own reaction to his nearness.

All he wanted was to take her against the nearest wall.

Since that was out of the question in her family-infested

home, he shrugged. "I came to find you, and they snared me. Your mother and son are inescapable. As you should know."

"Yeah, right, the unstoppable Richard Graves finally met his immovable objects."

"Very much so. Your mother and son are intractable. Your sister and her little urchins, too. What should I have done in your opinion to deter their determined attentions? Bared my fangs and snapped at them?"

"Gee, I'm sure they'll be thrilled with your opinion of them. But, yeah, one look at your real face and a swipe of your forked tongue and they would have run screaming. But you sat there purring all night like a lion ingratiating himself to a naïve, male-starved pride."

This time he guffawed. Their unlikely situation had made her think of that parable, too. "What can I say? Your mother's cooking can soothe even me, and your little tribe is quite…entertaining. They're such an exemplary audience. And they're yours, so it wasn't in my best interests to scar them for life with the sight of my hood spread out."

"News flash, playing nice with my family wouldn't ingratiate you to *me*, since that's the one thing I won't forgive you for." Before he could answer, her lips thinned. "Enough of this. Give me your word you won't come again."

His eyebrows rose. "You think my word is worth anything?"

"Yes."

Heat surged in his chest. She seemed to believe that, when she shouldn't believe he had any code of honor.

Not willing to corroborate her belief, he said, "Then, maybe you don't know anything about me after all."

Before she could blast him again, he brushed against her as her mother and sister walked in. He promised he'd be back in answer to their new invitation, then took his leave. The women saw him to the door and stood there until he drove away.

Isabella remained in the background. He was sure she was killing him a dozen horrific ways in her mind.

The stimulation of her murderous intentions only lasted a few blocks before reality all came crashing over him again.

He should heed her warning, should walk away. He'd seen her, he'd had her, and after he made sure she stayed away from Rose, he should disappear from her life again.

It shouldn't matter he felt he'd suffocate if he didn't have more of her. It shouldn't matter she'd had his son. A boy who provoked a thousand unknown stirrings inside him. For what would he do with those aberrant feelings?

She hadn't told him she'd had his son, seemed bound on never letting him know. Even without knowing what he *really* was, she knew she mustn't let him near a boy that age.

And she was absolutely right.

For the past seven years he hadn't known Mauricio existed, and Mauricio hadn't known he did.

He would keep it that way.

Six

After Richard left, her mother and sister pounced on her with questions. Isabella expended every drop of ingenuity she possessed into dodging them and validating none of their suspicions.

Those ranged from his being a suitor she wouldn't let close for reasons they couldn't imagine—since as did every woman on earth, they thought him a god and/or a godsend—to the truth. Her mother was the one whose eyes contained the suspicion…the *hope*, that he was Mauri's biological father.

She held it together until she was in her room, prepared for bed, then collapsed on it in a mass of tremors.

So much had happened so fast in that exhilarating, nauseating and terrifying roller coaster since he'd exploded into her life last night. Now his incursion had reached inside her home and within inches of the secret she'd thought safe forever. And it scared her out of her wits.

And that was before she considered that confounding evening he'd spent with them. Every second he'd spent charming her family like the snake he'd admitted he'd been labeled as, she'd felt a breath away from screaming with aggravation and swooning with dread. At the torture's end, she might have stood her ground, and Richard might have walked away, but she didn't think it would end that simply. He hadn't given his word he'd leave her family alone in his pursuit of her. And nothing involving Richard was without long-term repercussions. She was now terrified what his next blow would be and how he'd deal it.

At least she seemed to have steered him away from any suspicion he might have had about Mauri. His age alone must have been a red flag, and she'd gone light-headed holding her breath, expecting the worst. After all the suspense, he'd only made a passing comment and had taken her claim that Mauri was adopted without batting a lid.

But…maybe this very reaction indicated she was overreacting. Maybe even telling him the truth about Mauri would be the best way to end his infiltration of her life.

A man like him, who lived separate from humanity, without connections, who only cared about having the world at his feet, would probably be appalled at the news he'd fathered a son. His lack of curiosity, or the one that had been satisfied by a mere word, indicated that her assessment was probably correct.

Furthermore, this inexplicable visit itself might turn out to be a blessing in disguise. Maybe seeing her in her domestic milieu as a mother, especially to his biological son, would be a too-banal dose of reality, spoiling the fantasy of the wild affair he'd been planning to have with the mysterious femme fatale he seemed to think her. Maybe it would all douse his passion and make him walk away now, not later.

That sounded plausible. There was no way he would involve himself with her now that he'd seen her "tribe." Spending time with her family had probably been a quaint novelty to him, a field experiment in how the other half lived to add to his arsenal of analyzing human beings, to better devise strategies to control and milk them for all they were worth. But there was no way he'd want to repeat it.

He'd only said he would to punish her because she'd dared challenge him. But once he was satisfied he'd made her sweat it out long enough, he'd let her know he never intended an encore.

Once she came to this conclusion, exhaustion, emotional

and physical, descended on her like a giant mallet. She had no idea when sleep claimed her.

She woke up feeling as if she'd been in a maelstrom.

And she had been. Her dreams had been a vortex filled with Richard and their tempestuous time together, past and present. He'd always wreaked havoc inside her, awake or asleep. There'd never been any escaping him. Not in her psyche. She'd just have to settle for escaping him in reality.

By the time she headed to her office, her new conviction that he'd fade from her life again made her wonder if she should come clean to Rose and Jeffrey about her past.

She'd tried to after she'd left Richard yesterday, to deprive him of that coercion card. But their schedules hadn't allowed her to even broach the subject. So she'd scheduled a meeting with Rose first thing in the morning, the one sure way to get a hold of her.

But if Richard disappeared again, should she expose the ugly truth of her history to Rose and Jeffrey? Just the knowledge would scar their psyches. And what if they worried her past would catch up with her and they'd be standing too close when it did? *She* was certain there was absolutely no danger of that, or she wouldn't have taken their partnership offer. But what if they couldn't feel safe with her around?

She stood by her conviction they'd never judge her, would be more supportive than they already were. But if they worried about their family's safety at all, she'd have to leave.

And she didn't want to leave. Them, the practice, her new place. It was the first time she felt she had real friends, a workplace where she belonged and a home.

By the time she opened her office door she'd made her decision.

She'd wait to see what Richard did. If he disappeared again, that would be that. If he didn't…

No. She wouldn't consider that possibility until it came to pass.

Suddenly she found herself plucked from the ground and suspended against the door she'd just closed with two-hundred-plus pounds of premium maleness plastered against her.

"You're late."

A squeeze of her buttocks accompanied his reprimand before he crashed his lips over hers, invading her with the taste of him, the distillation of dominance and danger.

But he was invading more than her essence. He was breaching her last privacy, leaving her no place to hide. Just when she'd convinced herself he'd leave her alone, set her free.

She'd do anything to make him let her go. Even beg.

But his large hands were spreading her thighs around his hips, raising her to thrust his erection up at her core as he dragged her down on it. His tongue filled her again and again, drank her moans as they formed. Reality softened, awareness expanded to encompass his every breath and heartbeat. Nothing remained but Richard and her and their fusion.

"Richard..."

"Yes, let me hear your distress for me, make up for the agonizing night I spent, needing you under me, all around me."

Something shrill cut through the fog of sensations as he undid her blouse and bra, bent to engulf one nipple in his mouth. The first hot suckle almost made her faint with pleasure. Then the clamor rose again until she realized what it was—her mind screaming, reminding her of the threat he posed to her existence and everyone in it.

It finally imbued her with enough sanity and strength to push out of the craved prison of his arms and passion, to stumble away and put her clothes back in order.

"What are you doing here?"

At his question she turned to him with an incredulous huff. "I won't even dignify that by echoing it."

Lids heavy, his gaze swept her in ruthless hunger, strumming her simmering insanity. "I told you to end your partnership with the Andersons. And what did you do? You reported to work yesterday and again first thing this morning. When I made it clear this is the one thing I won't budge on."

She tossed him a contemptuous glance. "You don't have to budge. Only to bugger off, as you say in your homeland."

His lips twisted in that palpitation-inducing smile that seemed to come easier to him since yesterday. "Don't think that because I want you now more than ever I will bargain with you over this. It's not a matter of either you do it or you don't."

"You're right. It's not a matter of 'either or' but 'neither nor.'" At his arching eyebrow, she huffed. "You do know your grammar, don't you? The language *was* coined where you hail from. I will neither end anything with the Andersons nor start anything with you."

A theatric exhalation. "Pity. After everything that happened between us, I would have rather not forced you into complying. Oh, well."

He produced his phone from his pocket, pressed one virtual button. The line opened in two seconds and she heard a deep voice on the other end. She thought it said, "Sir."

Without taking his eyes off her, Richard got to the point of his call at once. "Murdock, I need a court order to shut down the Anderson Surgery Center in forty-eight hours."

With that he ended the call and continued looking at her.

So that was his extreme measure. If she wouldn't leave, he'd take everything from under her. And she had no doubt he could and would do it. And that would only be for starters. In case this somehow didn't work, he would only escalate his methods of destruction.

And none of it made any sense.

She cried out her confusion. "*Why* do you want me to stop working here? What is it to you? Is this even about me or…" A suspicion exploded in her mind. "Is this about

Rose? Did you discover her relationship to Burton and come here to clean up every trace of him, including anybody who knew him? If so, did you only want me out of the way so I wouldn't warn them about you? And now you've decided to strike directly since I didn't cooperate and spoiled your preferred stealth methods?"

As the conviction sank in her mind, from one breath to the next her desperation turned to aggression in defense of her friends. "Burton was a monster who deserved far worse than whatever you've done to him. But she was his victim. Besides that, Rose and Jeffrey are the absolute best people I've ever known, and I'd die before I let you near them. And that's *not* a figure of speech."

As if he hadn't heard her tirade, he cocked his head at her. "How did you come to know that couple?"

"Wh-what?"

"There was no evidence of when you met, or of your developing relationship, not even emails or phone calls, and I want to know how you did this."

"I—I met Rose in a conference in Texas four years ago."

"And? I want to know what led to their asking you to be their partner and not any of their long-term colleagues."

His icy focus shook her. Where was this interrogation heading? "I felt a…kinship to her at once. I guess she felt the same, since she told me her life story as we waited for a late lecturer. I was shocked to realize that Burton used to be her stepfather."

His eyes and jaw hardened. He gestured for her to continue.

"I didn't tell her about me, but that kindred feeling only grew when I knew both of our lives were blighted by that monster. Incredibly, she felt the same way. Afterward and for years, we talked for hours daily, using online video chat. We practically designed and decorated this place that way. She and Jeffrey kept pushing me to come live in the States and be their partner. The moment I could, I took my family and came back, thinking I was giving us all a new and safe life. Then *you* appeared to mess everything up."

His eyes grew heavier with so much she couldn't fathom. "I don't want to mess things up. Not anymore."

"Yeah, right. That's why you're going to shut down the practice Rose and Jeffrey worked for years to build and invested all their money in."

"It's all up to you. Walk out of here, and I do, too."

"You mean you'd leave them alone, for real? You wouldn't have done that eventually anyway?"

"I already said going after them was to force you to leave. I have no interest in sabotaging their business."

"So this isn't about Rose? You're not after her?"

"It is about her." Before his reply sent her alarm soaring again, he reached for her, dragged her against his rock-hard body. "But the one I'm after is you, as you well know. So I suppose we can negotiate after all. Taking everything into consideration, I'll make you a deal."

She squirmed against him. "What deal?"

"I want you out of here. And I want you, full stop. You want me, too, but need to be assured of your family's safety. So here's my deal. You will make use of everything I can give you, will be with me every possible minute that our schedules permit. And I promise to stay away from your family."

His hypnotic voice seeped through her bones with delicious compulsion, until she wondered why she'd ever put up a fight when being with him had always been all she'd ever wanted. And if he promised her family would be safe…

Then he added, "But only if you stay away from mine."

She pushed away to stare up at him, her mind shying away from an enormous realization.

Then he spelled it out. "Burton was my stepfather, too."

Richard had never intended to reveal that fact to Isabella. But he never did anything he intended where she was concerned. Nothing that was even logical or sane. He touched her, looked into her eyes, and his ability to reason was incinerated.

Not that he cared. As he'd told her, so many things had changed in the past forty-eight hours. His previous intentions weren't applicable anymore. He wanted her, had already decided to leave her family situation untouched. Laying down the card of his relationship to Rose now felt appropriate.

He'd always wondered if she'd ever worked out that his revenge on Burton had had a personal element, until last night when she'd made it clear she'd always thought it purely professional. He'd expected the truth to come as a surprise, but the avalanche of shock and horror that swept her at his revelation was another thing he'd failed to project.

Before he could think of his next move, the door opened after only a cursory knock.

And he found himself face-to-face with Rose.

His heart gave his ribs a massive thump as observations came like bullets from a machine gun. Rose's silky ponytail thudding over her shoulder with her sudden halt, the white coat swinging over a chic green silk blouse and navy blue skirt, her open face with its elegant features tensing and the eyes full of affection as she entered Isabella's office emptying to fill with surprise.

He'd checked her schedule, made sure she'd be occupied with patients during his visit. This confrontation hadn't been a possibility.

But it was a reality now.

And finding the sister he'd watched from afar for more than twenty-five years less than ten feet away was a harsher blow than he'd ever thought it could be.

Tearing his gaze away, he turned to Isabella, who was gaping at him as if she hadn't even noticed Rose's entry.

"I'll leave you to your visitor, Dr. Sandoval. We'll continue our business later."

He turned around and Rose blinked, moved as if coming out of a trance. "Don't go on my account."

He gave her his best impersonal glance. "I was just about to leave anyway."

Before either woman reacted, he'd almost cleared the door when Rose caught him by his sleeve.

Dismay soaring, he raised an eyebrow with all the cold impatience he could muster. He needed this confrontation to be over.

"Rex?"

Everything inside braked so hard he realized for the first time how people dropped unconscious from shock.

The sister who'd last seen him when she was six years old had recognized him on sight.

But it was still just a suspicion. Only he could solidify it. Or Isabella, now that he'd revealed his connection to Rose. But knowing her, she wouldn't be the one to do so. So it was up to him.

Feeling his insides clench in a rusty-toothed vise, he made his choice. "You must have mistaken me for someone else. The name is Richard. Richard Graves."

He flicked Isabella a warning glance, just in case. Not that he'd needed to. Isabella seemed to have lost the ability to speak or even blink. But when she regained the ability to talk, if she did tell Rose…

He couldn't worry about that now. He had to get the sodding hell out of there.

Not giving Rose a chance to say anything else, he turned and strode away, fighting the urge to break out into a run.

Once in his car, he drove away as if from an earth fissure that threatened to engulf everything in its path.

Which was a very accurate description.

Everything since he'd seen Isabella again *had* been like an earthquake that had cracked the ground his whole life was built on. He'd thought he could stem the spread of the chasms and return to a semblance of stability again.

But there was no fooling himself anymore. He'd set an unstoppable sequence of events in motion. And if he didn't stop the chain reaction, it would unravel his whole existence.

And everyone else's, too.

Two hours later in his penthouse, after a couple of drinks and a hundred laps in the pool, he had a plan in place.

He'd just gotten out of the shower when the intercom that never rang did.

The concierge apologized profusely, claiming that it was probably a false alarm, since he'd never allowed anyone up in the past six years, but a lady insisted he would want her up.

Isabella. She'd preempted him.

A wave of excitement and anticipation swept him as he informed the concierge that Isabella was always to be let up without question. He ran to dress, but she arrived at his door so fast he had to rush there barefoot in just his pants.

The moment he saw her on his doorstep, he wanted to haul her to bed, lose himself inside her and forget about all they had to resolve and all he had to do.

"Isabella…"

She pushed past him, strode inside. It took him a couple of minutes of following her through his penthouse to realize—to believe—what she was doing.

She was heading to his bedroom. And she was stripping.

Almost every surprise he'd ever had had involved her. This one almost had him launching himself at her as she passed one of the couches, tackling her facedown and thrusting inside her before they even landed on it.

He held back only because he wanted to let her take this where she wanted, to savor the torment of watching her disrobe for him, exposing her glory to his aching, covetous gaze. The contrast between the pitiless seduction of her action and her straitlaced stride made it all the more mind-meltingly arousing.

Once in his lower-floor bedroom, he could barely see her until he remembered he could turn on the lights with a whisper.

The expansive space filled with the subdued lighting he preferred, showcasing her beauty in golden highlights and arcane shadows. At the foot of his bed, she turned, wearing only white bikini panties and same-color, three-inch-heeled sandals. Her eyes were burning sapphires.

He approached, waiting for her to say or do something. She only stood there looking up at him.

Suddenly the urge to inspect her body, with the insight of new realizations, knowing she'd given birth to his child, overtook him. His eyes swept her voluptuousness, luxuriating in her as a whole before basking in each asset separately.

Her hips were lush with femininity, her waist a sharp concavity, her legs long and smooth, her shoulders square and strong. Every curve and line and swell of her was the epitome of womanliness, the exact pattern that activated his libido. Each inch of her had ripened to its utmost potential. He now realized it wasn't only time but motherhood that had effected the change.

Turning his savoring from visual to tactile, he caressed her buttocks, her back, leaving her firm belly for last. His skull tightened over his brain as he imagined her ripening every day with the child they'd made together during one of their pleasure-drenched deliriums. The idea of his seed taking root inside her, growing into a new life, that vibrant, brilliant boy who'd rocked the foundations of his world last night, turned his arousal into agony. He needed to claim her, to mark her with his essence again...*now*.

Wrestling with the savagery of his need, he skimmed his hands up to her breasts. Blood roared in his ears, his loins, as their warmth and resilience overflowed in his hands. He stared at the ripened perfection of her, the need to know if she'd breastfed Mauricio scalding him, the images searing him body and mind.

Unbidden, another image flared in his mind, heightening the imaginary inferno. Her, holding another baby, one he'd get to see her breastfeed.

Recoiling from the agonizing visions, he squeezed her supple flesh, his fingers unsteady with emotion and mounting hunger as he circled the buds he'd tasted during so many rides to ecstasy, thicker, darker now, and much more mouthwatering. And now he knew why.

Before he bent to silence the clamoring and engulf her nipples, she slithered from his hold and lowered to her knees.

Mashing her face into his loins, she kissed his erection, her hands trembling over the zipper, dragging his pants down.

"I didn't get to touch and taste you again…"

Her gasp of greed as he thudded heavily in her waiting grasp juddered through him. Relief and distress speared through him in equal measure as she worshipped him, the only touch and need he'd ever craved, measuring his girth, rubbing her face over his length, inhaling and smooching and nibbling. Then with a stifled cry of urgency, she opened her mouth over his crown, swirled her hot tongue over its smoothness, moaning continuously as she lapped up the copious flow of his arousal as if its taste was the sustenance she'd been starving for.

The sight alone, of her kneeling in front of him, of her gleaming head at his loins, of her lips, deep rose and swollen and wrapped around his erection, almost made him come.

Stepping out of what felt like burning cloth, he tried to savor it all, caressed the hair that rained over her face, held it away in one hand so he could revel in her every move and expression, bending to run his other hand over the sweep of her back, the flare of her hips. But she started rubbing herself sinuously against his legs like a feline in heat and he lost the fight.

He dragged her up, growling. Before he threw her back

on the bed and mounted her, she climbed him, wrapped her legs around his hips and ground her moist heat over his erection. He tore her panties off, digging his fingers into her buttocks, making her cry out, crash her lips into his.

Her tongue delved inside his mouth, tangling in abandon with his as if she was bent on extracting everything inside him. He let her storm him, show him the ferocity of her craving, rumbles of pained pleasure escaping from his depths.

Her voice, roughened by abandon, filled him. "Take me, Richard. Or should I call you Rex?"

He could swear he heard a crack as loud as a sonic boom. It was his control snapping.

He thrust up into her, invading her molten tightness, sheathing himself inside her to the hilt in one fierce stroke. Her scream felt as if it tore out of his own lungs. The very sound of unbearable pleasure, as his bellow had been.

On the second thrust he roared again and staggered with her to the bed, flinging their entwined bodies on it, loving her squeal as the impact emptied her lungs, then again as his weight crushed her next breath out of her.

He rose between the legs clamped over his back, holding her feverish eyes, tethering her head with a hand twisted in her hair, the other nailing her down by the shoulder.

Her swollen lips trembled over her anguished demand. "Do it, do it all to me."

He obeyed, pounding her, each ram wrenching from their bodies all the searing sensations they could experience or withstand.

Her shrieks of ecstasy rose until she mashed herself into him and he felt her shatter around him. Her inner flesh gushed hot pleasure over him, her muscles wrenching at his length in a fit of release. He rode the breakers of her orgasm in a fury of rhythm, feeding her frenzy.

"Come with me…"

He did, burying himself to her womb and surrendering to the most violent orgasm he'd ever known even with her, filling her with his essence in jet after excruciating jet.

Following the cataclysm, he couldn't separate from her. Couldn't imagine he ever would. He had to have her like this always, fused to his flesh through the descent, feeling her aftershocks and fulfillment.

He didn't think anything of her receding warmth until she shivered. Frowning, he rose off her to reach for the covers, groaning at the pain of separating from her body.

Securing her under them with him wrapped around her for extra warmth, he smiled in possession and satisfaction down at her. "I take it you've decided to take my deal?"

"No. This was actually the closure we both needed before I told you that I won't."

His hands, which had been caressing her back and buttocks, stilled. Her eyes were unwaveringly serious. She wasn't teasing or resisting. She meant this.

Then she told him why. "I can't have you in my life and hope it would remain normal. I've struggled too long and too hard, have too many people who depend on me to introduce your disruptive, destructive element in my life. I'm the pillar of my family and if you damage me, and I'm sure you will, everything will come crashing down. I won't have that."

Rising to look at her, he felt he'd turned to stone inside and out as she watched her rising, too.

"For closure to be complete, so we'd never have any loose ends tangling us in each other's lives, I'm also here to have everything out once and for all. It's the only way we could both finally let each other go. For good this time."

Seven

Richard let Isabella leave his side, a jagged rock in his throat. This felt real. And final.

Anything he did now to stop her would have to be true coercion. And no matter that he was losing his mind needing her, and she'd proved again she needed him as much, over-powering considerations had made her decide to quell that need. He *could* force her. But he couldn't. He had to have her not only willing, but unable to live without having him.

He watched her careful progress to the bathroom in only her sandals, what had remained on all through. She soon exited and, without looking at him, bent to pick up her panties, dropping them again when she realized they were ruined before walking out. Pulling on his pants, he followed her as she retraced and reversed her stripping journey.

Once beside the pool, she sat on the couch where they'd almost made love the first night and looked at him.

And the *way* she did…as if he was everything she wanted but could never have.

Before he charged her and overrode her every misgiving, her subdued voice stopped him in his tracks.

"I'll start." She stopped to swallow, her averseness to coming clean clearly almost overwhelming. "I'll tell you everything. My side of the story. But only if you promise you'll reciprocate and tell me the whole truth, too."

"What if I promise, and you tell me everything I want to know, but I don't deliver on my end of the bargain?"

Her shoulders jerked dejectedly. "I'd do nothing. I can do nothing anyway. The first truth I have to admit is that I am at your mercy. The imbalance of power between us is incalculable. I have so many vulnerabilities while you have none. You can force me to do anything you want."

He made her feel this way? Defeated? Desperate? He'd thought she needed his chase before she gave in to what she'd wanted all along. But if she truly hated it, this was as insupportable, as abhorrent, to him as when she'd thought he could harm her.

Feeling his guts twisting over dull blades, he came down to sit beside her. "You previously said you considered my word worth having. If you really think so, you have it. A caveat, though. You'll probably end up wishing you hadn't asked for the whole truth. It will horrify you."

"After what I've been through in my life, nothing ever would again." Her gaze wavered. "Can I have a drink first?"

Her unfamiliar faltering intensified his distress. He'd never seen her...defenseless before. Besides the shame that choked him for being what made her feel this way, a piercingly poignant feeling, akin to the tenderness only Rose had previously provoked, swamped him. For the first time he wasn't looking at Isabella as the woman who made him incoherent with desire, a woman he wanted to possess, in every meaning of the word, but a woman he wanted to... protect. Even from himself.

Especially from himself.

Stunned by the new perception, he headed to the bar and mixed her one of the cocktails she liked.

For a year after he'd left her, whenever he'd made himself a drink, he'd made her one, too, as if waiting for her to materialize and take it.

The day he'd thrown Burton in the deepest dungeon on the planet, he'd looked at the cocktail glass he'd prepared with such care and faced the stark truth that she never would. And he'd smashed it against the wall. Then he'd furiously and irrevocably terminated every method of communication she hadn't used. He'd been convinced she'd forgotten him. And he'd hated her then, with a viciousness he hadn't even felt for Burton. Because he hadn't been able to forget her.

And all that time she'd been running, pregnant with his child, giving birth to him, facing endless difficulties and dangers he could only guess at.

He didn't have to guess anymore. She'd finally tell him.

He poured himself a shot of whiskey, breaking his rule of not exceeding two drinks per day. He had a feeling he'd need as much numbness as he could get for the coming revelations.

It seemed she felt the same way as she gulped down the cocktail as soon as he handed it to her. Even with little alcohol, for a nondrinker like her, having it in one go would affect her as much as half a bottle of hard liquor would affect him.

As soon as he sat, struggling not to drag her onto his lap, she said, "To explain how I became Burton's wife, I have to start my story years earlier."

His every muscle bunching in dreadful anticipation, he tossed back his drink.

"You probably know my early history—that I was born in Colombia to a doctor father and a nurse mother and was the oldest of five siblings. My trail stops when I was thirteen, when my family was forced out of our home along with tens of thousands of others.

"Though we ended up living in one of the shantytowns around Bogota, my parents gave me medical training, while I home-schooled my siblings. Everybody sought our medical services, especially guerillas who always needed us to patch up their injured. Then one day, when I was nineteen, we went to tend to the son of our region's most influential drug lord, and Burton, who was there concluding a deal, saw me. He later told me I hit him here—" she thumped her fist over her heart "—like nothing ever had."

His own heart gave a clap of thunder he was surprised she didn't hear.

He wasn't ready to listen to this. Not just yet.

Rising, he strode to the bar to grab a tray of booze this time. He had a feeling he needed to get plastered. He only hoped he could achieve that.

He poured them both drinks. She took hers, sipped it, grimaced when she realized it was a stiff one, but took another swallow before she went on.

"He came to our domicile later to 'negotiate' with my parents for me. My father refused the 'bargain' point-blank and was so enraged he shoved Burton. Next moment, he was dead."

Richard stared at her, everything screeching to a halt inside him. Burton. He'd killed her father. Too.

She adjusted his deduction. "Burton's bodyguard shot him for daring to shove his master. Before I could process what had happened, Burton put a bullet through the killer's head then turned to me, apologizing profusely. My mother was frantically trying to revive my father, while I faced the monster who'd come to buy me.

"The sick infatuation in his eyes told me resistance would come at an even bigger price to the rest of my family. Though my soul wretched at being at this monster's mercy, I'd already dealt with the worst life had to offer and knew I could do anything to survive, and to ensure the survival of my family. And if I manipulated his infatuation, someone of his power could be used to save my family, and many, many others.

"So I swallowed my shock and anguish, said I believed he hadn't meant any of us harm, but to give me time to deal with my shock and loss and to get to know him. He was delighted my reaction wasn't the rejection he'd expected after the 'catastrophic mistake' of my father's murder and he promised me all the time in the world. And everything else I could want. I told him I only wanted my family to be taken to the United States, to live legally in safety and comfort. He told me that would only be the first of thousands of things he'd lavish on me.

"The next day I stood at my father's grave with the man who'd been responsible for his murder. Before Burton took us away, I promised my friends I'd be back to help as soon as I could."

His hand shaking with a murderous rage he'd never before suffered, he reached for the bottle. He took a full swig and savored planning the new horrors he'd inflict on Burton.

Isabella continued, "Within a year he got us permanent residences through an investment program. My sisters and brother were in school and my mother volunteered in orphanages and shelters. Burton pulled strings to equate my experience to college courses necessary for medical school. Then on my twentieth birthday, he proposed. Though he was like putty in my hands, from his murderous behavior with others, I didn't doubt he could kill us all if I wavered now that he'd fulfilled his end of the bargain. I was forced to accept. With an ecstatic smile."

This. The missing pieces. What explained everything. Rewrote history. Made everything he'd thought or felt or done not only redundant or wrong, but a crime. Against her.

And she wasn't finished telling him how heinous that crime had been. "After the lavish wedding, I played the part of the doting wife, capitalized on his abnormal attachment to me. Thankfully, I didn't have to suffer through many sexual encounters, as he rarely wanted full intimacy. I perfected the act of loving his constant pawing, though."

The rage that exploded inside him threatened to crack his head open as he imagined her succumbing to Burton's touch while her every fiber retched at the violation...

He hurled the half-finished bottle across the pool. His fling across dozens of feet was so forceful, the window smashed on impact, exploding outward. If not for the terrace, it would have rained shards on the street below.

Isabella's heavenly eyes turned black at his violence.

He gestured that he'd expended it, would rein it in now, and for her to continue.

So she did. "I was also thankful he'd had a vasectomy in his early thirties. When he said we could still have a child if I wished, I assured him my younger siblings always felt like my children, and I wanted to focus on my education, my humanitarian work, but mostly him. He was delighted, as he was with everything from me. I continued to perform the role of perfect wife to such a powerful man, appearing to make flamboyant use, as he wished me to, of his wealth, and managed to put aside millions. I wanted enough personal power, education-, money- and knowledge-wise, to plot my family's escape from this nightmare. Then you appeared in my life."

Before he found words to express the torrents of regret accumulating inside him, she looked away, eyes glittering.

"When you asked me to leave with you, promised to protect me, I believed you had no idea what you were getting yourself into, not knowing the extent of my vulnerability, or of Burton's power and obsession with me. I thought even if you'd managed to spirit my whole family away, he'd find us, and you wouldn't be able to protect yourself, let alone us, from his vengeance. Oblivious to your real powers, I thought you were no match for him, was certain I'd only doom all of us if I left with you.

"Then you were gone as I always knew you would be one day and I discovered what true misery was at last. It wasn't being trapped in this horror with my family eternal hostages, their lives depending on my ability to perfect my act forever. It was to know what passion was, then to lose it and return to my cage to pine for you forever."

"Isabella..."

Her hand rose, stopping his butchered groan. It seemed

she needed to spit this out, as she would venom. "When you put your plan in action, I knew once he became convinced I betrayed him, he would be as insanely vicious as he'd been irrationally indulgent, so I took my family and ran. Then around a year later, my 'lady in waiting' who was married to his new right-hand told me Burton's bank accounts had been emptied by unknown parties and he no longer had means to buy allegiance or even protection, and that just before she'd called me, he'd disappeared. She suspected he'd been killed.

"Not willing to gamble on that, I decided to go back to Colombia when friends enlisted my urgent assistance in relocating them. I employed all necessary secrecy methods, and used the money I'd taken from Burton to build shelters and medical centers for those I couldn't help personally.

"After three years of no developments, I dared to go back to the States for a conference, where I met Rose. Then four years later, when she kept persisting with her partnership offer, I made my most extensive investigations yet. It was then I discovered you'd thrown Burton into that off-the-grid dungeon for the world's most dangerous criminals and finally felt secure enough to come back. A week later...you appeared again. And here we are."

Richard stared at Isabella, every word of her revelations a shard shredding his guts.

He'd lived among corruption and perversion so long, he considered only the worst explanation for anyone's actions. He'd condemned her at face value, hadn't reconsidered when all his being had kept telling him otherwise.

But what she'd been through wasn't unique. He'd seen worse crimes perpetrated against innumerable individuals in the world he inhabited. It was what she'd achieved in spite of all the danger and degradation, the way she'd conquered all adversity, built unquestionable success and helped countless others that elevated her from the status of coping victim to that of hero.

And he was the villain. One of the major causes of her ordeals. Even worse, among her unimaginable sufferings, he'd been the one to cause her the most anguish.

And she had yet to mention what must have caused her the most turmoil.

"What about Mauricio?"

She turned, her eyes eclipsed by terrible memories. But there was no attempt to hide anything in them anymore.

"He's your son."

He'd already been certain. Still, hearing her say it was a bullet of shame and regret through the heart.

"I discovered my pregnancy just before Burton suspected I might have exposed his secrets. I would have had to run anyway even if he never did, since he would have considered I betrayed him in a way that mattered even more to him. I gave birth to Mauri four months afterward, almost three months before I was due. For weeks I thought I'd end up losing him or he'd suffer some major defects. It took the better part of a year before I was finally assured there were no ill effects of his being born so premature."

Their gazes locked over the knowledge of yet another crime on his record. Her emotional and physical distress as she'd escaped a madman's pursuit while carrying the burden of her whole family, not to mention her grief over losing him, must have caused her premature delivery. And what she'd suffered during and after… His mind almost shut down imagining the enormity of her torment.

"But as I said before, I hadn't put two and two together at the time. So I named him Ricardo, after you."

The consecutive blows had already numbed him. This new one gashed him the deepest. But he'd lost the ability to react to the agony, just welcomed suffering it.

"By the time I worked out what you'd done, and I couldn't bear being reminded of you every time I called him, he was two. It took him a year to get used to being called by his second name, my father's, and another to forget his first one."

So she'd cherished remembering him for two years every time she'd called their son, until she'd discovered his exploitation and the treasured memories had turned to bitterness and betrayal.

His eyes lowered, seeing nothing but a scape of roiling darkness where the most extreme forms of self-punishment swirled in his imagination like hideous phantasms.

"Now it's your turn."

Raising his gaze to hers, he no longer even considered not giving her the truth. Not only what she'd asked for, but *his* whole truth. Every single shred of it.

What no one else knew about him.

Isabella felt as if she'd just turned herself inside out.

But besides nearly collapsing after she'd poured everything inside her out to Richard, she felt…relieved. More. Freed. She'd never shared this with anyone. Even her mother and siblings. She'd protected them from the burden of the full truth. Though her mother suspected a lot, she'd never caused her the injury of validating her suspicions or inflicting the details on her.

Now only Richard knew everything about her.

His only overt reactions had been to bring half the bar over, guzzle down half a bottle, then smash a window fifty feet away. Apart from that, it was as if he'd turned to stone. He'd had no response to finding out Mauri was his.

He raised his gaze to her, his eyes incandescent silver, his face an impassive mask. And she knew he'd keep his word, would tell her his side of the truth. He'd warned it would horrify her. She'd claimed nothing ever could again.

But she'd lied. Her defenses were nonexistent where he was concerned. Anything with or from Richard devastated her. He was the only one who could destroy her.

Then he started.

"My father was in the Special Forces in the British army before he was dishonorably discharged. Bitter and suffering from severe financial problems after many failed investments, he joined a crime syndicate when I was six. He'd trained me in all lethal disciplines since I can remember, and I was so good that he involved me in his work. Not that I realized what we were doing for a couple of years. Then one day five years later, when Rose turned one, his partners came to tell us he'd been killed. Shortly thereafter, one of those partners started coming to our home. Then one day soon after that, my mother told me she and he just got married and the man—Burton—would now live with us."

Isabella sat forward, poured herself a drink, having no idea what it was. He'd already knocked her over with the disclosure that Rose was family and Burton had been his stepfather, too. She had a feeling she'd need anything to bolster her for the rest of his revelations.

"I knew Burton had killed my father because he wanted my mother. He'd been fixated on her as he had been with you. But because my mother was nowhere in your caliber, he soon began to mistreat her. And I could do nothing about it.

"Like you, I had a home filled with vulnerable targets, and though already a formidable fighter, I wasn't fully grown. Even if I could have killed him, that would have destroyed my family. I would have been put in a juvenile prison and my mother wouldn't have been able to carry on without me. So I did as you did. I played the part of the obedient boy who looked up to him, kept him placated every way I could. I tried to curb my younger brother, too, but Robert couldn't understand why I was being so nice to him. Rose soon took Robert's side, and it became Burton's favorite pastime to abuse them verbally, mentally and then, finally, physically. I hid my murderous hatred, channeled the perfect disciple, knowing it was the only thing that kept him in check, that he could easily kill them as he had our father."

She gulped down the horrible liquid in her glass, her eyes

filling. His gaze showed no indication of his thoughts as he continued recounting his atrocious past like a nuance-less automaton.

"When I was around sixteen, Burton started displaying signs of big money. I sucked up to him even more to find out its source, until he said he was now working for a major cartel just called The Organization, who turned abducted or sold children into mercenaries. He said he could make a bundle if he gave them Robert and Rose, that it would serve the two brats right.

"Knowing he'd do just that, I said surely their price would be a one-time thing, but if I became one of their 'handlers,' they'd pay me big money continuously, and he could have it all. Burton didn't like that it seemed I was protecting my siblings when I always said I could barely tolerate them. He also thought it fishy that I'd offer to give him the money I worked for. I allayed his suspicions, say-ing I considered it a benefit on all sides. I'd get out of the dump we called home, get rid of my clinging family, and get the best on-the-job experience. The money was in re-turn for giving me this opportunity, as I wouldn't be doing anything with it for years, with all my needs paid for by my new employers."

Isabella had heard of The Organization many times dur-ing her marriage to Burton. The magnitude of evil they perpetrated was mind-numbing. To learn that Richard had volunteered to basically be sold to them to save his siblings, to save Rose, was…too much to contemplate, to bear.

"Buying my rationalization, and knowing how much The Organization would pay for my skill level, Burton jumped on my offer. I knew I'd leave my family behind, but the al-ternative was incomparably worse. The last time I saw them was the day I left to join The Organization. Robert was ten and Rose was six.

"I intended to amass enough power to one day assassi-nate Burton untraceably and disappear with my family. But he kept guarding against any counterstrikes. I know I never let my loathing show, but Burton, being the self-preserving parasite that he was, moved my family to places unknown, kept obliquely threatening me with their safety, providing me with evidence they were all well. As long as the monthly flow of cash continued."

She had the overwhelming urge to throw herself at him and hug the helplessness he must have felt out of him. But Richard wasn't one for human compassion, giving or receiving it. And if he ever were, she wouldn't be the one he'd seek that from.

Oblivious to her condition, he went on, clearly bent on giving her the whole story in one go, as she had been.

"What made that first year in The Organization survivable was a boy two years younger than myself. They called him Phantom, considered him their star future operative. Then Burton noticed the friendship we thought we'd hidden. He monitored us and overheard Phantom saying he was working on an escape plan. Burton told me if I reported him it would mean a higher place in The Organization at once and more pay. *He* couldn't do it, because he'd have to say how he'd found out, and I'd be punished for not reporting my *friend's* plans, would be demoted, or worse, when Burton wanted my paycheck to move to the six digits already. He had a lot of investments going. He made it clear it was Phantom...or my family."

Isabella struggled to hold back the tears. She'd always thought Richard made of steel, that he'd never felt love or fear for others, let alone could be held hostage by those feelings. And for him to have been just that, by the same man who'd caged her in the same way, was too much to contemplate.

"I knew Phantom, being prized, would be punished, tortured, but not killed. My family were nowhere as valuable. And there were three of them. Burton could hurt or even kill one to have me toe the line the rest of my life. So I reported Phantom. I let him think I did it to advance my standing within The Organization so he'd hate me and show it, to further reinforce my coldblooded image, which everything depended on.

"Then I went all out to prove myself to be the absolute best they ever had. I applied my ruthlessness in ways you couldn't begin to imagine, my body count rivaling all the other operatives put together, until my monthly income was in the eight figures, with most of it going to Burton. I'd hoped to inundate him with far more money than he'd ever dreamed of so he'd let my family go, or at least treat them better until I got them out.

"But my escape and retaliation plans were further complicated when I was put in charge of another child—a boy they called Numbers, who reminded me so much of Robert. I couldn't leave him or Phantom behind. But I finally gained enough autonomy so I could search for my family. I found them in Scotland…only too late. I pieced together that my mother tried to escape with my siblings. Burton pursued her and she lost control of her car and drove off the side of a mountain."

Isabella lost the fight, let the tears flow.

Richard didn't seem to notice as he continued reciting Burton's unimaginable crimes against him and the ghastly sequence of events of his loss.

"From what I learned, Burton hadn't bothered to help or to report the accident. He'd just walked away, since they'd already served their purpose. My mother and brother had died on impact. Only Rose had survived. I found her in an orphanage and arranged for her adoption by a kind and financially secure couple who'd been about to immigrate to the United States. I've been keeping an eye on her ever since."

And that, Isabella realized, was how he'd found her again. Even though the paranoid way she'd conducted her relationship with Rose had kept her under his radar that long.

His dark voice interrupted her musings. "I never considered telling Rose I was alive. Then today… I can't believe she remembered me." He looked downward, his scowl deepening as if he was reliving those fraught moments. Without raising his face, he raised his eyes, impaling her with his glance. "What did you tell her after I left?"

She swallowed. "Nothing. I pretended I got an urgent call from my mother and ran out."

He only gave a curt nod. "It's best for her to remain ignorant of my existence."

She couldn't contest his verdict. Rose's life was the epitome of stability. The last thing she needed was his disruptive influence destroying her peace.

Although…he'd handled her crawling-with-kids-and-chicks household with stunning dexterity…

No. That had been a one-off. He'd sought her out the very next day to tell her he'd stay away from her family. Richard wouldn't want anyone permanently in his life. Not even his long-lost sister. Certainly not one who came with an extended family life right out of the textbook of normal and adjusted.

Considering he was done with that subject, he resumed his tale. "It was years before I could put my escape plan into action, after I made sure Numbers and Phantom and their team had escaped. I followed them, but as expected, they decided to kill me."

She gasped, blood draining. Phantom had been under the misconception he'd been his heartless enemy, a threat to their freedom and lives. As she'd been until an hour ago.

"Did you finally tell him the truth?"

He shrugged. "I saw no point."

"No point?" she exclaimed.

"Yes. I'd done everything they knew me to be guilty of, everything they hated me for. It didn't matter why I did it."

"Of course it matters. Knowing why always matters!"

He shook that majestic head of his in pure dismissal. "I don't believe so. I own my crimes, I don't excuse them."

He wouldn't ever think of asking forgiveness for them, either. "So if you didn't cite your extenuating circumstances to change their minds, how did you do it?"

"I told them it was in their best interest to back down, since it was them who wouldn't survive a confrontation."

A huff of incredulity escaped her. "I bet you weren't even exaggerating."

His look was what she expected a god would give a mortal who asked if he could smite him down. "I never exaggerate. They're formidable warriors, but their genius is in intelligence, applied sciences, medicine and subterfuge. My virtuosity is in termination."

"You're no slouch in intelligence and subterfuge yourself," she mumbled, remembering how he'd totally taken her in. Suddenly a terrible thought crossed her mind. "But since you survived without a scratch, does that mean...?"

An eyebrow arched. "You think I'd spend years planning to help them escape, only to kill them when they got their knickers in a twist?"

She exhaled in relief. "So how did it end with both sides alive, if you didn't put them straight and antagonized them in the most provocative method you could?"

"I was just stating facts. If they hadn't been using their macho hindbrains, they would have realized if I was the enemy, they would have all been already dead. Luckily, before I had to drive my point home, Numbers put himself between us and they backed down only for him. I let them continue thinking what they liked. I wasn't interested in becoming their friend, just in leading them in establishing our joint business."

"All your partners in Black Castle Enterprises are escapees from The Organization."

It wasn't a question but a realization. And it explained

OLIVIA GATES

everything. Those men were all larger-than-life; they must have been forged in the same hell Richard had been.

He nodded. "Once I made sure they were safe and our plan to dismantle The Organization was in motion, I could finally take my revenge on Burton. You know the rest."

No. She'd only thought she did.

It turned out she'd known nothing.

Now she did. And the more everything he'd just told her sank in, the more baffled and devastated she was. It *did* horrify her. But not in the way he'd thought.

He'd thought knowing he'd been the top executioner in such an evil establishment would validate her suspicions about him and…well, horrify her. What agonized her was realizing how much more nightmarish his life had been than hers. And that he'd had the best justification for all he'd done.

In fact, believing her to be Burton's willing wife, it was a wonder he hadn't punished her as viciously as he had him. It said a lot about the extent of his desire that it had curbed his killer instincts and stayed his hand.

Not that such desire mattered now. Those earth-shaking disclosures didn't change a thing.

While he might still want her, everything that had happened to him in the past had made him what he was now. If there was one man on earth who was unavailable for anything…human, it was him. That he hadn't said a thing about Mauri was proof positive of that.

So what she'd come here to tell him stood. She couldn't afford to have him in her life.

No matter that she craved him like a drug.

Her priority remained Mauri.

Inhaling a breath that burned like tear gas, she rose to her feet. He remained sitting, not even looking at her.

She waited until he looked up. "It's great we got things out in the open. But now you know my real history, you know I am not a danger to Rose, either myself or by association. Now we can go our separate ways, never to cross paths again."

Before he could say anything, she turned and rushed away.

It turned out she didn't have to worry. He just brooded after her in silence.

Once at the door, she remembered he had to open it for her. Before she could walk back to ask him to, the door opened. She hurried out, relieved, demolished.

This was it. It was over for good this time.

She'd never see Richard again.

Eight

When Rose entered her office the next morning, Isabella wasn't a mute, paralyzed mass like yesterday. She was a hopeless, miserable one.

She still struggled to smile as she received her treasured friend and colleague. Rose returned her kiss on the cheek before she pulled back, her blue-gray eyes filled with suppressed questions. She must be bursting to have her suspicion about Richard validated.

"Everything okay at home?"

In spite of the concern lacing the question, and the text message she'd sent her last night, Isabella believed Rose hadn't bought her excuse for running out yesterday one bit.

But Rose always made it clear that she was there for anything Isabella needed, and left it up to her to reveal any problems or worries. Isabella had never told her anything. Until now.

After she'd held it all in all these years, now that her family and those she'd struggled to help were safe, she could allow herself to consider her own needs. And now that the one she'd shared her innermost turmoil with had exited her life forever, she needed another confidante. Someone who wouldn't only listen in silence, offering not a word of sympathy or support, as Richard had. The only one who fit the bill was Rose.

She sat her down. "I need to tell you something—important. A lot of things, actually. About my past."

The worry hovering in Rose's eyes mushroomed into anxiety. "I always knew you were hiding something big, kept wishing you'd tell me."

Isabella reached for Rose's hands. "Before I do, I want you to promise to act according only to your and your family's best interests."

Rose grimaced. "Shut up and tell me everything, Izzy!"

And she did. Everything minus Richard.

All through her account, Rose's expressive face displayed her shock, horror, anguish and outrage on her behalf in minute detail. Her tears came at one point and wouldn't stop until Isabella fell silent and she hurled herself at her and crushed her in a nonending, breath-depleting hug.

"God, Izzy, you should have told me!" Rose sobbed between hard squeezes. "Why didn't you tell me?"

Isabella's tears flowed, too, as she surrendered to Rose's searing empathy. *This*...this was what she'd needed all these years, what she'd deprived herself of.

She thankfully let Rose inundate her with frantic reprimands before she finally pulled away, her tremulous smile teasing. "That's why I didn't tell you. I was afraid you'd drown me and flood the practice. Like you're doing now. When we've just finished decorating."

Rose burst out laughing. "God, Izzy, how dare you make me laugh after what you just told me?"

"Because it's all in the past. I just needed you to know everything about me, needed to share what I can't share with even my mother. But it is really all behind me."

Rose's resurging tears suddenly froze, her face filling with reproof again. "What did you mean by that prefacing warning? If you thought it a possibility this would change anything between us, you're stark raving mad!"

Isabella's heart expanded at the proof of her friend's magnanimity and benevolence. Then it compressed again. "Don't make any decisions now. Take time to think about it."

"The only thing I'll do with time is fume for months that you didn't come to me with this years ago!"

Isabella's lips spread at her friend's steel conviction. "At least wait until you see what Jeffrey thinks."

Rose's eyes widened. "You want me to tell Jeffrey?"

"I just assumed you would tell him."

Rose looked terminally affronted. "Of *course* I won't tell him!"

Isabella reached a hand out to hers. "I want you to tell him."

Rose snatched her hand, fisted it at her chest. *"No."*

It was Isabella's turn to burst out laughing at the growling finality in Rose's usually gentle, cheerful voice and the furiously obstinate expression that gripped her gorgeous if good-natured face. She looked like a tigress defending her cub. Isabella's laughter made her crankier.

Isabella tried to suppress her smiles. "I consider Jeffrey part of you. Not to mention a part of us, our team."

"I said no. You told *me* because you needed to purge the burden from your system by sharing it with someone who's strong enough to carry it with you, someone you fully trust."

"That's absolutely right, but Jeffrey—"

Rose cut her off. "You also needed to have someone fully appreciate what made you the wonderful human being you are."

"Uh…not that I'm not delighted you think I'm wonderful, but that's not how I…"

Again Rose bulldozed over her protests. "I tell Jeffrey all my secrets not because he's my husband and soul mate, but because they might impact him, so he's entitled to a heads-up. But if you really wanted him to know, and thought he should, as himself, not as a part of me or our team, you would have sat us both down and told us both all that. But you chose to tell only me."

Isabella shook her head at the incredible combination her friend was. The most romantic person on earth who melted with love for her husband, and the most no-nonsense prag-matist around. And as she'd always known, the best, strongest, most dependable friend anyone could aspire to have. She always felt the fates had chosen to compensate her for all the hardships of her life with Rose. And now she'd unburdened herself to her, not to mention knowing her relationship to Richard and therefore to Mauri, she felt the uncanny bond they'd shared from the start had become even deeper.

"And you did because I'm your closest friend. We're even closer than I thought. We both had our souls almost shattered by the same monster. And we both survived him." Rose's eyes shone with admiration. "Though I can't begin to compare our ordeals at his hand. I didn't fight for my life and that of my family for years like you did. I survived by accident."

Isabella now knew that wasn't true. Beyond escaping death in her family's car crash, Rose's survival had been no accident. She'd been saved. By Richard. He was the one who'd created her second chance in life. He was the real difference between their lives. She hadn't had a savior and champion like him.

She couldn't tell Rose that. The older brother who'd been looking out for her since she was ten didn't want her to know.

But although she'd always thought he'd played the opposite role in her life, that of conqueror and almost destroyer, it was still him who'd rid her of Burton forever. That made him the one who'd given her this new lease on life.

"What about Mauri? Is he…?" Rose choked. She couldn't even say Burton's name.

"*No.* I would have never let myself get pregnant by him."

But she *had* let herself get pregnant by Richard. When she'd discovered her pregnancy, even after he'd left, even knowing the danger she'd put herself in, she'd been giddy with delight that she'd have a part of him with her always.

So far, she'd risked it again. Four times, if she wanted to be accurate.

Rose's voice dragged her out of her turbulent musings. "Whew. It's a relief to know that monster didn't manage to perpetuate his genes."

Grabbing the opportunity to steer the conversation in a less-emotional direction, she pulled a face at Rose. "You should know me better than to think I'd inflict those on my child."

Rose pounced, hugging the breath out of her before pulling back. "But you're so amazing your genes would vaporize any dirt or perversion in any others. Mauri would have turned out to be the awesome kid he is just because you're his mom."

Feeling suddenly lighthearted, when she'd thought she'd never feel that way again after losing Richard for the second and last time, Isabella dragged Rose closer and smacked kisses on both her cheeks.

"Have I told you lately just how much I love you?"

Rose gave her a mock scolding glare. "When have you ever told me that?" When Isabella started to protest, Rose pulled her into another hug. "You never needed to tell me. I always knew. And I love you, too. Now more than ever."

Isabella hadn't expected to go home happy. But thanks to Rose, and to work, not to mention to Prince Charming Jeffrey, the day she'd predicted would be an endless pit of gloom had turned out to be the best she'd had in a couple of decades.

She didn't expect her buoyant condition to continue, knew misery would descend on her more aggressively than it had the first time she'd lost Richard. Back then, there'd been distractions vying for her mental and emotional energy, fractioning her turmoil over him. Now, without anxieties consuming her focus, she'd experience the full measure of it.

There was another reason she was certain her despondency would only deepen. Before she'd met him again, she'd had this vague hope she'd find love again. She now knew this was an impossible prospect.

Richard would remain the one who could make her turn off the world and lose herself in his ecstasy. She didn't want—couldn't stomach—anything less than that. So now she knew. She'd spend the rest of her life as a mom, a daughter, a sister, a friend and a doctor. But the woman part of her was over. Only Richard had the secret code to this vital component of her being. And he was gone. Forever this time.

Turning onto her street, she shook herself. She was sliding again, and she owed it to Mauri and her family not to expose them to her dejection. She'd promised them a shining new beginning and she'd be damned if she didn't deliver.

And then she had to count her blessings. She'd unburdened herself to Rose, their bond had become more profound, her family was safe, they loved their new home and she loved her new workplace. If she obsessed over Richard more than ever, if her body demanded its mate and master now that she could no longer swat her hunger away with hatred…tough.

She'd just mentally slapped some sense into herself when she saw it.

Richard's car. Parked—again—in her spot.

Her heart followed the usual drill when it came to Richard. It crashed to a halt before bursting out in mad gallop, stumbling like a horse on ice.

She didn't know how or where she ended up parking, or how she made it inside the house. The empty house. Where was everyone…?

Shouts burst from the kitchen. Her heart almost exploded from her chest as she burst into a run, then she heard… clapping. *Clapping?*

Screeching to a halt at the threshold, she saw…saw…

Richard was in her kitchen. He had every member of

her household at the huge semicircular counter island and he was…

Performing for them. Knife tricks.

He was swirling knives with such speed and skill, his hands were a blur; the feats he performed with four—no, five…*six* knives nothing short of impossible. He made it look effortless. His captive audience was openmouthed and glassy eyed.

She sympathized. She would have done the same if she wasn't shocked out of her wits.

With everyone hypnotized by his show, they didn't notice her. Only he slunk her a sideways glance, that half smile that reduced her brain functions to gibberish on his lips. She stopped behind Mauri, and Richard escalated the level of difficulty, catapulting knives above his head, behind his back, turning this way and that to show them the intricate, mesmerizing sequence.

At the crescendo of his routine, he tossed what looked like a fish filet in the air, threw the knives in blinding succession after it, slicing it to equal pieces in midair. After catching the plummeting knives in one hand and the fish pieces in the other, he spread his arms and took a bow.

A storm of applause and yells erupted. She almost clapped and cheered, too. Almost. It was a good thing she was still breathing and on her feet.

Everyone's excitement intensified when they noticed her. Richard slinked a tea towel over his shoulder as he approached her, his gaze unreadable, his mouth curved in that devastating smile. Her head filled with images of her winding herself around him, dragging that arrogant head down and taking those cruelly gorgeous lips.

"Did you catch Richard's unbe*lievable* show?" Amelia exclaimed.

"I caught a slice of it." Everyone laughed at her reference to his closing act. Including him. She wanted to be mad at him for crashing her home again, but couldn't. But that didn't mean she couldn't still reprimand him. "How will I convince the kids not to play with knives now?"

He waved away her concern. "I already took care of it."

"Oh, how did you do that?"

"I told them only I was allowed to do such things, as I spent more years than they've been on this earth practicing."

"And this convinced them?"

"They are extremely obedient cubs."

She blinked. "Uh, are we talking about the same trio?"

"*Or* I'm too intimidating even when I'm trying not to be."

Said trio was flitting around preparing the kitchen table, their awed eyes almost never leaving Richard. "They don't look intimidated, they look enthralled."

"Same result." His smile grew placating. "Don't worry. I got their promise they'd never try anything with sharp objects. I promised Mauricio I'd teach him to juggle. With environmentally safe plastic."

Before she could hiss his skin off for making Mauri such a promise, he turned to his audience.

"Now, to the second part of my show. Food."

Her mouth hung open as her mother and sister rushed to empty three huge brown bags on the other counter.

"Richard brought everything to make sure his recipe is just right," her mother explained, her smile so wide it hurt Isabella. "We're having a cooking contest. You'll grade his efforts tonight against mine in our first dinner face-off."

As Richard started preparing his ingredients, Isabella closed her mouth to keep her jaw from dragging on the floor.

Was that really him? Was this even her home? Or had she stepped into some parallel universe?

He wasn't kidding about this being the second part of the show. He turned preparing seafood into feats of speed and precision. She was sure he assembled weapons and dismantled bombs with the same virtuosity.

All the time he quizzed the kids about the seafood, spices, herbs and vegetables he used. Their excitement at the informative and entertaining Q and A session was almost palpable. She'd never seen them so taken with an adult. Mauri asked him more personal questions than she'd thought possible, down to how he chewed his food. Richard was a good sport, rewarding Mauri's boundless curiosity with amusing, frank, yet age-appropriate answers.

Seeing them interact the first time had been disturbing. Now it plain hurt.

After Richard started cooking, he said, "Somebody recently taught me that recipe. I was the sous chef during its preparation. Now I get to be the chef and, fingers crossed, I won't turn what was a magical seafood feast into a curse."

Amelia, who'd taken her eyes off Richard only to swing them to Isabella for a silent verdict on how things stood between them, piped in at once, "You have nothing to worry about. The aromas alone are a powerful spell."

"Who taught you this recipe?" That was Mauri, of course.

"A lovely lady called Eliana."

If he'd thrown that knife he wielded into her heart it wouldn't have hurt more. Hearing him mention another woman with such indulgence made something she'd never felt on his account sink its talons into her gut.

Jealousy. Acrid, foul. And totally moronic. She was the one who'd turned down his offer to continue their intimacies.

But…he'd never cooked with her!

Well, he was cooking for her whole family now.

As if he could feel her burning envy of that woman who'd taken him into her kitchen and made him follow her orders, his steel-hued gaze targeted her. "She's almost like a sister to me since married a man I consider a brother."

The tension drained from her muscles, forcing her to sit.

Mauri's next question came at once. "What's his name?"

"Rafael. Ah-ah…" Richard raised his hand, anticipating and answering Mauri's next batch of questions. "Rafael Moreno Salazar. He's from Brazil and he's my partner.

He's ten years younger than me. And *he* is a magician with numbers."

Numbers. The boy Richard wouldn't leave behind in The Organization, the one he'd postponed his own escape for.

Forever needing more info about Richard, Mauri lobbed him another question. "Do you have other friends?"

"I have six partners, including Rafael. One I considered my best friend. He doesn't like me back now."

And that had to be Phantom.

Before Mauri pounced to extract that story, Richard gave him what she could only call a man-to-man look that said, "Later." And wonder of wonders, it worked. Well, almost.

Mauri swerved into another tack. "What's his name? Where's he from?"

"Numair Al Aswad. That means *black panther* in Arabic. He's a sheikh from a desert kingdom called Saraya."

Everyone's eyes got even wider. It was still Mauri who asked what she thought was on everyone's mind. "Is each of your friends from a different country?"

Richard chuckled as he began to distribute food on plates. "Indeed. Black Castle Enterprises is a mini United Nations. We also have a Japanese chap, a Russian, an Italian and a Swede. My right-hand man, Owen Murdock, is an Irishman. I trained him like I trained Rafael."

"Like you'll train me?"

It felt as if everyone, except Benita and Diego, who chose this moment to bicker, held their breath for Richard's answer.

He considered Mauri for a moment. "We'll see if you've got what it takes first."

"I got it!"

The kids giggled at Mauri's impassioned claim but stopped at once. It wasn't Mauri's scolding look that made them look so sheepish and contrite. They never reacted like that to his "older brother" exasperation. It was Richard. He didn't level any disapproval or reprimand at them, just a look.

She fully sympathized. Just a look from him took control of her every voluntary and involuntary response.

Her mother and sister intervened to end Mauri's bombardment of Richard, and they all sat to eat.

It did turn out to be a magical meal, on all counts. The food was fantastic, making everyone want to meet the Eliana who'd invented the recipe, with her mother the first to declare Richard the winner of their contest. The constant mood was one of prevailing gaiety and excitement, again thanks to Richard. He was a maestro in handling people of all ages, compelling, constantly surprising, making each person feel they had his full attention, and causing them to fall over themselves to win his approval.

Although she knew this was just his expert manipulation skills, she couldn't help but enjoy it. Delight in it. But both his behavior and her reaction to it made her more nervous.

What *did* he want?

Then she was finally getting the chance to find out.

After dinner, her mother and sister insisted she and Richard retire to the living room while they cleaned up. Mauri agreed to stay behind only after Richard promised a drawing session afterward.

The moment they were out of earshot, she pounced. "Any explanation for…all of this?"

A smile that should be banned by a maximum-penalty law dawned on his face. It was different from what he'd flooded her family and house with all evening. A mixture of wickedness and provocation. One of those would have been more than enough for her to handle. Together, as with everything about him, they were overkill.

He only answered after he sat. "Your family invited me, remember?"

"And since when do you answer anyone's invitations?"

"You have no idea what I've had to do in the past months with Rafael's marriage. Then Raiden, another of the Black Castle blokes, the Japanese-by-birth guy I mentioned, followed suit. Both their weddings had me putting up with human beings all the time. Then came Numair's. That one rewrote the fundamental rules of existence for me. He was the one I thought would be the last man on earth to succumb to the frailties of our species or fall into the trap of matrimony. Nothing was sacred after that, and I've been open to anything ever since. Even cooking dinner from a minitribe of women and children."

So all his friends had married. Was that what was making him dip his foot in the land of domesticity? To see if it was for him? And he thought her household was the most convenient testing ground, since he already had a son and a lover there? Did he think she'd let him experiment on them?

Gritting her teeth, she sat beside him. "You said you'd leave my family alone."

"That was only in return for leaving mine alone."

"But you now know your concern for Rose is misplaced."

"I do. I no longer want you to stay away from Rose."

"Well, *I* want you to stay away from my family."

"I no longer want to do that, either."

"Why? You only involved my family as a pressure card."

"I did?" He cocked his head at the grinding of her teeth. "By 'family' you mean Mauricio. You want me to leave *him* alone."

"Who else?"

At her exasperated answer, he shrugged. "I don't want to do that, either."

"Why?" she snapped. "What's new? You didn't bat a lid when I told you he was your son."

"I didn't because I've already been immunized against the shock, having contracted it full-force the day before. I knew he was my son the moment I saw him."

"No *way* you knew that. He looks nothing like you."

He produced a picture from his inner pocket, handed it to her. If she wasn't certain Mauri never had clothes like that, and this photo was in a place they'd never been and looked from another era, she would have sworn it was him.

"That's my younger brother, Robert. He looked exactly like our mother. I took after my father. Rose was a mix of the two."

Stunned, she raised her eyes, a memory rushing in. "Rose once told me Mauri so reminded her of one of her dead brothers. I didn't make anything of it, as it never occurred to me to tie you to her."

His face darkened. "So she believed I was dead."

She swallowed. "She did only because it was the only thing to explain why you didn't search for her."

His jaw muscles bunched. She winced at the pain she felt for both Rose and him. This wasn't right. That he'd deprived Rose of knowing he was alive. Rose suffered the loss of her biological family even now. And he might have suffered even more watching her from afar.

"But she didn't hesitate to identify you, which means she's been clinging to the hope that you're alive. You probably look very much like she remembers you."

"I was sixteen. I looked nothing like this." He lowered his gaze, as if remembering those moments they'd all been frozen with shock, each for their own reasons. "Did she ask you about me again?"

"I didn't give her a chance. I told her everything about me, so she was too busy with my revelations to think of you. But I'm sure she will. What do you want me to say when she does?"

"What do you want to tell her?"

That was the last thing she'd expected he'd ask. "I...I honestly don't know. I think she deserves to know the brother she loved and clearly still misses terribly is alive. But you probably have nothing in common with that brother, so maybe it's not in her best interests to know you. It's your call."

"Don't tell her."

Hating that this was his verdict, but conceding it was probably the right one, she nodded.

Then her original point pushed to the forefront again. "So you knew about Mauri all the time you were here before, and as I told you everything about myself. Yet you gave no indication that you were in the least interested."

"I wasn't." Before her heart could contrarily implode with dismay, he added, "I was flabbergasted."

That astounded *her*. "I didn't know anything could even surprise you."

"Finding a seven-year-old replica of my dead brother on my ex-lover's threshold? That's the stuff strokes are made of."

The "ex-lover" part felt like a blow to her heart.

Sure, she'd walked away this time, saying it was over. But was that what he already considered her? What he'd decided she was? When they'd made love…had earth-shattering sex…just yesterday? If he wasn't here to pursue her, then why was he here?

"I walked out of here intending not to come back."

"And that was the right decision. Why are you back?"

"Because the facts have been rewritten. Now instead of wanting to end your friendship with Rose, I want to be your and your family's…ally."

Ally? *Ally?* That was downright…offensive after what had happened the past couple of days. Not to mention in the past.

"I don't need allies."

"You never know when and how you might. Having someone of my influence on your side can be more potent than magic."

She tamped down the need to blast his insensitive hide off his perfect body. "I have no doubt. But I don't need magic. I work for what I have. And I have more than enough to give my son the best life and to secure his future."

"Even if you don't want or need my alliance, you don't

have the right to make that decision for Mauricio. The fact remains, he's my flesh and blood. And my only heir."

After a moment of gaping at him, her nerves jangling at his declaration, she choked out, "Are you here because you decided to tell him that?"

Mauri chose this crucial moment to stampede into the living room. "I got all my drawing stuff!"

Before she could say anything more, Richard turned his attention to Mauri.

Brain melting with exasperation and trepidation, she could only watch as father and son ignored her and got engrossed in each other. She had to wait to get her answer.

A no would mean resuming her life as it was. A yes would turn it upside down. And it was all up to Richard.

As it had always been.

Richard had swung around at Mauricio's explosive entry, infinitely grateful for the distraction.

As heart-wrenching as the sight of him, the very idea of him, still was, right now he'd take anything over answering Isabella's question. Since he didn't have an answer for it.

He had no idea what he was doing here, or what he would or should do next.

In the distraction arena, Mauricio was the best there was. The boy—his *son*—wrenched a guffaw from his depths as he hurled himself at him, dropping his armful of drawing materials in his lap.

Crashing to a kneeling position at his feet, Mauricio anchored both hands on his knees and looked up at him with barely contained eagerness. "Tell me your opinion of my work. And teach me to draw something."

"You can draw?"

That was Isabella. She would have asked if he could turn invisible with the same incredulity.

Richard slid her a glance. "I have many hidden talents."

"I'm sure." She impaled him on one of those glances that

made it an achievement he hadn't dragged her out of that kitchen and buried himself inside her.

Mauricio dragged his focus back, and his angelic face, overflowing with inquisitiveness and determination, sent a different avalanche of emotions raging through him.

His throat closed, his voice thickened. "Why don't you show me your best work?"

Mauricio rummaged through the mess on his lap, then pulled out one sketchbook and thrust it at him. "This."

With hands he could barely keep from trembling, Richard leafed through the pages, his heart squeezing as he perused each effort, remarkable for a boy of his age, testimony to great talent…and turmoil.

Had the latter manifested itself in response to their lifestyle, as Isabella kept relocating them to keep them safe? He was sure she'd shielded her son and family from the reality of their situation. But he believed Mauricio was sensitive enough he'd felt his mother's disturbance, and felt the dangers she'd paid so much of her life to protect him and their family from.

There was also a searing sense of confusion in the drawings, an overwhelming inquisitiveness and the need to know, what *he'd* experienced firsthand. Was that a manifestation of his growing up fatherless? Was he constantly wondering about the father he'd never known, or even known about? Did a boy of such energy and intelligence miss a stabilizing male influence, no matter how loving and efficient the females in his life were?

He pretended to examine each drawing at length, trying to bring his own chaos under control.

At last he murmured, "Your imagination is quite original and your work is extremely good for your age."

Mauricio whooped. "You really think I'm good?"

Though the boy's unrestrained delight made him wish to give him more praise, he had to give him the qualification of reality. "Being good doesn't mean much without hard work."

"I work hard." Mauricio tugged at Isabella. "Don't I?"

Her eyes moved between them, as if she was seeing both for the first time. "You do, when you love something."

Richard retuned his gaze to Mauricio before he plunged into her eyes. "When you *don't* love something, you must work even harder. When you're lucky to love something, it only makes the work *feel* easier because you enjoy it more. But you must always do anything, whether you enjoy it or not, to the very best of your ability, strive to become better all the time. That's what I call 'got what it takes.'"

Mauricio hung on his every word as if he was memorizing them before he nodded his head vigorously.

Isabella's gaze singed every exposed inch of his skin.

The burning behind Richard's sternum intensified as he turned a blank page. "What do you want me to teach you?"

Mauricio foisted the colors at him. "Anything you think I should learn."

Richard gave him a considering look. "I think you need a lesson in perspective." As soon as the words left his lips, Richard almost scoffed. No one needed that more than him right now.

"What's that?" Mauricio asked, eyes huge.

"I'd rather show you than explain in words. We'll only need a pencil, a sharpener and an eraser."

Richard blinked at the speed with which Mauricio shoved the items in his hand then bounced beside him on the couch, bubbling over with readiness for his first drawing lesson.

Gripping the pencil hard so the tremor that traversed him didn't transfer onto the paper, Richard started to sketch. Mauricio and Isabella hung on his every stroke.

Before long Mauricio blew out a breath in awe. "Wow, you just drew some lines and made it look like a boy!"

Richard added more details. "It's you."

"It does look like me!" Mauricio exclaimed.

Richard sketched some more. "And that girl is Benita."

"But she's not that much tinier than me."

"She's not tiny, she's just far away. Watch." He drew a few slanting, converging lines, layered simple details until he had a corridor with boy in front, girl in back. "See? We have a flat, two-dimensional paper, but with perspective drawing, we add a third dimension, what looks like distance and depth."

Mauricio's eyes shone with the elation of discovery, and something else. Something he'd once seen in Rafael's eyes. Budding hero worship. He felt his lungs shut down.

"I get it!" Mauricio snatched another sketchbook, showed him that he did before raising validation-seeking eyes to him. "Like this, right?"

Richard felt the smile that only Mauricio, and his mother, provoked spread his lips. "Exactly like that. You're a brilliant lad. Not many people get it, and most who do, not that quickly."

Mauricio fidgeted like a puppy wagging his tail in exultation at his praise. "*I* didn't know anyone could draw so quickly and so great! Can you do everything that good?"

"As I told you, whatever I do, I do to the best of my ability. I'm the best in some things, but certainly not in drawing. Plenty can do far better." Mauricio's expression indicated he dismissed his claim, making his lips widen in a grin once again. "There *are* people who make it seem as if they're pouring magic onto the pages. But what they and I can do comes from a kernel of talent, and a ton of practice. The talent you have. Now you have to practice. It will only become better the more you do it."

Isabella's gaze locked with his and the meaning of his motivational words took a steep turn into eroticism. It had been incredible between them from the first, but only kept getting more mind-blowing with "practice." That last time had been their most explosive encounter yet. He couldn't wait to drag her into the inferno of ecstasy again.

Suppressing the need, he continued to give Mauricio examples while the boy emulated him. Isabella watched them, the miasma of emotions emanating from her intensifying.

Mauricio finally exhaled in frustration, unhappy with his efforts. "You make it look so easy. But it isn't."

"You'll get there eventually. What you did is far better than I expected for a first time."

Mauricio eyed his drawing suspiciously. "Really?"

"Really. Draw a lot, draw everything, and you'll be superlative, if you want to be."

"Oh, I want!"

"Then, you will be. Trust me."

"I trust you."

A jolt shook Richard's heart. Hearing Mauricio say that again, with such conviction, made him want to go all out to deserve that faith and adulation.

Should he be feeling this way? Was it wise? Could he stop it or had he put in motion an unstoppable chain reaction?

"I want you to teach me everything you know."

Richard laughed. The boy kept squeezing reactions of him that he didn't know he was capable of. "I doubt you'd want to learn most of the things I do."

"I do!"

He slanted a glance at Isabella. "I don't think your mother would appreciate it, either."

"Because it's dangerous stuff?"

"To say the least." Before Isabella burst with frustration he looked at his watch. "And that's a discussion for another day, young man. We agreed we'd do this until your bedtime. Now you need to go to sleep and I need to get going."

Without trying to bargain for more time, Mauricio stood and gathered his things, looking like a stoic knight's apprentice. He had an acute sense of dignity and honor. Once he gave his word, he kept it. It made Richard...proud?

Before he could examine his feelings, Marta came to take Mauricio to bed. Handing his grandmother his things, he came back to say good-night. After he hugged his mother, he threw himself at Richard, clung around his neck.

"Will you come again?"

Feeling the boy's life-filled body against him, the tremor of entreaty in his voice, was like a fist closing over his heart.

Richard looked over the boy's head at Isabella. Her eyes were twin storms. She was terrified. Of where this might lead. Truth be told, he had no idea where it would. And was just as afraid.

But he had only one answer. "Yes, I will."

Planting a noisy kiss on Richard's cheek, Mauricio slipped free, flashing him a huge grin before skipping off.

The moment she could, Isabella hit him with the burning question she'd postponed for the past hour. "*Do* you intend to tell Mauri the truth?"

There was only one answer to that, too.

"No. Not yet."

Nine

Not yet.

Every time those two words reverberated in Isabella's mind, which was all the time, it made her even more agitated.

Not yet implied he would tell Mauri the truth eventually.

But he'd also implied that even if he did, it wouldn't mean anything would change. Mauri would only know he had a father, and would get the benefit of all his wealth and power.

As if *that* wouldn't change everything.

Before he'd left that night, he'd confessed he hadn't thought this through, didn't know what to expect himself. But the fact remained that Mauri had a right to everything he had as his only heir. While he...he only wanted to know his son. Only time would tell how that would translate into daily life or in the long term. They'd just have to wait and see how things worked out.

She had no other choice but to do just that. Now that he'd expressed the wish to know his son so unequivocally, she'd been unable to deny him his desire.

Ever since that day three weeks ago, she'd succumbed and gone along for the roller-coaster ride of having Richard in her family's everyday life. And he'd been with them every possible minute. After their workdays, from early evenings to past the children's bedtime, he'd been there. And he'd shocked her more with each passing minute.

His unstoppable charm continued on full-blast. But she could no longer believe it to be anything but genuine. Though he dazzled them all, she was now certain it wasn't premeditated. He clearly liked being with her family. He really was interested in all of their concerns and indulgent of all their quirks.

But with Mauri, he was something she'd never seen a man being toward a child, not even her own loving father.

That almost tangible affinity they shared had disturbed her, worried her from that first day. It shook her to her core to see it growing every day, in Richard's eyes, in his vibe. Such absolute focus, such a heart-snatching level of emotion.

What shook her as much was seeing *him* through new eyes. There was far more to him than the lethal seducer who'd taken her heart and body by storm, or the merciless void who'd taken Burton apart, or the ruthless manipulator who'd threatened to tear her life apart when he'd first returned. There were depths and passions in him she doubted even he knew he possessed. And no one seemed more surprised to discover these hidden qualities than Richard himself.

Just today, he'd done something she was certain he'd never contemplated within the range of possibilities.

He'd taken them shopping.

She'd agreed only after he'd promised no splurging. After the fact, she'd kicked herself for not defining *splurging*. To him, it could be keeping it under a million dollars.

As it had turned out, she shouldn't have worried.

Thinking they were shopping—rightfully so—with the genie of the lamp, the kids had asked for things they wouldn't dare ask of their family. She'd bated her breath, hating to have to shoot him down in front of them if he succumbed to their demands. But he'd only given them the most subtle but stern lesson in needless excess and its detriments. After that, they'd let him choose, and he'd picked reasonably priced stuff they'd been delighted with, but would also truly enjoy *and* benefit from.

Mauri was the one who didn't ask for anything, excessive or otherwise. He was overwhelmed each time Richard picked something out for him that he revealed he'd intensely wished for. What he'd never asked her for. Mauri never asked for anything, as if he was aware of her burdens and never wanted to add to them, even when she entreated and cajoled him to ask for anything. It forced her to try to predict his desires. Clearly very inaccurately. It upset and stirred her in equal measure that Richard, after such short if intense acquaintance, was the one to read him so accurately.

After the shopping for the kids was concluded, she told Richard he was forbidden from buying the adults anything. He again said she didn't have a right to dictate terms on the others' behalf. She grudgingly conceded that his relationship with her family should remain independent of theirs.

Especially since *that* was now nonexistent.

Ever since he'd come offering his so-called alliance, there'd been no hint of the voracious predator he'd been. Each day, each *hour* that passed without him bringing up his desire for a continuation of their affair left her partially relieved...but wholly distraught. For she wanted him now, this new him she could admire and respect, far more than she'd ever wanted him before. But it seemed her earlier assumption had been correct. The reality of her being the mother of his son, the domesticity of her life situation, seemed to have doused his passion irreversibly.

Just as she was considering putting herself out of her misery and asking him what his intentions were, she found Rose and her family right in their path.

Rose hadn't asked her about Richard again. To her relief. And astonishment. Isabella surmised she hadn't because she feared Isabella knew nothing about his real identity, and didn't want to cause him trouble since he was hiding it.

Following the same rationalization, Rose probably wouldn't bring up her suspicion again in everyone's presence.

As Jeffrey and their kids, Janie and Robbie—named after Rose's mother and brother, Janet and Robert, as Isabella only now realized—rushed to greet them, Rose stood behind, staring at Richard. Richard, after shaking hands with Jeffrey at Isabella's brief introduction, stared back.

After her mother and sister took the kids and went to the food court, only the four of them remained. Jeffrey's animated conversation petered out when he realized it was a monologue and finally noticed the turmoil in his wife's eyes as she stared at the stranger.

Before he could react, Rose threw herself at Richard, clung to him with all her strength.

Isabella's lungs almost burst. Richard looked as if he'd turned to stone the moment Rose touched him.

Then Rose's incoherent whimpers started to make sense. "Don't tell me you're not Rex...don't you dare."

Richard squeezed his eyes shut, bared his teeth as if straining under an unbearable weight.

Rose suddenly pulled back, features shaking out of control, eyes reddened and pouring tears as she grabbed his arms in trembling hands. "You're my brother. *Say* it."

Richard breathed in sharply, emptied his massive chest on a ragged exhalation and nodded. "I'm your brother."

A sob tore out of Rose's depths and she flung herself at Richard again. Among the cacophony filling her ears, Isabella heard Jeffrey exclaiming a string of hells and damns.

As Rose wept uncontrollably, mashing her face into her brother's chest, this time Richard contained her in his great embrace, stroked her gleaming head soothingly, his hands trembling. Isabella remembered to breathe only when she felt the world dimming.

Richard had decided to stop hiding, to let his sister have him back.

A week ago she'd asked him why he'd never done that.

He'd said so he wouldn't taint Rose's life with his darkness. When she'd said that same fear should apply to her and her family, he'd assured her he'd installed every precaution, would never impact them negatively in any way. When she'd countered he should do the same with Rose and come clean to her and his response had been a silent glance, she'd figured it was only a matter of time before he did.

Suddenly it hit her. This was all his doing. He was the one who'd chosen the mall and decided when to stop shopping and walk around. He must have known Rose and her family were coming, had wanted to set this up to see where it would lead. But it seemed Rose had still surprised him with her unrestrained reaction.

Richard now stepped back from the sister who clutched him as if afraid he'd disappear again if she let him go. What Isabella saw in his eyes almost knocked her off her feet.

Such…*tenderness*.

She'd seen nothing like that in his eyes before. Not even toward Mauri. With him there was indulgence, interest, and when no one noticed, stark, fierce emotions that left her breathless. He'd certainly never looked at her—before his current careful neutrality—with anything approaching this…sheer beauty. She hadn't thought him capable of it.

But she'd never inspired such depth and quality of emotion in him.

His voice was a gruff rasp as his gaze moved from Rose to Jeffrey and back. "We have much to talk about. How about we do it over lunch? Isabella wanted to have sushi today."

Nodding feverishly, looking up at him as if at everything she'd ever wished for had come true, Rose clung to his arm, let him steer her away. Isabella and Jeffrey followed the newly reunited siblings in a trance.

Richard spent the first hour telling the Andersons everything. The next two were consumed with Rose's nonstop questions and his attempts to answer each before she hit him with the next.

He left out strategic areas. Such as how many monsters he'd eliminated. And how he'd gotten the info to bring Burton down, making it sound as if Isabella had cooperated knowingly, as if there'd been nothing beyond this goal between them. Rose must have been too dazed to remember her earlier observation that Mauri looked like their dead brother to come up with the right conclusion. But Isabella felt it was only a matter of time before she did. Or before Richard told her.

Jeffrey finally shook his head. "So you removed every obstacle from our path in our known history! I thought we were plain lucky, but Rose always said she had her own guardian angel, and me by association. Turns out she was right."

Richard huffed. "More like a guardian devil."

Rose's eyes filled again as she squeezed his hands. "You've always been an angel to me, from the first moment I can remember, till that day you went away. But I always felt you watching over me, and that's why I never believed in my heart that you were dead. It's only because you never came forward that I had to tell myself that you were. But I lived feeling I'd one day see you again. That's why I knew you the moment I saw you. Because I've been waiting for you."

"I'm glad you did." Richard's smile was tight with emotion. "And I'm sorry I made you wait that long."

She lunged across the table, knocking things over to plant a tear-smeared kiss on his cheek before subsiding. "Never be sorry. I'll be forever grateful you're alive, that you found me back then and that you're here now. I can't ever ask for more than that."

"Can *I* ask you to forgive me for ever doubting you?" Jeffrey hugged his wife to his side lovingly before returning his gaze to Richard. "Rose always talked about her biological family, but mostly about you. Though she had more years with your mother and brother, she remembered you most of all. She always said you were the best at everything, couldn't believe you *could* die. She painted this Superman image of you, and what do you know? She was right. I have a bona fide double-oh-seven for a brother-in-law."

"I bet Rex would put him to shame…uh…" Rose stopped and smiled goofily at Richard, squeezing his hand again as if to make sure he was really sitting across from her. "I don't know if I can get used to calling you Richard."

His free hand cupped her cheek, and the look in his eyes almost uprooted Isabella's heart all over again.

What she'd give to have him look at her that way.

"You have to in front of others." His gaze suddenly turned deadly serious. "It's beyond vital I'm never associated with Cobra, The Organization's operative. Though I wiped every shred of evidence they had on me, changed radically from the bald-shaven, crooked-nosed, scarred boy and man they knew, and no one suspected me in the past ten years, I can't risk any mistakes that might lead to my exposure. The consequences to everyone I know would be unspeakable."

At his ominous declarations, what shook her most was finding out he'd been mutilated by his years as his father's, Burton's and The Organization's weapon. She'd only known him after he'd fixed the damages—at least the physical ones—but now she realized more than ever how deep they'd run.

At the couple's gaping horror, he exhaled. "This is why I didn't want to burden you with my existence. Maybe it's advisable that I continue watching over you from afar without entering your lives at all."

"No!" Rose's cry was so alarmed, so agonized, it was another blow to Isabella. "I *must* have you in my life. We'll do everything you need us to do." She tugged at her husband, eyes streaming again, imploring. "Won't we, Jeff?"

Jeffrey nodded at once, eager to allay his wife's agitation. "It goes without saying, man. Your secret is our secret." Then he grimaced. "But what are we going to tell the kids?"

"Oh, God...I hadn't thought of that," Rose sobbed, the realization bringing on another wave of weeping. "We can't tell them you're their uncle!"

Richard engulfed her hands in his, as if to absorb her anguish. "It's not important what they think I am as long as I become part of their lives." Richard looked at her, no doubt correlating how the same applied to Mauri. Turning his gaze back to the distraught Rose, his lips crooked in a smile. "Tell them I was your dearest friend when you first got adopted. They'll end up calling me uncle anyway."

Just as tremulous relief dried Rose's tears, Isabella's mother and Amelia came back with the kids for the second time. Richard suggested they all adjourn to his place for the rest of the evening. Everyone agreed with utmost enthusiasm, Rose and Jeffrey's kids squealing in delight when Mauri told them he had a pool in his apartment.

As they all headed for their cars, Isabella hung back, looking at Richard. This lone predator who was now suddenly covered in family. And appearing to delight in them as they did in him.

Only she felt like the odd woman out. As she was.

If he no longer wanted her, and it was clear he didn't, she'd always be left out in the cold.

Over the next few weeks it seemed as if an extended family had mushroomed around Isabella's immediate one. Rose's adoptive family, Richard's friend Rafael and his wife, Eliana—the recipe fairy, as she'd come to be known in their household—and Isabella's own siblings. With the latter now living abroad, two in France and one in Holland, they'd all come to visit on her return to the United States and were delighted with her new status quo.

She was the one who suffered more the better things got.

Not that she felt alienated by everyone's focus on Richard. *That* pleased her, for him, and for everyone else. It was Richard's distance from her that was killing her inch by inch every day.

Today, as with every Saturday, Richard was coming to take them to spend the day with everyone who could make it. He'd been taking them on outings that only a man of his imagination and influence could come up with and afford. She'd cautioned him he'd been overdoing it, building unrealistic expectations that he'd always be that available, that accommodating.

His answer had shaken her, since it was the very reason she wanted to make every second with Mauri count. He said that Mauri would be seven only once, that soon he wouldn't think it cool to hang around with him or be as impressed or as easily pleased by him. But he had another reason she didn't. He had seven years of absence to make up for.

He'd ended the discussion by reassuring her that Mauri understood he might not be able to keep up this level of presence, that he'd managed to clear his calendar to spend this time with them, but that that might not always be the rule.

Then she'd tried to call him out on his extravagance. Though his trips were fun and enriching for all of them, they cost a ton. He'd waved her concern away. He already owned the transportation and commanded most of the personnel and services involved. He'd insisted she sit back and enjoy someone doing things for her for a change.

She would have enjoyed the hell out of it, had it been meant for her. Or even partially for her. But she was incidental to him as Mauri's mother. And she could no longer take it. If he wanted to be with his son, he should be, without dragging her along.

Decision made to tell him this today, she rushed to hide the signs of her tears when she heard the bell ring. He was already here.

Mauri stampeded down the stairs to open the door to the man he now lived to anticipate.

Tears welling again, she listened to the usual commotion of father and son meeting. This time it was even more enthusiastic, as if it was after a long absence when they'd seen each other forty-eight hours ago. Yesterday was the first time in weeks Richard hadn't spent the evening with them.

When she brought herself under control, she walked down to excuse herself from their planned outing. Both of them would probably welcome that, must be unable to wait to be alone together.

Before she took the turn into the living room, she froze. Mauri's voice carried to her, serious, almost agitated.

"Do you know that my real name is Ricardo? Today I discovered it's Spanish for Richard. Mom used to call me Rico until I was two, then started calling me Mauri. But I always hated Mauri. I always wanted to be Rico."

Slumping against the wall, tears stung her eyes again. She hadn't even realized that Mauri—Rico—remembered. What had she done to her own son to ameliorate her own suffering?

There was absolute silence. Richard, for the first time, had no ready answer.

So Mauri…Rico just hit him with his next question.

"You're my father, right?"

That question had come much later than she'd anticipated. Her knees still almost gave at finally hearing it.

Every nerve quivered as she waited for Richard's answer.

By now she knew anything she'd ever feared on Mauri's…Rico's behalf would never come to pass. Richard, for all his darkness and complexities, was proving to be a better father to Rico than she could have ever wished for. He was beyond amazing with him. She believed he either loved their son or felt all he was capable of feeling for him. Rico would be safe and cherished with him. And Richard had revealed himself to be a tremendous role model, too.

Powerful, resolute, committed, brilliant, everything a boy could look up to and wish to emulate. Not to mention that she didn't think Rico could go back to a life without him.

What she feared now was all on her own behalf.

If Richard revealed the truth and demanded to be in his son's life indefinitely, she could only continue to do what she'd been doing. Make his presence in their lives as welcome as could be. She wanted Rico to have his father.

But his desire for her had come to an abrupt end the moment she'd gone from black widow in his eyes to hardworking doctor and the steadfast mother of his child.

She could have lived with that, if only she didn't yearn for him. More than ever. For against all her efforts and better judgment, what she felt for him made her previous emotions fade into nothing. If she'd loved him before, she worshipped him now, while he'd never felt anything beyond desire for her. A desire that had ceased to exist.

But she might have been able to put up with seeing him regularly, as she'd been doing so far, even knowing he'd rather she wasn't part of the equation. What made it untenable was the thought that he might, probably would, one day find the one woman for him, fall head over heels in love with her as his friends had with their wives and marry her.

How could she survive watching him with another woman up close for the rest of her life, the life she knew she'd spend alone if she couldn't have him?

A one-note ring made her jump. She felt around in her pocket frantically before she realized it was Richard's phone.

He answered at once. "Numair?" After moments of silence, he exhaled. "Mauricio…Ricardo, I'm sorry, but I have to run. Numair, the partner I told you about, said it's an emergency. I don't know if I'll be back in time to have our outing, but we'll continue our discussion later, I promise."

Isabella stumbled away, ran into the study. Listening to him practically run out of the house, she sagged down.

She'd thought Richard would finally tell Rico the truth

and she'd start dealing with the new reality, for worse, or worst, and be done with it.

Now she had to wait. For his return.

To start a new chapter with his son.

And to close hers forever.

Ten

Richard didn't know whether to feel thankful or enraged at Numair's summons. He'd interrupted one of his life's most crucial moments.

But there was one rule they lived by in Black Castle. If one partner called, everyone dropped everything *at once* to answer.

But what would he have done if Numair's call hadn't taken precedence over even Mauricio's…Ricardo's…*Rico's* question?

He'd wanted to snatch him in his arms and tell him, *"Yes. I'm your father. And I'm never leaving your side ever again."*

Now he'd never know if he would have.

Those past weeks with him, with Isabella, had turned him inside out. He felt raw, giddy, ecstatic, off balance. And terrified. As much as he'd once been for his family's safety.

He'd been scared of making one wrong move and shattering that unexpected perfection that had sprung between them all. He'd battered his way through every personal situation in his life, because he'd been dealing with men who thrived on adversity, equals who only got stronger with conflict. But mainly because he'd known when all was said and done, he'd mattered to no one. So nothing had really mattered.

But although he'd been in constant agony needing Isabella, he'd been unable to reach out and take her. Even if she still wanted him, he'd feared reintroducing such tempestuous passion would destroy their delicate new status quo, messing up this harmony he hadn't dreamed they could ever have.

That had only been his initial fear. He'd progressed to worse possibilities soon after. That if he pursued her, she'd let him have her again, but that intimacies would never let her see him beyond sex. Knowing the real her now, that would have never been enough. He feared she would have pushed him away sooner or later, but remained always near for Rico's sake. He had no doubt someone as magnificent as her would have eventually found someone worthy to worship her.

He didn't want to imagine what he was capable of doing if he saw her in another man's arms.

Everything inside him roiled until he reached Numair's penthouse.

The door opened before he rang the bell and, without a glance, Numair turned and left Richard to follow him inside.

A melodious voice heralded the approach of what he'd once thought an impossibility. Numair's bride.

Before she noticed his presence, Jenan clung to her husband's neck and they shared a kiss like the one he'd seen them exchange at their wedding. A confession of ever-present hunger, a pledge of ever-growing adoration.

The sight of his former friend so deliriously in love with his princess bride had been a source of contentment before. Now it tore the chasm of desolation inside him wider.

He longed to have anything even approaching this bond with Isabella. But there was no chance for that. He'd done her so many wrongs, he couldn't dare hope she'd ever forgive him, let alone love him as he loved her.

Yes, he'd long admitted the overpowering emotions he felt for her were love. Far more. Worship and dependence that staggered him with their power. He believed he'd always felt all that for her, with the events of the past weeks turning their intensity up to a maximum. He'd only spent years telling himself she was nothing to him so he could live on without her. But while he'd destroyed Burton, he'd also damaged something infinitely more vital. Isabella's budding love. Which had only been possible when she'd been oblivious of his true nature. He'd made reclaiming it far more impossible since he'd barged into her life…

"Richard, what a great surprise!"

He blinked out of his oppressive musings as Jenan strode toward him, still spry in her third trimester of pregnancy. Her hand embraced her husband's, as if they couldn't bear not connecting. She glowed with Numair's love, her body ripe with its evidence. It was literally painful to look at her.

He'd missed it all with Isabella. He hadn't been there to cherish and protect her while she'd carried their child. Instead, his actions had put her in distress and danger. If not for her strength and resourcefulness, the outcome could have been catastrophic. As it was, he'd caused her years of strife and misery, had caused Rico's premature birth. He could have caused his death, and Isabella's.

"If my presence is a surprise—" he growled his pain "—then your beloved husband neglected to tell you that he made me drop a crucial matter to answer his clearly fraudulent red alert."

Jenan pulled a leave-me-out-of-it face. "*And* that's my cue to leave you colossal predators to your favorite pastime of snapping and swiping at each other." Planting a hot kiss on her husband's neck, she murmured, "No claws or fangs, hear?"

Numair's love-filled gaze turned lethal the instant he directed it at Richard. "No promises, *ya habibati.*"

Chuckling, supremely confident in her husband's ultimate benevolence, Jenan passed Richard, dragging him down for an affectionate peck before striding out of the penthouse.

The moment she closed the door, Numair growled, "What the *hell* is the matter with you?"

"With *me*?" Richard's incredulity immediately turned to anger. "Numair, you've never caught me at a worse time—"

"Tell me about it," Numair interrupted.

"*And* it's not in your best interest to provoke me after—"

Numair talked over him again. "After I almost took a bullet for you."

Everything went still inside Richard. "What?"

"I trust you remember Milton Brockovich?"

Richard frowned, unable to even guess at the relevance of Numair's question. He had no idea how he knew of Brockovich.

Four years ago Brockovich's older brother had raped and almost killed a client's daughter. Richard had saved the girl, would have preferred to take the scum in, but he'd pulled a gun on him. So Richard had put a bullet between his eyes. He'd seen the younger unstable Brockovich in the precinct, and he'd ranted that he'd get even with him.

Richard had considered liquidating him as a preemptive measure, before dismissing him. He'd decided the airtight security measures he constantly varied would take care of Brockovich if he ever developed into an actual threat.

"And do you remember forcing me to pledge to fulfill any one demand in return for information leading to Jenan's whereabouts when she disappeared?"

"You mean when she discovered you were using her?"

Numair sneered. "I hated being indebted to you. So when Rafael told me of your domestic adventures with those suburban doctors, I knew something was wrong. I watched you, looking for an opening to do something big enough, preemptively, to fulfill my obligation to you. And I discovered you've converged massive security on those people, for no apparent reason...and neglected your own."

Richard frowned. Numair was right. His personal team did nothing without constantly updated orders. The ones he'd forgotten to give them...for weeks now. Not that this should matter. His personal security was a matter of paranoia on his side, not an actual necessity.

Numair went on. "I know you're probably one of the most unassailable men on earth, but I had a bad feeling about this. Knowing you're at your headquarters early on Saturdays, I decided to confront you. I caught up with you as you left the building—just in time to see Brockovich pull a gun on you. The Cobra I know would have sensed him a mile away. Wouldn't have let him breach that mile in the first place. You didn't even notice him as he passed you. He turned to shoot you and I was on top of him, diverting the bullet and knocking him out. You were gone by then without noticing a thing. I put him someplace where he won't cause anyone trouble again, but I got this—" he held up a bandaged forearm "—from a ricocheting piece of pavement. And I had to lie to Jenan about it."

Richard could only stare at him.

"You didn't hear the silenced gunshot or notice the commotion behind you in an almost empty street."

Richard shook his head, dazed. "You saved my life."

Numair gave a curt nod. "And since you saved mine when you reconnected me with Jenan, this repays my debt."

Unable to stand anymore, Richard sagged on the nearest horizontal surface, dropping his head in his hands.

Numair came down beside him. "What the *hell* is going on with you, Cobra?"

He slanted him a glance without raising the head that felt as if it weighed half a ton. "Don't tell me you care."

"To borrow what you said—when you helped me resolve Zafrana's debts, saving Jenan's kingdom and its king, her father—if I didn't, I wouldn't have intervened on your behalf."

"You didn't do it for me. You were just discharging your debt. You're terminally honorable that way."

"That notwithstanding, and though I might have seriously considered killing you before, I wouldn't want your life to end at the hands of such a worthless scumbag."

"You think I deserve a more significant end, eh?"

"Definitely a spectacular one." Numair's expression suddenly grew thunderous. "Will you tell me what the hell is wrong with you? Are you...sick?"

Richard's breath left him in a mirthless huff. "You can say that." Before Numair could probe, Richard sat forward, deciding to end this meeting. "Thanks for bringing this to my attention. And for saving my life. I'm in your debt now. You know the drill. You can ask for anything and it's yours."

"Again, to echo what you said to me before, I'll collect right now. Answer my questions."

"Why? Really, Phantom, what do you care?"

"Let's say now I've found this hugely undeserved bliss with Jenan, and you do have a hand in it, I can no longer hang on to my hatred of you. I don't want to. I want to wipe the slate clean, don't want to let old animosities taint the new life where our child will be born. Especially since you turned out to be human after all, apparently wanting a woman so much you've been putting up with her family and friends for weeks on end. Not to mention slipping up like mortals do. So just tell me the truth, dammit."

Richard had long thought it pointless to tell Numair why he'd betrayed him, causing him to be punished within an inch of his life for two months straight. But he wanted to stop hiding from him, as he'd stopped hiding from Rose, and from himself. He needed to resolve the issues between them, once and for all.

So he told him the truth. About everything.

To say Numair was stunned would be an understatement.

Suddenly heaving up, Numair dragged him with him by his lapels, his teeth bared, his shout like thunder. "All these years...you *crazy* bastard...you let me think you betrayed me, made us live as enemies...*all these years*."

This wasn't among the possible reactions he'd expected. Numair was enraged...but not as he'd thought he would be.

Richard swallowed the thorns that had sprouted in his throat. "I did betray you. I almost had you maimed. I did get you scarred. And it didn't matter why I did."

Shock expanding in his eyes, Numair shook him, hard. "Are you mad? Nothing else mattered. You had no other choice. Your family had to come first. You did the only thing to be done, sacrificing the one who could take the punishment for those who couldn't. I'm only damned sorry it didn't save your family. I would have taken far more damage if it had ultimately spared their lives."

Richard tore himself from Numair's furious grip, sagged again to escape the contact, the crashing guilt, the crushing futility. Numair's hands descended heavily on his shoulders.

"Look at me." He did, letting Numair see the upheaval filling his eyes. Numair winced. "I went mad all these years, hated you as fiercely as I once loved you for never giving me an explanation, not for the betrayal itself. You were the first person who ever gave me a reason to cling to my humanity, the one I looked up to, the one who gave me hope there'd one day be more for me than being The Organization's slave. Because there was more with you, a friendship that I thought would last as long as we both lived. I hated you, not because I got scarred, but because I thought you took all that, my belief in you, in our bond, the strength and stability it brought me, away from me."

Moved beyond words, Richard stared up at Numair, the stinging behind his eyes blurring his vision.

Numair sat, fervor replacing the fury on his face. "But I have my friend back now. And you have me, too. It's twenty-six freaking years too late, but better late than never. You damn self-sacrificing jackass."

Richard coughed. "That was no self-sacrifice. I just believed there was no forgiving my crimes. I only hoped you'd consider, after all I did over the past ten years, that I atoned for them, at least in part. But you're as unforgiving as your homeland's camels."

Numair arched a teasing eyebrow. "What, pray tell, did you do to atone? It was *I* who deigned to put my hand in that of my betrayer to build Black Castle Enterprises for us all."

"You deigned nothing. You couldn't do it without me."

Numair's face opened on a smile Richard hadn't seen since he'd been fourteen. "No, I couldn't. And I now believe what Rafael kept telling us all these years. That my escape plan wouldn't have worked, certainly not as perfectly as it had, without your help." Suddenly a realization dawned in Numair's eyes. "You waited until we were all out before you left, too, didn't you?"

Letting him read his answer in his eyes, Richard attempted a smile. "We didn't do too shabbily for sworn enemies, did we?"

Numair clapped him zealously on the back, imitating his accent. "We did splendidly, old chap."

The knife embedded in his chest only twisted at Numair's lightheartedness. "At least, you did. You're there for the woman you love every moment she needs you, to love and protect her. You'll share with her every up and down of childbirth and child rearing. You'll never leave her to face a merciless world alone, like I did with Isabella."

Numair frowned again. "You had reasons for your actions, and she understands them like I do now. The fact that she let you in your son's life attests to that."

"She may understand, even forgive, but she'll never forget, not what I did in the past, or what I did when I first invaded her life again. She'll never love me again."

Numair grabbed his shoulder, turning him fully to him. "When has *never* been a word in your vocabulary? You keep after something until it happens. So you lost seven years of your son's life…"

Unable to bear Numair's placation, he tore his hand off, stepping away from him. "I didn't lose them, I *threw* them away. When I didn't give her the benefit of the doubt, didn't trust my heart about her, when I left her in the hands of the monster who'd destroyed my family. I almost cost her, and Rico, their lives…"

"Stop it, Richard," Numair roared, bringing his tirade to an abrupt end. He'd never called him Richard before. "You won't serve them by wallowing in guilt. From now on, you'll live to make it up to her, and to your son. From what Rafael tells me, the boy worships you. And she's trusting you to be around him. This says a lot about her opinion of you as you are now, and of your efforts to *atone*. Keep at it, prove to her how much you love her and your son. When she realizes the best thing for her is to open her heart to you again, she will. Hang in there. When she bestows her love and trust on you again, nothing will ever touch that blessing. I know."

Richard only nodded so Numair would let this go. He couldn't bear one more word on the subject.

Satisfied that he'd talked him down, Numair let Richard divert their conversation to their own shattered relationship. Numair did more than wipe the slate clean. He pushed a re-start button where they'd left off as teenagers.

Numair finally let him go two hours later, and only one thing he'd said looped in his mind until it almost pulped it.

When she realizes the best thing for her is to open her heart to you again, she will.

What Numair thought would bolster his hope for a future with Isabella had only pulverized it, since she undoubtedly realized the best thing for her would be to never open her heart to him again, to stay as far away from him as possible.

When he finally worked up enough nerve to go back to Isabella's home, it was she who let him in. She'd sent Mauri out with Rose's family and stayed behind to talk to him.

With foreboding descending on him like a suffocating shroud, he followed her into the living room.

Once they sat, the voice he now lived to hear washed over him, a tremor traversing it.

"I overheard you and Mauri…and *Rico*…earlier today."

So she'd heard their son's desire to be called Rico again. And his demand for Richard to admit that he was his father.

Would she forbid him to do so, revoke his privilege to come to her home and spend time with Rico? Would she cast him out?

Isabella's hushed words doused his panic. "If you need my blessing to tell Rico the truth, you have it, Richard. I will accommodate your every desire to be with him."

The delight that detonated within him almost blanked out the world.

She wasn't casting him out but letting him further in. As Numair had said, she'd grown to trust him with Rico, was giving him the ultimate privilege of claiming his son.

But…was she telling him that was the extent of their relationship? He'd only be Rico's father, but…nothing to her?

In the past he'd been worse than nothing, her bane, steeping everything between them in deceit and manipulation, then in lust and degradation. If he'd intentionally set out to destroy her feelings for him, he couldn't have done a more complete job. If she wanted something real and lasting with a man, she'd look for it anywhere else but with him. She *deserved* the real thing. The best there was. And he wasn't it. He had sinned against her beyond forgiveness, was tainted beyond retrieval.

But since he was, what right did he have to Rico? Wouldn't he be better off without a father like him? It was even worse now that his turmoil over them could have gotten him killed today. What would that have done to Rico if he'd already known Richard was his father?

Why he invaded their lives? What had he been searching for? Redemption? When he'd long known he was beyond that? Love? When he knew he didn't deserve it?

If he loved them, and he loved them far beyond anything

he'd thought possible, he had to make them happy. To keep them safe. There was only one way he could do that.

He rose, in an agony worse than when multiple bullets had torn through his flesh, looked down into Isabella's searching gaze and dealt himself a fatal injury. That of saying goodbye. Forever this time.

"Actually, I think you were right not to want me near your family. I'm glad that interruption stopped me from making an irretrievable statement, gave me time to realize it's not in Rico's best interests to have me in his life. Nor is it in Rose's and her family's. I'm sorry I forced myself into your lives and disrupted your peace, but I promise to leave all of you alone from now on. Once you tell Mauricio I'm not his father, he'll reconsider being called Rico, and there won't be any irreversible damage when I disappear from his life."

Shocked to her core, Isabella watched Richard walk away, feeling as if he was drawing her life force out with him.

Then the front door clicked shut behind him and everything holding her up snapped. She collapsed on the couch in an enervated mass.

She'd thought he'd be delighted with her blessing, had been about to follow it with a carte blanche of herself, if he'd consider her as a lover again.

She'd been ready with assurances that whether or not it worked out between them, it wouldn't impact the lifelong relationship she'd been sure he'd wanted with his son. The worst she'd thought would happen was his rejection of her, had been prepared to put up with anything, even watching him find love with another woman, so Rico would have his father, and she'd have him in her life at all.

She hadn't even factored in the possibility that within hours he'd decide he didn't want Rico, either.

There was only one explanation for this. He'd given the domestic immersion a go, and when the moment of truth had come, he'd decided he couldn't have her and Rico in his life on an ongoing basis. He didn't need them the way they both did him.

So he'd decided to walk away, thinking it the ideal time to curtail damages. Little did he know he'd been too late. Mauri was already so deeply attached she dreaded the injury the abrupt separation would cause him.

As for her, he'd damaged her eight years ago. But now...

Now he'd finished her.

On Mauri's return, she rushed to her room to postpone the confrontation until her own upheaval had settled. But he came knocking on her door, something he never did, bounding inside, asking when Richard would be coming the next day.

Sticking hot needles into her flesh would have been easier than telling him Richard wouldn't come at all.

Rico's reaction gutted her.

He wasn't upset. He was hysterical.

"He wouldn't leave me!" he screamed. "He promised me he'd come back to tell me everything. It's you who never wanted to tell him about me. You don't like him and keep silent when he's here, no matter how nice he is to you. You kept looking at him with sad eyes until you made him go away. But I won't let him go. He's my father and I know it and I'll go get him back!"

"Mauri...darling, please..."

"My name is Rico!" he screamed, and tore out of her grasp.

It was mere seconds before she realized he hadn't bolted to his room, but downstairs and out of the house. She hurtled after him, spilled outside in time to see him dart across the street. She hit the pavement the moment a car hit him.

Eleven

It was true that catastrophes happened in slow motion.

To Isabella's racing senses, the ghastly sequence as her son flew into the trajectory of that car, the shearing dissonance of its shrieking brakes, the nauseating brunt of its unyielding metal on Rico's resilient flesh and fragile bones was a study in macabre sluggishness. It had been like that when her father had been shot dead a foot away from her.

Then her son's body was hurled a dozen feet in the air, with all the random violence one would toss a scrunched piece of paper in frustration. He impacted the asphalt head-first with a hair-raisingly dull crunch, landing on his back like one of his discarded action figures. At that point, everything hit an insane fast-forward, distorting under the explosion of horror.

She hadn't moved, not consciously, but she found herself descending on him, crashing on her knees beside him, her mind splintering.

The mother in her was babbling, blubbering, falling apart in panic. The woman whose life had been steeped in tragedy and loss looked on in fatalistic dread. The doctor stood back, centered, assessing, planning ten steps ahead.

The doctor won over, suppressing the hysterical mother under layers of training and experience and tests under fire.

From the internal cacophony and external tumult rose her mother's voice, as horrible as it had been when her husband lay dying in her arms, shouting that they were a doctor and a nurse, and for everyone to stand back. Everything stilled as she accessed the eye of the storm inside her, examined her unconscious son as detachedly as she would any critical case.

Her hands worked in tandem with her mother's as they zoomed through emergency measures, tilting his head, clearing his airway, checking his breathing and circulation. Then she directed her mother to stabilize his neck and spine, stem his bleeding while she assessed his neurological status. The ambulance arrived and she used all its resources and personnel as extensions to her hands and eyes in immobilizing, transferring and resuscitating Rico.

Then there was nothing more to do until they reached the practice. Nothing but call for reinforcements.

She knew she should call her partners. But the first call went to the only one she needed with her now.

Richard.

Even if he'd walked away, half of Rico remained his. Even if he'd chosen not to be Rico's father, he'd once told her he wanted to be her ally. Only an ally of his clout would do now.

While she was a pediatric surgeon with extensive experience in trauma, this was beyond her ability alone. Rico needed a multidisciplinary approach, with a surgeon at the helm who counted neurosurgery as a top specialty. Only one surgeon with the necessary array of capabilities came to mind. Someone only Richard could bring her.

The line opened at once and a butchered moan escaped her lips.

"Richard, I need you." This sounded wrong, was irrelevant. She tried again. "*Rico* needs you."

The moment Richard felt his phone vibrate he just knew it was Isabella. Even if the look in her eyes as he'd walked away had told him he'd never hear from her again. If he was right, and it was her calling him now, then something terrible must have happened.

Then he'd heard her voice, sounding like the end of everything. *Richard, I need you. Rico needs you.*

He listened to the rest and the world did come to an end around him.

Rico. His son. Their son. In mortal danger.

Without preliminaries, she ended the call. The worst possible scenario lodged into his brain like an ax.

No. No. *He's fine. He* will *be fine.* She'll save him. *He'll* save him. Antonio. He *must* get Antonio.

Barely coherent as he tore through traffic on his way to her, to his son…to his *family*, he called Antonio. He was Black Castle's resident omnicapable medical genius, who'd saved each member of the brotherhood, except him, as he'd never been part of it, from certain death at least once. After Isabella herself, he'd trust no one else with his son's life.

As per their pact, Antonio answered at once. In his mounting panic, everything gushed out of him. Antonio calmly estimated he'd be in New York with his fully equipped mobile hospital in an hour. But if the condition was critical, they must start without him.

Richard called Isabella back, including her in a conference call so she could give Antonio her diagnosis directly, as the expert, and the one who'd been at the accident scene.

But that had been no accident. He'd done this. Every time he came near her—them, he almost destroyed them.

In a fugue of murderous self-loathing he heard Isabella give Antonio a concise, comprehensive report of Rico's injuries and her measures to save him, her voice a tenuous thread of control.

Isabella… This miracle fate had given him when he'd never deserved her, who'd given him another miracle, only for him to throw her—throw them away, time and again.

His mind fragmenting under the enormous weight of guilt and dread, he'd almost succumbed to despair when

Antonio's authoritative tone dragged him back to focus with the first ray of hope. His verdict.

"From his signs, your diagnosis of a subdural hematoma with a coup-counter-coup cerebral contusion is correct. From his vitals, your measures have stabilized him and stopped the brain swelling, which will resolve over time. But he will need surgery to drain the hematoma and cauterize the bleeders. It's not as urgent as I feared, so I can be the one to perform it. Bring him to the tarmac. I'll have the OR ready."

The terrible tension in Isabella's voice rose. "We're already at the practice, and I wouldn't move him again. Our OR is fully equipped. I'll prep him and wait for you there."

Antonio didn't argue. "Fine. I'll bring my special equipment. Continue to stabilize him until I arrive. Richard—send a helicopter to the jet."

Emerging from the well of helplessness, latching on to something useful to do, Richard pledged, "I'll get you to the OR ten minutes after you land."

Once at the practice, Rose intercepted him, restraining him from stampeding in search of Rico and Isabella.

They were in the OR, and the most she could do was take him to the lounge where surgical trainees observed surgeries, *if* he promised not to distract Isabella or to agitate her, when she was miraculously holding it together.

Ready to peel his skin off to bolster Isabella, he gave Rose his word. Once they arrived, nothing could prepare him for what he saw through the soundproof glass. It would scar his psyche forever.

Rico, looking tinier than the strappy, big-for-his-age boy he adored, lying inert and ashen on the operating table. Isabella in full surgical garb, orchestrating the team swarming around him: Jeffrey, Marta, other nurses, an anesthesiologist.

Then Isabella raised her head. The one part of her visible,

her eyes, collided with his. What he saw there before she turned back to their son almost brought him to his knees.

"He'll be fine." Rose caressed his rock-tense back, tugging him to sit on the viewing seats.

His eyes burned. "Will he?"

Assurance trembled on Rose's lips. "She already saved him from the worst at the accident scene. The surgery is necessary, but I believe the life-threatening danger is over."

A rough groan tore from him, and he dropped his head into his hands, unable to bear the agony of hope and dread.

"She's amazing, isn't she?"

Rose's deep affection made him raise his head and look down at Isabella once more. He wondered again how fate had found it fit to bless him with finding her. His only explanation was so he'd lose her, the worst punishment it could have dealt him. But that was what he deserved. Why had fate chosen to punish *her* by putting him in her path time and again?

"Look at her—functioning at top efficiency even though it's her son on that table. I don't think I would have held together in her place. But Isabella's survived and conquered so much, she channeled that strength to take on the unimaginable responsibility of Rico's life."

Realizing she'd just said Rico's name, he looked at her.

A smile of reproach quivered in her tear-filled eyes. "I almost fainted when Isabella finally told me the truth. It's why I am up here, not down there." A beat. "Not that I didn't know it from the first moment I saw you together. I kept hoping you'd tell me all this time. Why didn't you?"

"I...I...left it up to her to tell you." It hurt to talk, to breathe, to exist. And he deserved far worse, a life of constant agony. "I was on probation, and she didn't know if I'd work out. I didn't. I was a catastrophic failure. I was leaving them, leaving all of you. I'm the reason this happened. I almost ended up killing my son."

"You were leaving? God, Rex, why—?"

Rafael, Eliana, Numair and Jenan walked in, cutting off Rose's anguished exclamation.

Eliana rushed to hug him. "Antonio called us."

Rafael hugged him, too, and he saw in his eyes that Numair had told him everything. But there was no surprise there, just reaffirmed faith. Rafael had always believed in him, no matter the evidence against him.

"I called him as I walked in, and he said he'll be landing in a few minutes," Rafael said. "My helicopter is waiting beside his landing lane. He said he'll drop off with his gear outside the practice like he does on missions. I coordinated with the police so they don't pursue him or my pilot."

Numair added, "The others are on their way. Is there anything else we can do?"

Richard shook his head, choking on too many brutal emotions to count. His son lying there, his fate undecided. The love of his life doing what no mother should, fighting for her son's life. The unwavering support of Isabella's and Rose's families. All his friends rallying around him.

Yes, friends. Brothers-in-arms. Just…brothers.

And he again wondered…how he deserved to have all these people on his side when he'd done nothing but waste opportunities and make horrific decisions.

Suddenly, Antonio rushed into the OR already gowned. And as if they'd always worked together, he and Isabella took their places at the table. After Isabella filled him in as he set up his equipment and examined scans, Antonio looked up, gave Richard a nod, a promise. His son would be fine.

Isabella looked up, too, sought only his eyes, and he wanted to roar for her to leave it all to Antonio. She'd suffered enough. But he knew she'd see it through, could only be thankful his son had such a mother.

"All right, everyone…" Antonio's voice filled the lounge. "Out." Before Richard could protest, he pinned him in his uncompromising gaze. "Especially you, Richard."

Everyone rushed out immediately, but Richard stood rooted, even as Rose and Rafael tried to pull him away. He couldn't leave Rico. He *wouldn't* leave *her*.

He'd never leave either of them again.

His gaze locked with Isabella's, imploring her.

Let me stay. Let me be there for both of you.

Her nod of consent was a blessing he didn't deserve, but he swore he'd live his life striving to.

She murmured and Antonio exhaled. "Dr. Sandoval decrees that you stay. But make one move or sound and you're out." At Richard's eager nod, Antonio looked at Rose. "Sorry I kicked you out with the rest, Dr. Anderson, but I did only so you'd keep your big brother on a leash. Now you'll do it in here."

Rose's relief was palpable as she dragged him to sit down. He sank beside her, clinging to Isabella's eyes in one last embrace, trying to transfer to her his every spark of strength, pledging her every second he had left on this earth, whether she wanted it or not. She squeezed her eyes, as if confirming she'd received it all.

Then the procedure started.

Richard had been in desperate situations too many times to remember. But none had come close to dismantling him like the two heart-crushing hours before Antonio announced he was done, and they wheeled Rico to Intensive Care.

Richard found himself there, pushing past Antonio as he came out first. "I must see him."

Antonio clamped his arm. "I let you watch the surgery against my better judgment already, because Dr. Sandoval needed your presence. But if I let you back there, she'll go back, too, and I barely managed to tear her from your son's side. I don't want her around him while he's still unconscious one more second. She's been through enough."

As Richard struggled with his rabid need to touch his son,

to feel him breathe and to spare Isabella further anguish, Antonio's gaze softened as she and the others came out.

"The surgery went better than even I projected. Seems Rico has his father's armored head." Rose and his Black Castle friends who'd caught up gave drained smiles as Antonio's gaze turned to Isabella. "But seriously, Dr. Sandoval's impeccable damage control presented me with a fully stable patient." His gaze turned to Richard, hardening. "Without her, the prognosis wouldn't have been the perfect one it is now. Rico is a lucky boy to have his mom's healing powers and nerves of steel."

Another breaker of guilt crashed over Richard. He wanted to snatch Isabella in his arms, beseech her forgiveness. Only knowing she wouldn't appreciate it held him back.

Antonio extended a hand to Isabella. "It was a privilege working with someone of your skill and grace under fire, Dr. Sandoval, though I wish it wasn't under these circumstances."

Seeming to operate on autopilot, Isabella took his hand. "Isabella, please. It's me who's eternally in your debt. You were the only one I could trust my son's life with."

Antonio waved him off. "Any neurosurgeon worth his salt would have done as good a job. His condition, thankfully, didn't require my level of expertise. But it was a privilege to operate on him. He's sort of my nephew, too, you know. Whether Richard likes it or not, he's been drafted into our brotherhood."

Richard stared at him, overwhelmed all over again as everyone murmured their corroboration.

Antonio turned to Richard. "Any debt here is all yours, buddy."

Richard's nod was vigorous. "Unequivocally. I'm indebted to *everyone* here, and to the whole world, an unrepayable debt in the value of Rico's invaluable life."

Antonio chuckled, no doubt enjoying seeing Richard,

who always antagonized everyone, so ready to be everyone's eternal slave.

Richard only dragged him into a hug. He even kissed him.

Pulling back, blinking in surprise, Antonio laughed. "Whoa. Who are you, and where's the lethal and exasperating Richard Graves I know and love, and occasionally loathe?"

Richard exhaled. "He doesn't exist anymore."

Antonio laughed. "Nah, he's still in there. But I bet he'll never again emerge around our current company." He wiggled an eyebrow at him. "I would have loved to squeeze you for an installment on your debt, but there'd be no fun in that when you're beyond collapse." He pulled Richard's hand, wrapped it around Isabella's. "Go get some rest."

"But…"

"But…"

Hand raised, Antonio ended their protests. "I'll hold the fort here, not that I need to. Rico is stable, but I'll keep him sedated until his brain edema totally resolves. I'd rather you don't look ninety percent dead, as you both do now, when he wakes up." He shoved them away. "Go home…now."

Twelve

All the way to Isabella's house she sat beside him, unmoving, unresponsive. Not that he'd tried to make her respond. She'd been shattered, had put herself back together so many times, he could barely breathe around her in fear that she'd finally come apart for good.

Once inside, she stopped at the living room, her eyes glazed, as if she was envisioning their evenings spent there. Without warning, a sob tore out of her, sounding as if it actually ripped things inside her to break free.

She'd held it all in until this moment. Before another thought or reaction could fire inside him, she was a weeping heap on the ground.

Crashing to his knees in front of her, he wrapped himself around her, reciting her name over and over, hugging and hugging her, as if he'd integrate her whole being into his own, or at least absorb all traces of her ordeal.

She suddenly exploded out of his arms. His heart almost ruptured. She hated his touch, couldn't bear his consolation.

But instead of pulling away, she tackled him. Stunned for seconds before relief burst inside him, he let her ram him to the ground, needing her to take her revenge, expend her rage, cause him permanent damage as he'd done to her. Hoping he'd finally atone for a measure of his crimes against her, he opened himself completely to her punishment.

She only crashed her lips over his.

Going limp with shock beneath her, he surrendered to her

as she wrenched at him with frantic, tear-soaked kisses that razed whatever remained intact inside him. Then she was tearing at his clothes, clawing at his flesh in her desperation, bathing him in her tears, her pleas choking.

"Give me...everything...I need it all...now, Richard... *now*."

That was what she needed? To lose herself in him, to ameliorate her ordeal and douse her pain?

This was an offering he didn't deserve. But it was the least of her dues. To have everything that he had. He'd give it all to her, now and forever, to do with what she would.

The barbed leash he'd been keeping on his need snapped. He completed her efforts to tear his clothes off, ripped her out of hers and surged to meld their naked bodies, squashing her against him as if he'd absorb her.

Nothing, starting with him, would ever harm her again. Or Rico. Not while he had breath left in his body.

She met his ferocity halfway, the same remembered horror reverberating in her every nuance, the same need to extinguish it driving her. She sank her teeth into his lips, whimpering for his reciprocation. Giving her what she needed, he twisted his fist in the silk of her hair, imprisoning her for his invasion. She fought him for more, urged him deeper until the stimulation of their mouth mating became distress. Tearing her lips away, she bit into his deltoid, broke his skin as she crushed herself to him. Growling his painful pleasure, the bleakness of despair shattered inside him as her unbridled passion pulsed in his arms, dueled with his, equal, undreamed of. He'd do anything...*anything*... to make it permanent.

He heaved up with her bundled in his arms. "Bed—Isabella...where's your bed?"

"No...here...I need you inside me...*now*."

Her keen sent the beast inside howling to obey her. Running to the closest horizontal surface, he lowered her there, flung himself over her even as she dragged him down. Madness burgeoned between them as she rewarded his every nip and squeeze with a fiercer cry, a harder grind of her core into his erection, a more blatant offering of herself. Her readiness scorched his senses, but it was her scream for him to *fill* her that slashed away his sanity, made him tear inside her.

He swallowed her scream, let it rip inside him as her unbearably tight flesh yielded to his shaft, sucking him into their almost impossible fit, hurling him into the firestorm of sensation he craved. The carnality, the reality, the *meaning* of being inside her again… This was everything.

And he'd always cede everything to her, the one he'd been made for.

He withdrew, his shaft gliding in the molten heat of her folds. She clung to him, demanding his return, her piercing cry harmonizing with his tortured groan.

Sanity receding further, he thrust inside her once more. She collapsed beneath him, an amalgam of agony and ecstasy slashing across her face, rippling through her body, hot passion gusting from her lungs.

"Give me all you've got… Don't hold anything back…"

Her need rode him, making him ride her harder. The scents and sounds of her pleasure intensifying, her flesh became an inferno around him, more destructive than everything he'd ever faced combined. And the one thing that made him truly live.

With every squeeze of her flesh welcoming him inside her, needing what he gave her, another fraction of the barrenness of his existence, the horrors he'd seen and perpetrated, dissipated. The poignancy, the liberation, sharpened until he bellowed, pounding into her with his full power. Crying, begging, she augmented his force, crushed herself against him as if to merge their bodies.

Knowing she was desperate for release, he sank his girth inside her to the root. She bucked so hard, inside and out it was like a high-voltage lash. It made him plunge ever deeper inside her, sending her convulsions into hyperdrive, suffocating her screams. The gush of her pleasure around his thickness razed him, the force of her orgasm squeezing his shaft until her seizure triggered his own.

His body felt as if it detonated from where he was buried deepest in her outward. Everything inside him was unleashed, scorching ecstasy shooting through his length and gushing deep inside her as if to put out the flame before it consumed them both.

At the end of the tumult, she slumped beneath him, unconscious, her face streaked in tears. He could barely hang on to his own consciousness enough to gather her and go in search of her bedroom.

Once there, he laid her on her bed, every vital piece of him that had gone missing without her back in place. She'd tell him when she woke if they were back for good, or only temporarily. If she'd bestow another chance at life, or if she'd cut it short.

Isabella felt for her phone before she opened her eyes.

Finding it on her nightstand, where she didn't remember putting it, she grabbed it in trembling hands, sagged back in a mass of tremors, tears overflowing. There were a dozen messages from her mother and Antonio throughout the night, the latest minutes ago. Rico was perfectly fine.

Before she could breathe, another blow from her memory emptied her lungs again. *Richard.*

She'd almost attacked him, made him take her…then she remembered nothing. The explosive pleasure his possession had given her had knocked her out. Afterward he'd put her in bed and…left?

Before mortification registered, a silent movement did, making her sag deeper in bed. Richard…in only pants, walking in…with a tray. The aromas of fresh-brewed coffee and hot croissants made her almost faint again. She was that hungry.

She was hungrier for him. Not that she'd jump his bones again. The overwrought situation, her excuse and what had ignited him, was over. He'd decided to walk away, and she had to tell him he was free to go. She'd be damned if she clung to him through his guilt over Rico, or any obligation to her. Being unable to stop wanting him was her curse.

Suffocating with heartache, she struggled to find words to breach the awkwardness as Richard put the tray beside her then sat on the bed. His eyes downcast under a knotted brow, he silently poured her coffee, buttered a croissant, adding her favorite raspberry jam. His heat and scent and virility deluged her, hunger a twisting serpent in her gut.

Cries bubbled inside her: that he didn't need to stick around, or coddle her, that she was okay now—*they'd* be okay. Before any escaped, he put the croissant to her lips. But it was the look in his eyes that silenced her, made her bite into the delicious flaky warmth, her senses spinning.

It felt as if he was showing her inside him for the first time. It was dark and scarred and isolated in there. A mirror image of her own insides. She'd already worked all that out, but she'd thought he'd grown so hardened, was so formidable, that his demons were just more fuel for his power, that he didn't suffer from his injuries the way she did. But he was exposing facets of himself she would have never believed existed—wounded, remorseful...vulnerable.

Enervated by the exposure, she could only eat what he fed her and drown in his gaze, in a world of aching entreaty, and what she'd despaired of seeing directed to her... tenderness.

Then he began speaking. "I've been damaged in so many ways, been guilty of so much, I can't begin to describe it. But Rico...he's purity and innocence and love personified. And you...by God, Isabella, *you*. Against all odds and in spite of all you've suffered, you are all that and everything that's shining and heroic. And while I can't breathe without you..."

That statement was so…enormous it had her pent-up misery bursting out. "B-but you didn't come near me for weeks!"

His gaze flooded with incomprehension, then incredulity. "Didn't you feel me *warring* with myself not to?"

She shook her head, every despair she'd been resigned to evaporating, bewilderment crashing in its place. *"Why?"*

"Because I spoiled everything, in every way possible. In the past and in the present. But even after I discovered the extent of my crimes against you, you still gave me another chance—but only for Rico's sake. I was going out of my mind needing you, but though I knew you wanted me still, physical intimacy had so far only driven you further away, made you despise me, and yourself. And I didn't blame you. I didn't know if I had more in me than what you already rejected. So I enforced the no-touching rule on myself to see if I could offer you what I never did, if I had something inside me that was worthy of you, of Rico…of the extended family who'd reached out and accepted me as one of their own because of you."

Every word unraveled the maze of confusion she'd been lost in, shattered the vice of anguish gripping her insides.

He'd been holding back. He still wanted her.

He went on, dissolving the last of her uncertainties, giving her far more than she'd dared dream of. "But as I fully realized the extent of my emotions for you, I started to worry about the sheer depth of my attachment to Rico, the staggering *force* of my love for you. I started to fear myself. Then Rico asked if I was his father and Numair summoned me, and it all spiraled out of control in my mind."

The staggering force *of my love for you… My love for you.*

The words revolved in her mind, spinning an all-powerful magical spell, enveloping her whole being.

Richard loved her.

As mind-blowing and life affirming as this realization

was, the more pressing matter now was his distress. The need to defuse it was her paramount concern. Her trembling hand covered his fisted one. "What happened? I could have sworn you'd come back to tell him the truth."

He continued staring at her, adrift in his own turmoil. "I was so lost in you, in my yearnings for a future together as a family, I totally dropped my guard. I almost got myself killed. And I didn't even notice it. Numair saved my life unbeknownst to me."

Each nerve in her body fired, every muscle liquefied. A wave of nausea and horror stormed through her at the idea that he could have been...been... The images were... unbearable, unsurvivable...

"That was the last straw. It made me believe that whatever I do, just because of what I am, I'd only blight your lives, cause you even more untold damages. I had to keep you safe, from myself most of all. That was why I had to walk away."

Another surge of dread smashed into her.

He believed his love, his very life, would be a source of threats to them? And that was why he'd still walk away?

His eyes were haunted, desperate, as they left hers, searched space aimlessly. "I thought my control and strength of will limitless. But it all crumbled in the face of my need for you. What can I do now when it's beyond me to leave you?"

The heart that had been pulping itself against her ribs did a full somersault. She swore.

And she did what she'd told herself she couldn't do again. She launched herself at him, over the tray, knocking everything over, tackling him down to the bed, bombarding him with kisses and raining now-ready tears all over him.

"You can do only one thing for the rest of our lives. You can love, love, *love* me, and Rico, as much as we love you."

Richard, lying speechless beneath her unrestrained passion and relief, looked as if he was coming out of a fugue.

"You *love* me?" If she'd told him she could stick to walls he wouldn't have looked more stunned. "*You* love me? How? When I did everything to deserve your loathing?"

His guilt, his hatred of himself, his conviction he didn't deserve her love felt so total, she knew he'd need a lengthy argument to persuade him otherwise. She wasn't up to that now.

She wanted to get to the good part at once. At last.

So she asked one simple question. "Do you love us? Me?"

And if she had any doubt, what came into his eyes now put it all to rest forever. It *was* staggering, the purity and totality of emotions that deluged her.

"I far more than love you. *You.* I've *always* loved you… from the first moment I saw you. But I thought you never really wanted me, and that was why you didn't come with me, never sought me again. I fought admitting my love for years, so I could move on. But I was done fighting weeks ago. I only want to worship you forever, and be the father Rico deserves, and never let you go."

Crying out, she snatched a kiss from those lips that had been the cause for her every ecstasy and agony.

"You want to know how I could love you? *That's* how. I loved you from the first moment, too. I must have *felt* your love, and it kept me bound to you, even through the misconceptions and estrangement." She melted caresses over the planes of his rugged face, sizzling in delight at the open adoration in his eyes. "And if I loved the old you with all my heart, I adore the new you that Rico unearthed, the magnificent man and human being your terrible life had buried deep within you, with all my being."

He shook his head adamantly. "Rico only melted what remained of my deep freeze, but the one who brought the whole iceberg crashing down into tiny fragments has always been you. The moment I saw you again, it was over for me." He heaved up, had her beneath him in a blink. "I want you certain of one thing. I would have admitted it sooner rather than later that I wanted nothing but to be yours, to make it all up to you, even if we didn't have Rico." His face twisted. "But we do have him, and you saved him... You saved all of us."

He buried his face in her bosom and she felt another thing she'd never thought possible. His tears.

Crying out, as if they burned her, she dragged his head up, her hands and lips trembling over his face, needing to wipe them and the pain behind them away.

No longer hiding anything from her, his emotional state or anything else inside him, he worshipped her in return. "This perfection makes me even more terrified. I don't deserve a fraction of it. How could I possibly have all this?"

After another fervent kiss, she looked into his eyes, intoxicated with the freedom of showing him everything in her heart. "You better get used to it. You have all of me forever. And Rico. And you also have Rose and her family. And my family. *And* your best friend back. Not to mention that army of partners who drafted you into their brotherhood."

His eyes turned into shimmering pools of silver. This time she knew it was with joy and gratitude.

His next words confirmed her suspicion. "It's too much."

Wrapping his massive frame in a fierce embrace, she pressed his head to her fluttering heart. "No, it isn't. You see only the bad things you did, when you had overpowering reasons...or at least was under as powerful misconceptions. But you also did so many incredible things for so many people. You sacrificed yourself for your family, then for Rafael and Numair and their—your brotherhood, then you gave Rose a second chance and watched over her all her life."

He pushed himself off her, as if unable to bear her exoneration. "But what I did to you..."

She pulled him back, never intending to let him go again. "I don't care anymore what you did when you thought I was Burton's accomplice. Neither should you." He shook his head, face gripped in self-loathing. She grabbed his face, made him look at her. "What matters is that you gave me everything."

A spectacular snort answered her claim.

It made her burst out laughing. His scowl deepened, not accepting that she should make light of it. Her lethal Cobra had turned out to be a noble knight after all.

Grinning so widely it hurt, she stabbed stinging fingers into the mane he'd let grow longer, as she loved it, which she'd been dying to do since he'd imposed the no-touching ban.

"You have," she insisted. "You've given me passion and pleasure like I never dreamed possible. And you did something else no one could have—you freed me from Burton, opened up my life to new possibilities."

"That was totally unintentional!" he protested.

She overrode his protest. "You did try to save me, and if I hadn't been so busy protecting you, I would have come with you, or I would have at least sought you, and you would have protected me." As he looked about to reject her qualifications, she tugged on his hair, stopping him. "But the greatest gift you gave me is Rico. And since your return, you've given me our own small family, and an extended one. Now you're giving me your love, this incomparable gift you've never given another."

Listening to her enumerate his countless contributions to her life, his expression softened with that tenderness she was already addicted to.

"I'm giving you *everything* I have and am. You already have it, will always have it. You can weed through the mess and extract only what you like. You can toss out the rest." Just like that, he was the uncompromising Richard Graves again.

Laughing, her heart hurting with too much love and exultation, she stormed him with kisses again. "I'm hoarding every single thing about you. I love every gnarled shred of what makes you the man I worship."

He only got more serious. "I mean it, Isabella. Just tell me everything on your mind the moment you think it, and whatever it is, it's yours, it's done or it's gone."

As he melted back to the bed, taking her with him, she luxuriated in his sculpted magnificence, her pleasure magnified unto infinity now that she knew this majestic being was hers as she was his and she'd always have the right to revel in him.

"As long as this is a two-way street and you tell me anything you want different."

"You're beyond perfect just the way you are." He looked alarmed. "Never change!"

She chuckled, delirious with his new transparency. "I guess I'll have to one day. I'll grow older."

"I already told you, you will only grow better."

"It's *you* who is growing so much better with age. There should be a law to curb your improvement." She nipped his chin, caught his groan of pleasure in hungry lips. "I constantly want to devour you."

Hunger blazing in his eyes, he pressed himself between her spreading thighs. "Devour away. I'm self-regenerating." He suddenly groaned, grimaced. "I didn't promise you the most important thing."

She wrapped her legs around his hips, pulling him back to her. "Nothing is more important than having you."

"Yes, there is. Safety. Yours, Rico's and that of everyone you love. I promise you my near-fatal slipup will never be repeated. If I feel I can't be sure of that, I'll scrap this identity and start from scratch."

Terrified all over again, she clung to him. "Oh, God, Richard, how did it happen?"

He told her and she sank back in relief. "You don't have other people who want to kill you, do you?"

"Actually, it's in everyone's best interest to keep me safe...so I can keep them safe."

"If so, what's with your security fetish?" At his rising eyebrows, she grinned. "Yes, I've noticed our security detail everywhere. I know if I'm being watched. Comes from my years in Colombia and then on the run."

He groaned, the knowledge of her ordeals something she knew would hurt him forever. "It's been a well-established paranoia since I escaped The Organization. Knowing what it would mean if they ever found out I defected, and who I am now, I'd rather always be safe than sorry."

"But you *are* generally safer than anyone on earth, barring that aberrant situation, which could have happened to anyone."

"It should have never happened to me."

"And it won't happen again, if I know anything about you. So we're not in any danger by association. What are you worried about, then?"

His lips twisted, as if she'd asked him why he breathed. "I'll *always* worry, because you and Rico are not inside my body, where I can monitor where you are at all times, and where I can keep you safe every second of every day for the rest of my life."

After another ferocious hug, she pulled back, grinned up at him. "Welcome to love. And to parenthood."

He squeezed his eyes, gritted his teeth. "It's always that bad, isn't it?"

"Far worse."

His eyes opened, blasting her to her marrow with his adoration. "I love it. I love *you*. Darling…"

Her phone rang. They froze for a heartbeat before they both lunged for it.

It was Rico. Shaking, Isabella put him on speaker. He sounded sleepy, but exactly like their perfect little boy.

"Uncle Antonio told me who he is and what happened and that he didn't expect me to wake up so soon, and that my head is as hard as my father's. You're my father, Richard, right?"

Richard covered his face with his hands for a second, dragged them down over it, his eyes filling again. "I am your father, Rico. And *Father* is what I want you to call me from now on. I'm sorry I left, but your mother and I are coming right now, and I'll tell you everything as soon as you can handle long talks. But I want you to know one thing. I'm never leaving you again. *Ever.*"

Rico's squeal of delight was cut short before he slurred for them to hurry up. Antonio came on and told them to come only if they were rested, as Rico was already asleep again.

With the call over, Richard looked at her, his eyes reddened, his expression disbelieving again. "This *is* too much, my love. Too many blessings."

Overwhelmed by everything, too, Isabella clung to him. "Can you handle one more? You might have to make space inside yourself for one more person who'll love you forever." He pulled back, eyes wide in shock. She bit her lip, pulled at a patch of his chest hair. "I suspect we made another baby."

"You suspect?" he rasped, looking shell-shocked.

"Want to find out for sure?"

He exploded from her side, cursing that he'd shredded his clothes, called Murdock, told him to get him intact ones and the helicopter.

She giggled at seeing him all over the place, flustered, no doubt, for the first time in his life. "What are you *doing*?"

"I'm going to buy a pregnancy kit."

"By helicopter?"

"That's to go to Rico."

"But we're not in such a hurry anymore." He looked as if this possibility hadn't even occurred to him. "And there's a kit in the top drawer of my bathroom cabinet."

Before she finished talking, he hurtled to where she'd indicated, coming back with it in seconds.

Trembling, she rose, took it from him, her smile shaky. "I had to go to the bathroom anyway."

"Why?" Then he groaned. "Bloody hell, yes, of course, by all means. I think my mind has been irreversibly scrambled."

She planted a kiss on his chest as she passed him. "No way. But I love you even more because it's scrambled now."

Heart drumming madly, she ducked into the bathroom. In minutes, she exited, the strip held tight in her hand.

"Tell me." His voice was a ragged rumble.

She walked into his arms before she held up her fist. "I wanted to find out with you."

"Do it."

She opened her fist. The two pink lines were as clear as they had been when she'd found out she was pregnant with Rico.

On a triumphant growl, Richard crushed her to him.

Many hot tears and kisses later, Richard raised his head, scorched her to her soul with the power of his love. "I'll always live with the regret that I wasn't there for you when you were carrying Rico, that I lost the first seven years of his life." His finger on her lips silenced her protest. "But now fate has given me more than the everything it has already given me—another miracle, and a chance to fix all my mistakes. Now I get to share our new baby with you, and with Rico, from the first moment. I will be there for you, for all of you, every single second, for the rest of my life. This time, I'll do everything right."

Aching with thankfulness, she clung to him, the man she was fated for, the father of her son and of her unborn baby. "Just love me, just love us. You're all I need. All our children will ever need. If we have you, everything will always be right with the world."

Looking down at her, that god among men who loved her, he lavished hunger and tenderness and devotion on her, his every look and word a pledge. "I will live to love you. And you have me, all of me. I'm all yours, forever."

* * * * *

LET'S TALK
Romance

For exclusive extracts, competitions
and special offers, find us online:

f facebook.com/millsandboon

◎ @millsandboonuk

𝕏 @millsandboon

Or get in touch on 0844 844 1351*

For all the latest titles coming soon, visit
millsandboon.co.uk/nextmonth